say

when

Also by N. Gemini Sasson:

<u>The Faderville Novels</u>
Say No More
Say That Again
Say Something

<u>The Sam and Bump Misadventures</u>
Memories and Matchsticks
Lies and Letters
Threats and Threads

<u>The Bruce Trilogy</u>
The Crown in the Heather (Book I)
Worth Dying For (Book II)
The Honor Due a King (Book III)

<u>The Isabella Books</u>
Isabeau: A Novel of Queen Isabella
and Sir Roger Mortimer (Book I)

The King Must Die:
A Novel of Edward III (Book II)

<u>Standalones</u>
Uneasy Lies the Crown:
A Novel of Owain Glyndwr

In the Time of Kings

say
when

A Faderville Novel

N. GEMINI SASSON

cader idris press

SAY WHEN

Copyright © 2018 N. Gemini Sasson

ISBN 978-1-939344-15-1 (paperback)

Library of Congress Control No. 2018914316

This is a work of fiction. The names, characters, and incidents portrayed in it are the work of the author's imagination. Any resemblance to actual persons, living or dead, events or localities is entirely coincidental.

All rights reserved. No part of this publication may be reproduced, stored in a retrieval system, or transmitted, in any form or by any means, electronic, mechanical, photocopying, recording or otherwise without the prior written permission of the Author.

For more details about N. Gemini Sasson and her books, go to:
www.ngeminisasson.com

Or become a 'fan' at:
www.facebook.com/NGeminiSasson

You can also sign up to learn about new releases via e-mail at:
http://eepurl.com/vSA6z

Editing by Cynthia Shepp
Cover art by Ebook Launch

*For every dog that has ever been misunderstood—
and every person who gave them a chance anyway.*

(P.S.—Parts of this story are partly true.)

SAY WHEN

A second chance at life—and love.

Sooner isn't the perfect dog, but she's finally found the perfect home with owner Brandy Anders—until one tragic day when life goes from hopeful to hopeless.

Grayson Darling has never believed in fate; he's just down on his luck for now. Recently divorced, downsized, and soon to be without a home, his move to Faderville is supposed to be temporary. All he has to do is sell his uncle's farm, then he can return to success and civilization in New York City.

The farm he inherited, however, comes with unforeseen responsibilities. When his ex announces her engagement and the job he'd hoped for falls through, Grayson figures his luck has completely run out. He can't deal with life anymore.

Then, fate intervenes in the form of a dog. Sooner only needs a foster home while her owner recovers, so it's not a long-term commitment anyway. But the dog turns out to be more of a challenge than Grayson bargained for.

Sooner proves, however, that a dog can give you a second chance at life—and love.

chapter 1
Sooner

The world raced by as we whizzed down the highway in the minivan. Spinning in a tight circle, I tried to find my tail, but no matter how many times I looked, it wasn't there. I rubbed my sides against the wires of my crate, spun some more, and barked for the sheer joy of it.

I love my life! I said. *I love it, love it, love it, love it…* (breathe) *love it, love—*

"Sooner, stop," Brandy admonished from the driver's seat. "You're hurting my ears."

Perplexed, I tipped my head from side to side. She'd said something about ears. And to stop. But stop what? Stop using my ears? That was absurd. How could I listen if I stopped using my ears? I told her so.

Silly, Brandy! Silly, silly, silly—

"Okay, okay! I get it." When she leaned her head to the side so I could see her face in the rearview mirror, she was smiling. She did that a lot. It was how I knew she was different from the others when I first saw her. How I knew she was meant to be my person. "You're happy, huh, girl? I'm proud of you. You did good today."

Good, yes. I am always good. Always. I am the best! The brightest! The greatest!

For emphasis, I rattled the metal bucket in the corner of my crate with my nose. Water sloshed everywhere. Had I done that? I bopped it with my head. More water spilled over the edge. I think I did. Yes, I did!

Oh, wait. She might not like that. I should cover it up. Since I had nothing to cover it with, I clawed at the newly formed puddle in the pan of my crate in an attempt to spread it around.

When we got home, maybe Brandy would let me swim in the pond just down the road from our house. I loved the pond! Loved how cool the water was, and how it smelled of algae and mud and fish. I hadn't caught a fish yet, but I would. Someday.

Brandy shook her head, her messy red curls twisting and tangling in the wind. She had the windows down for me. Brandy always had the windows down if it wasn't too hot or too cold. She knew I liked to smell things. If she would let me out of this metal crate, I could stick my head out the window and *really* inhale.

"Know what, Sooner? I've had six obedience trial champions, four top-level agility dogs, five different breeds—and I know you're barely two years old, so it's probably crazy of me to say this—but I believe you may be the smartest one yet. The day I brought home my first Australian Shepherd—you—was the best day of my life. Those other people who'd returned you to the breeder, they just didn't understand Aussies need a job—and you've excelled at every job I've given you. You are one super amazing dog. How did I ever get so lucky?"

I had no idea what she was saying, but I kind of had to pee. I woofed at her to let her know we needed to stop somewhere.

"That's right, girl. I'm talking about you. You are the best, Sooner, the absolute best. Don't know what I'd do if anything ever happened to you. You're every dog I've ever wished for. Maybe I should clone you, huh, just in case?"

I woofed again. She kept driving. Humans weren't always as smart as they pretended to be. How could she not know the difference between a happy playful bark and one that meant I was going to squat and let go of the full contents of my bladder if she didn't get a clue?

"You like hearing your name, doncha, girl? Sooooooooner, Sooner, Sooner, Soooooner."

What the heck? Was she howling now? She was terrible at it. We'd sort that out later. I'd teach her the proper way, but right now I had to *go*! I stared at the back of her head, hoping she'd take a peek in that mirror and see my distressed expression, but she was now singing along to the radio, oblivious.

We were getting closer to home—I could tell by the low mountains that had risen up around us. They resembled the ones around Brandy's house, with lots of trees covering them and sometimes a rocky bluff overlooking a river valley. But the smells weren't familiar yet, so I knew we still had a ways to go.

Woofing again, more softly now, I tried to keep my tone sober. Surely she'd catch on that it was a different bark.

"What's that, girl? You need to go potty?"

I barked louder, twice. *Yes! Potty!*

There was hope I could train her up right after all.

"Hang on, okay? We're ten miles from the next exit. I can't just pull off to the side of the interstate in these parts. Semis in the next lane, cars barreling past at eighty miles an hour, and practically no shoulder. Crazy drivers." She glanced through the opposite car window. "Yup, no shoulder at all. Highway butts right up against the mountainside there. Amazing how they cut through solid rock like that so they could build a highway, isn't it? Simply amazing. Daddy was a civil engineer. Used to build bridges. Course, he worked in an office mostly, but sometimes he'd go out to a job site, just to see how things were coming along and…"

The pressure between my legs was killing me. I shouldn't have drunk so much water. Then again, I hadn't known we were going to be in the van for so long. And I'd been thirsty when we'd left the dog sh—

Whoosh!

Whoa! What was that?

I watched out the window with fascination. A giant box with lots of wheels rumbled along in the lane beside us. I think Brandy had called those things semis. Or was it trucks? Humans had too many names for things. Anyway, it was big. And noisy.

Now what had I been thinking about? Had to pee. Thirsty… Oh yes, the dog show.

I brightened at the memory. It *had* been a good day. A great day. Brandy had started training me as soon as she took me home. Easy stuff at first: sit, lie down, stay, come, heel. In the beginning, I got a treat every time. Sometimes, honestly, I was just guessing, but I eventually began to understand that different words meant she wanted me to do different things. Then it gradually became more complicated. 'Come' didn't just mean barrel in her general direction. She wanted me sitting in a certain spot, not far enough away she couldn't touch me, but not so close my nose was shoved between her legs. When I heeled alongside her, I wasn't allowed to lag behind where she'd lose eye contact with me, nor wander in front where I could trip her. I had to keep my shoulder by her knee—which was a tricky thing for a dog to grasp. I had to figure it out on my own. Food and play helped me learn, though. Sometimes I got things wrong, but Brandy never punished me for trying.

Folding into a sphinx position, I rested my head on the cool surface of the crate pan. I was trying to be patient, I really was, but this was urgent.

I whined.

"Just a few more—"

I howled. *Arooooooooooo, arooooooo, arrrrr-arrrrr-roooooooo.*

"Okay, okay, okay."

Brandy whipped the van onto the narrow shoulder. Tires crunched over gravel. After we rolled to a stop and she'd unbuckled herself, she got out and came around to the rear where my crate was. She opened it and clipped my leash on, then gently lifted me out. I strained in her hold, eager to do my business, but she seemed frightened somehow—and that worried me. As soon as she put me down, nature took over and relief flowed from me.

"Good girl, Sooner. Good girl. Hurry up, though, okay?"

We were between mountains, the area beside the road green with grass, and a metal and wood barrier running parallel to the road. Beyond it, the earth plunged steeply. Kicking up some dirt to cover my mess, I strained to see what was down there. Trees, grass, more trees, lots of dirt, water somewhere, and—

My nostrils quivered. What smell was that? Some animal, perhaps? Curious, I lurched toward the slope.

"No!"

Brandy yanked me back so hard my collar hit my trachea. I retched.

"Sorry, girl, but you don't want to go down there. You'd break all your legs before you got to the bottom."

I coughed a few more times, just for effect. Brandy knelt, pulling me to her side.

Cars buzzed past on the highway. A truck roared into the distance. The ground vibrated under my feet. More cars. More trucks. Gigantic beings, hurtling over the asphalt, racing to unknown places. Hot wind blasted my face with each passing. The rumble was almost deafening.

Brandy hugged me to her chest. "Oh, baby. You're shaking. Those great big trucks must look terrifying to little ol' you. It's okay.

I'm here. I won't let you get hurt. But do you see why I didn't want to stop here?"

Her babbling was only prolonging the amount of time we remained in peril. I wanted back in the van, and I wanted to go home. Stretching upward, I placed my paws on either side of her neck, then clambered into her lap.

Grunting, she scooped me up and clutched me tightly. My gangly legs dangled from the sling of her arms. "Let's go home."

Upon hearing the word 'home,' I licked her face to let her know I agreed.

At the van, she urged me toward the open door of the crate, but I didn't need encouragement. I jumped in. The space was safety, security. Even as much as I hated being confined in it sometimes, it was my little den—the place where I slept and ate. It was my sacred space. My quiet and comfort.

As she latched the door shut, I licked the salt from her fingers.

"You want some of my pretzels, huh, girl?"

I licked harder, not sure what she was asking, but she tasted good. She stepped to the front of the van, opened the door, and reached for something between the front seats. The plastic bag crinkled as she lifted it. I could hear that sound a mile away.

"Probably not good for you—heck, I eat so many of the dang things, they're probably not good for me, either—but you deserve a special treat today. Maybe I'll stop in town at the drive-thru before we go home to get you your very own cheeseburger. Would you like that, Sooner? A cheeseburger?" She returned to my crate, then slipped a pretzel between the bars. I took it gently from her fingers as she'd taught me, before wolfing it down in two bites. Her eyes sparkled as she gazed at me. "I am so, *so* proud of you. You got your first two legs in elite agility today. Come next spring, we'll finish your first championship title. The first of many. We've got a lot more work to do, but there's no limit to what we can do together. We're a team,

Sooner. A fantastic team, you and me."

I'd understood all of two words: home and my name. It baffled me as to why humans were allowed to talk nonstop, but if I tried to express myself, I got scolded. There was something very lopsided about that.

"Hey, girl. Know what?" Leaning in close, she kissed the tip of my nose. I returned the affection with a big wet slurp, which made her laugh. "Aww, thanks. I love you, too. More than the sun and the moon and the stars."

I knew that one word, all right: love. It meant a lot of things, but they all gave me the same wonderful feeling.

Brandy slipped two more pretzels between the wires of my crate before returning to the driver's seat and pulling back onto the highway. I snarfed them down in seconds, hoping she'd toss back a few more, but she just kept on driving.

I sat upright, leaning against the side of my crate, watching the cars and trucks go by, some speeding ahead, some falling behind. Shifting, I yawned and pressed my eyes wide, but no matter how hard I tried, they kept drifting shut.

In time, I could no longer resist the pull of sleep. My feet slid forward, and my belly sank to the cool pan. The zooming became a white noise that lulled me toward nothingness. In my dreams, bees buzzed at a distance. The sun spilled down from a cloudless sky. Grass tickled my paws. I saw jumps and tunnels around me. Up above, there were planks to race over and peaks to climb. I sailed from obstacle to obstacle, my legs full of boundless energy. And beside me, Brandy ran, trying hard to keep up, to get the words out, her face alight with joy.

Team, yes. I think I knew that word, too. We were a team, Brandy and me. Together.

Brandy understood me better than any other human could. I knew this because I'd been returned to the breeder by two different owners at a very young age. The little I remembered of those places wasn't good—a lot of yelling and unhappiness and the words 'untrainable' and 'hyper' and especially 'bad dog' being repeated over and over again. It had shaken my confidence and confused me, which only made me try harder to do something right. But if I ever did, it went unnoticed or wasn't good enough. The fault was always mine for not understanding, never my owners' for being unclear.

My dreams drifted back to Brandy and all the things about her that made me feel loved and understood. The twinkle in her eyes. The dimples in her cheeks when she smiled at me. The calming feel of her hand stroking my back. How she laughed when I played. How her voice pitched high when she approved of what I did, then sank low when she didn't. There was far more of the former than the latter, which was precisely how I liked it.

For a while, I thought of nothing, dreamed of nothing. My mind was blank, my body resting. I was still young and needed lots of sleep, so I could wake up full of energy. For now, though… for now I rested, trusting in Brandy to take us home.

—o0Oo—

The nightmare started with an abrupt jar and a rib-rattling shudder. My teeth slammed together, pinching the edge of my tongue. Then a terrifying moment flashed by in which the world tumbled and shook. At the edge of my consciousness, I became aware of an awful noise—the moaning crunch of metal as it compacted and the screech as it was twisted by unnatural forces, all followed by the drawn-out wail of a dying monster.

My eyes shot open, although they couldn't focus in the chaos. Everything was on its side, then up, then down, then sideways again. The training bag Brandy took everywhere with us spun and flopped about inside the van, its contents spilling wildly. Bits of treats pinged on every surface. My toys flew haphazardly about. A jug of water burst open, dousing my face as I was slammed on my back, the crate upside down, the pan lying on top of me.

I tried desperately to find Brandy, but it was hard to know where to look, to see anything at all. Daylight had given way to the murkiness of nightfall, color and clarity replaced by muted tones and obscure shades of silver and gray.

For a minute, everything lurched in one direction, forward, including the crate with me inside it. That was when I saw Brandy—or at least the reflection of her face in the rearview mirror—eyes wide in horror.

The front end of the van dipped forward and down. A ravine gaped below, its slopes dangerously steep and punctuated with jagged rocks. At the bottom wound a barely trickling creek bed, its thin ribbon of water glinting in the phantasmal glow of the van's headlights.

And then... the van tipped over the edge and plunged into the chasm far, far below.

chapter 2

Brandy

Brandy's world flipped upside down, spiraling dizzyingly around her. She observed it all with a mixture of horrifying fright and detached fascination. Almost as if she were not in her own body. A cyclone of papers, cups, pretzels, coins, and sunglasses swirled around her, pelting her, clinking against the windshield.

With a bone-hammering thud, everything came to a halt. Brandy was aware of her heart paused in its beating, her breath trapped in her lungs. Her limbs had been tossed about like the loosely sewn-on legs and arms of a shaken rag doll. Her head had slammed backward against the headrest, her spine twisted as the axis of her orientation came to a rest. She knew all this and yet… she couldn't feel a thing. Except for the sensation of hanging with her head down. Like a bat.

Darkness cocooned her. All sound, all smells, all sights faded from her awareness. She was… and she wasn't.

Somewhere, at the edge of her universe, another being existed.

A creature connected to her own spirit and yet wholly unlike her. Simpler. Purer. Untainted by life's harsh lessons.

Sooner?

The dog cried out to her.

She reached for her. Felt the faintest sweep of fur beneath her fingertips, the soft leather of a nose, and then… it was gone. Darkness returned. Time stalled. Hands grasped her. Laid her down. Covered her in cloth. A great bird lifted her up, up, up. Her body lightened. Her spirit broke free.

For a time, she floated through a mist-choked void. Wind whispered in her ears, carrying on it the voices of all those she had known throughout her life. Light permeated the edges of her vision. Filled the space above her. Faces cast in shadows gathered around her, sharpened. Young faces, old. Wrinkled, smooth. Some pale as the moon and others dark as night. She knew them. She must. Friends? Family? No names came to her. Only feelings of warmth, kindness, caring, friendship… and loss, disappointment, abandonment, grief.

The barking of a dog startled her. Snapped her back to awareness. She listened, concentrated on it. It wasn't an alarm bark, but a joyful one. A familiar bark.

Her energy centering, solidifying into physical form, she moved toward the sound. Pushed her way past the gathered figures, their images dissipating, vanishing, as she brushed not against, but *through* them.

Brandy staggered toward the barking, then ran clumsily as pain awakened in her feet and legs. The dog… *her* dog—it was running away. With someone. A man.

Although she tried to run faster, to catch them, she couldn't keep up.

Sooner… wait! Stop!

They kept running. Away. Their forms now nothing but fading images in the distance.

And then, just as Brandy's resolve threatened to collapse… they turned. Waited until she came closer. Close enough to see them more clearly.

Sooner?

The dog ran partway to her. Then stopped suddenly. Glanced back over its shoulder. And returned to the man. Again, they ran. Faster than she could manage.

Finally, the barking was no more. They were gone.

Still, she kept going. Searching. Calling out into the never-ending nothingness.

Until no words would form in her throat. Until her feet stopped moving. She couldn't go on anymore. Could not, despite wanting to. Lost for hope, she sank to the ground and covered her head with her arms.

And then a hand alighted on her shoulder. A man's hand. Beside her, a set of paws appeared.

Wiping away tears, she looked past the dog, up into a face she did not recognize… yet.

She only knew that when she met him—if he existed at all—she would know him by the goodness in his heart… and the dog at his side.

chapter 3
Grayson

If Grayson Darling was successful, he could fool himself into believing the admiration of others equaled friendship. So far, it hadn't.

If he stayed busy, he reasoned, he could ignore whatever weighed down his heart and it would eventually go away. It never did. He wasn't even sure, for the longest time, what that discomfort was.

In the end, he realized what he was—and had always been—was lonely. Even though he had been surrounded by people his entire life.

The biggest heartache came from knowing what he had lost with his wife of twenty-five years. When they were young grad students raging with hormones, he'd loved her curves and her too-thick, bouncy hair. The fact she'd made a point of seeming unimpressed with his posturing had only made her more desirable. And so he'd gone to great lengths to get her attention: working out, dressing his best, always keeping his hair neatly styled, and speaking to her in the most respectfully polite and flattering terms he could manage without crossing the line of objectifying her.

Fiona Baumgartner—or Fee as everyone called her—hadn't been

an easy catch. And yet, he'd managed to take her for granted once she was all his. Not right away, of course. The shift had been so gradual he hadn't even been aware of it. Fee had tried to bring it to his attention. Subtly at first, by suggesting they go on a trip to somewhere they'd never been before to rekindle their romance. He'd argued for staying home and saving for their golden years. She'd acquiesced, settling for dinners out at a not-too-expensive neighborhood restaurant while he talked of work.

Eventually, she'd brought his inattention up in conversations, how she wished he'd make more time for their marriage, how she wanted to go away, just the two of them. Unwilling to argue any longer, Grayson had yielded. They'd jetted to far-off destinations and Fee had looked forward to each trip with the wonderment of a six-year-old seeing the ocean for the first time. For Grayson, however, they were interruptions in his climb up the corporate ladder, as well as drains on their finances. Meanwhile, he'd attended to every call for help from work as urgently as if a babysitter were keeping them in the loop on a sick child.

In the beginning, she'd been tolerant. Then came the eye rolls, the sighs of disgust, the walking away. Finally, the frequent correspondences with work that interrupted their dinner dates, vacations, and evenings in front of the TV at home had resulted in arguments. At the time, he'd believed her outbursts were merely dramatic ploys for attention. He was with her—shouldn't that be enough? They weren't twenty-two anymore. They'd settled down, aged, grown comfortable with each other. To him, everything had seemed just fine.

He hadn't realized how serious she was until he'd come home to an empty apartment.

That evening, he'd sat alone in front of the TV until late into the night, absorbing the hollowness surrounding him. There was no one to complain to about the department accountant's gross calculation error or to comment to about how the remodeling of the break room was disrupting everyone's productivity. Yet the more he thought about it, the more he realized it wouldn't have mattered. Fee had stopped listening a while ago, but only because he had stopped caring about her long before that. Stopped caring about them.

That wasn't to say he didn't care if she got hurt or was sick. He wasn't inhumane. It had simply become too much effort to put her wants and needs before his. There was only so much of him to go around. It seemed so much simpler to laser his focus on work. Anyway, getting into a woman's head was far too complicated a matter to attempt. Never mind she'd tried to tell him directly what it was she needed from him.

And so, he found himself alone. If she wanted to find a reason to leave, he was clueless about how to stop her.

After they'd settled on the terms of divorce—all of which went fairly amicably, according to both attorneys—he'd only had one question for her: "Why, Fee? Why did you leave?"

She closed her eyes, shook her head. The attorneys had left them alone in the room minutes before. When she met his gaze, it was with a pained, doleful expression. "You still don't understand, do you? Marriage isn't about just living together and sharing finances. Shouldn't be, anyway."

"But... what did I do?"

Fee tilted her head, the sweep of her bangs cutting a dark angle across the lines in her brow. "It's what you no longer did, Grayson. You stopped seeing me. Stopped looking at me the way you used to. Stopped noticing if I colored my hair or wore a new dress. And I tried to get you to notice. Believe me, I tried. One day, I realized I may as well have been a hologram. I just felt... invisible." She pinched her coral-colored lower lip between her teeth for a moment. "And I didn't want to feel that empty anymore. I wanted to share my life and my future with someone who had it in his heart to cherish every moment."

"Is there… is there someone else?" he asked, fearful of the answer either way.

"No, there's no one else. Not now, anyway. Someday, though…?"

In her mind, she'd already replaced him with someone she hadn't yet met. Or was there a friend or coworker she was subconsciously attracted to—someone more appealing than him? Even so, he believed her when she said there was no current 'other'. But it was the fact she'd decided to leave purely because of him—that was worse than if some other man had swooped in and dazzled her with his charm and good looks. *That* he could've understood.

"Tell me," he'd said, "tell me what I could've done differently."

Not could do. Could *have done*. Past tense. In saying that, he realized, he was admitting defeat. There was no going back.

"Could have done *differently*?" Fee regarded him quizzically, as if she didn't understand the words he was using. "You would've had to have done something in the first place for me to suggest a change, Grayson. The thing is, you just weren't… there." She waited for him to speak, but when he didn't, she added, "Love is a reservoir, Grayson. You have to repair the cracks and plug the holes when they happen, certainly, so it doesn't all drain away in a rush. But you also have to keep filling it daily. Because if you don't, it will evaporate little by little. Eventually, you'll have nothing left but a big empty hole."

It was too much for him to get his head around. To admit he didn't quite understand would've made him feel stupid, so he merely said, "I see."

But he didn't see at all. Didn't fully understand what she was getting at. He wanted to, though. Maybe in time he would. But by then, it would be too late. It already was now.

"Let me ask you this," Fee said, tempering her frustration. "When are you going to start engaging in the here and now? When are you going to stop and look around you at what is and realize this world, the people in it—they're worth holding on to? Because tomorrow, or sometime down the road, they might not be there anymore. When, Grayson?"

When? He couldn't say when he barely understood the question.

He'd still been trying to process it all and form an acceptable response when she picked up her purse from the giant cherry wood table and walked out the door. And out of his life.

With no reason to get home in time for dinner, he'd immersed himself in his work and it had paid off. His bosses had noticed. They'd praised his hard work, referred clients to him. Which worked great—until the day it no longer did. Like so many other hardworking, experienced, and well-educated people in the workforce, he was downsized. The company was struggling. Longtime employees were being let go. It wasn't anything personal, they said.

Single and out of work, he threw himself into the job-search pool, exhausting his personal network and coming up empty at every turn. His whole life, he'd saved for his retirement and for a rainy day, but the last twelve months had been an endless series of rainy days.

So when the letter from an attorney in Kentucky arrived, he considered it with curiosity. His uncle had died, leaving behind a house and farm. As Skip Dalton's closest living kin, the estate had been bequeathed to him. He couldn't remember ever having been there. His first impulse was to simply sell the place at auction. That, at least, would put some money in his pocket until a job offer came in.

The next day, he received a phone call. He didn't recognize the area code, and he almost didn't answer it. But on the off chance it was a response to an employment ad, he did.

"Hello?"

"Howdy! Is this Grayson? Grayson... *Darling*? Is that really your last name?"

It was an older woman with a distinctly Southern twang who was overly friendly, none of which appealed to him.

"It is. Why are you calling? And… what is *your* name, if I may ask?"

He doubted it was a job offer. Probably a political survey with too many skewed questions or a pitch for a low-interest credit card that had hidden fees attached. He was about to hang up when she spoke again.

"Oh, sorry. I'm Loretta Hoberty. I hate to ask, but any idea when you'll come down and take over your uncle's farm? I've been feeding the animals for over a month now and cleaning up after them—and let me tell you, I feel it in my back. Not that I'm allergic to hard work, mind you, but I'm not a spring chicken anymore. Anyway, I had plans to go see my grandkids in Jacksonville real soon. I'd arrange someone else to help, but, well… I can't really shell out of my own pocket for something not mine. You understand, right?"

He did, and he didn't. If there were animals involved, they weren't really his either. Although if viewed from a legal standpoint… "Oh. Thank you, I suppose. But I hadn't realized there were any animals. I only learned of the farm passing to me yesterday. I thought maybe the farm produced grain, hay, that sort of thing. So, what kind of animals? How many? I'll compensate you for your time, of course."

Although he was reluctant to say that, it seemed the right thing to do. It was still summer. If there were a few cows in the field, surely they'd be grazing on some of that Kentucky bluegrass out in a pasture and drinking from a stream? How hard could that be to take care of?

"So you have no idea what he did for a living?' Loretta asked, no hint of judgment in her tone. "None at all?"

He didn't feel like explaining to her that his mother and uncle, while not entirely estranged, hadn't been all that close.

But the more Grayson sifted through his memory, the more he realized he didn't really know anything about his uncle, other than he'd been much older than his mother and had stayed in Kentucky, where their family originated from. He certainly had no knowledge of the man's livelihood.

"No, I'm sorry, I don't know. Did he raise cattle? Swine? Sheep, maybe?"

He had no idea how to take care of any of those. The woman sounded desperate for relief. She'd done the neighborly thing, stepping in. He couldn't take advantage of her good graces any more than that.

"Horses—race horses, at first. Had a couple of big winners, put them up for stud, but that was ages ago. Over the last decade, he branched out. Basically anything with a lineage worth investing in. He loved the differences in each breed. Traveled the country. Had friends and customers all over the world. Yep, quite the spread ol' Skip built here, but I can't say it's the lifestyle I'd want anymore. Been a horse gal all my life, but I recently retired. Nowadays, I just want to play with my grandbabies—when I can see them, that is."

He got the hint. Besides, relieving her of the burden was the ethical thing to do.

"I can be there by Friday. Is that all right? I don't mean to impose on you any further, but I have to conclude some business here in New York"—purging his walk-in closet of outdated business attire had been next on his list, although he wasn't sure how he could afford to replace even a portion of his collection of tailored suits—"but I'll get there by then, if possible."

"Oh, thank you! I hope I can hang in there until then. I'm feeling that pinch in my lower back. Got a disc that pops out of place when I overdo it. That can lay me up for weeks. I didn't want to talk about it, make you feel put upon, but… I'm so relieved. Thank you, Mr. Darling, sir. Thank you!"

Her gratitude was so effusive that, for a moment, he wondered if it was genuine or this was some kind of scam to lure him to… He couldn't even remember the name of the town, just that it was somewhere in southern Kentucky. Regardless, he put his suspicions aside and arranged to meet the woman at his uncle's farm on Friday so she could 'show him the ropes,' as she put it.

Grayson didn't have the slightest idea what that might entail, but even as he began to pack his suitcase, he made plans of his own: to contact the estate attorney and get the name of a reliable auctioneer, as well as someone to transport the livestock to a sale yard.

Then, once employment was obtained, he could get back to living his life—however dismal and isolated that might be.

—o00o—

Grayson raised his eyes from his lap. He'd wanted to avoid this announcement, but it had to be made. "I suppose I should tell you— I'm going out of town. To my uncle's farm in Kentucky. Seems he left it to me."

It was the end of another weekly counseling session with Dr. Philipot, a man so average looking as to be forgettable. Thin and pasty, he had a bland voice that bordered between soothing and sleep-inducing. Grayson had begun seeing him almost two years ago at Fee's suggestion, just a few months before she asked for the divorce. She'd implied Grayson had attachment issues, that maybe there was something in his past that precluded him from getting in touch with his emotions. In reality, he hadn't seen them as all that necessary. Hadn't felt the need to react to every little thing.

Oddly, it wasn't until Fee left him that he felt... *something*. An emptiness. A heaviness. A feeling of being pulled downward. And then later, when his job evaporated one otherwise-sunny day, he felt a bothersome sense of something being wrong, out of his control, like a bicycle speeding downhill, no brakes, a brick wall at the bottom he had to avoid but didn't know how to.

If Fee no longer loved him, who could?

It had taken him weeks to describe those feelings to Dr. Philipot. Months more to understand where they might have stemmed from.

Even then, knowing hadn't seemed to help all that much. 'Depression' Dr. Philipot had called it. Grayson didn't see it that way. He was simply down in the dumps. What man wouldn't be when his wife had left him and his employer had seen fit to cut him loose? Things would get better. Eventually.

"I'm sorry for your loss." Dr. Philipot sat back in his leather swivel chair, his head tilted to one side.

It took a moment for Grayson to understand he meant his uncle's death, not his divorce. In reality, Grayson felt as much loss as if he'd read the obituary of a stranger in the newspaper. He hadn't known the man, not really. Could barely remember meeting him the once—or was it twice? For certain at his mother's funeral. Had his uncle come to his college graduation, too? He couldn't recall.

"Was it unexpected?"

Grayson snapped back to the present. "Yes, yes, it was. I didn't even know he had a farm."

"I meant his death. I assume he was older."

How much older had his uncle been than his mother? Grayson couldn't recall. "I don't know. In his eighties, maybe? I didn't know him that well." Barely at all, actually.

"Perhaps you'll get to know him, in a way." Dr. Philipot leaned forward, then moved a stack of papers to one side as if to signal their time was at an end. "A person's belongings can reveal a lot about them."

Grayson cringed inwardly. What if the man was a hoarder? He detested clutter, had always tried to live simply, buying for himself and his wife what was practical and priced fairly. His frugality had been yet another of Fee's complaints. At any rate, physical belongings could be donated to charity, valuables sold at consignment shops or auctions. The rest could be dumped in the garbage. The animals, however, were another matter.

Dr. Philipot glanced at his watch, then scribbled on one of the papers. "How long will you be gone?"

"I don't know." Grayson said that a lot to Dr. Philipot. "A week. Maybe two?"

"Hmmm." Dr. Philipot tapped his pen on the desk. "Sometimes these situations are more complicated than they seem, especially if there are legal or financial matters to clear up. Are there other relatives?"

"No, I'm it." That was one thing he was sure of.

"After you get there and get a feel for the situation, why don't you get in touch with me? And if you need to talk with me for any reason, feel free to call, please. If I'm with a client"—Grayson noted he always called them 'clients' and not 'patients'—"you can leave a message with my receptionist and I'll call you back as soon as I can. Let her know if it's urgent. When you return, we can resume our normal visits."

Grayson assured Dr. Philipot he would. But in the back of his mind, he hoped this was the last he'd see of the doctor. Maybe a temporary change of scenery would lift the darkness from his life and he wouldn't need a shrink anymore.

chapter 4
Sooner

I opened my eyes to chaos scattered about in darkness. Everything was everywhere. And yet, I seemed to be nowhere, surrounded by nothing.

Every bone in my body ached. My head hurt. My spine was stiff. Lifting my head, I glanced around. It was all so fuzzy. So unfamiliar.

Where is this place? How did I get here?

I laid my head back down on a mat of leaves and grass. Closed my eyes. Inhaled. The scents were strange. Harsh. Startling. I had to think about what they were. Oil. Metal. Wood and earth. Gasoline… Blood?

Brandy!

I snapped to alertness. Pushed myself up. A cough spilled out of my lungs, compressed by bruised ribs. I retched bile onto dirt soaked with gasoline and oil. The van lay in a twisted heap at the base of a steep hillside. Halfway between was my crate, mangled and warped, the wires splayed, some protruding skyward, others bent back around on themselves.

I limped toward the van, unable to bear my full weight on one of my hind legs. The scent of blood in my nose was remarkably strong. It was hard to see. There was no moon, only a faint sprinkling of stars veiled by clouds.

I barked. *Brandy? Brandy? Brandy?*

It took all my might to force the sound from my chest and throat. I barked again. *I'm here, Brandy. I'm here! Here!*

Only the crickets answered. *We're here, too*, they seemed to say.

After a few more steps, I stopped to rest. It was hard going. The ground slanted. It was loose and uneven, littered with rocks and branches, crowded with weeds as high as my chest. But I kept going. Toward the van. To Brandy.

When I found her, it looked like she was asleep.

But she wasn't. Something was terribly wrong.

The van was on its side, the empty passenger side crumpled against the ground. The glass of the front windshield was cracked in a spiderweb pattern. But I could see Brandy through it. She was still buckled into her seat, suspended a few feet up, her body limp like one of my well-worn toys with the stuffing pulled out.

I could see her, but I couldn't get to her. Not from the front, anyway.

I hobbled toward the back. One door was flung open. That must have been how my crate had flown free. The other was half off its hinges, angled like a bird's broken wing.

The bin containing my food was upside down in the open doorway, the lid popped loose. Bits of kibble lay here and there, but I wasn't interested in food. I needed to check on Brandy, to wake her up. Climbing, I fought my way through the mess. The foldable soft crate I used for indoors at the shows blocked my path. I tried to push it out of the way with my nose, but it was too big. When I tried to pull it back with a front paw, I discovered it was tightly wedged in place. My bad rear leg was preventing me from bearing my weight on both back feet and I couldn't gain enough leverage to move it. So I grabbed the edge of the frame with my mouth, then pushed and pulled and pushed some more until it gave just a little. After, I forced a shoulder past it and shimmied through. I thought I was clear, but my hips, being broader, got stuck. The frame pinched my bad leg, and I yelped.

Movement caught my eye. It was Brandy! She moaned low, and I could tell she was badly hurt.

I barked to let her know I was there, that I would help and take care of her. But she made no more sounds.

Despite the pain, I dragged my body past the soft crate so I was crammed in a small space behind the front passenger seat. Brandy's head and right arm hung down in the space between the seats, her hair partially covering her face.

Standing on my one good hind leg, I placed both front paws on the empty seat and raised up to sniff her. I smelled traces of fear and panic. Snuffling her face, I whimpered softly, hoping she would open her eyes and smile reassuringly at me. Pain stabbed through my leg, but I ignored it. Stretching my neck as far as I could, I licked her face and arm. Licked and licked and licked. Until my mouth and tongue went dry. Until my leg, my neck, my body told me to stop. And then I licked some more.

But Brandy didn't respond. Didn't open those sparkling eyes, always so full of love. Didn't speak my name. Didn't smile. Didn't so much as flinch or mumble.

My body trembling, I sank back down. Rested. Thought about what to do. What I *could* do.

Stay. It was what Brandy often told me. Just… stay. Be there for her. For when she would wake up.

It was so hard for a young dog like me to be patient. To trust she'd come back whenever she went away. But she always had before. And to stay was what she had taught me to do.

I will not leave you, I whined. *I will be here. For you. Always.*

—o0Oo—

For a dog, the smallest measures of time are breaths and heartbeats. There were many of both as I waited for Brandy to awaken, to acknowledge my presence, to see I was every bit as loyal as she would have expected.

But as I lay there in that lopsided van, Brandy's battered body dangling in the harness attached to her seat, I wondered if she might remain there forever, helpless. Clearly, I could not free or revive her. Even if she woke up, could she free herself? Would my presence alone be of any use? As much as I tried to deny it, I knew it would take another human to get her out and take her somewhere she could be cared for. But how would anyone know she was here?

Through the shattered front window, I could make out the faintest hint of daylight. Had we been there the whole night? How could someone not have seen it happen, not have come?

Wake up! Wake up!

Her hand was cooler now, her breathing faint.

Brandy?

If I didn't find someone to help, she might not ever awaken.

So I left the van, difficult though each step was. Struggled up the hill, following a path of broken branches, bits of debris, and deep gouges in the earth where the van had rolled and bounced.

It took a very long time. Too many heartbeats to count. By the time I made it almost to the top, I could see the bright ball of the sun and feel its warmth beating down on me. A dull roar grew in my ears—the highway.

I focused on the top of the hill. Almost there. Then glanced back to where I'd come from. Far below, through a tangle of shrubs and small trees, rested the mangled cube of metal that was Brandy's van. From up here, it would have been easy to miss. The smells, however, were strong: the musky scent of broken wood, the crushed vegetation, the tang of metal, the stink of oil and gas.

I pushed on. With each step, pain flared in my rear leg. It came from a deep cut, probably from the wires of my crate as I'd been tossed about in the van and then thrown out the back. I tried to remember what had happened, but after I saw Brandy's face in the mirror, no more pictures came to mind.

The earth beneath my paws vibrated. Fear flowed through me, gripped my heart. I smelled the reek of diesel coming from the highway. Tires hot from many miles spinning over asphalt. The fluids they poured into the metal beasts.

The rocks near the top were jagged, the slope so steep I fought not to slide back down. Below, if I had fallen, it would have been into dirt and brush. Here there were stones as big as my head and gravel that shifted beneath my weight.

The tear in my back leg gaped more and more, air stinging across the line where blood was freshly flowing. It hurt! But I had to go on. To find humans. Show them where Brandy was.

When I made it, finally, it was just as terrible as the day before. The mindless beasts flew along the smooth path, intent on going wherever it was they had to go. Were they all going to dog shows? To the pet store for more kibble? Or the place where they kept food for humans and gathered it into plastic bags? Why did they need to travel so far or so often? Most of all, why did they feel the need to get there so quickly?

Standing next to a gap in a length of metal supported at intervals by stubby posts, I kept my distance at the edge of the road for a long while, unwilling to venture too close to danger. If any of them saw me, they didn't bother to stop. Why would they? How could I let them know their help was needed?

I went closer. Onto the edge of the road. Waited, hoping. Car after car sped by. But no one stopped. No one even slowed.

There were no houses close by. No buildings where they might have handed food out the window or any of those horrendously smelly places where they fed the wheeled beasts. Far, far in the distance, though, I could see a tall sign with symbols on it. They meant nothing to me, but to humans, they were a representation of something. Maybe if I went that way—

The wail had been on the edge of my senses for several heartbeats before I took note of it. It was coming closer. When I turned in the direction of the sound, I saw… pulsing lights? Their message was clear: *Get out of the way!*

As I moved back toward the post where I'd sat when I first topped the hill, I finally realized the metal piece between two of the posts was torn away. Had the van gone through there? I sniffed the ground. Rubber, yes. I caught the air scent leading down the hill. Yes, it had.

The scream of the car with the blinking lights got louder. Shriller.

My ears pinned to my head, I folded to the ground and flattened myself there. Normally such a sound would have sent me running. I was keen to things out of the ordinary, alert to the slightest movements or changes in my surroundings.

The screaming car came closer. Slowed. Rolled past where I lay. Stopped.

A door flew open. A woman wearing a hat and sunglasses jumped out. Slammed the door shut. She tapped a small black box above her breast pocket as she walked my way.

"I think I've found it. Mile one-fifty-three on the mark. There's a…" She caught sight of me, paused. Her eyes immediately skipped to the gap in the metal band. She wandered to it, very close to me. I backed up, but she wasn't studying me now. She was staring at the van down below. Or what was left of it.

"Holy cow," she murmured.

"Deputy Langley? Is everything all right?"

The box crackled.

"Deputy Langley?"

She pressed a button on the box. "Send all available rescue units. We have a vehicle in the ravine. Looks like a single car accident. I'm not sure how long it's been there."

A long string of words came out of the little box just below her shoulder. Other voices. Urgent. Concerned. I didn't always understand all the words, but I could sense the emotions behind them.

"Are there any victims?" the box asked.

"At least one. Someone was driving it. But I don't know if they survived. I don't see how anyone could."

"Someone should be there in a few minutes. Can you reach the vehicle to assess the extent of the victim's injuries?"

The woman's gaze shifted to me. "I... could, but I don't think it'd be safe. Best to wait for someone with ropes. Tell them to bring the rappelling gear."

"Affirmative. Sit tight."

"Will do."

The small voice in the box kept on talking, but the woman in the hat seemed to have tuned it out. Her attention was on me. I backed away, never taking my eyes off her.

I was wary of strangers at first meeting. Always had been. But I seldom let it show unless I sensed danger. Before, Brandy was always with me. From her reaction, I could gauge friend or foe. Mostly it was somewhere in between. So I would remain polite and well-mannered, neither overtly friendly nor unfriendly. Just watchful. As I was now.

She crouched, extended her hand. I took another step back. Sharp rocks dug into my raw pads.

"It's all right... girl?" She tilted her head sideways. "You are a girl, right? I don't see any boy parts. You have a girl's face. Pretty girl."

A quickly stolen glance told me the next step back would be treacherous if I wasn't careful.

"Scared?"

My muscles tensed, ready to dart away.

"You don't need to be. Really. I won't hurt you. I want to help." Her voice was soft, but there was a nervous quiver to it. She wasn't sure what to make of me. Wasn't sure she trusted me. Dogs knew these things. And since she didn't trust me just yet, I didn't trust her either. She pulled her hand back, rested her elbows on her knees, then nodded toward the gap where the van had gone through. "Is your owner down there?"

A giant truck rumbled by. I jumped back. My hind feet landed on the gravelly slope and slid. I scrambled to regain my footing, digging my claws in.

The woman shot to her feet. "No, don't!"

Pivoting, I ran farther down the slope, my nerves jangled. That word... 'no,' Brandy almost never used it—and that had made all the difference for me. But when I was younger, I'd heard it often. It had frequently been accompanied by flying objects like shoes or fingers that grabbed me by the scruff, along with more angry words.

"Please, I didn't mean—"

I paused to look up at her. She hadn't followed, seeming afraid of going down the hill.

"Good girl. Gooood girl."

I knew those words, too. Brandy said them to me every day.

"Yes, you're a good girl to stay with your owner."

Stay? I cocked my head. I also knew that word. I sat, waiting for the next command.

"Good girl. *Very* good." She moved past the jagged length of metal, lowered herself a step onto the rocks, and then another. "Stay there. Stay. Good, good, good."

As she picked her way down the hill, I could hear the sound of another vehicle on the road above, coming to a stop. Doors shut. Feet stomped. Not one human. Two. Heavier. Men.

"Langley, yo! Where are you?" called a gruff voice.

I hunkered low.

Langley extended a palm in my direction. "It's okay, girl. It's okay. Just... stay. Stay, okay?" Then she shouted up, "Yeah, down here!"

"Where?"

What sounded like a herd stampeded toward the gap. Two men appeared, their jaws hanging slack as they took it all in.

"Holy Mother of—!"

"Anybody alive down there?" the second man said. He was smaller than the first, less boisterous.

"Other than the dog?" Langley answered, glancing at me. "I don't know yet. Is rescue on the way? I don't think I can get much closer."

"What the hell you doing down there, anyway?" the bigger man said.

"Trying to get the dog to come to me."

"Ah, hell, you're going about it all wrong." He readjusted his belt. A black metal object hung from it. Then he began to pick his way down to where Langley stood, grunting with the strain of each movement.

"Preston, I don't think it's a good idea for you to—"

"See, what you need is some of this here." He pulled a skinny stick from his back pocket, then bit at the top of it with his teeth. The plastic wrapping crinkled as he tore it loose. He waved it about.

It smelled vaguely like... pepperoni? Brandy used to pick them off her pizza and feed them to me when we ate our dinners together. She lived alone. Her only friends were the other people at the dog club, most of them women, but there were a few men. We spent several nights a week there, practicing our obedience and agility with the other dogs and handlers. Afterward at home, Brandy always fed me first before she fixed her own supper. When she sat down to eat in front of the TV, she'd toss me bits of her meal—carrots, hunks of potato, bits of shredded chicken, melted cheese, bread—but only ever a little.

My favorite was always when she had pepperoni pizza. I lived for those greasy little circles of meat. I could swallow them whole. Why waste time chewing?

In the distance, another piercing wail sounded, coming closer. Its shrill cry cut through the wind and tore the sky.

The big man ripped off a piece of meat stick, then lobbed it in my direction. It hit me in the chest and I jumped, startled. I'd begun to trust the woman, but this man… he just didn't understand. I dived behind a tall clump of weeds to peer cautiously between the stems.

"Preston, stop. You'll scare her away."

"Naw. Dog's gotta eat. She'll warm up to me once she figures it out." He blundered his way through the tall grass. His jacket snagged on a thorny bush. He cursed at it and jerked his arm away, tearing his sleeve. "God bless it! Second one this week. First, it was hauling that hobo out of a dumpster and now—"

His head and shoulders went backward, his feet flying out from under him. His body hit the ground with an ungraceful thud and tumbled down, down, down. Toward me.

I ran. Sideways along the hill, following a path laid by some small animal. Then down again, but slightly away from the van, keeping my eye on it.

Into the gulley, I flew. Away from the van. Over the broken branches and crushed weeds. Around rocks and trees and brambles thick with thorns.

Ran and ran and ran. My legs heavy. Muscles burning. Lungs bursting. Heart pounding, pounding, pounding in my ears.

Until I could not go one more step.

chapter 5
Sooner

It was a long time before my heartbeat returned to normal. My leg was wet with blood. I had curled onto a bed of grass beneath a scraggly sapling to lick my wound clean. With each swipe of my tongue, it stung anew.

Water. I needed water.

I sniffed the air. Smelled mud somewhere. Where there was mud, there was often water. Crawling out from my hiding place, I lifted my nose to the wind. The mud... it was farther downhill from where I was now.

Where was I? I looked around, listened. Far away, I saw a ridge. Along it, cars and trucks zoomed. But where was the van? Where was Brandy?

I had to go back the way I'd come. So I put my nose down and followed my own tracks. But my scent was light. I'd raced over rocky places and patches of dirt and had even run on a gravel road for some distance. I remembered only snatches of it. Something deep inside had told me that running meant escaping—and escaping meant safety.

A twig cracked, and I nearly leapt out of my skin. But it was only a branch snapped by the wind.

The wind—it was blowing harder now, coming from behind me. It made it difficult to follow my trail. The farther I went, the harder it became. My scent was fading. Other smells mingled with it. Several times, I stopped to get my bearings, but this was a strange land with strange sounds and strange scents and danger everywhere.

My throat ached for water. I sniffed the air again. Listened. Heard, somewhere, the chime of water rippling over stones. I started that way, then stopped. If I went to the water, would I find my way back to Brandy?

Brandy. I had to find Brandy. Needed Brandy more than I needed water or food or rest.

So I lowered my nose to the ground and inhaled deeply, concentrated. Followed my trail until I could hear the boom of human voices and the groan and squeal of their machines.

The van! I could see it now.

So many people. Some climbing carefully down the hill with ropes attached to them. Others standing, overlooking the site from above. Still more below, milling about. A few were kneeling near the front of the van, next to a lump with a light-colored blanket covering it. They were using small machines and devices to—

It was Brandy!

I started forward, then just as quickly stopped myself. They were helping her. They would take her somewhere safe.

Very carefully, I wandered closer, keeping to the brush and tall grass. No one gave any indication they saw me.

I wanted to go to her, to let her know I was there. But this was all so terribly strange and frightening. I didn't understand it all.

So I watched and waited, all the while growing more tired and thirsty. By now, my leg was throbbing. I licked it some more, cleaned away a sticky white goo seeping from the scab that wouldn't stay closed.

A noise. A great and awful noise from above. I crouched low. Looked at the sky. A mechanical bird whirred up high, swooping from far away to right overhead in mere seconds. Like a hummingbird or a bee, but so much bigger, so much faster. It hovered until it was directly over where Brandy lay. A long basket attached to cables descended from it to the people collected around Brandy. They gently lifted her and strapped her into it, then grabbed the hooks on the ends of the cables and clipped them to the basket.

One human waved to the big bird and up Brandy went. Dangling above the ravine like a fly caught on the strand of a spider's web.

Brandy, no! Come back! I barked. *Come back!*

My protests were drowned out by the hum of machines, the roar of the wind, and the clamor of voices. Still, no one looked my way.

Gradually, Brandy was pulled up, up, up. Until she was over the road where the vehicles with pulsing lights were. The basket was pulled into the mechanical bird, which flew away.

She was gone.

My heart went cold inside. My Brandy was *gone*. How would I find her again? Would she come back to get me? How long would I have to wait?

I didn't know the answer. But I would wait as long as it took.

—o0Oo—

The sun climbed higher, heating my fur, drying out my throat and lungs. My thirst was all-consuming. Never in my life had I craved water so much. I would have drunk from a puddle, but it hadn't rained in more days than I could recall. The vegetation, although still the green of summer, was dry and crinkly. The grass and trees thirsted, too.

If I left and Brandy came back, I might miss her. So I stayed, sheltered by the dappled shade of a grove of small trees, my tongue hanging, my rear injured leg heating from the inside out.

They brought a giant machine to the road's edge at the top of the hill. It had a tower of metal extending outward from its body, and from that dangled another cable with a big metal hook at the end. The hook was lowered, then affixed to the van. Several men heaved at the van until they pushed it upright. Then, through a series of maneuvers and after an even longer time, the van was dragged up the hill by the cable.

I wondered why they were bothering. It didn't seem to be of much use anymore. Humans threw so many things away. Why save a smashed-up vehicle?

The van, mangled and twisted, was put on the bed of a truck. They took it away. Gradually, the people all left.

It was almost night now. I was alone. Didn't know what to do. Whether to stay or go.

Water. If only I had water. And maybe a little to eat.

But if I left...

I stayed. For now.

When Brandy returned to get me, she would see what a good dog I'd been. That I'd stayed, even though she hadn't told me to.

I would rest while I waited. But I would not leave.

My chin upon the ground, I stretched my feet out. Dirt dug into my cut. I flopped over onto my good side. Watched the top of the hill for the longest time. While more and more cars went past. Until I saw only the cones of light they threw before them. And heard the steady roar of their engines and the hum of tires spinning...

—o0Oo—

"Sooner! There you are. Are you ready to go?"

I bounced in place. Higher, higher, higher.

See, Brandy? See? I barked. *I stayed. I stayed! Right here. I didn't go anywhere.*

"Let's go then!"

Brandy took off running. Faster than any rabbit I'd ever seen. Her steps so light she barely touched the earth. Which was a funny thing, because Brandy didn't run without good reason.

I tried to run after her, but my feet kept landing in the same place. So I tried harder. But my muscles wouldn't do what I wanted them to.

Perplexed, I watched as Brandy jumped over the van, then vanished between the trees.

Wait, Brandy, wait!

The giant metal monsters came to life, squealing and groaning and belching smoke. They rumbled and churned and turned toward me.

I wanted to run. Knew I should. But I couldn't go... anywhere. Couldn't run. Couldn't follow Brandy. Couldn't hide or walk away or even lie down.

The hair on my neck stiffened. I raised my head, aware of something above. A shadow. The stir of air. A pulsing.

A mechanical bird swooped down from the sky—

—oOOo—

The sky was as dark as the darkest night. Crickets sang their nighttime songs, as crickets everywhere did. Clouds cloaked the stars. A soft wind stirred the tree branches and rustled the grass. They were all sounds I'd heard before. But not at home in my bed. There, it was quiet. As quiet as quiet could be.

At home, lying on my own soft bed inside a crate at the foot of Brandy's, I could relinquish my vigil. All demons were banished. All duties absent. I could sleep, undisturbed, secure in knowing nothing would harm us.

The moment Brandy stirred in the mornings—a gentle turning, her foot stretching beyond the edge of the mattress, a sigh—it was time to sound the alarm.

Wake up, wake up, I'd whine. *I have to pee.*

Sometimes, she resisted.

"Too early," she'd mumble. "It's only six AM."

A dog's bladder waited for no one.

Wake. Up.

A groan from beneath the covers.

I'll pee in here, I'd yip. *And then you'll be sorry.*

And that was how I trained Brandy. I started with the quietest command I could, escalating only when my person refused to listen. Most of the time, however, I let Brandy think she was getting her way. Dogs were smarter than most humans gave them credit for.

—o00o—

Eventually morning came, gray and with the smell of dampness on the air. The wind strengthened, the constant rush of it drowning out all the smaller sounds. It was both welcome and unwanted.

The humans who had so busily cleaned up our mess had not returned. If not for the random broken-off pieces of the van still lying about and scraps of our belongings strewn about in the branches, I could almost imagine the night before had never occurred.

As I watched and waited, it became increasingly apparent. Brandy was not coming back. I would have to find her.

So I padded through the weeds, walked around where the van had been, sniffing hard to pick up her scent. There were so many other smells, though. Strong, offensive smells. The wind was mixing them together, making it hard to detect one from the other. The more I sniffed, the more confused I became.

Finally, I came to the base of the hill and followed the path they'd dragged the van up. By the time I reached the highway, I realized the rumbling was not just the cars and trucks speeding by. It was thunder. And with thunder came the flashes of light that jangled every nerve in my body.

As I began along the road, keeping to the ditch that ran parallel to it, the first drops of rain came softly. But the longer I went on, the harder they came and the louder the rumbling got. Until my fur was soaked, and I had to squint to see at all. The cars and trucks did not slow down, sending huge sprays of water out. The rain had begun to collect in puddles, and I paused to drink from one at the road's shoulder. With the first lap of my tongue, I recoiled. It had a dirty, oily taste to it. So I went on, faster and more determined.

Until I came to a bridge.

The road narrowed to span the distance. Below, a river cut deeply. There was water down there. Water to drink. But above was the way to more humans. To wherever they had taken Brandy. And perhaps, to home.

As I stood there, pondering what to do, my skin prickled. The sky lit up, then darkened again, light and dark alternating faster than I could blink. With the next flash came the sizzle of air on fire—a crack and a boom so deep it knocked me off my feet.

I lay stunned, my insides buzzing. I couldn't move, couldn't think. Every inch of me, inside and out, tingled. It felt as though my heart had exploded, disintegrated.

A long while later, I returned to awareness, gained control of my muscles. I flopped onto my back. Stretched. Breathed in. Out. In time, I struggled to my feet, but my legs were weak and wobbly.

Another rumble vibrated the earth beneath my paws. Fear propelled me forward. I ran clumsily. Down, away. Looking for cover. As if I could outrun the storm itself.

Near where steep earth met the moving water was an overturned boat. I flattened to wiggle beneath its cover. The space was small, dark, and smelled of stagnant muck and traces of fish, but it was safe there. Safer than outside, anyway. It was dry at least, and I could not see the flashes as they came, except for the slightest flicker through the tiny space through which I'd come. The ground still shook. The sky still boomed. The air still crackled with invisible sparks.

I stayed there forever, it seemed. So tired I ached from the inside out, and so hungry I felt the hollowness of my belly drawn back into my spine. Brandy had taken me out on boats before. To fish on the lake with her father when we visited him. At first, I'd been scared of the rocking motion and the water all around, but Brandy had patiently taught me to swim and put a vest on me just to be safe. Brandy did special things like that with me. Many dogs were not so lucky.

Water trickled beneath the edges of the boat to pool in a little divot. I lapped greedily as it filled, more thankful for the drink than I was discomforted by being so wet. It was gritty with dirt, but that didn't matter. It satisfied my thirst for now.

Later, as the thunder rolled off into the distance, I slept. Until the pounding and then the patter of rain ceased, and the daily sounds of human activity rose around.

When I finally came out from under the boat, I wasn't prepared for what I saw.

This wasn't home. Not even close. Our home was in a small neighborhood in a small town, surrounded by rolling fields and patches of woods and weathered barns and old farmhouses.

This was a city, stretching the length of the opposite bank. With buildings both tall and squat. Streets and sidewalks and cars, cars, cars. More goings-on than a living being had any use for.

But where there were people, there was food.

Just like water and sleep had been everything not so long ago, it was food I now craved with fierce determination. I needed to find food more than I needed to find Brandy.

Because without food, I couldn't go on, could never find Brandy.

chapter 6
Grayson

Grayson needed to eat. It didn't matter what. He just needed sustenance to keep him going. A glance at the clock on the dashboard revealed it had been a whole four hours since he'd last eaten. He'd been pressing the pace to get to his uncle's farm, which meant he'd been limiting his bathroom breaks, despite the number of caffeinated beverages he'd consumed since leaving the city.

The *thwop-thwop-thwop* of chopper blades drew his attention momentarily skyward. He glanced through the tinted upper part of the windshield of his rental car to see an emergency medical helicopter sweep across the sky. Those were never good. The helicopter veered northward, away from the interstate, disappearing after a time beyond the treetops of a distant ridge.

Soon after, traffic slowed. As the highway dipped into a broad valley, Grayson could see the long line of cars and trucks bogging the road ahead. Highway patrol car lights flashed and twirled beyond a point where the vehicles were being funneled into a single lane.

Grayson flipped his signal on and squeezed into an opening in the left lane. For close to an hour, he inched forward, stopping and going at intervals, until he could see a crane lifting a mangled van from the ravine off to the right side of the road. A nearly unrecognizable mass of metal. If the driver or any passengers had survived, it was a miracle. Someone had, though, or else they wouldn't have bothered to bring in the helicopter.

Finally, Grayson cleared the point where the van had smashed through the guardrail. The highway opened back up into two lanes, freeing the space between the vehicles. Pushing his car back up to speed, he set the cruise. The car was a rental he'd selected based on affordability. His only requirements were something fuel efficient with cruise control and automatic transmission. He got that and little more: a two-door silver economy car with a radio and plain black interior. The suspension was stiff and the ride noisy, but he'd had to make precious few stops for gas along the way—a fact he was grateful for. It was cramped, but he didn't plan on having it long, anyway.

Although the accident had temporarily diverted his attention, his hunger had returned in full force. The fullness of his bladder made the need for a break even more urgent. He focused his attention on finding an exit with services. It had been forty miles since the last one. He hadn't been hungry then.

Judging by the online map he'd examined before he left, it hadn't seemed all that far—only a few inches. The number of miles from Manhattan to Faderville, Kentucky had seemed irrelevant. He'd get there when he got there. Settling matters would take as long as needed and not a day more.

The cramp in his lower right leg had become unbearable. His knee and ankle ached to the point he found it hard to concentrate on his driving. Residual effects of being struck by a car just before his senior year in college, he'd been told. After his leg had healed, he'd refused prescription medication, even though the pain still lingered decades later. The only help, he'd been told by more than one doctor, would be ongoing physical therapy. The schedule had been too disruptive to his work, the exercises too rigorous for what seemed to make only a tiny difference. It was easier to accept his limitations than to try to overcome them.

At times like this, however, he remembered what it had been like to feel the immortality of youth, to be strong and fast and undaunted by the most demanding physical endeavors. Now, however, he felt older than his years, broken and compromised.

When the next exit came up, he got off. The only food was at a truck stop and fueling station. After putting gas in the car, he went to the restroom, washed his hands, then came out to order a greasy burger and overly salted fries. When he asked for water, the clerk slid a bottle with a fancy label across the counter.

Grayson regarded it with disdain. "Just water. In a cup, please. Not that. Water shouldn't cost two dollars. It comes out of the tap for free. Or close to free, anyway."

He hadn't meant to sound so terse. It wasn't normally his manner. But she'd assumed he wanted to pay extra for the convenience of a plastic bottle with a screw-on cap and a label that proclaimed its purity.

The teenage girl squinted at him. Keen enough not to argue, though, she re-rang his order, handed him back the two dollars, and gave him a paper cup. "There's a sink in the bathroom."

He didn't have the time or motivation to make this into a learning moment. The sooner he got on with this trip, did what he came to do, and made it home, the better.

Back in his car, as he ate the first few bites of his sandwich, he tallied the miles to go. Not far, but still too many. He yawned between mouthfuls. Although he was most of the way there, he wasn't accustomed to driving for so many hours at a time.

As he drove on toward the small town called Faderville, clouds dark with rain loomed on the horizon, reflecting his mood.

Ten months without a job. Ten months of sending out resumes, researching businesses, poring over the *Wall Street Journal* every day, a dozen nibbles resulting in personalized e-mail replies—he wasn't counting the automated ones—maybe half a dozen preliminary phone interviews, two real interviews, both ending in regrets and good wishes for better luck elsewhere as they selected another, probably younger, candidate…

Ten months of dashed hopes and mounting rejection.

Longer than that living alone.

Even though he and Fee had had busy professional lives, there had been a comfort in her presence: the dresses hanging in the closet, her toothbrush next to his, her collection of shoes heaped by the front door, the warmth of her body beside his as they sat on the couch in the evenings together.

And yet… it had become incredibly mundane. As bland as pureed oatmeal. They hadn't fought in the beginning, so they hadn't needed to kiss and make up. Much as Fee had kept her feelings to herself, so had he. Grayson had never told her how gray the world seemed to him, how tasteless every bite of food, how disappointing his once-favorite things had become, how he struggled to find even the slightest traces of joy or causes for laughter. To admit those things would've seemed unmanly and weak.

His troubles hadn't kept him awake, though; every night, he'd slept soundly, lulled into slumber through the magic of a pill. They'd been a habit he hadn't been proud of, but without them, his nights were restless and his days a mind-numb slog through quicksand. Those uneventful precious eight hours were sometimes the best part of his day. Still, he didn't feel the need to broadcast his dependence on them. He'd lied, just a little, to Fee about the pills. Just like he'd lied when she asked if he felt sad or hopeless sometimes.

Depression seemed like such a gloomy word. So pervasive. He might be a little down in the dumps, but he wasn't… *depressed*.

Depressed people moped and complained. He did none of that. They withdrew, stopped showing up to work, abandoned their families. Sometimes they even killed themselves. He couldn't imagine taking such an extreme measure. The thought of it scared him too much. He didn't have the stomach for it.

There'd been a time when he'd been happy, though. Even before Fiona had stolen his heart and made him mad with desire. When he was young and vibrant and, in his own mind, undefeatable.

When he'd been a runner. A good one, at that.

It had all ended one misty morning, the summer before his senior year in college. Bowerman University was a mid-sized school in upstate New York, far removed from any metropolis, deep in the forested foothills of the Adirondacks, close to the Vermont border. It was an institution long on academic excellence, but newly upward in the world of collegiate distance running. The climate and terrain had hardened a burgeoning team of determined runners, many of whom had been overlooked by the traditional powerhouses. Coach McCafferty had built his program from the ground up, setting the bar high for his runners. In his ten-year tenure, he produced several Olympic athletes. Grayson had been spoken of in the same light. He was a workhorse, unimpeded by injury, unbroken by the many hundreds of miles of training, undaunted by challenges from the fiercest competitors.

Born to run, Grayson reveled in the rhythm of it, the cadence of his stride, each arm swing, lungful of air, and labored heartbeat. The oneness with the world around him. The feeling of floating on air, of hurtling through time.

The depth on his college cross country team had been nothing short of astounding. As a junior, Grayson was the championship meet runner-up to a senior. During his final season, he was expected to lead his teammates to a national team title. Nothing was a given; he knew that. But he would do everything in his power to do his part.

Late August—just like it was that day as he drove south and west from West Virginia into Kentucky—was his favorite time of year. The workouts were just beginning. But on most days, it was still the quiet and solitude of the long run. Up just after dawn, he'd hit the roads, sometimes alone, sometimes with a teammate or several. On that fateful day, he'd been out with Justin Zarecky, the number-two man on the team. Roommates and training partners, they had become best friends by circumstance. Neither was a talker, which was why Grayson enjoyed his company on early mornings so much. He had no desire to make meaningless small talk before his brain was fully functioning.

They were almost done with the eight-mile hill loop as it descended Fagan Road. The shoulder was gravelly and narrow, the ditches deep with weeds. The road hugged a cutout into the rocky earth on one side.

"I've been thinking of asking Caroline to marry me," Justin said soberly.

"Eventually, you mean?" Grayson pulled in a deep breath. They'd kept up a good clip, faster than was necessary for an easy day, but the mist had given the woods around them a mystical quality. It was like running on a cloud, their steps light, hearts quick. "Like after the next semester, when you graduate?"

"No, like tomorrow night. I've been thinking all summer—she's the one. *The* one. I know it. So I figure... why wait? If she says yes, we could be married by this time next year. Besides, that would give her—I mean us—time to plan."

"You don't have a job yet."

"Yeah, so? Neither do you."

"I'm not contemplating marriage." Grayson hated being the practical one, but Justin was too smart a guy not to think things through. He just felt an obligation, as his friend, to point out the obvious.

"Anyway," Justin went on as they began into the last turn, "it would give me some incentive to find a job. A good one. Her, too. If we both got offers in different cities, though…"

Grayson wasn't paying close attention at that point. Justin was merely thinking out loud, maybe looking for a little reassurance. He wasn't going to dampen his hopes any further. Caroline was a great gal. His friend would be stupid to let her slip away. He'd be even stupider to get hitched before he had his life plans in place, but he couldn't tell a guy that when he was blind with love.

"Don't you think that's the way to go, Grayson?"

"Sure. You're a couple of smart cookies. You'll make it work." Even as he said it, Grayson had no idea what he'd just encouraged him to do.

The hill fell away behind them, but the woods closed in tighter. They had less than half a mile to go. Justin had a bounce in his step and a smile to match. It was annoying.

Grayson checked his watch to gauge their pace. Too fast. He'd pay for it tomorrow. Justin looked at his in sync.

"Ah, damn." Justin wiped the spit from the corner of his mouth. "I have anatomy in fifteen minutes. If I'm late, Dr. Horton will lock the auditorium doors and I'll have to knock to get in. Bastard."

Then he took off like his shoes were on fire. Grayson, foolishly, took off after him. But his friend had a head start. Swinging close to the curve, Justin took a hard left.

Grayson saw the car before he ever heard it. It was going too fast. A blur of gray, careening over the white line. Justin dived to his left, toward the ditch. But physics and mathematics and geometry had unchangeable laws. Justin's attempt to alter course at his relatively lower speed was not enough to avoid the trajectory of the car.

Its front grill impacted with Justin's legs in a bone-crushing *thump!* He smashed into the hood. Then his body flew into the air, did several flips, and hit the asphalt on the opposite side of the road.

Lagging behind, Grayson had dodged to the right. But the car's driver, reacting too late, overcorrected the steering. The car spun partway before heading back toward the ditch to Grayson's left, but not before the bumper clipped his left knee.

Grayson was thrown back, twisting as he reached to break his fall with his hands.

The next thing he was aware of was the driver kneeling at his side on the road.

The man, dressed in a navy button-up shirt and matching pants, laid a hand on his shoulder. His embroidered name badge said, 'All-Seasons Heating and Cooling,' and below it, 'Steve'.

"Don't move, man. Don't move." Steve glanced at Grayson's legs and winced. "You... Are you okay? Can you understand me?"

Grayson stared at his legs. Whose foot was that, pointed at such an odd angle? Was it... his? "Okay... I guess." He was more concerned about Justin than himself. Besides, he couldn't feel anything wrong. Not yet, anyway. He tried to turn his head to find his friend, but he couldn't see him. Everything around him was spinning and out of focus. "My friend...?"

The driver's gaze slid to a place Grayson couldn't see. "Um, I... I don't know." His face was a mixture of horror and wide-eyed panic. "I was just changing the station on the radio. When I looked up... he was there. I couldn't..." His eyes, full of tears, met Grayson's. "I'm sorry, man. I didn't see him in time."

In the end, Grayson survived, his lower leg cleanly broken, his kneecap shattered. He hadn't run a step since that day.

Justin, mercifully, had died instantly.

chapter 7
Grayson

The thing that struck Grayson was how many miles there were between towns and houses in this part of the world. He hadn't been outside Manhattan in almost a year. There, there were so many people everywhere he got used to not looking them in the eyes unless he needed something. Here, nearly every driver he'd passed since leaving the interstate had lifted their hand in a wave. He wondered if the car he was driving, a nondescript silver coupe, resembled a local's.

Faderville hadn't been terribly far off the highway, but the farm was tucked away in the remotest part of the county. The town itself had been quaint, to put it nicely, with a tiny post office, a two-story courthouse with a central dome, and a collection of small shops downtown. The hotspot seemed to be a family restaurant just off the interstate. But he'd long since left that momentary glimpse of civilization and was deep into what he'd call the boondocks. The scenery was appealing, but that was about the extent of it. Now late in the afternoon, the sun had scorched away the morning's mist and left in its stead a suffocating blanket of humidity.

Not a day for any sort of outdoor activity. All the more reason for Grayson to be in disbelief when he saw them in the distance, nearly a mile away: a pack of runners, high schoolers judging by their lanky builds. As his car crested a low ridge and he moved over into the other lane to give them space, they broke into single file for added measure. Their shirts were soaked with sweat, their beardless faces slack in prolonged discomfort, their legs and arms swinging synchronously. Behind them, an older man with a paunch and a fringe of snow-white hair covered with a baseball cap huffed on his bicycle.

The boys, lost in friendly banter, paid Grayson no heed as he drove past. But the old man—their coach, he guessed—touched his fingers to the brim of his cap. A wave or a nod was a common practice done to show one's gratitude for providing a clear and safe passing distance, yet Grayson knew firsthand it would only take one distracted driver, one selfish person in a rush, to thoughtlessly violate that space and put them in danger.

By the time he actually turned onto Troutwine Road, he'd made so many turns and gone so many miles he was sure the GPS on his phone was leading him on a wild goose chase. Eventually, he reached the address the attorney had provided. He looked on in awe.

Uncle Skip's farm was like a feature spread out of *Southern Living* magazine. In reality, he'd been mentally prepared for a rundown shack or two to shelter the animals and a ramshackle cottage with peeling paint. Maybe even a mobile home. But this... this was not what he'd envisioned.

He drove down the winding lane, smoothly blacktopped, lined on either side with a white board fence and a sentry of shade trees. A handful of horses were pastured on one side. On the other was a hayfield. Off to the right stood a well-maintained, sprawling white barn trimmed out in dark green with a green metal roof and three cupolas. Atop the center cupola was a wrought-iron weather vane with a trotting horse.

The house was more modest in size but no less immaculate, its colors mirroring that of the barn. A wraparound porch encircled the structure.

It wasn't until Grayson stopped the car and got out that he saw the man lazing in the rocking chair by the front door, his weathered boots propped on the railing and a battered white cowboy hat covering his face.

"I'd say you're late, but time kinda stands still out here, don't it?" The man lifted his hat from his face and smiled in greeting, although it was hard to tell if he was actually smiling with that thick handlebar moustache of his. "Then again, maybe I was early."

Limping as he made his way to the porch, Grayson fought a grimace. The pain flared sometimes, but if he moved around, it tended to loosen things up. He checked his watch. It was half past four. "Mr. Franzen? I'm sorry, had I arranged to meet you here today?"

It was the estate attorney who'd sent him the letter. The man not only resembled Sam Elliott, the actor—he sounded like him, too. That or Tom Selleck.

"Call me Rex." He swung his feet down, stood—all probably six-feet four-inches of him—and reached over the railing. "Loretta told me you'd be by sometime late on Friday."

Grayson shook his hand. "Grayson."

"Well met, Gary."

Grayson cringed. Normally he corrected people when they got his name wrong, but he didn't intend to see much of this man, so it wasn't worth the bother. "Likewise... Rex." Turning around, Grayson gestured toward the barn. "You didn't let on that Skip Dalton had money enough for all this."

"Would you have been here sooner if I had?" Rex's silver moustache tilted in a smirk.

Grayson shrugged. "Maybe."

If Uncle Skip had enough money to run a modestly successful

horse farm like this, he probably had a respectable lump of cash in the bank. Enough to tide Grayson over until the next job came through at least. That wasn't why Grayson had come here in the first place, but it was a pleasant bonus for the inconvenience.

"So he had a will then? He named me in it, did he? I'm sorry, you'd think I'd know this, but he and I weren't close. Your call came as a surprise to me."

"I'll get you up to speed, Gary." His jaw muscles working as he chewed a stick of gum, Rex picked up the suit jacket he'd slung over the porch rail, then motioned for Grayson to follow him inside.

Pain flared in Grayson's lower leg like a bullet tearing through flesh. He almost cried out—and had he been alone he might very well have—but pride prevented it. Instead, he drew in a sharp intake of breath, held it, and paused only for a moment before forcing himself up the steps. Mercifully, the pain ebbed to mere discomfort with each stride.

The screen door banged shut behind them as they walked into what Grayson could only describe as a 'parlor'. The furniture was of an older style, like something in a museum, but if it was indeed old, it had barely been used. He circled the room. It was filled with antiques: a marble-based clock with Roman numerals, a scroll-top secretary's desk, a mahogany sideboard with claw-feet legs, and an upright piano complete with sheet music for "America the Beautiful." Atop the mantel, however, there was a trace of dust. Without thinking, Grayson ran his finger over it.

"I let the maid go." Tossing his suit jacket over the sofa arm, Rex settled down next to a floral-patterned end cushion, legs spread wide, elbows on knees, hands clasped. "It seemed the prudent thing to do. Until the finances are settled, anyway. No sense doling out money to keep up a house no one's inhabiting. But now that you're here…"

Maids cost money. Grayson was feeling less optimistic now about his uncle's net worth. "That won't be necessary. I don't intend to stay long. And I'm perfectly capable of cleaning up after myself in the meanwhile."

"Huh." Rex tugged at the end of his mustache.

"Huh, what?"

"Pardon?"

"You said 'huh'. Like there was a thought behind that."

Rex sat back, scratched his neck. "You got something at home to get back to—wife, job, a pet?"

Grayson didn't know how to respond. The correct answer would be 'No, to all the above,' but that was really none of this guy's business. Instead, he changed the subject. "Something to drink?"

"If you don't mind. Glass of ice water would be fine."

It was only after he'd made the offer that Grayson realized he had no idea what might be in stock in the kitchen or how old any of the food or beverages might be. His uncle had been deceased almost a month now, although from Grayson's understanding he'd been relatively healthy for a man of his years until the end when a ruptured aneurysm in his brain took his life. Water and a little ice from the freezer seemed like a safe bet.

Once in the kitchen, it took him a few minutes to find the glasses, rinse them out, and fill them up. The ice cube tray was exactly where it should have been.

Back in the living room, he handed Rex a glass and cut to the chase. "Was Skip over his head in debt?"

"Mighta been." After placing his used gum back in its wrapper and tucking it in a pocket, Rex downed half the glass, then held it at arm's length to catch a beam of sunlight through the cut crystal, turning it at angles to send prisms of color bouncing off every surface in the room. "Hard to say."

"What does that mean?"

Rex pointed to the sitting chair next to the sofa. Upholstered in brocaded red velvet, it looked like a relic from the Victorian era.

"Maybe you oughta sit down."

Grayson's first impulse was to walk out the door and go back to Manhattan. But he'd come this far. Might as well find out what the situation was really like.

"You have any idea what Skip Dalton did for a living?" Rex asked.

"You want me to guess?"

"Why not? Give it a whirl."

"He bred horses?"

"I take it Loretta filled you in. Anyway, that's what he did the last couple of decades. Before that, he owned restaurant franchises. Lived a comfortable life. Modestly successful. Enough to land him this spread. As far as horses go, he had ambitious plans, loved his animals, and took wonderful care of them." On the end table next to him was a circular crystal coaster in the same pattern. He set the glass on it, tugged his tie a little looser, and rolled up the sleeves of his dress shirt. "Let me say this, though—he didn't know the first thing about breeding, training, or bloodlines. He invested in them, you could say. Bought a few, sold a few. Had a winner or two along the way. But breeding horses and dealing in them takes a certain amount of business savvy, scientific study, and a whole lotta intuition—and even more luck. Mostly, he sank a boatload of moola into what turned out to be a rather risky investment."

Having dealt in numbers his whole life, Grayson wasn't about to take this man's assessment as a condemnation of his uncle's business acumen. When Rex got around to showing him the reports and spreadsheets, Grayson would take it for what it was—good or bad. He hadn't expected anything when he came here, so if he left with nothing, the only thing lost was his time.

Rex waved a hand in a vague circle like he was trying to indicate something beyond the room they were sitting in. "You see all these fancy horse farms around here and you figure those folk must be making money hand over fist. What you don't know is that, for most of them, it's just an expensive hobby. Something they're passionate about, sure.

"But the truth is the ones who can afford the often-mountainous losses are usually successful in other aspects of life: they own multimillion-dollar businesses, are surgeons, real estate investors, a few media moguls, and celebs. Very few actually make a living buying and selling horses. Horses eat a lot of hay and feed. When they need a vet, it ain't cheap. They need trailers to be transported in and big, powerful trucks to haul those trailers, barns to house them, fences that need maintenance…

"Hell, my youngest daughter wanted a pony when she was little. Her heart was set on it. It was all she could talk about for three solid years. Pony this and pony that." A smile of fond reminiscence crinkled his weathered cheeks. "Like the good daddy I am, I caved. The money I poured into trading up rides for her as she grew, the lessons, the entries for shows, the costumes, the tack… I could've sent her to college twice over by the time she graduated high school. Hindsight being what it is, I wish we'd encouraged her to pursue sports or dance instead. She coulda played the harp, for all I care. Point is, Skip likely spent more money on the horses than he was bringing in."

"So he… he lost a lot of money?"

"Most likely. Bought a lot of expensive horses, paid some exorbitant stud fees. Like any business, you gotta invest, but there's a point where you learn to cut your losses. Skip never got to that point. You see, Skip had a tender spot in his heart for the ones whose racing careers ended too early or the ones that didn't pass the muster."

"He took them in then?"

"On his own dime, he did. He may not have been good with animal husbandry, but he was a good man."

That was nice to know, but it wasn't much consolation.

"Be straight with me," he told Rex. "Was he in over his head? Did he owe more than he was worth?"

"Well, that's hard to say."

"Give me your best guess. If I sell those horses at auction and put this farm on the market, is there likely to be anything left?"

"You want a quick sale?"

"Ideally, yes."

"Then no."

Just as he feared. Coming here hadn't solved anything. He should've stayed home. Should've just declared this was none of his doing, then let the probate court handle it.

"And if I want top dollar for this farm? How would I go about doing that?"

"Traditional sale. I could hook you up with a good agent. Someone who specializes in farms, whether functional or hobby. But I gotta be honest, Gary—a transaction like that… could happen right away, could take a while."

"As in… weeks, months?"

Rex shrugged. "Or years."

"Years?" Grayson went to stand by the fireplace. "Why years?"

After getting up from the couch, Rex came to put his hand on Grayson's shoulder. "Gary, I'm the rare kind of lawyer who tells people the truth. And the truth is I don't have any idea in hell how long it'll take to sell this place. It could get snapped up tomorrow. It could sit for years, even as dandy a place as it is. Lord knows I'm no expert on the real estate market." He walked over to the sideboard, then tapped on a stack of papers there. "I'm going to leave you with all this boring paperwork to look over. Meanwhile, I have a lot of Skip's documents to sort through, so maybe I can give you a better answer when we meet again. Next week work for you?"

"Not tomorrow?"

"I'm a lawyer, Gary. Not a convenience store clerk. As much as I'd like to help you get all this settled lickety-split, I have other clients with more urgent affairs. We small-town attorneys wear a lot of hats." He tugged at the brim of his, then handed Grayson a card. "Call my office Monday and set it up. Oh"—he put his suit jacket on and patted first his right pocket, then his left before producing a set of keys—"you'll want these. Not that anybody locks their doors around here, but it might be good to do for the time being. Last month up in Lexington, there were four homes broken into of people who'd died recently. Criminals like to hunt through the obituaries for their next target, figuring dead people won't put up much of a fight."

Grayson saw Rex out the door. Just as the lawyer was getting in his truck—a late-model crew cab with all the bells and whistles—Grayson stopped him.

"The horses... I don't know how to take care of them."

"No worries there. I'm sure Loretta will be by before sundown. Usually is. She can walk you through the whole routine." He pounded Grayson on the arm reassuringly. "As much as she complains about seeing after the critters, she loves 'em like her own children."

Grayson couldn't see how it was possible to place animals on the same level as humans; nonetheless, he was grateful for the neighbor's help. All he had to do was keep the horses healthy until someone took them off his hands.

As Rex Franzen's truck disappeared into the distance, Grayson took a second look around. How many gallons of paint and how many days would it take to paint all that fence? Had his uncle taken care of the grounds himself—or had he had a groundskeeper as well as the maid? The upkeep had to be incredibly time-consuming.

For Grayson, however, the thought of taking all this on himself was too much. He wouldn't know where to start, even if he'd known what to do.

After a short walk around the property, during which he observed the horses for a time—and they him—he headed for the front door to explore the house, the strangely heavy set of keys jangling in his pocket. He had his foot on the first step to the porch when his phone rang. He didn't recognize the number, but it was a New York call. His heartbeat quickened. The financial firm he'd last interviewed with almost three weeks ago had told him they'd be making a decision about now. Could it be them?

"Hello?"

"Mr. Darling?"

"Yes, speaking."

"This is Terrence Hawkins with Attovan Investments. How are you today?"

"Good, thank you." He felt the slightest spark of hope. This day could turn out well after all. "And how are you, Mr. Hawkins?"

"Fine, thank you," Hawkins replied about as enthusiastically as if he'd just had his wisdom teeth pulled. "I want you to know we've made a decision about the position you applied for."

"That? Oh, of course. And?"

"Your qualifications were beyond adequate: education, experience, recommendations..."

A few seconds lapsed. Papers rustled in the background. Grayson's heart began to sink. It wasn't the pause, it was the word 'were'—*Your qualifications were...* A clue, tiny but glaring. If the man had called to offer him the job, he would've used present tense.

Grayson lowered himself to sit on the bottom step. He felt the need to take this sitting down.

"We've offered the position to another candidate. He's given a verbal affirmative, but he hasn't signed on yet. We want you to know in the event he backs out, you are first on our list of alternates. I'm just calling to check you're still available and open to the job, should our first selection fall through."

"Uh... yeah, I mean yes. Please do keep me in mind. I'd be delighted to work for Attovan... if you need me."

After he hung up, he sat there staring out at Kentucky farmland for what must have been an hour, dejected and numb. Although he told himself he should feel hopeful, he wasn't. Because he'd begun not to care. About anything. Even himself.

If he'd been a drinker, he would've gone inside to see if his uncle had a stash of liquor somewhere, but alcohol made Grayson sick. He didn't touch the stuff. Which was a pity, because he could've used the escape from reality about then.

His life wasn't even mediocre. It was dismal. Had been ever since Fee left him. Maybe before. He'd tried to turn it around, but every chance, every glimmer had proven fruitless. It was as if a toxic cloud surrounded him and everyone but him saw it.

If he ceased to exist at that very moment, would anyone know or care?

He couldn't think of a single soul that would. Unless…

Grayson opened his contacts. Fiona Baumgartner—still first on his list. She'd reverted to her maiden name after the divorce, claiming it was necessary for her to start fresh, but in reality, it was like she was denying ever having been joined to him. He hit the call button. Almost hung up when he heard the first ring go through. And then before the second one—

"Grayson? What a pleasant surprise. Can't say I was expecting to hear from you today."

"Fee, hey…" He smiled just a little. She still cared. He didn't want to get back together with her—well, actually he would've liked that—but that wasn't his intent in calling her. He just wanted to hear her voice. To matter to someone. "How are you these days?"

"Really good. Really, *really* good. I'm glad you called."

"You are?" This was going even better than he'd hoped.

"Yeah, I am. There's something I've been wanting to tell you."

Hope and joy fled at the tone behind her words. That sinking feeling from a short while ago returned to his gut.

"I'm engaged! Can you believe it? I can hardly believe it myself. I didn't want you to find out from someone else, but Mark and I are planning to get married in Italy on New Year's and..." The overt enthusiasm she'd started with dissipated, like it had finally sunk in that there was no good way to tell him.

He knew she'd been dating, although not seriously last he'd heard. This was more than a surprise—it was a shock. But he couldn't let on about that. "That's great, Fee. I'm, uh... glad you're happy and, you know, moving on with life."

"Right. Grayson, I'm..." She stopped herself from apologizing. It wasn't needed. "So, why did you call? Did that job with Attovan come through?"

Although they rarely spoke anymore, they sometimes texted short messages to each other. Important things. The interview had gone so well they'd all but offered him the job on the spot. He'd assumed it was merely a formality that they hadn't. "Actually they passed me over. Just today."

"Oh, I'm sorry, Grayson. Really, I am."

He knew she was. Just like he knew she was sorry they'd grown apart and divorced. They both were. But she *had* moved on; he hadn't. Probably never would.

"Is that why you called?" she asked. "To tell me?"

The truth was he'd called to tell her he was in Kentucky because of his uncle's farm. He'd wanted to tell her about the horses and how much land there was and how much work it seemed like. He'd been hoping she'd offer some insight that would help him cope with it all. Or that she'd point out some silver lining. Fee had always been good at that. But none of that seemed to matter when the person you'd once loved with all your heart and soul delivered a punch to the gut.

"Yeah, uh, I suppose so. I'm still looking though. I've sent out a dozen more resumes, gotten some responses... I've even been thinking of starting my own financial consultation service."

"That's a great idea, Grayson! Why don't you?"

"Maybe I will." But he wouldn't. He'd only said that out of desperation, to make his abysmal life seem more promising than it really was.

Somehow, he found his exit and they said goodbye.

He knew, without knowing why, that he wouldn't hear from her again in a long, long time. If ever again.

chapter 8
Sooner

I sat there a long time, watching the river flow by. I hadn't given up on finding Brandy, but I couldn't go on without food. My stomach hurt. My legs were wobbly. I could barely stand, let alone run or even walk for miles.

I knew what I needed to do. I just didn't know how to do it. Or if I even could.

If I went back up the riverbank to the highway, I could cross the river and go to the city that way, where there was bound to be something to eat. But there wasn't much room on the edge of that bridge. The danger was too great. No, that wasn't an option.

I could swim across. After all, Brandy had taught me how. But my hunger had made me especially tired and the river was wide, the water flowing fast. I wasn't sure I could make it.

The water churned and bubbled at the river's edge, a brown foam collecting in small pools where the rocks had trapped it. It wasn't clear like the lake where Brandy had taken me fishing with her father. It was brown and smelly.

For a while, I paced along the bank beneath the bridge. If there was any chance of finding Brandy, I had to just pick a direction and go.

Finally, I turned to follow the river farther up, away from the highway bridge. I spotted another metal structure beyond a bend that seemed to span the river. The closer I came to it, the more I realized my good fortune—there were no cars or trucks on it, just two pairs of metal strips running parallel and beneath them, broad, weathered slats of wood.

It didn't take all that long to get there, but my observation was confirmed—cars did not go this way. My path across was clear. The convenience of it was stunning.

Partway up the embankment, two boys appeared. I was never quite sure what to make of children—especially the half-grown ones like these.

"Logan, look—a dog."

The other one rushed to the concrete barrier that ran along the road next to the river. He hopped up, then dangled over it. "Hey, puppy, come here. Here, puppy, puppy, puppy!"

I stayed where I was. Under other circumstances, if Brandy had been with me, I might have said hello, but it was better to stay safe for now.

"That's not a puppy."

"I know that, Becker. But what else am I supposed to call it? Not like it's gonna tell me its name or anything."

"Yeah, I guess. What kind of dog do you suppose it is?"

"Looks like a mutt to me. I reckon its tail got run over, and they had to amputate it."

"You think so?"

"I bet."

"I heard some dogs are born without tails. Some cats, too."

Humans and their incessant babbling. These two were starting to irritate me. If I continued up the bank to the bridge, I'd have to go right past them. Too close.

They stood there a while, talking more words that made no sense, calling to me at intervals.

"Think we should tell someone, Logan?"

"Tell who what?"

"That there's a dog down there. Maybe it's lost or something."

"Maybe it's wild and has rabies."

Enough of this. Turning, I started to run back the way I'd come, even though my leg hurt so badly now I couldn't help but limp. Far enough away I had a good head start, just in case they did come after me. Finally, I turned around to look, but they'd already lost interest and gone on.

When I was sure it was safe, I returned to the bridge. I had to squeeze beneath a metal fence between the river and the road. It snagged my fur, pulling clumps loose.

At the bridge, I paused. This road was different. The twin strips of metal ran across it and on into the city. In the other direction, they ran out into a field, seeming to go on forever. The wooden slats beneath the rails had gaping spaces in between them. I'd have to be very careful where I put my feet. If I missed a step—

My toes tingled. The ground beneath my feet buzzed. Soon, the ground shook.

Far off in the general direction I'd come from, a long mechanical beast with no end in sight snaked along the metal tracks. It was headed for the bridge.

If I didn't go now, I might never get to.

I started off at a stilted trot, hindered by my bad leg. The throbbing increased with every stride. The shaking from below grew stronger. I tried to hurry, worried the beast would beat me to the end and I'd have to jump over the edge into the murky water. Then I came to a spot where a board was missing. I stopped, looked behind me...

shouldn't have.

It *was* getting closer. Through the pads of my feet, I felt the rumble of its roar and knew it was after me.

It was too late to turn back. I had to go on, had to concentrate. When I focused ahead, it was as if the bridge were suddenly twice as long as it had been only seconds before.

I gathered myself, leaped, landed on my front paws, pitched forward—

My rear foot slipped. My leg went down in the hole, nothing but a roiling river far below. I tumbled, fell on my side, my bad hind leg twisting.

Pain was nothing when danger bore down. I pulled myself up—bad leg and all—and continued. Step by step by step.

My heart beat strong and fierce. My lungs drew air, deep and life-giving, fueling my muscles. Fear propelled me—faster, ever faster. Each stride growing longer and stronger, my feet barely grazed each board before pushing off and flying forward again.

A drawn-out blast slammed inside my ears. The ground shook, vibrating every bone in my body. I cast a glance behind me, seeing it had reached the start of the bridge. If I stayed my course down the middle, there was no escape. Shifting toward the side, I ran fast now, but the thing chasing me was impossibly faster.

Something in the river below caught my eye. The water flowed and splashed around a fallen branch… I lost my rhythm, placed a foot too far forward, wobbled.

For the briefest moment, I lost my balance. My shoulder hit the metal structure framing the bridge. Terror filled me. I scrambled to get my legs underneath me, each foot in the right place. Claws digging in, I veered back toward the center and raced on, never glancing back.

I ran until my heart threatened to explode. Ran until I thought my lungs would burst and my legs give way.

Until bridge met earth again.

Leaping free of the tracks, I tumbled down another embankment covered in loose rocks and scratchy weeds.

When I came to a stop, I swung my head toward the tracks just as another blast sounded. The beast thundered by, its wheels gliding over the smooth tracks. Closer up, I could see it was not just one beast, but many beasts trailing the leader. A strange thing. Just like the mechanical bird.

When it was long gone, I straggled out from the brush, more battered and bruised than before. The city sprawled far and wide.

And in its midst, the heady smells of food *everywhere*.

—oO0o—

That day and the next, I ate plenty by stealing cat food off porches and turning over trash cans. I slept in a cluttered garage one night and a stuffy crawl space the next. With a full belly and plenty of rest, I should've felt better, yet I was anything but.

I missed Brandy. Missed the sound of her voice, the gentle scratches under my chin, and the crunchy treats she used to feed me that tasted of cinnamon and apples. Somehow, I had to get back to her.

Although I wandered the city in search of her, deep down inside, I knew she wasn't here. I needed to go back to where she'd left me.

First though, I'd eat one more time while I could. So I went to a yard with overgrown bushes, where it was easy for me to hide until it was clear. After I squeezed under the chain-link fence, I crept carefully through the tall grass. Beneath the tree in the center of the yard was nothing but a patch of dirt. I sniffed the trunk. It reeked of urine.

A dog had been here not long ago. I peered around, ready to bolt. It wasn't there now, so I peed to leave my scent. As I kicked up dirt, I noticed a metal chain hanging from a clothesline.

I crept closer to the porch, watchful. I lapped at the stale water in the first algae-stained bowl. Then, as fast as I could, I ate the large chunks of kibble in the second.

Greedy, I ate and ate, until I was full and happy.

Until the back door of the house swung open… and the biggest, ugliest dog I had ever seen blustered out and locked eyes with me.

Face to face with Death itself, I froze from the inside out.

His jowls hung from a sagging face heavy with wrinkles. Tiny ears flanked the top sides of his overly large skull. They weren't really ears so much as little flaps of hide where his ears should be. His eyes were a piercing gold, the irises half hidden beneath drooping lids. His coat was a shiny blue-gray, the color of metal. His leg bones were gnarly like the trunks of a tree. The knuckles of his toes splayed on the weathered planks of the porch. Two of me could fit beneath him.

A rumble vibrated in his throat. He licked his lips. His spine bristled.

I was going to die. Today. Cruelly. Painfully. My guts ripped from the softness of my bloated belly. My insides laid open for the buzzards. He'd leave my skeleton there as a warning to any others who dared to trespass.

I lowered my head below my shoulders in a signal of submission. His lip curled up, quivered, revealing yellowed fangs. He lifted a giant paw, took a step toward me. Drool dripped from his jowls in steaming globs. Behind him was an older man in nothing but his boxers and a stained undershirt, half-stooped with the burdens of old age and decrepitude.

"What's 'at, Beau? Some damn mutt eatin' yer grub?"

The monster dog licked his lips, then growled again. The old man cackled.

It wouldn't matter how much I groveled. This was fight or flight. Since this dog was four times my size and could fit my head inside his mouth, well, running away was the best option.

Turning tail, I made for the gap under the fence. Speed and agility were my best traits, but sometimes even those were not enough. After I crossed the yard in six strides, I dove for the opening, knowing my pursuer would be too big to follow. I ducked low. The links, some of them bent open and sharp, scraped at the top of my head, but I wasn't about to stop to avoid a few scratches.

The problem, however, was my collar—the pretty green-patterned collar Brandy had bought for me at a dog show when I was an older puppy. My traveling collar, she'd called it. It had a tag on it with symbols that meant something to humans. Whenever she loaded up the van, she'd buckle it on me, and off we'd go on some adventure.

A wire from one of the fence's links hooked beneath it as I rammed my head through the opening. The bottom of the collar hit my windpipe, choking me. A twist of my head only tightened it more. I couldn't go through, couldn't pull back. The entire rear portion of my body was exposed, vulnerable.

The monster dog thundered across the ground. Low woofs boomed from his throat. Up on the porch, the old man goaded him onward.

"Git 'em, Beau. Git the sucker!"

I pushed and pulled and thrashed side to side, all the while aware if I called out, I would surely mark myself as fallen prey. Panic rose in my chest. Fright filled me.

Clods of dirt thwacked against me as the dog slid to a halt. I didn't see what came next. I felt it. Deep and wounding.

His teeth sank into my haunch, that fleshy part just in front of my good rear leg near my belly.

I whipped my head back reflexively with a strength I hadn't known I had. The collar slammed against my windpipe again. The snap broke. The release was so sudden I didn't have time to think about it. I only knew I was free—and that flight had turned to fight.

Teeth snapping, I whirled and dodged, hitting each foreleg in turns, then his throat and jowls. He was strong and big, but I was a tornado that couldn't be contained. *Bite, bite, bite.* Sounds I'd never before made ruptured from deep within. *Bite!* I would not stop until I'd won my freedom—and if I injured or killed him in the process, so be it.

I would win this fight or die trying.

Thinking was not something that consciously happened when life could end at any moment. I bit and tore and bellowed. Growled and twisted. Reacted to his every action. It was instinct. Survival.

As I took hold of his throat, pinching with all the force of my jaw, he went down and rolled, pinning me beneath him.

A madness took hold of me. Snatched my mind and carried it to a dark and forbidding place.

Never. Give. Up!

Fury consumed me. Emboldened me. Latching onto his lip, I shook my head back and forth.

With a yelp, he released me. I sprang to my feet. Ran. Bounded onto a trash can next to the fence—and sailed over. I hit the ground on the other side, tumbling forward. In the next heartbeat, I was up and running again.

The old man's shouts followed me, empty threats fading as I ran. Through streets, across yards and parking lots, and past busses teeming with humans. I ran across the bridge where the beast had chased me. Back along the river. To the highway.

Not until the wounds of my skirmish took hold of my senses did I stop for rest. I crawled into a large pipe that ran beneath the road. Muck and stagnant water choked the tunnel. But it was dark there. Out of sight of human eyes. Away from predators.

There I lay on a narrow flat of soft mud. Afraid. In horrible pain. Until night came.

Then I mercifully slept, while my body healed in small and seemingly insignificant ways. Safe and alone.

—o00o—

A fire raged inside me. Too stiff to move from the tunnel, I licked my wounds slowly while every inch of me burned. I stopped often to sleep more, unable to resist. Couldn't have moved on even if the monster dog had been on my heels again. Whenever I woke up, it was only long enough to lick the deep puncture wounds clean, see whether it was day or night or if anything had changed, before I slept again.

At some point, I drank from one of the fetid pools of water. I regretted it a hundred times over when I puked up every last bit of food I'd eaten that day—or maybe it was the day before. I didn't know anymore.

How many days had passed since Brandy's van had crashed? Had she gone back to look for me? Was she okay?

Would I *ever* see her again? I was beginning to doubt it.

As I lay inside that tunnel, my energy ebbing, the fire inside me draining away my strength, something within me shifted. Tomorrow and yesterday didn't matter as much as today. And today there was only pain and misery and shattered hope.

So I did what my body demanded: I rested. For days. My belly drew up tight. Mouth went dry. My eyesight blurred, senses dulled, and muscles grew so weak I stopped trying to stand or move to the edge of the tunnel to look out.

I had so many dreams. Of Brandy and me. Of running fast and free through a meadow. Chasing a Frisbee and bringing it back as she praised me. Climbing and jumping over the obstacles Brandy gave names to: teeter, walk-it, frame, over, tunnel…

Tunnel. Like this place in a way, but not nearly so long or nasty inside.

I dreamed of doing obedience with Brandy—heeling at her side in precise position, my head craned up to watch which way her shoulders moved and to better hear the commands she gave.

I hadn't stayed. I hadn't been loyal. I'd thought I could find her, but I couldn't.

If I ever saw Brandy again, I would *never* leave her.

—o0Oo—

Brandy's hand lifted my chin so she could stare into my eyes.

"I told you to stay."

Ashamed, I averted my eyes. *No, I don't think you did tell me that. But yes, I should have stayed.*

She shook her head. "Why? Why did you leave, Sooner?"

To find you.

"They came back to look for you—my friends did. They called and called for you. But you were gone, to heaven knows where. What have you been doing all this time, huh, Sooner?"

Just trying to make it to the next day. To survive. So we could be together again.

"Nothing can keep us apart, Sooner. We were meant for each other. You have to believe that." She leaned over and kissed me on top of my head. "Now let's go. It's morning. Time is wasting. You can't lie around like a log all day."

—o0Oo—

Morning. The light that poured in was a pale pink. The air smelled of dew.

Brandy wasn't with me. She hadn't been. It had only been a dream. A wish. A vision born of hope.

Why had it felt so terribly real, though? I'd felt the brush of her fingers beneath my jaw. Looked into her eyes. Heard her voice as if she were standing right before me.

My heart ached for her. For what might never be again.

I stretched my legs. Some of my wounds had closed over. But blood had matted my fur and formed scabs in more places than I cared to know. The fire inside me, however, was gone. In its absence, I felt the tiniest bit stronger. Like I might not die after all.

On quivering legs, I stood. When I was sure I wouldn't fall over, I took a step, then another, and another… until I stood at the opening of the tunnel.

It took some time for me to realize the buzz I heard was from the vehicles on the road above. It took even longer to figure out which way to go.

The going was slow, but I went. It didn't matter how long it took. What mattered was I was going back to wait for Brandy.

Because even though I hadn't done what I should have, I was sure she wouldn't give up on me.

"Love you, my Imperial Princess Sooner," she'd say every night at bedtime. "More than the sun and the moon and the stars."

All I knew was that meant she loved me a lot.

And me? I would *always* love Brandy. More than bones and squeaky toys and Frisbees and food and sleep. No matter how far away she was or how long it had been since I'd last seen her.

I'd loved her from the first moment I saw her—and I would love her even if I never saw her again.

Because even though love had a beginning and started from nothing, it had no end and no limit.

chapter 9
Grayson

When had she stopped loving him—and why?

Leaning against the trunk of his car, Grayson realized he could never ask Fee that question. Not now, anyway.

After she'd left him, he learned the worst part of it was just being *alone*. No one to report to about his day. No one to share a meal with. No one to remind him to put his dirty clothes in the hamper. Just his own steps echoing down a bare-walled hallway as he headed to an empty bedroom to sleep solo in a king-sized bed.

'When' wasn't so much a definitive moment as it was a process, he decided. Like falling in love. If he didn't believe in love at first sight, then he couldn't accept that falling *out* of love was like flipping a switch off. It happened over time.

After exploring the house, Grayson had come back outside. He wasn't sure why, other than he didn't quite know what to do with himself. He was too tired from driving to start sorting any of his uncle's belongings, but it was far too early to go to sleep. Turning in a circle to take in the view, he wished he'd asked Rex where the property line was so he could get a better idea of how big this estate actually was.

He drew a deep breath, then let out a prolonged sigh. It smelled so different here: the purity of dew forming on damp grass and the headiness of cut hay, the muskiness of ageing wood and the perfume of rose petals. It was also an uncluttered landscape of undulating hills, distantly situated barns, and animals grazing undisturbed.

Despite the simple beauty around him, however, he drew little peace from it. Inside, he was deeply troubled. Not just because of his job situation or the desirable apartment and comfortable lifestyle he might have to give up. But because of who he had become without his ever realizing how or why.

Fee had always been the interesting one, the optimist, the funny one, the person who made friends easily. He had been the antithesis of all that. He'd always considered himself to be the realistic one. Now he wondered if pessimistic hadn't been a more apt term.

The question then wasn't when, but *why* had Fee stopped loving him? For a long while, he'd avoided pondering the question, but time had afforded him a clearer perspective. He hadn't made time for Fee or paid attention to her. He'd stopped appreciating her in innumerable ways—stopped doing a lot of things over the years, like saying the words 'You're beautiful,' 'I missed you,' and more simply 'I love you'.

It just seemed she'd always be there. And for a long time she was… until she wasn't.

Grayson pushed away from the car and wandered toward the barn, following a path in the grass his uncle must've taken daily.

There was no way of winning Fee back again. But if he ever had another chance at love, he'd go about it differently. He'd do better. He'd remember how precious and transient it could be, and he vowed he'd make every moment count.

Love was a thing that had to be done every day, every moment.

Not something placed on a shelf like a possession.

It was an act, not an object. A verb, not merely a noun.

And he'd been an utter failure at it.

—oOo—

"You look lost."

A woman well into her sixties with whitish-blond hair down her back sauntered into the barn, then pulled a feed sack off a teetering stack piled atop a pallet. She carried it to a plastic feed bin sitting between two stalls, ripped the top open, and began pouring it in.

Grayson stepped away from the stall he'd been inspecting, moving to pull another sack from the pile. It was heavier than he expected, but he tried not to show he was struggling as he brought it to her.

"You must be Loretta." He set the sack down beside the bin—he didn't have the strength to lift it high enough to empty it—and offered his hand. "Hi, I'm Grayson Darling, Skip's nephew."

She shook his hand, her grip surprisingly strong, then emptied the second sack. "Pleased to make your acquaintance, Mr. Darling. Grayson, is it? That what you go by?"

"Yes, thanks for asking, A lot of people just assume…" He was aware how patronizing it might sound if he lectured her about his umbrage on people's assumptions. Not wanting to make a poor impression, he started over. "Thank you for coming by. I could use some guidance. I'm not really experienced with animals."

"I could tell that when I walked in here." She scanned him from head to toe, squinting. "First off, I'd suggest a change of clothes."

Loretta had shown up in jeans with holes, worn boots, and a faded T-shirt. Grayson, on the other hand, had on a pair of pleated khaki slacks and one of his better polo shirts. Not exactly business attire, but he'd figured since he'd be meeting new people today, he might as well look presentable. Nonetheless, her comment suddenly made him self-conscious. "Why's that?"

"Because you're going to get dirty. Horses snot like nothing you've ever seen, poop mountains, and pee lakes. They can also bite and kick, but don't let that scare you. They only do those things to you if you're an idiot." She grabbed a bucket off a hook, scooped some feed into it. "You're not an idiot—are you, Grayson?"

She was joking. He was pretty sure of it. Or maybe she had him pegged for a clueless city slicker who didn't belong here. He played along. "Depends on who you ask."

She smiled—a broad, heartwarming smile—and he immediately felt at ease. As she handed him the bucket, she said, "I like you, Grayson Darling. I imagine we can get you trained up just fine. Might be a bit rough, seeing as how I'm leaving town in about a week, but I'll give you my number if'n you have any questions. And there's always Doc Hunter."

"Who?"

"Dr. Hunter McHugh. He's the vet around here. The best one, anyway."

After scooping out another bucketful, she dumped part of it into a trough. His first inclination was to do the same with his, but she hadn't fully emptied her bucket yet, so he followed her to the next stall where she poured out a little more.

"That doesn't seem like enough to feed a horse," Grayson observed.

"It's not their dinner. They've been out in the pasture all day. This is just to tempt them inside quicker; otherwise, they'd stay put. They know the routine. But if I don't give them a little extra grain, they tend to take offense and call my bluff the next time."

"Ah, I see."

"Say," Loretta said as she moved on and poured more, "you haven't seen a dog around here, have you?"

"Skip had a dog?"

"No, not his. A lost dog. There was an accident on the highway yesterday. A van went into a ravine not far from here. Apparently, the driver's dog was thrown free and ran off. It was even on the news. Just thought you mighta seen it around. An Australian Shepherd, if I remember right. A red tri named Sooner."

"I don't even know what that would look like."

"Medium-sized. Kind of like a Border Collie, but a bobtail instead of a bushy tail. And red tri means mostly red, but with tan and white. Seen anything like that?"

He shook his head.

"Her name is Sooner. Like an Oklahoma Sooner, I guess."

"Sorry, I've only been here a few hours, if that. No sign of a dog. *Any* dog."

"Okay. Just figured I'd mention it."

When she finally emptied the bucket in the last stall, Grayson wasn't sure what to do with his.

"Follow me." She headed toward the pasture. At the gate, she flipped the latch up and stepped inside. Grayson joined her. Maybe there was a trough in here to fill.

Loretta pressed her pinkies together in a V, slid them between tight lips, and blew. Her whistle was shrill enough to scrape the paint off a barn wall. The horses, which had been ambling casually toward Loretta and Grayson when they first entered, lifted their heads and hooves to fly at them in a gleeful gallop, their manes twisting in the lazy summer breeze, their silken tails streaming behind them.

Grayson dropped the bucket on the packed dirt, grain spilling onto the ground as he sought an exit. At the gate, he fumbled with the latch, unable to figure out how to release it. The horses charged closer. Panic energized him. Clambering over the gate, he dropped onto the other side, safe.

Loretta shook her head. "They ain't a wildebeest stampede,

y'know." Even as the horses thundered at her, she didn't move. "Get back over here. You need a proper introduction if you're gonna care for these critters. And if'n you don't calm down, you're gonna have a lot of trouble on your hands. Animals pick up on your vibes. Trust 'em and they'll trust you right back."

As the first of the horses neared her, it slowed, making a wide arc around her and tossing its head with a nicker.

"Hello, Goliath," she returned. "I'd ask if you're hungry, but you always are. Now Persephone, on the other hand..."—Loretta indicated a cautious-looking chestnut mare with wide eyes—"she thinks everyone's out to get her until she gets to know them. Kind of like you."

Sufficiently shamed, Grayson wiggled the latch. It wouldn't give. He pulled harder. Tried to move it in the opposite direction.

With a disgusted sigh, Loretta came to the rescue. She pushed on the latch. It popped open easily, and Grayson joined her. "There are all sorts of latches. Once you know how to work 'em, they make sense. Just curious, but what kind of work do you normally do?"

"Banking. Financial consulting. Loans, mostly." He had, anyway. Lately, he'd been a professional resume author. Judging by the results, he wasn't very good at it.

"Well, you're about to learn what calluses and a sore back are." When a third horse approached and went for the bucket, Loretta corrected it. "Ach! You mind your manners."

The horse, an Appaloosa—Grayson knew that much—twitched her ears and snorted.

"Always gotta comment, don't you, Spark? You're a feisty one, ain't ya?" She patted the horse's cheek. "Just like me."

After they had all gathered, Loretta finished the introductions. When the one named Clifford started to nuzzle Grayson's neck, he froze.

"Can you call him off?" he said. If this went on much longer, he was going to do something embarrassing, like pee his pants.

"He's telling you to hurry up. You'll figure them out soon enough if you pay attention. Each one has their own personality, their own way of getting their point across."

Hot horse breath steamed the inside of his ear. If the thing bit him, it could do considerable damage. "And what exactly am I supposed to do?"

"Pick up the bucket, then lead them inside the barn."

"Do *what?*"

"You heard me just fine."

He didn't move. "No, I—"

She picked up the bucket, gave it to Grayson. Then she popped the latch for him, pushing the gate wide. "Let me save you some trouble."

They were all eyeing him with barely contained patience. The sheer size of Goliath, some sort of draft horse, he surmised, was enough to make him want to keep his distance. If Goliath wanted to, he could smash Grayson's skull with a single hoof as if his head were a rotting pumpkin.

"While you're standing there making up your mind, just remember a week from now I won't be around. You best figure this out. Now just do what I say. Walk this way."

With that, she turned and went toward the barn, leaving him alone in the pasture with four horses circling him, hungry looks in their eyes.

"This is not what I signed up for," he muttered.

"I heard that!" Loretta hollered from the barn. One by one, she opened the stall doors. A couple of horses swung their heads her way, but then returned their attention to Grayson, closing in on him. Spark stretched her neck, nibbled at the rim of the bucket. More grain landed on the ground. Goliath barged his way past to claim the spoils.

Grayson was moments away from just dumping the bucket and

claiming it was an accident when Loretta barked, "I ain't got all day!"

Before he could lose all courage, Grayson went to the barn, his arm held out stiff like a clothesline. Goliath kept knocking the bucket as they went, feed spilling out in a long trail. Two of the horses stopped to snack. Goliath hit the bucket harder, over and over like a petulant child.

By the time Grayson got to the barn, Loretta was standing there with her arms crossed, her head cocked to one side. It was the same look his mother used to give him when he hadn't done something right.

When he glanced behind him, he was almost bulldozed by Goliath.

"He goes in that first stall, but he always acts like he doesn't know that. He just thinks he can go eat the other horses' feed if he wants, but don't give him the chance." She took Goliath by the halter and pointed his nose in, then gave him a soft whack on the rump.

Grayson wondered if that wasn't a dangerous thing to do. Then one by one, she got the next three situated. The last one, Clifford, went in on his own.

"Best to do it in that order." She repeated what she'd just done, which was a good thing because Grayson had been more concerned about his own safety than any prescribed order.

He asked her to write it down for him.

"You're serious?"

"Well, I was hoping they had their names on the stall door or something, but I don't—"

"Fine, fine. I'll add it to my instructions." After pulling a folded set of papers from her back pocket, she wrote on one with a pencil she took from an empty can resting on a small table in the aisle. "This probably ain't everything, but it should get you through the basics."

Handing it all over to Grayson, she went on to explain each point. It was well over ten pages, single-spaced. Everything from daily feeding schedules, to how to scrub down and refill the water tanks, to which farrier to call and how often, to grooming particulars like brushing and checking hooves…

The words blurred. Feeling the beginnings of a headache, he pressed his fingertips to closed eyelids.

"Hey, you all right there? You look a little peaked. Then again, hard to tell. You do have a pasty complexion."

He opened his eyes to see her surrounded by a halo of dust. The last of the sun's rays were filtering in through the far end of the barn.

"I think the best thing for me to do would be to find homes for them. This isn't what I…" He stopped himself, not wanting to sound callous. "I just think it would be best. How do I go about selling them to someone who's better suited than I am to take care of them?"

She appeared a little crestfallen. "All of them?"

"Yes. It's just that, well, I don't know anything about horses and I'll need to return to Manhattan."

"Oh. How soon?" She wandered over to Goliath's stall, then reached between the iron bars to stroke his neck as he munched at his grain. The horse stared back at her, nothing but gentleness and gratitude in his large brown eyes. They had a bond, those two.

"Not right away, but the sooner the better, I suppose." It pained him to think of sending that horse away. But horses were sold and bought all the time, he told himself. They lived a long time. He'd heard a carriage driver say so once when Fee had insisted they go on a ride through Central Park. Even then, he'd wondered how the horses adjusted to each change, if they ever missed their old homes, or longed for past owners. "You've been taking care of them a long time now—a month?"

"Three weeks and four days. Twice a day. But I've been around off and on for years whenever Skip needed a hand. Neighbors around here do that. I don't know what it's like where you live."

Where he lived, he didn't know most of his neighbors well

enough to ask for a cup of sugar, let alone to lend a hand with farm chores.

"What I'm getting at is…" he said. "The thought crossed my mind, anyway, that I could give you one. Goliath, maybe."

Her breath hitched. She turned slowly. "You'd do that?"

He shrugged. "Sure, why not? As repayment for your help."

What he didn't want was for her to refuse out of politeness. As magnanimous as the gesture might appear outwardly, he also had a selfish motive—it would be one less horse to have to sell. Plus, he'd know where Goliath had gone and that he'd be well cared for.

Loretta's whole face crinkled. She sniffed back a tear. "Thank you mightily, but… why Goliath?"

"Isn't he your favorite?"

The tears came then, quiet but steady. She fished in her pockets for a tissue. When she couldn't find one, she stretched the end of one of her short sleeves and wiped her eyes on it, nodding. "I reckon so. Although you probably shouldn't talk that way in front of the group—they're like kids. They get jealous if they sense you have a favorite. But the reason… the reason he and I have this connection… it's because we're both getting older. He can't pull a wagon or a plow anymore. He's just a big ol' pasture ornament, as Skip used to say. He bought the old coot for two hundred and fifty bucks five years ago. He's worth less than that now."

"Oh, it seems like your time's worth more than that. Do you want Spark, too? Or one of the others? Pick one. I don't mind. I'd like you to have them before anyone else."

Despite his insistence, she emphatically shook her head. "No, no. Told you, horses can live a long time. All the rest, they're young to middle aged for horses. I can't commit to ten or twenty years. I could never give up an animal, for any reason. No, I'll take Goliath. I've got just enough land and a nice shed for him. My kids used to raise goats for 4-H, but that was years ago. If Clayton fixes it up good, it'll make a fine retirement barn for Goliath." The more she talked, the more her weathered face brightened, but in her pause, a cloud overcame her features. Her smile dipped and her hand went over her heart. "But... I'm going to visit my daughter. Was, anyway. I suppose I can call her and tell her that—"

"Don't even think of it," Grayson interjected before she could finish the thought. "I'll see to his needs. Everything he needs is right here. I'll figure it out. He'll be fine. I'll be fine. Really, don't worry. He'll be here when you return."

Rather abruptly, she bridged the space between them and gathered him in a brief hug.

"Thank you," she whispered into his ear, then let him go, stepping back suddenly and averting her eyes as if the gesture had surprised even her.

"It's no problem, really." But even as Grayson reassured her, he was thinking about all the manure he'd have to shovel and sacks of feed to carry. "So you're leaving next week?"

"Yep."

"When do you return?"

If she'd said, he couldn't remember, but maybe his memory was foggy with so much new input in one day.

"Six weeks was the plan. This is so generous of you."

Six weeks? *Six. Weeks?* He couldn't possibly stay here that long. "Oh. Why so long?"

"I thought I said. Maybe not. Sorry, I've talked to so many people about it. Anyone who'll listen, really. My daughter's having bunion surgery. She won't be able to do much the first month or so. And she has five kids. Baby Payton is thirteen months. Her husband works fifty, sometimes sixty, hours a week to help make ends meet. I promised to help her a long time ago, before Skip died. Her surgery was actually supposed to be two weeks ago. Because of me being needed here, it got rescheduled. But I can't ask her to do that again—

and I can't not go. Besides, I've been looking forward to this trip for a long time. I haven't been to Florida to visit her since they moved there two years ago. Do you know how hard it is not meeting your youngest grandkid?"

Grayson had never felt a compulsion to hold a fussy, crying baby. Both Fee and he had agreed on that matter. It wasn't that they'd ruled out children entirely, but that it had never seemed like the right time to start a family. Then one day, they were over forty, then approaching fifty, and it seemed too late. By then it was—for reasons other than their age.

"I hope you enjoy your time with your grandchildren," he told her. "I'll keep you updated on how things are going here."

Why he'd made the offer, he wasn't sure. It would make it even more difficult when he had to return to Manhattan and make other arrangements for Goliath's care.

As for what to do with placing the other horses, maybe he could call this Dr. McHugh and ask him. By the time Loretta came back, except for Goliath, they'd be long gone.

So would he, if all went as planned.

—o0Oo—

A rooster's crow obliterated the peace of a pre-dawn haze. Rudely awakened, Grayson went to the window, but couldn't discern the source of the reveille. Living in the city, noise was a constant—even in the depth of night, up on the tenth floor. Out here, the quiet was what made such a sound disruptive. He'd have to download one of those white noise apps to drown such things out.

Energized by his irritation, he put on a shirt and went out to the front porch to discover the source. The familiar stabbing in his lower leg and ache in his knee lessened the more he moved around.

He scanned the landscape. The nearest house had to be close to half a mile away, but it was up on a hilltop, so the sound carried as clearly as a tornado siren mounted on a tall tower.

Nothing he could do about it now, short of marching over to the neighbor's and insisting they dispatch with the offending bird.

So he went into the kitchen to make himself a pot of coffee. It took thirty minutes to find an old-fashioned percolator, a bag of coffee beans, and the grinder. He started the coffee and headed out to the barn. As he drudged through his morning chores, re-reading Loretta's instructions to ensure he did nothing wrong, the responsibility of it burdened his conscience. How Loretta had managed by herself for so long, he didn't know, but she was made of a different fabric than he was. If he was finely woven linen, she was denim.

He'd thought the morning routine would take him fifteen minutes at most, but it devoured two hours. Two hours during which he hadn't finished the coffee in his pot, consumed his morning dose of TV, read his newspaper online, showered, or eaten. By the time he sat down to toast and a second cup of coffee, he was more miserable than when the confounded rooster had startled him from his slumber.

At five minutes past nine, he called Dr. Philipot's office and left a message. He needed to talk, to make sense of this unexpected mess he'd allowed himself to get mired in. For close to three hours, he bumbled around the house, pulling open drawers, peeking inside closets, even climbing the ladder into the attic. Skip—uncle seemed like too familiar a term for a man he barely knew—had accumulated his share of items, but most were quality goods, some antiques even. A tag sale would have gotten rid of most items quickly, but some, Grayson guessed, had value. It would be wiser to have someone look at them who could tell—an auctioneer or—

His phone rang.

"Dr. Philipot, hello."

"Grayson. You're in Kentucky now, I take it?"

"Faderville, to be precise."

"Where's that?"

"Somewhere between Nothingville and Nowheretown."

"Ah. A bit of culture shock, perhaps? Tell me about the situation."

"Do you have an hour?"

"It's not our usual day or time for a session, but I can work you in. I'm always concerned about your welfare, and I'm glad to walk you through any difficulties you may be experiencing."

Grayson knew that meant the doctor was going to bill him. He hadn't expected anything less. Unloading on a friend would have been free, but all his had gone the way of his ex-wife and his ex-job.

"Let me just fill you in on yesterday. It's a doozy."

And Grayson told him about everything—how debts may have compromised his uncle's finances, how Attovan Investments had chosen not to hire him, and how he'd called Fee hopeful for a sounding board and had instead been hit with the news of her upcoming nuptials.

After each incident, Dr. Philipot would offer up some version of, "And how did that make you feel?" Then Grayson would respond in some manner of, "Not particularly good."

Until he came to the four horses he was now charged with tending and how he'd impulsively decided to gift the aged draft horse to the neighbor who'd taken care of them.

"That's quite a lot to take on, Grayson, but I suppose you'll manage. How do you feel about your present situation?"

Grayson thought about it. It was hard to untangle the threads of his emotions, especially when a pervasive feeling of failure clouded everything. "I'm not sure... Mostly overwhelmed. Resentful, too, I suppose. And..." He struggled for the proper word. It was an unfamiliar feeling.

"Take your time. Can you describe it?"

"Better." Not an adjective. More of a comparison really.

"Better than what?"

"Just… better. To do something for someone like that. It made me feel a little bit better. For a while, at least."

"You don't still?"

"I'm not sure. I just expect things will get worse again. That something will go wrong or fall through. It seems to be a trend lately."

"That sort of thinking is a bit fatalistic, don't you think?"

When Grayson didn't answer—because he wasn't sure if it was an honest question or just psychobabble rhetoric—Dr. Philipot added, "What if it's a turning point, Grayson? What if, from here on, things get better for you, all because you reached out and made someone else's day better?"

"I saw that episode of *Oprah*, Dr. Philipot. I don't believe in karma."

"Pardon?"

"*The Secret*. It's a book where they basically espouse you can change your life just by sending good vibes out into the universe and by envisioning a certain future you can attract it to you. You know, do unto others…"

"Oh, I know what you're talking about, but that wasn't really what I was getting at. I'm just saying if something makes you feel better, more hopeful, then maybe you should do it again. From time to time, anyway. Altruism is powerful."

Good for the recipient, but it wasn't going to get Grayson a job, save his apartment, or get Fee back.

"Thank you for returning my call, Dr. Philipot. I'll let you get back to whatever it is you were doing."

"No bother, really. And we still have ten minutes left if—"

"Actually, I think one of the horses has his head stuck in between the boards of the fence." A lie, but he didn't want this call to last another moment. "I'd better rescue him."

"Oh, yes. Go then. And call again whenever you need to. Even if something good happens. Just one more thing, while I'm thinking of it…"

"Go ahead," Grayson reluctantly prompted.

"This is based on some reading I've been doing lately, put out by one of the professional societies I belong to. But for people suffering from chronic low-grade depression, there's compelling evidence a pet can be extraordinarily helpful."

"A pet?"

"Yes, dogs seem to be the preferred pet. They're most responsive to their owners' moods, and they're excellent at providing comfort. Other animals—cats, rabbits, horses, miniature pigs even—can fill that role, too, but which is most suitable depends on the person, really. Sometimes they're referred to as 'emotional support animals'. As I said, though, dogs seem to be the most effective."

"A dog, right. I'll keep that in mind." Immediately, he dismissed the notion.

"Look, I know I've offered you medication in the past, but—"

"Yes, and I've turned it down every time. I haven't changed my mind since the last, if that's what you're getting at."

"I'm not. I just wanted to suggest an alternative. Something new. There's a reason why people have dogs, Grayson."

"I'm sure there is." He hated it when Dr. Philipot kept circling back to the same point. Like he couldn't let it go. So he threw in a diversion. "Actually, though… I was thinking of taking up a new hobby. Or resuming an old one."

"You are? What would that be?"

"I'll let you know when I decide."

After Grayson hung up, he sat on the porch and watched the horses. For hours. Mostly wondering what in the world he was going to do with them.

He had no intention of calling Dr. Philipot again. Possibly ever.

A dog? How could he ever accommodate a dog while working ten-hour days and living in Manhattan? Time to stop paying his therapist for useless advice. He'd keep more of his money that way, too.

chapter 10
Sooner

For most of that day and the next, I wondered if I would ever get back to the place I'd last seen Brandy. I even began to wonder if I'd gone the wrong way, but from time to time, when I'd stop long enough to take in my surroundings, I'd recognize some feature of the landscape that stirred a memory.

How many days had it been? Usually, I kept track of such things by counting the number of sleeps. But while the fire had burned inside me, I'd slept in long bouts, through darkness and daylight. It made it all impossible to sort out.

When I finally did arrive, the scent of our things was so faded, so overcome by other scents, that I realized how badly I'd erred by leaving in the first place.

The ache in my heart grew. If Brandy *had* come back to search for me, she'd long since moved on because I hadn't been there.

Maybe tomorrow, though, she'd come. And if not tomorrow, then the day after. I wouldn't leave this time. Not even for food. Because I couldn't imagine Brandy not coming back for me. She would!

SAY WHEN

The sun sank behind distant hills. The valley in which the van had once lain in a twisted heap shifted from shadows to total darkness. Stars pierced the night sky. The buzz of insects mingled with the whoosh of cars barreling down the highway.

Somewhere far away, the howl of my wild kin called to my primal side. A song of solitude and the longing to connect.

A lone coyote had begun the chorus, until one pack and then another joined in. I lifted my snout and sang with them, until my throat hurt, my head was light, and I'd forgotten why it was I started. When their song faded, I lay down to rest.

—oO0o—

Later, I was stirred from my sleep in the bushes by the sound of many feet tamping down the dry grass.

I raised my head, peering into the darkness for the movement of shadows. My heart quickened. Fear filled my chest. I sniffed the air. I couldn't see them, but… they were there—the coyotes.

When I saw the first pair of golden eyes glint in the blackness, I didn't stop to think about what to do.

I ran.

And they chased.

Up the hill I went, struggling through low branches and a tangle of woods, dodging broad tree trunks and sprawling shrubs, while loose ground gave way behind me.

I didn't stop to count how many they were or how close. Whether there were two or ten didn't matter. Before the accident, I'd been quick and strong, but my adventures had taken their toll. The farther up I went, the more I slowed, the more my lungs heaved for air.

They yipped with glee, closing in on me. The terror propelled me up the last of the hill and over its crest. Leaping the metal rail, I landed on the edge of the road.

Cones of light hurtled down the highway in both directions. A horn blared so close by I jumped back, my rump hitting a post.

While the sounds had drowned out the galloping of their paws, I was aware of them. Knew they were still there, still coming after me.

But I also sensed they were cautious of humans, rightly so. I'd seen Brandy's dad pick up a rifle and shoot at one from the porch of the cabin by the lake. Humans no more trusted coyotes than coyotes did them.

A truck blasted by, hitting me with a wall of air so forceful it pushed me back more. Hugging the rail, I trotted its length. But when I came to the end of it, what I saw made my heart go cold.

Two—no, three—coyotes were waiting for me. And if I had to guess, I'd say there were some behind me on the other side, too.

The smaller of those in front of me lowered her head and slunk toward me, as if in submission.

Don't trust her! a shrill voice inside me screamed.

The ones behind crept closer. I sensed them.

When I'd lain in the tunnel not so long ago, my body heavy with fatigue, I could not have fought them off. Not even one. I still wasn't sure I could. The scars the monster dog had inflicted on me were still raw, the bruises deep. I was hungry and weary and weak.

Right now, I couldn't even outrun them. I had so little left.

The female crawled on her belly to me, licking her lips and curling her body as she kept her head down. Her soft whimpers begged friendship, as if to say, *Join us. We will show you where the food is and the safe places to hide. Be one of our pack.*

I wasn't fooled, though. The evil glimmer in her eye was clear. I heard the quiet steps of her companions. Sensed they, too, hungered—and I was the prey.

I was trapped: three before me, others behind and beside me, the highway on the other side.

There was only one way out.

I bolted across the highway. Headlights blinded me. A horn sounded. Rubber and steel bore down on me. Still, I continued, barely avoiding one car as I crossed a lane and then another before finding myself in a wide grassy swath. But in a shallow gully was a concrete barrier. I couldn't stop to see if they were still following. I leaped over it, landing in yet more grass.

On the other side was another strip of highway, the metal beasts zooming in the other direction. I went across, mindless of the bright lights. A car swerved, barely missing me. Another horn. More cars, more horns.

On the far side now, I peered over the edge. It was a long way down. On the other side where I'd come from, the pack watched, calculating if they should follow. I trotted along the edge, my lack of strength now pulling at me like a heaviness I couldn't beat. As long as I stayed off to the side, I knew I wouldn't get run over. The road rose and fell, so I went slowly, ever watchful.

For a long time, they followed me. I kept on going, if only to get away from them.

After a while, I stopped checking to see if they were there. Until I forgot about them. Until I thought I couldn't go on anymore.

The pads of my feet were raw and tender. Every step was agony. They had been like that for a long time, but fear had caused me to block out the pain. And for the first time I noticed it was well past daybreak.

I gazed across the highway, but they weren't there. There was no sign of them. As if they'd never been there. Had they? Or had I merely imagined them?

I'd long since grown oblivious to the passing vehicles. I almost sank down and slept right there next to the highway when I saw, not so far away, a small farm.

Better to rely on humans than to leave my fate to the coyotes.

—o0Oo—

I'd hoped it would be something other than what it was. Farms generally had animals: cows, chickens, pigs, horses, cats, dogs. Animals needed to be fed. There was a rusty tractor with a flat tire sitting out in the open and a small barn in need of repair, as well as a modest house with a detached garage, all surrounded by overgrown pasture. But no animals, which meant no food. If there'd ever been animals, their scent was long gone.

Still, it was worth checking out. Not like I had other options.

I explored the perimeter, slowly working my way closer. No trash cans in sight, no buckets filled with feed, no bowls of kibble, not even cat food. I sniffed around the car parked in front of the garage, checked for open doors in the outbuildings. All closed. The smell of humans was strong, so I remained watchful.

And then I saw… a tree with fruit, the branches bowed toward the ground. Beyond it, more fruit trees. I went to the first one, found the lowest fruit and pulled it loose. Ahh, the most delightful thing I'd ever eaten. Sweet and juicy. Almost like the apple slices Brandy fed me, but not as tart, with a gritty texture and odd shape, fatter on the bottom than the top.

A banging startled me. The fruit fell from my mouth as I stared toward the house. A woman with pale hair stood on the wooden steps outside the back door.

"Damn coyote. Get away from my pear—" She narrowed her eyes, but didn't come closer. Just stood there, studying me. I readied myself to run, even though I barely had the energy to remain upright. "You're no coyote, that's for sure. Something about you seems mighty familiar. Wait there."

She went inside, but I kept an eye on the door as I started on a second piece of fruit. I ate it in three bites, then began a third. Not as filling as my kibble, but I could survive on this if I had to. I tried a piece lying on the ground, but it had the sour smell of rot to it and several flies were buzzing about it. My nose told me to move on. I circled beneath the tree. There weren't any that were low enough to pluck from where I was, so I backed up for a better look. There, a little higher. Ripe, no worm holes, no flies. I coiled and sprang upward, but my body was so weak I could barely get off the ground. I backed up more, ran at it. My teeth barely nipped it. The fruit remained up high, out of reach.

Lowering my sights, I sniffed about for more fallen fruit. I found another that was only half rotten. Exhausted, I collapsed to the ground, the fruit between my paws.

Bang! The door slapped shut behind the woman. She held a piece of paper up. Gazed between it and me. That was a peculiar thing to do. I could never understand why humans studied their flat objects—computers, TVs, books, newspapers—with such fascination. They were so uninteresting. Except sometimes for the TV. Because it made sounds with pictures that moved. Even so, humans spent way too much time in front of them.

"You're one of those Australian Shepherds," the woman said. "Doc Hunter has one kinda like you. Different color and markings, though. Says here your name's Sooner."

I perked. How did she know my name?

"Sooner. Is that your name—Sooner?"

I hadn't heard my name in so long, but I resisted going closer.

"And your owner's name was Brandy Anders."

Brandy? She knew Brandy! I stood. My nub wagged uncontrollably. Was Brandy inside?

I wanted to trust this woman, but—

"Clayton?" she called. When no one answered, she opened the door and called again. "Get out here, will you, Clayton? I asked you to take a look five minutes ago. That dog's still here."

Moments later, a man—almost as wide as he was tall—joined her on the steps. The first thing I noticed was he kept one arm stiff at his side, like it didn't work quite right. His hair was bushy and on the longer side. A thick gray beard hid most of his face. He might have frightened me on his appearance alone, but his eyes told a different story. They were bright and kind.

"Lookie there, will ya?" He lifted the brim of his cap to get a better look. As the sun fell fully on his face, I saw his eyes crinkle with a smile. "Pretty dog—or was once. Looks like it's been through hell and back, though."

The woman shoved the paper in his face. "Think this is the same dog? I saw this on Facebook a few days ago. Took me a while to find the post."

He pulled his head back, squinted. "You know I can't see squat without my glasses, Loretta." He took the paper from her and held it at arm's length, then studied me again. He handed the paper back to her. "Yup, probably is. What's them words below the picture say?"

"Says lost dog. Two-year-old female Australian Shepherd, red with copper and white markings." She tilted her head at me again. "Looks more golden than red to me, but that could be all the mud and from being out in the sun."

"So who's searching for her?" Clayton asked.

Loretta frowned. "Says her owner was involved in an accident… That must've been the wreck out on the interstate last week. Heard they flew the woman in a helicopter to Lexington."

"Did she live?"

After a few more moments reading, Loretta shook her head. "Doesn't say here, but I can look it up on the computer. It does say the dog has a collar and a microchip." She glanced at me. "No collar, but I suppose she could've lost it. Doc Hunter can scan her for a microchip."

Clayton barked a laugh. "Good luck catching her. Dog looks frightened to death. Anyway, what're you going to do if that's not the dog? We're headed to Florida tomorrow. We can't keep her."

"Yeah, yeah, I know. Maybe Doc Hunter will know what to do, though. Even if she's not this dog, I can't take her to the shelter. Any loon could take her home, and those dogs aren't right for just anyone. She seems like a smart one. Smart enough to have kept herself alive for over a week. Just need to figure out how to get a hold of her without spooking her."

The man turned to go inside.

"What're you gonna do, Clayton?"

He went inside, then returned with a plate. My sniffer immediately went to work. I could smell it from here—meat! Cold meat, but I smelled bone marrow, too.

"Those are last night's ribs," Loretta said. "I was gonna make us sandwiches for lunch. You're not gonna give that to the dog, are you? We got bread and cheese. Why don't you try those?"

He rolled his eyes. "If you were near to starving but didn't trust someone, which would you go for?"

"I don't—"

"Just watch." He put the plate on the railing, then shredded the meat from the bone—which wasn't an easy task with only one good hand. When he was done, he stepped down from the stairs and tossed a hunk in my direction. It landed halfway.

I stayed where I was. I knew the ruse. Besides, he was still too close for comfort.

"Well, that didn't work now, did it?" Loretta scolded.

"Patience, my dear." Clayton returned to the porch, then held the door open. "Give her time. Come on inside."

"What if she runs away?"

"If she were going to run, she'd've done it by now."

Scoffing, Loretta brushed past him. "We'll see about that."

"Indeed we will." When Loretta disappeared, Clayton said softly to me, "Eat up. There's more where that came from."

I waited a good long time before I darted to the meat, grabbed it, and ran off a safe distance around to the other side of the barn, where I snarfed it down in two bites. My tummy had never been so happy—it was the best food I'd ever eaten. Still hungry, I crawled to the corner to watch the house. Maybe he'd throw some more food out. Humans were so wasteful. I couldn't even say how many times Brandy threw perfectly good food in the trash to let some men in a big truck carry it off.

Not long after, Loretta spied me through a window. "She's out behind the goat shed."

Nothing happened for a while. I was lying down, my eyelids growing heavy. I was still hungry—and thirsty—but I also needed to rest. Seemed I needed a lot of that lately.

And then... Clayton came outside with a bucket. At the back of the house, he turned on a water spigot. Water rushed out, filling the bucket. Carrying it to the garage with his good arm, he opened the small door on the side, then put the bucket just outside the door and went inside. I couldn't tell what he was doing besides making a lot of noise, but when he came out again, he glanced at me.

"Don't mind me," he said calmly. "Just taking care of the honey-do list."

More time passed, during which I slept, stole another piece of fruit, and slept some more. Finally, I could no longer resist. Skulking around the outside of the building, my eyes glued on the door he'd gone in and out of, I went to the bucket and drank my fill.

Throughout the morning, I got used to Clayton coming and going about the yard. Each time, he left a small hunk of rib meat on a plate outside the garage, moving the plate from time to time, which made me highly suspicious, but as hungry as I was, I took my chances.

And then, he placed the plate *inside* the garage.

How dumb did he think I was?

I ambled off into the woods, where I slept some more. Safe, but

SAY WHEN

still very hungry.

—oO0o—

The sun rose in the sky, arced overhead, and began its lazy descent. At some point, the woman got in her car and drove away. But I knew Clayton was still in the house because he hadn't left with her. Maybe he'd gone to sleep or busied himself with the many senseless tasks humans immersed themselves in, like bathing.

I'd go into the garage, take as much meat as I could gulp in a few bites, and be on my way. Maybe I'd come back later, maybe not, but if there was food to be had, I wasn't going to leave it uneaten.

Or maybe… maybe I'd stick around. As long as he was going to put food out for me every once in a while…

While the pull of sleep had lifted for now with the prospect of filling my belly, getting up and moving was hard. I was stiff, my steps small and slow. My head was fuzzy, too. The sharpness of my thoughts and reactions weren't what they used to be. I'd been fast once. I could jump high, run swiftly, and turn in a blink. Over bars, up A-frames, and through tunnels. But crossing that yard took impossibly long. It was as if the distance had increased in the brief time I'd been resting.

Finally, I went to the bucket of water and drank. I stopped just long enough to breathe. Then I drank some more. Which made me wonder—how long had it been since I'd peed? I couldn't remember.

The smell of food called to me. I saw the plate sitting alone in the middle of the garage, heaped with meat still on the bone. The wise thing would have been to grab one and run. But I needed every fiber of that meat. Needed the bones to lick the marrow from and to clean my teeth. Needed more than one. Anyway, I hadn't seen any sign of the man for some time now.

So I crept inside and settled with the plate between my paws.

Gorging myself, I tore every fiber of meat from the bones and licked the insides clean.

Until darkness fell across the shaft of light pouring in through the open door.

"Y'like that, Sooner?"

I popped to my feet. Clayton stood in the doorway, a great shadow shutting out the sun's light. Moving inside, he squatted, elbows resting on his knees, his plump cheeks bunching in a smile beneath the whiskery gray forest of his beard.

"Been through a lot, haven't you? Someone's been looking for you."

In warning, I lifted my lip at him. Although I desperately wanted to trust this man, I didn't know him. I wanted a soft bed in a dry place, clean water, and food every day, preferably an endless bowl of kibble topped with table scraps. I wanted to sleep where I knew I was safe, where no vicious dogs or a pack of hungry coyotes could do me harm. Where I could be safe from the lightning. I wanted to run and play where no cars would run me over.

A car. I heard a car coming up the driveway. I crouched, ready to spring.

"Don't worry, Sooner. It's just Loretta. She ain't all that scary."

A door slammed outside. Human feet padded across the ground. Another door opened and shut. Then, for a while, nothing happened.

Clayton patted the floor as he lowered himself to his knees. "I'm not gonna hurt you. Promise."

Mostly, I wanted a scratch behind my ears or a hand softly stroking my tummy. A face I could look into and know I was loved and cared for. Anyone's face.

And I wanted to hear my name again.

"Sooner, it's okay." He took a rope from his back pocket, the end looped like a collar. Setting it down, he took a plastic bag from his shirt pocket and opened it with his teeth. For the first time, I noticed the arm he kept so close and didn't move wasn't a real arm, but some sort of plastic. Slipping a piece of bologna from the bag, he held it out. More softly, he said, "It's okay. Nobody's gonna hurt you, Sooner. Promise."

My name was like a magical spell, lulling me to him. I was tired of running. Tired of hurting and starving and thirsting. Tired of being on my own. On my belly, I crawled to him.

Partway there, I stopped. I still wasn't sure.

He extended his hand, the bologna dangling like a worm on a hook. As I crept closer, he placed it on the ground. I watched his hand slide to the rope, saw him gather the loop.

"It's okay, Sooner. You're hungry, right? Come and eat."

I wanted to, but—

The door burst open. The shape of a woman, slightly padded with the comfort of later years, stood silhouetted in the doorway.

"Clayton? What are you...? Is that her?"

"Loretta, shut the door!" he growled.

Startled by the volume of his voice, she gasped. Just as she recovered and reached behind her to push at the door, I darted past.

Out into the daylight. Away. To safety.

Again, I ran.

Voices faded into the distance. My name echoed. But they weren't people I knew. They weren't Brandy. I wouldn't let them capture me.

For two more days, I ran, sometimes even into the night. I ran until my lungs burned and my heart was near to exploding and my muscles would go no more. Until my belly was as empty as it had ever been.

I sensed danger everywhere. Nothing was familiar or welcoming. It wasn't my home. More and more, I lost my bearings. At times, I could've sworn I'd been in a certain spot before, but I was never entirely certain. One hill looked like so many others. Maybe I was going in circles.

On the third day, I could no longer run. I walked, stumbled, fell, and walked some more. And then—

A big sprawling barn ahead. Food, possibly water.

A place to lie down… for as long as I needed. Forever, maybe.

Every bit of me hurt. My heart, especially.

On quiet feet, I sauntered into the barn. Giant beasts—horses—raised their heads and nickered at me from their stalls. But I ignored them. Either they would come out and kill me, or they wouldn't.

At the end was a stall, the smell of corn and oats strong. When I stumbled in, my rump brushed against the open door. I saw a bin, its lid loose. Nudged it open. Heard the *whomp* of the door slamming shut behind me.

I was trapped! I barked in frustration.

In the next stall, the biggest horse snorted and kicked at the walls with his hooves. The structure shook. The bars above the door, the hinges, and the latch rattled. Spinning circles, he let out a high-pitched whinny. I couldn't see him, but I could hear his fury, could sense his enormous strength. I barked again, if only to feel fiercer than I was.

After a series of yips, I stopped. I didn't have the energy. Didn't care if I was stomped to death.

I curled myself tightly into the farthest corner, defeated, no will left. I couldn't continue. Couldn't stand the loneliness, the hopelessness, the fatigue, hunger, and pain.

I'd given up—on finding Brandy *and* on surviving. I just wanted to sleep. Forever.

chapter 11
Brandy

Brandy dangled at the edge of sleep. A long, troubled sleep. She resisted waking. Somehow, she knew it was better where she was. Better not to invite the outer world into her awareness. Not yet. Instead, she sank back into her dreams. Slipped into the past.

The day she met Sooner, she knew they were meant to be. The pup, half-grown and all legs, was a wild thing. Darting about, running up to say 'hi,' and bouncing off her chest with all four paws before kangarooing off again.

"I'm so sorry." Violet, the puppy's breeder, offered Brandy an old towel. "She has no manners. They didn't teach her a thing. The first home decided they just didn't have time for her. The second owner declared she was untrainable."

Brandy took note of the muddy pawprints on her shirt. Ignoring the towel, she bent down. "I haven't met an untrainable dog yet." She clapped her hands. "Sooner, come!"

The gangly puppy loped to her. While the dog was still a few feet away, Brandy produced a treat from her pocket. She held it slightly above the puppy's head between her thumb and forefinger.

The puppy focused on the treat, her hind end wiggling uncontrollably. She skidded to a halt at Brandy's feet and sat, staring into Brandy's eyes, then at the treat, then back at her. The message was clear: *I did it! Treat?*

Lowering her palm, Brandy let her have the treat. She understood the look behind the pup's bright green eyes, felt her own heart bursting with love. "See, she came."

Before Brandy had finished the last word, Sooner took off again.

Violet shook her head. "Ah, but she didn't stay."

"I didn't ask her to. Anyway, she doesn't know that command yet. We'll get to it."

"I don't know. Sometimes I watch her and... How do I put this? She *is* smart. I've seen her figure things out no other dog could, but... she can't slow down enough to stay focused. It's like she has to do everything at light speed. *Act first, think later*—that's her motto. I'll be honest, you'd have your hands full with her. She's almost six months old, but barely knows what a leash is. I know what you've accomplished with your dogs, Brandy, and I know you have big plans. Maybe you'd be better off with one of my younger pups. They won't be ready to go home for a couple of weeks yet, but you'd have a clean slate with them, not a dog with baggage. I'm not sure yet what the best situation for her is, but maybe I'll just hang onto her for a bit longer and—"

"So are you saying I can't have her?"

"I'm not saying that. You're more experienced than most of my puppy owners, but I don't want you to feel obligated to prove a point. If you do take her and it doesn't work out—"

"No, I want her. And if you'll let me take her home, I'll keep her forever. I'm sure of it."

In fact, she'd never been more positive about anything. She'd loved this puppy at first sight, if that were even possible. Loved her not because she would be easy to train, but because she would learn from this dog more than any other and become not only a better trainer, but also a better person for it.

It was almost as if Sooner was a part of her that she hadn't known was missing.

A dog. How can a dog be part of your soul?

Brandy drifted toward wakefulness, pondering the thought. Dogs might have been different from humans—they didn't follow politics or practice religion, they couldn't understand the value of money, and didn't seek more than they needed—but one thing Brandy knew for sure was dogs did indeed have souls.

A faint rustle was followed by a soft whoosh of air. Brandy felt her head being raised, then lowered onto a gentle cloud.

"There you go," said a kind voice. "Comfy now?"

She homed in on the direction of the voice. Her head wouldn't turn, but... Slowly, her eyelids parted. The world around her was as distorted as a child's tempera painting. A face leaned closer, words falling from a pink-rimmed mouth in a slow buzz. She could only make out some of them, but pieced together, they carried her into the present: *van, accident, helicopter... hospital.*

As images around her began to register—an IV drip, the metal railing of a hospital bed, a blue curtain pushed back into folds hanging from the ceiling, a collection of vases with brightly colored flowers on the windowsill—her other senses also awakened. The acrid burn of antiseptic filled her nose. The buzz, she realized, was emanating from the fluorescent lights overhead and the flow of electricity through the machines surrounding her. The cloud was a bank of fresh pillows, propping her up.

She also felt pain. Deeply intense, bone-wrenching pain. She was here, alive, and yet... she didn't recognize the source of her pain. All she knew was she couldn't bear it. Not yet.

Make it go away, she tried to say, although she was sure neither her tongue nor jaw worked properly. She closed her eyes, yearning toward the darkness, the nothingness.

Something—fingers?—tapped her wrist. Words tickled the insides of her ears, but they bounced around before drifting off. She felt a warm stinging sensation flow up her arm. Moments later, the pain began to ebb mercifully away.

Her body felt light again. Like she was floating in a warm pool of water. Colors swirled around her, gathering into shapes. She was standing now, gazing over a meadow of the most vibrant green she had ever seen, buttons of dandelions dotting the landscape beneath a cloudless sky. In the center of her awareness, one shape grew larger, came toward her, and then stopped at her feet.

When she finally saw what it was, her heart swelled.

Sooner, she said, crouching to take the dog's chin in her hand. *Where have you been? I thought I told you to stay.*

chapter 12
Grayson

At fifteen minutes past ten AM, Grayson had checked his e-mail five times already. Maybe six. He wasn't sure why he'd bothered. In order to get a rejection—or an offer, even, for another interview—he would've had to send out more resumes. But he was still hoping some of the employers he'd already applied with might've had a change of heart or that the person they'd picked first had taken a better offer.

It was Tuesday morning. He should've put another call into Rex Franzen, since no one had responded to his message requesting a meeting. Should have, but he hadn't. Probably wasn't going to, either. He had other things on his mind that had been bothering him for a long time.

He'd tried not to think of them, to keep himself occupied with the animals and the house. Since his arrival, Loretta had come by a few more times to help before leaving for Florida. She'd been helpful, but he couldn't help but feel inept and unprepared for the responsibilities that had been heaped on him. He hadn't asked for this. It wasn't part of his plan.

He stumbled to the bathroom, a retro decorator's nirvana of subway tiles and copper-plated fixtures. He picked up his razor to shave, the pad of his thumb lightly grazing the edge of the blade. Several seconds passed before the sting of a cut permeated his senses. He flipped the faucet lever on, cold water running in a weak stream from the spigot, and then watched his blood tint the water pink as it swirled around the bowl of the marble sink before finally disappearing down the drain. Just like his life.

What he couldn't understand was what it was about him that was so unappealing. Was he caught in that limbo of being too old for an entry-level position, yet not quite experienced or educated enough for a higher rung? Had his references said something bad about him? He couldn't think of what that might be. Maybe he hadn't been personable enough, driven enough, savvy enough, or insightful enough. Intangible qualities. Maybe he'd given off an air of detachment. Or been too serious, too obsessed with the details of minutiae to adopt a healthier big-picture outlook.

Still bleeding, he wrapped a length of toilet paper around his thumb and proceeded to shave five days' worth of scruff. The safety razor scraped over a whiskery chin and throat. Every once in a while, he ran the razor under the spigot and watched the stubble wash off. Halfway through, he decided this was the last time he'd shave. There wasn't any point in being clean-cut when he might not see another human being for days. Besides, even if he did, what was the purpose in trying to impress them? The clerk at the local mom-and-pop grocery store was going to sell him a jug of milk no matter his appearance.

Finished with his final shave, he pressed a folded square of toilet paper to his cut and thumbed through his contacts as he briefly considered calling his former bosses and coworkers to ask what he could have done better or where he'd failed. In the end, he didn't have the courage. Didn't want to know. Because the reality was it didn't matter. He was unemployable. His skills were obsolete. He hadn't kept up with the times. Wasn't anything special… to anyone.

The weight of that flattened him.

Being jobless wasn't even the worst of it. Fee hadn't seen enough in him that was redeemable to stay by his side, even when he'd had a respectable job. The one person he thought he could count on. And now he was displaced, too. His uncle's farm was a beautiful place—but he was entirely out of his element. To Grayson, a farm was a picture on a calendar, a passing scene from the highway, the place where filet mignon or a loaf of bread originated from. Something looked at briefly with fleeting appreciation, not a place to invest in or call home.

The whole point of his musings was that Grayson was alone. Loneliness—it was the worst feeling he could imagine. He was worthless. Unimportant. A nobody. He didn't matter to anyone. Never really had. He hadn't been integral to or touched anyone's life. He'd only been concerned about his own. He wasn't… connected.

Tossing the bloodstained toilet paper in the wastebasket, he opened the medicine cabinet without even knowing what he was searching for. His bottle of sleeping pills was the first thing he saw.

If he went to sleep right now, today, and never woke up, how long would it be before anyone noticed? Would anyone care?

Probably not.

Eventually, Loretta would return from her trip and come check on the horses. She'd find them in the field, their tails and manes tangled, their feed troughs empty, their water tanks thick with scum, and she'd come to the house, knock on the door, then let herself in—because he hadn't locked it, he realized. He almost never did while he was at home.

Home? Had he just thought of this place as home? No, it wasn't that. It was just a farm he was trying to sell so he could get back to the life he'd known.

A life that didn't exist anymore.

He filled a glass with water, getting ready to brush his teeth, but set his toothbrush aside. What was the point in that? The point in anything? All his efforts went to waste. Just got tossed back in his face with rejection, abandonment, and isolation.

Then, from the lower shelf, he took out the bottle of pills, closed the lid on the toilet seat, and sat. For minute after excruciatingly long minute, he held the bottle in his palms, reading the warning on the label. Very grim. Fatal, even.

With his thumb, he popped the lid. Blood ran fresh and bright down the pad of his thumb, pausing in the crease before continuing to stream down his wrist. He'd cut himself more deeply than he thought. He wiped it on his pants, then lifted the bottle, opened his mouth, and tipped his head back. A handful of caplets fell on his tongue. He tapped the bottom and more poured in. Scooping up the glass of water, he brought it to his lips—

A commotion outside. He turned his head to hear better. The horses. A series of frantic whinnies. Hooves stomping. And then… the bark of a dog?

He hadn't gone out yet that morning to let the horses out of their stalls. Getting out of bed had been a chore in itself. If he swallowed the pills, if he died… they'd die, too.

The bark again.

A neighbor's dog left loose? He hadn't been in the area long, but he'd observed it was common practice to allow one's dog to roam freely, as if building a fence to keep it contained was some kind of inhumane punishment. In Manhattan, people didn't dare take their dog out without a leash unless they were in a fenced-in dog park.

More barking. More protests from the horses.

If he was going to do this, he had to give them a fighting chance at survival. His despondency shouldn't be their death sentence, too. He had to let them out, so they could graze in the pasture and drink from the creek. After he chased the dog off.

Standing, Grayson spat the pills into the toilet and flushed it. No sooner was he watching the pills swirl down the drain than he wished he'd spat them into a towel or empty glass for later. It was the last of his stash. He'd have to get a refill on his prescription or buy something to replace them.

Which robbed him of the impulsivity of the moment. It had been one thing to decide to end his life when he was stuck in the hopelessness of a fleeting moment. It was another thing entirely to plan it out for later.

Rushing down the stairs, Grayson realized he needed some kind of weapon, some means of chasing the dog off. He opened the door to the hall closet to look for a bat or tennis racket, pushed his uncle's winter coats aside, and was met with the odor of moth balls. Where was—?

His hand knocked against a length of solid metal and wood. A rifle clattered to the floor. He knelt, grabbed the box of bullets tucked in the corner, and pulled the gun out. Had he sought it out for the dog—or for himself?

The metal felt cold in his palms, and he couldn't fathom ending his life by pulling the trigger. A rifle would be tricky; a handgun more convenient, although he hadn't uncovered one of those in the house. Still, what if he wasn't entirely successful and only blew away part of his face, disfiguring himself for life, and enough of his brain to render him a vegetable? Even if it worked, it was too violent a death for him. Besides, what about whoever found him if he did succeed? Someone would have to clean the mess: brains splattered against the wall, shards of his skull everywhere, blood staining the floorboards.

He listened for a moment. Had the dog gone away on its own? No, the horses were still announcing the presence of an unwelcome guest. One who, he was afraid, might be doing them harm.

Standing in the front foyer, he stared at the rifle and bullets, vague as to how to even load the thing, let alone aim and shoot. Only once in his life, when he was twelve, could he recall ever having held a firearm. A friend of their father's had groused about Canadian geese wandering up from the lake and gathering on his lawn. After retrieving his rifle, the friend told Grayson to follow him. While they stood behind the corner of the woodshed, he placed the weapon in Grayson's hands, told him how to hold it, how to unlock the safety, sight the target, and fire. Grayson shook his head and handed the rifle back. As he walked away, he heard the boom of the gun, followed by a clapping of wings and alarmed honks. The flock rose into the sky. He forced himself to turn around, hopeful the shot had sunk into soft earth. But lying half in the water was a mound of downy feathers. A life extinguished. He couldn't—

This was different, though. He was protecting the horses.

He opened the chamber, put in just two bullets, and closed it.

Then he marched out to the barn, the gun held before him in the lightest grip he could manage without dropping it.

Entering the barn, he let his eyes adjust to the shaded light. A quick scan of the stalls told him where the problem was. Most of the horses looked alert but undisturbed, their heads held high, their ears twitching at every sound.

In the second to last stall on the right, however, Goliath was circling, his head bobbing in a dance of bluster. Occasionally, he slowed to peer toward the end corner of his stall. Grayson walked that way. Goliath stopped and glanced at him, then back to the corner. The horse pulled his lip up, showed his teeth, stomped a hoof several times.

The door to the last stall wasn't latched on the outside, but it had swung shut. Grayson had noticed the first day how it hung at a slant and if not propped open with a full bucket, it tended to shut itself. It was where bales of alfalfa were stored for easy access, along with the everyday tack and the bins of grain.

The dog had gone in there, maybe for food, and accidentally shut itself in. If the dog was feral and near starving, it wouldn't think twice about biting. If it was rabid… Yes, there were plenty of wild animals in these parts to spread the vile disease.

As quietly as he could, Grayson approached the stall, the rifle raised to shoulder level. He stopped next to Goliath's stall. That alone seemed to calm the gentle giant. It also gave Grayson the chance to listen for a low growl or the pacing of frantic feet.

He heard nothing except the soft, slow whoosh of indrawn and exhaled air.

Lowering the barrel, he crouched to keep his head below the open part of the door, then crept closer. When he was close enough, he rested the rifle next to the door and took hold of the handle. Sliding the latch closed, he peered over the top of the half-door.

Startling eyes of golden green stared back at him. In the far corner of the stall, pressed against a plastic tub of horse feed, huddled the most pathetic-looking dog he'd ever laid eyes on. Creamy tan eyebrows twitched alternately as it gazed back at him with equal amounts of fear and apprehension. Its coat was burnished at the ends and a deeper, richer red at the roots, almost mahogany. Patches of hair were missing around obvious scars, recently acquired. In the haunch of one rear leg, a deep gash had barely scabbed over. Even from ten feet away, Grayson could see the knotted mats behind its ears and the ragged feathers of its forelegs. He could even discern a few puncture wounds on its legs and face.

The dog had nearly been mauled to death. But by what? Another dog, a pack of coyotes? Had it been attacked by a bear or some other wild animal?

Whatever had happened to it, it needed help.

Grayson raised himself up to his full height. The dog cowered. Its legs wobbled from exhaustion. He watched it for a minute, weighing what to do—whether to go in and soothe it or call an animal control officer. It could be diseased. It could try to bite him.

If he called the county dog catcher, they'd come with their noose at the end of a long pole, lasso the poor thing by the neck, and then drag him or her off to a steel cage in the back of a truck. Then they'd take it to the shelter, where they'd quarantine it, take blood, and start shots.

There would be no comfort for the poor creature if he did that.

The dog's eyes drifted shut. It swayed.

"Hey there," Grayson whispered.

It opened its eyes. Barely. Just enough for Grayson to see they were glassy with fatigue before it turned its head away as if to signal it offered no challenge to his authority. This dog had no fight left in it. So far, it hadn't tried to bolt or shown its teeth. Mostly it just seemed like it wanted to be left alone... whatever the outcome.

Grayson hurried into the house, then rummaged through the kitchen. Five minutes later, he returned with a mixing bowl full of water and a plate heaped with cheddar cheese, turkey slices, and half a baked sweet potato that was left over from last night's dinner.

Ignoring the rifle still propped next to the stall, he opened the door slowly and cautiously, ready for the dog to try to escape. But it had wedged itself even farther into the corner. After setting the bowl and plate inside, he closed the door behind him, but didn't latch it.

He knelt, not wanting to appear too big and imposing to an already-fearful animal. The dog tucked its head down before slowly folding to the floor. It was trembling all over.

"Where did you come from? What happened to you?" He knew the dog wasn't going to answer. They were just questions spoken aloud. It was a beautiful dog—or had been once. Medium-sized, it looked vaguely like one of those herding dogs, a Border Collie, he thought they were called, but its head was a little squarer, its body frame slightly stockier, and... it didn't appear to have a tail. Just a little nub. An Australian Shepherd, maybe? Its main coat color was a dark red, but coppery tan marked its cheeks, eyebrows, and legs. Its feet and chest were trimmed in white.

Of all its features though, the eyes stood out most. It was as though their gaze could pierce his very soul. He turned away, not wanting her to see what was in there. Not today.

A minute later, curious, he stooped lower to get a better look. The hair on her belly was scant. And yes, he could see it was a girl dog. Then it occurred to him that this was the dog Loretta had spoken of, the one people had been searching for. Yes, this could very well be her. Loretta's description fit this dog. And it certainly looked like it had been on its own for some time.

Something compelled him to help her. To let her know that all hope was not lost. That things could and would get better.

It took a minute before he remembered the name Loretta had said. "Sooner? Are you Sooner?"

But the dog gave no reaction.

"I'm Grayson. And I'm going to help you."

Carefully, Grayson rose and let himself out, making sure she couldn't slip past. He'd left the house in such a rush he didn't have his phone on him. So he went inside and retrieved it from the nightstand beside the four-postered bed.

For a good five minutes, he sat on the edge of the oversized mattress, staring at the screen of his phone, unsure who to call. Definitely not animal control. The sheriff? No, that didn't seem right either. He'd been to the grocery store just yesterday to see if anyone had taken his cards down for the horses, since he hadn't gotten any calls the past few days. They'd still been there. He couldn't recall any for a lost dog, just a couple of cats that had been found.

If Loretta was around, he'd ask her. Today, though, if Grayson remembered correctly, was the day of her daughter's scheduled surgery. He couldn't call her.

There was only one person left he could think of. After looking it up, he dialed the number for Dr. Hunter McHugh.

"Yes, hello. This is Grayson Darling. I've found a dog. She needs to see the vet. It looks like she's been in a fight. She's also underweight and lethargic. I think this is the dog they've been searching for—the Australian Shepherd called Sooner."

The woman who answered asked him questions, most of which he couldn't answer based on his brief encounter with the dog.

"Can the vet come to the farm?" Grayson asked, his sense of urgency building. "He's been here to take care of my uncle's horses before. It would be easier for the dog if—"

"If you'd like him to examine the dog as early as possible, your best chance would be to bring her here. In order to make a farm call, he'd have to cancel several other appointments and I'm not sure how we would make that work. Do you think you could be here in…"—fingers tapped at a keyboard—"say half an hour? He has an opening then. Actually, it's his lunch, but if it's an emergency, we'll work you in."

"I'll be there. Where are you located?"

She gave him the address before he could find something to write with, so he rushed to the bathroom, grabbed a sliver of soap, and wrote it from memory on the bathroom mirror. When he'd hung up and dressed himself presentably, he transferred the address onto the map app of his phone and got the directions. As he turned to leave the bathroom, he inadvertently kicked the trash can. It toppled over, its contents spilling onto the floor, including the empty pill bottle.

Shame flushed through his chest. How could he have considered that a solution to his fleeting problems?

He picked up the bottle. After righting the trash can, he tossed it back in. As for his sleeping problems, he'd have to find another answer for that. He didn't want the pills around anymore.

Halfway down the front porch steps, he paused to take everything in—the rolling hills dotted with cattle, sheep, and horses; the patches of woods teeming with wildlife; the houses and barns, some diligently maintained, some in varying stages of decay; the winding roads and distantly spaced mailboxes; the sprawling oaks that shaded so much of the lawn surrounding the house; and the china-blue sky laced with clouds of purest white. He'd seen it all multiple times before, known it was there. And yet, he hadn't really *seen* any of it until just now.

Then, he went to save the dog that had first saved him.

chapter 13
Sooner

I floated through a wasteland of gray oblivion and muted sounds. At the edge of blissful forever sleep and unwelcome wakefulness. Unaware of my body, yet trapped inside it.

Half of me wanted to let go, to detach from all the pain and loneliness I'd so recently known; half of me wanted to fight my way back, despite all I'd suffered. Unfeeling nothingness… or struggle and uncertainty. I knew what was easier.

Yet somewhere, at the brink of my awareness, a familiar voice reached me through a twisting fog.

Sooner, are you paying attention to me? I told you, we were meant to be together.

Brandy? I fought my way through the mist. Listened. There, ahead of me. The faintest circle of light amidst a cloud of darkness. *Where—?*

You and me, Sooner. You… and me.

The light dimmed, faded away.

Where are you, Brandy?

A new pinpoint of light appeared. Brightened. Swirled outward.

Flared like a sunburst. I had to look away.

Right with you. Well, you're with me, anyway. I told you to pay attention. Now look at me!

I opened my eyes to a grid-work of metal bars and the stinging scent of antiseptic.

Too tired to get up, I waited for my eyes to focus. For Brandy to appear. I waited and waited, but she never came. Her voice didn't sound again.

Only an occasional whimper and plaintive meows broke the quiet. I wasn't alone. There were others nearby, but I was isolated from them in a box of sorts. Two small metal bowls were affixed to the wire door. One was a water dish. Life-giving water.

I needed to drink. Nothing mattered more.

It took all my strength to raise myself up, then to bend my head to the bowl. Cool water trickled down my throat, filled my insides. After a few more laps, I slid back down onto my belly and became aware of a peculiar stiffness in various places on my body. Where I'd had poorly mending wounds before, there were now shaved areas with the cuts and punctures stitched closed. I felt the urge to lick them because they were itchy, but I didn't have the energy. How was it there were now pieces of thread holding me together? The last thing I remembered was crawling into the stall to hide among the hay bales. A man had appeared, spoken to me, stroked my fur, and…

My memory went no farther. Everything beyond that was overshadowed by a haze of nightmares. Of flying through the air upside down in the van. Of Brandy's face in the mirror, her eyes wide with fright. Headlights bearing down on me, the trumpet of horns deafening in my ears. A city with buildings so close together I could barely squeeze between them, and so high they blocked the sun. Giant-headed dogs with yellow fangs dripping venom. An old stoop-backed man with a heinous laugh. A dark and endless tunnel, full of frogs and bugs and rank muck up to my chest. Coyotes with eyes of fire, howling ghoulishly in the night, circling me...

"*Sooner?*"

I heard Brandy's voice once more, but couldn't discern where it was coming from.

"*Sooner... come!*"

My whole body jerked. I was awake again. Awake and alert now. Not running anymore, but someplace indoors, someplace... safe? I couldn't be sure.

It was nighttime. A faint light glowed in a hallway, and another small light shone from a fixture on the wall opposite where I was. I couldn't make much sense of my surroundings, but the man had brought me here; I guessed that much. I was in the care of humans. Safe from coyotes at least.

When I had rested some more and felt strong enough, I sat up to drink again and get a better look around. The first pale light of morning spilled from the hallway, where there must've been some windows or a door. I could hear other animals beginning to stir beside and above me. A kitten meowed inconsolably. The dog above me scratched at his floor.

As I drank some more, I noticed there was a small amount of kibble in my bowl. I ate slowly, savoring every piece, never more grateful for a square meal than I was at that moment. Too soon, I reached the bottom of the bowl, so I curled up and waited for the humans I knew would come.

When a door somewhere opened and shut, an old hound next to me began baying—long, throaty cries of joy and anticipation. Moments later, the whines and yips became a chorus seeking attention.

I was cared for that morning. Tended to with gentleness and patience. I was still very scared, still reluctant to trust. How I wanted to! But when I'd been chased and bitten and almost died a dozen times in as many days, it was hard to let go of the fear that had kept me alive.

A man with wavy golden hair came by a few times, barely glancing my way. The fourth time, he stopped to check the piece of paper affixed to the outside of my crate. He gazed at me kindly, spoke softly. I tucked my head toward the corner of the cage, trying to ignore him so he'd leave me alone. But he stayed, persistent. His fingers reached through the wires to touch my paw. I flinched, but I didn't pull away. He stroked my foot a few times and said, "Everything's going to be just fine, girl. You'll feel better soon. I promise."

Then, to my relief, he left.

Fear had made me strong and fierce when I was never those things before. Fear had made me fast, when I had nothing left to run on. Fear had made me cautious and kept me alert, so I saw the danger coming.

As the people came and went, fed and walked me, changed my bandages, and applied a stinging liquid to my mending wounds, I let go of that fear just a little each time, not because it hadn't kept me alive, but because holding on to it was so exhausting.

—o0Oo—

He looked as though he was afraid of me—the man now staring at me through the cage door. He stood back a bit, the smell of nervousness seeping from his pores. What was he afraid of? I wouldn't bite him. Not if I could run. Which I couldn't do. So—

Something about him, though… His face was familiar. Vaguely. It wasn't until he spoke that I began to piece it all together.

"Hello, Sooner." He knelt, still a safe distance away. "You look better. Relatively speaking. Remember that day on the farm—when I found you?"

I sniffed the air, drew in his scent more fully. He smelled faintly of… ah yes, horses and hay. Now I remembered. After Clayton and Loretta had tried to capture me—and failed, thanks to my quickness and guile—I'd run over the hills to a farm with horses. The giant creatures hadn't been welcoming when I'd wandered into their barn, but I was desperate enough to risk it. When the door swung shut behind me, the large horse in the next stall made a terrible ruckus. I thought for sure he was going to burst through and stomp me to smithereens, so I retreated behind some hay bales for refuge, too terrified, too hopeless, and too drained to seek escape.

Yet I hadn't gone there merely to hide. I'd gone there to die. In peace. Alone.

Because I was sure I'd never find Brandy again. And that made going on any longer more unbearable than I could tolerate.

Her love had been my sun and my moon and my stars. Now they were dimmed. Dark as darkest night.

So I'd closed my eyes once more, my will to stay or go… gone.

Until I'd heard his voice.

"Sooner? Are you Sooner?"

I am. Who are you?

"I'm Grayson. And I'm going to help you."

Then he'd gathered me in his arms and brought me here. Where I could get better.

I trusted this man. Not because I had to, or because I might otherwise have died that day. But because I sensed something familiar in him. Something we shared. A loneliness. A need. Something… incomplete?

There was strength in surviving on my own. Independence required courage and confidence. But there were times when what I was capable of by myself was not enough to overcome that which bore against me.

As a young pup, I had sought to be my own being, eager to teach my first two human families what it was I wanted them to do. But that had made them unhappy. They hadn't understood me. I thought I knew so much. Brandy had taught me otherwise—that together we could do more than we ever could alone. But this man, Grayson, he needed me just as I needed him. In ways very different from what Brandy had required of me. Simpler ways. Which was a good thing, because there wasn't much I could do right now, as battered as I was.

He scooted closer. Gazed at me not with pity, but sympathy. He spread an open palm against the wire door. I touched it with the leather of my nose, gave his fingers two short licks, then laid my head back down. His hand moved to my paw, which was pressed against the wires. He rubbed my toes gently.

"Maybe taking care of you is just what I need," he said, more to himself than to me. "Only until your owner gets better, though."

I lifted my head to listen and watch his face better. There were more words coming and I intended to capture them all, just in case he spoke one I knew, so I could make some sense of what was going on.

"This is crazy, I know. But it's only for a few weeks. Maybe a month. Two at most. She should be better enough then to take you back. But you can't go see her now. Not like you are, not like she is. So I'll do my good deed. Help someone out. Her, you. I don't know if what Dr. Philipot keeps telling me is true, that you get back what you put out in the world, but... well, it's not like I have much else going on, so I might as well do something, right?" Withdrawing his hand, he sat back. "Maybe one day I'll understand why you showed up when you did. Right now, though... yeah. Me with a dog? That's the last thing I would've expected."

I tipped my head one way, then another. Besides the word 'dog,' I hadn't understood much of it. But I did understand more about him—that he was hurting, too, only in a different way. And because of that, maybe I could help him, just as he had helped me.

What did I have to lose?

—o0Oo—

He took me home that day. To *his* home, that was.

First, though, he put a new collar on me, carried me outside the clinic to pee, and then to his car. I wanted to watch out the window, memorize the route we were taking, but while my energy was rebounding, the memories of the accident were still too fresh in my mind. Without my crate, I felt even more vulnerable. So I plastered myself flat on the backseat, too scared to look out.

When we finally stopped and he opened the door to help me out, I was shaking terribly. I couldn't stop. A puddle of drool soaked the seat beneath my head. Would he be angry at me for making a mess?

"You don't look well," he said without judgment.

At which point, I threw up.

He covered his mouth and nose with a hand. "Ugh," he mumbled into his fingers. Then, "Stay there a minute. I'll get something to clean this up." He shut the door.

I wasn't embarrassed so much as I was relieved we'd stopped moving. Feeling better enough now to peek out the window, I watched the door, but was surprised when he came out of the house a different way. He had a pile of towels in his arms and a small bucket of cleaning items. After he opened the other door in the back of the car, he gently urged me out that way so I wouldn't have to step through my own puke.

"Let me take you inside and get you situated first. I just hope that stain isn't permanent. This car is a rental. They'll charge me five times the normal rate if I don't return it in the same condition they gave it to me."

I had no idea what he was saying most of the time, but I liked that he talked to me. Brandy used to use a lot of words I knew, like 'good girl' and 'come' and 'heel' or even just 'let's go'. This guy didn't seem to know any of that. When I saw the opportunity to point it out, I put the brakes on, even though I knew very well how to walk on a leash.

Oblivious as he was, he hit the end of the leash ahead of me with a jerk. It nearly knocked him off his feet.

"Come on, Sooner. This way, all right?" He pulled on the leash, gently at first, then more firmly.

I locked my legs. He pulled harder, made little kissing sounds, slapped the side of his leg, and said my name over and over. With each word, the tension in his voice rose.

"Don't do this to me, girl. I know you know all this. You were supposed to be some spectacular performance dog. Had a lot of titles for your age. I have no idea what they all mean, but you couldn't have gotten them if you hadn't gone through a lot of training. So don't act like you don't know how to walk on a leash, okay? Because I know you do."

Sometimes a statement had to be made. Like who was in charge. Best to get that straight from the get-go.

I lowered my head to the level of my shoulders. The collar he'd put on me at the vet's began to slide over my head. It had almost slipped over one ear before he gave up the fight and just scooped me off the ground.

"I know this is all new to you, but whether you realize it or not, I'm doing you a big favor."

As I lay stiff in his arms, he carried me up the porch, then set me down before the front door and made my collar a little snugger. When he opened the door, I studied my surroundings, on the alert for danger. Those horses had been far off in the field when we arrived, but what if there was a cat inside—or another dog? It took a great deal of coercion before he got me through the doorway and into the living room.

"Wait here," he commanded wearily.

Then he did something strange. He unclipped my leash, then walked into another room. I heard water running.

Hold on. What if he was going to give me a bath? Oh no! No, no, no, no. No way. Ever.

I jumped at the front door, trying to push it open, but it wouldn't give. Desperate, I clawed at it. This had all been a trap! The scratches, the gentle words, the trip in the car. This was a groomer's. I was going to tear down this door if it took me all day to do it.

"Whoa!" Grayson's hand hooked through my collar. He dragged me back. "Where are you going? Just relax. Did you think I was going to give you a bath?"

I twisted in his hold. If I spun hard enough, he'd have to let go. But he threw an arm around me and tried to pull me to him. I was panting now, frantic, my heart going so fast it was hard to tell one beat from another.

"I was just running water to offer you a drink. Don't worry, Sooner. You can't have a bath just yet with all those stitches, anyway. All you need to do is just hang out with me, get used to things. I know this is all new to you."

Blah, blah, blah, Sooner. Blah, blah, was what I heard.

"You're trembling again." He knelt beside me and held me until my breathing slowed and my body stopped shaking. Even when I lay down and put my head in his lap, he stayed there with me, stroking my neck and speaking softly. "I know you're scared. I know. You want things to go back to the way they used to be. For the bad things never to have happened. We have more in common than you know, girl. Just that the changes in your life took place a whole lot quicker and more drastically than mine. But we both ended up alone, huh? So what do you say we help each other through this rough patch? Then, by the time you can go back to your owner and she's happy to see you, maybe I'll feel like I made a difference in someone's life." Scoffing, he shook his head, the whole time scratching my chest and neck. "That's what Dr. Philipot tells me, anyway. That I can't just anonymously donate to a charity or randomly volunteer. That I should personally help someone who really needs it. Like you, Sooner. And this Brandy, whoever she is."

Brandy? He knew Brandy? I stared him hard in the eyes, trying to send a message I wanted to hear more—that the word 'Brandy' meant more than all the rest.

Brandy, I woofed. *Tell me more about Brandy.*

Laughing, he ruffled the fur on top of my head.

"You're a character, Sooner. Let me show you where your bed is for now. I think you'll like it."

Grayson got up and left again. I followed him. Just to make sure he didn't disappear. I kept my distance, though. I didn't want him to think I was getting attached or anything.

He went through a doorway and into the kitchen, glancing over his shoulder every so often to see if I was behind him. I sat in the entrance to the room. This was close enough. Besides, I didn't see an alternate escape route, just in case he decided to stick me in the big farm sink and give me a bath. Brandy had done that when I was younger and went swimming in the lake—to 'wash the fish stink off me,' she'd said. I'd always cooperated, but made sure to give a good shake before she was done just to get her all wet and let her know my opinion on the matter.

"You can hang out in here while I'm doing chores outside. Eventually I'll let you follow me around, but not until you're all better and I can trust you not to run off. You can also sleep in here. See, I got you a bed." He pointed to a giant pillow tucked into the corner. I'd have the stuffing out the first time he disappeared. Challenge accepted. "Whatever you do, though, don't chew on this table. I checked, and it's over a hundred years old. Hand carved, one of a kind." He thumped on the table, then pointed at me. "I'll get you some bones as soon as I get to the grocery, but that won't be for a day or two. In the meantime, do *not* chew on the table. It's an antique. Got that?"

I understood 'table' and 'chew'. The table was for chewing. Got it. Nice of him. This guy and I were going to get along just fine.

He went to the fridge and opened it. I took a couple of steps closer. The fridge was where the best food was—leftovers. Drool filled my mouth. I licked my lips and swallowed, but some of it spilled onto the floor.

"Let's see. What do we have here? Bologna... You like bologna, Sooner?" He dangled a piece in the air.

Bologna! I love bologna! I inched closer. Close enough to smell it was the kind with little flecks of cheese in it.

Wait... this was another trick. I could tell. What did he really want to do—give me a bath, cut my nails, give me a shot? Nope, I wasn't going to fall for that.

"Want some?" He waved it back and forth. When I didn't budge, he tore off a strip and ate it himself. "Mmm, mmm, mmmmmm. Best bologna ever."

Oh, that was cruel. He wasn't going to eat it all... *was he?*

He ate another piece.

My nose quivered. Bologna aroma filled my nostrils, danced across my taste buds. I lay down, put my chin on the floor. He lifted yet another piece to his mouth. I put a paw over my eyes, not able to watch this any longer.

"Is that a trick you know?"

Trick? Yes, I knew tricks. Brandy had taught me a lot of tricks to keep my mind busy. I waited for him to give a command, but he just stared stupidly at me. So I played dead.

"That one's not very convincing. Your eyes are still open."

This was when he was supposed to tell me 'good dog'. A little praise tossed my way didn't cost much. This guy was going to take *forever* to train—if he could even be trained at all.

He ate the last piece of bologna. "Come to think of it," he mumbled as he chewed, "I didn't have lunch today."

Selfish b—

"What? Why are you staring at me like that? You don't look very happy." He opened the fridge again, then took out an entire new package of bologna and a brick of cheese. After he made himself a sandwich, he rolled some of the cheese in bologna, put it on a plate, and set it on the floor.

And then... he walked around the table and got himself a glass of water.

This was my chance. Darting to the plate on the floor, I gobbled down the bologna and cheese. If he thought I didn't notice the nasty little pill he'd tucked inside, he was mistaken. I managed to catch it at the back of my tongue before it went down and spit it out under a chair, where I hoped he wouldn't notice it. Then I finished the rest as he bumbled about the kitchen, putting away dishes from beside the sink and peering into cupboards like he wasn't sure what went where.

"Liked that, did you?" From a jar on the counter, he scooped out a spoonful of peanut butter and put it on the plate. Then he put the jar back in one of the cupboards, set the plate on the floor, and stepped away.

I just about died right there. After making sure he was busily distracted, I sniffed for pills. Deciding there were none, I licked the plate. Creamy smoothness filled my mouth. I swallowed pure happiness, and it slid down to the utter delight of my stomach. I licked every inch of that plate. Licked it across the floor and under the table.

How long had it been since I'd had a treat like this? How many days had I been content to find cold meat with congealed fat or soggy green beans in a Styrofoam container or a partially filled plastic tub of yogurt on the verge of turning rancid? This wasn't just fresh food, good food. Peanut butter was my *favorite* food. Ever! I would do anything, anything at all, for peanut butter. If this was—

Click.

I spun around to see him standing outside the kitchen on the other side of a baby gate. Humans and their tricks. Why had I not been paying closer attention? Testing the latch, he grinned smugly. The traitor. I knew all about those things. My second family had tried to confine me by putting them up in almost every doorway. What they hadn't counted on was how determined I was to find out what was on the other side.

"You stay here, Sooner," Grayson said. "I have some chores to do outside." He thumped the heel of his hand against his forehead. "I can't believe I'm saying that—chores. My coworkers at the bank would never have envisioned me shoveling manure. I'd give anything to be back in my stuffy suit, sitting at my desk in the air conditioning, preparing reports for my clients. But no, I've traded in Armani for Levi's, polished marble floors for muddy linoleum, a leather swivel chair for a cracked vinyl seat on a tractor." His sigh seemed to come all the way from his gut. "Well, things to do. Sit tight."

Somewhere in there, I'd heard the words 'sit' and 'stay'. Okay, maybe he did know something. But I was still unimpressed. He could be confusing.

So I sat and stayed—for a little while, anyway.

I had to know what he was up to. I also wanted to request more peanut butter, because he hadn't given me nearly enough, so if I could train him to give me more when I wanted some, life around here might be pretty darn sweet.

Waiting long enough to hear the front screen door slap shut and his footsteps pounding down the porch stairs, I then assessed the situation. The gate wasn't the kind I was used to, with small squares in which I could slip my toes and climb over, meaning that option was out. No, this one had vertical bars. Hmm. I hooked a paw over the top bar and pulled, but it was securely latched in place. So I pushed against it with the side of my body. No luck there, either. After jiggling it back and forth some more with nothing happening, I limped in a slow circle around the kitchen table, thinking.

As I glanced at the gate from the other side of the room, I realized it wasn't all that tall. Up until recently, its height wouldn't have been a problem for me. I'd been a well-conditioned agility dog. But I had a lot of cuts and bite wounds and stitches piecing me together. My joints were still sore and my muscles weak. Right now, walking was a hard-enough thing to do, let alone taking a running jump at a gate, clearing it, and landing deftly on the other side.

Still, I had a point to prove. If I got hurt in the process, so what?

Taking a few more laps around the table to loosen up, I summoned my courage. The more I moved about, the more limber I felt, relatively speaking. He'd probably be impressed I was so talented and determined, not to mention athletic. I took two more laps to build speed, which was hard because the floor was slick and I couldn't get much traction. On the third round, I changed trajectories and went for it, knowing if I didn't time this right, it could be disastrous.

My claws dug into the floor. I pushed off and up, tucking my feet to my belly and bending my spine to arch gracefully. Which I didn't quite do. The graceful part, I meant. I'd lost my stretch and my spring. My body went flat. My front feet cleared the top bar of the gate, but I'd jumped too soon and was already descending as my rear legs came over. Too low, my hind feet clipped the gate, wrecking my momentum.

The gate came crashing down, landing on top of me as I slid onto the wooden floor of the dining room. If it hadn't been for the rug anchored in place by the dining table, I'd have kept sliding right into the china cabinet.

Clumsy, but I was on the other side. Not like I hadn't crashed a few jumps in my earlier days of running agility. Just never this badly.

I wiggled from beneath the metal gate and stood. Nothing broken, but I'd landed hard on my shoulder. Gimping across the dining room, I headed to the living room where only a screen door stood between me and freedom. But that wasn't my goal. I'd had enough of being on my own. This situation with Grayson wasn't a bad deal if I could figure out how to work it to my advantage. I stopped before the door to outside.

This was too easy. He'd left the main door open. The screen door was shut, but it opened with a handle, rather than a knob. I'd figured this one out a long time ago. Another, and perhaps the final, reason I'd been ejected from my second home before I finally ended up with Brandy.

Reaching up, I hooked my nails over the handle and pulled down. It took me a few tries, but it finally released. I bopped the door with my shoulder to shove it open, remembering my injuries too late. My shoulder throbbed for a moment, but the ache quickly faded.

I was halfway across the porch when I saw Grayson trotting across the yard, a rake in his hand. Good, he was coming back. All I needed was for him to—

"Sooner?" Throwing the rake down, he began running. Not well, I might add. He was just as lame as me. "What in the world?"

I sat, patiently waiting.

As he came closer, he slowed. "It's... okay... It's okay, girl." His chest heaved. He stopped, put his hands on his knees. After a few ragged pulls of air, he half-straightened, swaying like he might topple over from his brief sprint. "How did you... get out of the... house, huh?"

He extended a palm, approaching me cautiously like Clayton had, like he was afraid I might bolt at any second. If I'd wanted to leave, I'd have been long gone already. Since he was having a hard time figuring out why I was sitting out here, I went to the screen door and scratched at it gently.

"Do you...?" Confusion clouded his brow. "Do you want something inside?"

Woofing softly, I scratched again. I was going to die of starvation if this guy didn't get with it.

He opened the door and followed me to the kitchen, where I sat beside the cupboard with the peanut butter in it. After fetching the used spoon from the sink, he took the peanut butter out and fed me, spoonful after spoonful.

"You're a good dog for not running away. If you'd taken off..." His face twisted with anxiety. "Just don't run away, okay? Just... don't. I owe you more than you'll ever know."

He'd said, 'good dog'. He'd *finally* said it. That must have meant he was impressed with how I'd managed to let myself out of the kitchen and the house—I thought. I raised my paw in a high five.

"Good dog, Sooner." He tapped my paw with the flat of his palm. "Good dog."

When he'd screwed the lid back on, he knelt in front of me so we were eye to eye. "Sooner, I'm not entirely sure what I'm going to do with you, but I think you're going to keep me on my toes more than I'd like. Just go easy on me, okay, girl?"

Okay! I barked. That word meant I was free to do whatever I wanted. Sitting, I held up my paw for another high five. This trick always seemed especially pleasing to humans. Brandy had taught me to greet new friends this way. Little kids especially loved it.

Laughing, he high-fived me again. "Okay, okay."

A little bubble of happiness exploded inside me. I spun in a circle one way and then the other. Another trick, but he seemed not to understand.

"Whoa, settle down. Don't get so excited. You still have stitches. It's a wonder you didn't pull any loose when you knocked that gate over." He held up his hand again. "High five."

I complied, which delighted him. When I showed him some other tricks, he didn't know the names of those. Not the most trainable of humans, but there was hope yet. We'd take it one thing at a time. Small steps.

At some point, his laughter dissipated. He regarded me soberly. "They scanned you at Hunter's clinic. If the microchip number matches up, we'll know you belong to Brandy Anders, but I'm pretty sure you're the dog."

Lifting my chin, he studied my face. "I feel like I have no idea what I'm doing with you. Been a long time since I had a dog. A very long time. I'd forgotten what it was like." His chest expanded, then deflated with an expelled breath. "The article said her back was broken. That could be bad. *Very* bad. You were the lucky one." He pinched my cheek affectionately. "Maybe I was, too."

I licked his wrist. Partly because I was starting to like him. Just a little. But also because I wanted him to let go of my face. Besides, he'd been staring at me for way too long and it was getting uncomfortable.

After I took a long drink to wash the last of the peanut butter down, he clipped a leash onto my collar and made sure it was secure, but not too tight. "I bought this collar and leash brand new for you, Sooner. They didn't have much of a selection at the dollar store in Faderville, but I saw this neon green set and thought it would go with your eyes. You have the prettiest golden-green eyes. Do you know that?"

I listened, even though I wasn't sure what he was saying. Because that was what he seemed to need. Someone to sit close to him and listen.

One thing I was sure of—if any human ever needed a dog, it was Grayson.

chapter 14
Brandy

More than anything, Brandy wished she had her dog beside her now. It had been a grueling day. A dog like Sooner was the best therapist a person could ask for. Today, she needed that endless source of love to reassure her that everything would be okay.

Hours after Brandy had awoken from her second surgery, the one where they put the screws in her hip, she'd expected to find her father. Two days earlier, her dad had told her he'd make the drive and wait through her surgery, but he hadn't shown up, before or after. While the post-surgery haze of anesthetic was still lingering, her brother had told her over the phone about her father's massive stroke the night before.

Her dad had promised to be here for her. But now in *his* time of need, she couldn't do anything for him. Nothing at all. Not today. Not tomorrow. Not anytime soon. She hated being so weak and useless. Hated not being there for the man she loved most in the world. He was the one who'd taught her to be strong and independent, yet here she was, laid up in a hospital two hundred miles away, unable to even get out of bed.

There weren't enough drugs in the world to erase her misery.

Her father was everything to her, her greatest supporter and most demanding critic, her best friend and protector. Even after the shocking tragedy of her mother's death, her dad had held the family together. He'd never wavered in his love for his children, even as he must have been breaking on the inside.

And now, he was impaired, likely permanently, unable to walk, feed himself, or speak. As sorry as Brandy felt for herself, at least she could talk and hold a spoon. She may not have been physically whole, but she had her mind. Her brother had said their dad didn't even seem to recognize him. Given her own current state, it would be some time before she could visit him. She wasn't sure how much more she could take, but she kept telling herself if she had survived the accident, she could get through anything. It was a sentiment easier spoken than believed. Because right now, she needed someone to—

"Brandy?"

A pair of older women stood in the doorway of her hospital room—one slight and spry with chin-length hair in a mousy brown, and the other full-bodied with a shock of white tresses gathered into a messy bun.

"Jae? Shirl?" Brandy pushed the hair from her eyes. If she could have, she would've sat up, but she didn't feel like moving. Plus, there was the back brace. She barely had enough energy to talk. "What are you two hooligans doing here?"

Shirley rushed forward to grab her hand, then gave her a peck on the cheek. "We came to see you. Why else would we be here?"

Jaelynn, the heavier woman, produced a bouquet of flowers: sunny yellow-faced daisies and cheery mums in orange and pink. "Brought you something to brighten the place up. Plus, been house hunting with my son, and he can't find anything in his price range he likes. So seeing you is a welcome break."

Jaelynn and Shirley practically lived at the dog club. Jae's children, all grown, had all moved away except for her youngest son, and Shirl, although she'd been a bachelorette all her life, lived a full life. The dog club was their family. Not only did they devote countless hours to teaching classes, but they chaired obedience trials and volunteered at community events like the Dog Jog and the Greater Lexington Pet Expo. They even organized the annual Adoptathon just after the Christmas holiday, when influxes of unwanted pets were dumped at the shelters. In some ways, their constant altruism had made Brandy feel selfish for taking a more competitive approach to dog sports, yet they'd never for a moment made her feel anything but welcome and worthy of their friendship. And now, there they were, paying her a visit. Just as if she *were* family.

It had taken Brandy years to realize these people had created their own connections through a shared passion. Much like others did by attending a church or belonging to a softball team or community theater group.

"How ya feelin', gal?" Shirley asked.

"Truthfully?" Brandy forced a smile. "Better than I expected. So long as the drugs don't wear off." She'd made a joke of it, but it was the truth. She could easily understand how people got addicted to painkillers. Hopefully she'd be able to cope without them eventually, but she knew the longer she stayed on them, the harder that would be.

"For someone who's been through what you have," Jae said, "I'd say you look pretty damn good." She handed an oversized 'get well' card to Brandy.

Brandy slipped the card from its envelope and unfolded it, but even that menial task took all her concentration. Her head was still foggy, and her fingers felt thick. At first, it looked like a collection of scribbles and smudges. Then Brandy realized she didn't have her contacts in. She held the card at arm's length, waiting for the words to come into focus. She could just make out the names of dozens of club members and their well wishes.

And alongside the names of the club members, they'd each written the names of their dogs.

"Thank you. I…" She didn't know what to say. Couldn't speak. Her breath came in ragged gasps.

Brandy shut her eyes tight, trying to hold back the flood, but the tears fell anyway, rushing down her cheeks, clogging up her throat.

"I'm sorry, Brandy." Jae plucked a tissue from the box on her nightstand, then waved it in front of her. "We didn't mean to upset you."

Brandy blew her nose. Loudly. More than once. Jae gave her a handful more.

Shirl rubbed her arm lightly, as if she were afraid too much pressure might break yet another bone. "What's the matter, hon? You can tell us. Don't hold back."

It wasn't the card that had Brandy choked up. It was what Jae and Shirl hadn't said.

"They haven't found Sooner yet, have they?" A rhetorical question, but still, she held onto the slightest glimmer of hope.

Frowning, Jae shook her head. "Sorry, no."

Brandy mopped at her eyes. "I don't know why, but I still sense she's out there somewhere. You're going to think this is silly, but I've dreamed about her every day since the accident. I can hear her thoughts in my dreams, almost like we're having a conversation." She blew her nose again. "Now that I hear myself say it out loud, it does sound like the craziest thing ever. Forget I said it."

Jae and Shirl glanced at each other.

Shirl touched Brandy's shoulder. "We believe you."

"About a dozen of us went down there for several days after the accident," Jae said. "Combing the woods and hills for her, asking around, putting up flyers."

"No leads at all?" Brandy asked.

"Just one. A woman who said they had her in their garage, but she claims the dog got out."

"It was her? Did the description fit? Did they check her collar, the tags?"

"They said she didn't have a collar on, but the description fit."

"And no one told me—why?" It came out sharper than Brandy intended, but she was alarmed no one had informed her. How could they not?

Shirl shrugged. "I'm not sure what the search team decided, whose job it might have been to let you know, but at the time, I think you were still in a pretty bad way. At any rate, that was more than a week after the accident. Sooner hasn't been seen since."

Brandy stared out the window. It was night now. The parking lot lights blotted out the stars. "Someone must have her. She's a friendly dog. She'd go home with anyone."

She knew, however, that under the circumstances, Sooner might be scared. Too scared to trust just anyone. Someone had already tried to take her in, and she'd run away. Other dogs had been known to roam lost for weeks before finding a way back home. Still, she had to believe Sooner would eventually be desperate enough to look to a human for food. "Someone has to have seen her. Or have her. I can see someone taking her in, thinking they'd found this smart, pretty dog. But who'd just take a dog in and not try to find its owner? She has a microchip. All they'd have to do would be to take her to a vet or shelter and have her scanned. It wouldn't be that hard."

Jae and Shirl nodded, agreeing how thoughtless it would be for someone not to check around or post on social media to try to find the owner.

As her friends shared stories about acquaintances whose dogs had gotten lost and then been found, doubt pushed forward from the back of Brandy's conscience. Something in the timeline of events didn't quite connect. Her phone had been destroyed in the accident. In order to find her father and get a hold of him, the highway patrol had needed to sift through the wreckage to find some entry forms she'd had in the van that had her father's phone number listed as an emergency contact on them. He'd come to the hospital then, but she'd remained unconscious for two more days. She hadn't even been aware of his visit. Her first surgery had taken place soon after that, and it was another week before she was cognizant enough to ask for a new phone. By then, her father had had his own medical troubles. More time went by before her brother was able to fly in for a visit, then secure a phone for her. She wasn't sure how long it had actually taken, but if not for the matter of her dog being lost, she might have dismissed replacing her phone altogether. She had more important things to worry about. Her health for one. Her father's for another.

Precious time had been lost. Time during which her dog could've roamed farther afield. Time in which her phone hadn't been working. A gaping window during which someone could've tried to reach her.

What if someone *had* tried to call her then?

chapter 15
Grayson

Grayson was thankful this fostering situation was only temporary—although he still didn't know what constituted 'temporary'. Doc Hunter's receptionist had called recently to confirm the dog was indeed the Australian Shepherd, Sooner, owned by the Brandy Anders who'd been in the accident. The microchip company, however, hadn't been successful in reaching her by phone, and e-mails to her were bouncing. Given she'd been in a fight for her life, it was no surprise. Grayson was prepared to keep the dog for a couple of weeks if needed, until a friend or family member could be found to come get her. How long could that take?

At any rate, he didn't really need a dog in his life right now. Not long term, anyway. Being responsible for Sooner only complicated what had lately been a downwardly spiraling period for him. If someone called him with a job offer back in New York, what would he do—take the dog with him? Hopefully she'd be back with her owner long before that. What was he supposed to do if he did go home and her owner later wanted her back—drop everything and drive nonstop back here to deliver her? Besides, how would he care for a young, energetic dog until then while being gone all day at work? Doggie daycare had to be expensive in Manhattan. He could hire a dog walker to come by twice a day, but the dog would be climbing the walls out of boredom in between.

Which became obvious the first time he left her alone.

Sooner greeted him at the back door in the kitchen, not in the normal you've-been-gone-too-long-oh-how-I-missed-you happy dog wiggle and bounce, but in a submissive creep, her head low.

Grayson set the grocery sack on the kitchen counter before turning in a slow circle. The overstuffed dog bed he'd bought for her at the farm supply store before bringing her home had exploded. Tufts of downy stuffing lay everywhere: under the kitchen table, around and over the throw rug that used to be by the back door but was now crumpled next to the fridge, and in a long haphazard trail leading into the dining room. He didn't even want to look there. Mixed in with the stuffing was three days' worth of garbage. Sooner had managed to topple the trash can, flip the lid open, and scatter the contents. Undoubtedly, she'd picked through it and eaten her fill of day-old chicken scraps, potato skins, and bread heels, along with a variety of supposedly inedible trash.

Despite the mess, his first thoughts weren't ones of anger at Sooner's misbehavior or remorse at his own stupidity—after all, the dog was bored and he'd been dumb enough to leave her unattended for hours in the house while he ran errands—but concern over whether there'd been anything toxic in the trash that she might have ingested.

He dropped to his knees, sorting through the bits of trash for clues. There were shredded scraps of paper towels, junk mail, soggy tea bags, pieces of plastic packaging... Could those block her digestive tract?

Trembling, he took out his phone and dialed Doc Hunter's

emergency number as he continued to sift through the refuse with his free hand.

"Dr. McHugh speaking. Can I help you?"

The empty sleeping pill bottle. Grayson turned it over in his palm, chicken grease smeared over his fingertips. How had he gotten to that point? Sure things were bad, not what he'd planned, but—

"Hello? Who's there? Is this an emergency?"

"Um…" Grayson swallowed, clenched the bottle in his fist. His gaze fell on Sooner, who was flattened to the floor beneath the table. "Sorry. Yes, this is Grayson Darling—Skip Dalton's nephew. You were here—"

"I remember. Are the horses okay? Is there a problem?"

"The horses are fine. They were as of this morning, anyway. I called because… well, I'm not sure if it's a problem or not. The dog I'm taking care of, Sooner… seems she got into the trash. Looks as though she chewed up some plastic. I'm not sure if she ingested it or not, but she's being unusually sedate. Could that cause her problems? If she did eat it, I mean."

"It could. Solid objects can block an animal's digestive tract—"

"I was afraid of that." He sat, the gravity of his careless mistake bearing down on him. A ragged edge of the plastic bottle poked into the meat of his palm. "Will she need surgery? Should I bring her in right away? I don't know how long ago—"

"First of all, stay calm. Surgery is a last resort, provided there is a blockage. And you said yourself you're not sure if she did actually ingest something dangerous. Just this week, one of my client's cats ate half a dozen rubber bands. She gave it some hydrogen peroxide, and the cat regurgitated all but one."

"What happened to the last rubber band?"

"It came out the other end. Most things do."

"Did she see the cat eat them?"

"No, but they were there on the end table one minute. The next, they weren't, and the cat had a very sorry look on his face."

"Animals don't experience guilt"—he gave Sooner a sidelong glance, but she looked more like she was suffering from indigestion than remorse—"do they?"

"Only if they've been found out. Otherwise, no. Anyway, tell me, how does the dog look right now?"

"Unusually calm... for her. Not that I've had her that long, but I was under the impression that she's not what you'd call a laidback dog, given her background."

"Probably true. See if you can get her to walk around. Let me know if she seems cramped up or in distress in any way. I'll hold while you do that."

"Are you sure it's not a bother? I don't want to pull you away from another client if you don't think it's urgent."

"No problem. I'm just driving in between farm calls. Besides, I'd rather handle it now than at three in the morning."

"All right. Hang on." Grayson put the phone down, then crawled closer to Sooner. She lifted her head, and he was momentarily hopeful she would bound to her feet. "Sooner? Come here, girl. Let me take a look at you."

Her head sank back down between her paws, and his heart with it. He patted the floor, called her name, but she wouldn't budge. When half a minute of gently coaxing her didn't work, he retrieved the peanut butter jar from the cabinet. She refused to be tempted. So he crawled underneath the table, pushing the chairs out of the way. He half expected her to try to elude him when he got close, but she stayed where she was, inert. Gently, he took hold of her collar and pulled her out. She was reluctant, but not defiant. He walked her around the table once. Other than looking like she wasn't having much fun, she didn't seem like she was having trouble moving. He gave the vet a report.

"That's encouraging," Hunter said. "Now touch the leather of her nose. Is it hot?"

"No, seems fairly cool."

"Good. Open her mouth, then tell me what color her gums are."

Despite his misgivings, Grayson did as told. Sooner's jaws opened easily. She even yawned once he let go, as if she didn't mind at all once she realized there were no pills involved.

"Reddish-pink, I'd say. Is that normal?"

"As long as they're not pale. Pale is bad."

"They're not pale."

"Good, good. Now gently probe her belly. Any obvious protrusions, a distended abdomen, or indication that being touched in that area is uncomfortable for her?"

Grayson took his time feeling her stomach. "No, nothing unusual. I wouldn't even call her abdomen 'distended', just... pudgier than normal."

To be truthful, she resembled a kid who'd overdone it on the Halloween candy and was ready to hurl. At this point, he wished she would.

A turn signal clicked in the background. "Tell you what—I'm not sure you have anything to worry about, but I want you to keep a close eye on her. If she shows any other signs of discomfort, has diarrhea, or stops eliminating altogether—call me. Additionally, if she does have some kind of gastrointestinal obstruction, she may start vomiting, dry heaves included. That's not necessarily a bad thing. She's trying to eject whatever it is she swallowed. Since you say she seems a little lethargic for her, let's try to help that along."

"Help what?"

"Help her vomit."

"Excuse me?" Grayson imagined sticking a finger down the dog's throat to trigger her gag reflex. It seemed a dangerous thing to do, considering she had fangs. "Is there an alternative, Doc? Can't I just monitor her... her poop?"

"You're going to do that, too. But you can't necessarily make her defecate on command. Besides, it could be a while before any foreign objects work their way through her system. For now, I want you to give her a homemade remedy that's as good as anything I could administer, just like the cat owner did." Hunter directed Grayson to look in the medicine cabinet for hydrogen peroxide, then told him how much to give her and at what intervals.

Grayson wrote it all down. When he'd confirmed the dosage, he asked exactly how he was supposed to convince the dog to swallow something that probably wasn't the least bit enticing.

"With a syringe."

"With a what?" Grayson grasped the edge of the counter "No, I'm not giving her shots. You need to—"

"Not with a needle. You give it to her orally. Sorry if that wasn't clear. The syringe is just the plastic part that holds the liquid and has measurements on it. If you don't have that, a medicine dropper will work, too. You'll see the markings on the side. Just dispense the hydrogen peroxide into a bowl or cup, suck it up to the amount I told you, then squirt it down the back of her throat and hold her muzzle shut until she swallows. She may not like it, but that's not the point."

After repeating a few details and assuring Grayson several more times he was just as capable of handling the situation—and at far less expense than the clinic's staff—Hunter signed off, having reached the Appleton's goat farm, where he was checking on a set of newborn kids.

Although lacking Hunter's confidence, Grayson carried out his instructions implicitly. He suddenly understood what it was like to be a new parent with an infant running her first fever. Yes, most survived it just fine, but what about those few who didn't? What if something went terribly, horribly wrong? And then this Brandy Anders would forever blame him for being unfit to be a dog's caretaker, irresponsible, negligent, uncaring…

As soon as she was in the clear, he was going to head into town and find a trash can with a lid that latched shut. To be extra safe, he was going to put the trash can under the sink and place a childproof lock on the cabinet door—or better yet, put the trash can in the pantry behind a closed door. She'd have to have opposable thumbs to make her way through that many barriers.

Having a smart dog in the house was difficult enough. Add boredom and it equaled the workings of a savant with ADHD.

Something less complicated, like a Basset Hound or a Chihuahua, might have been a better choice for a novice like him to foster. Forget Australian Shepherds. He wasn't up to the challenge.

And yet… there was something different about her from other dogs. Different in a good way. Even when she'd done bad things, like upending the garbage and helping herself to it. At times, she seemed empathic. Like she could read his mood without having to ask him all the details of his day. She knew when to offer comfort and when to try to entice him to play. She also knew when to hang back and just let him be, as if she understood that some matters resolved themselves in their own time and without interference.

Sooner was also a problem-solver, and he admired her ingenuity. She'd been hungry, and, lured by the intriguing scents, had decided to do something about it. Granted, sometimes her deeds were misdirected, but she was a dog after all. She couldn't read a clock or fix herself lunch. His task, from here on, was to figure out how to prevent such mishaps.

First though, she wasn't looking too swell. Having given her the home remedy, he watched and waited. Waited while nothing happened. She didn't look worse, but she wasn't getting better either.

After another unproductive hour, he gave her another dose. He took his dinner in the kitchen while he listened to the evening news on the TV as it played in the living room. At intervals, he offered her water and a dog biscuit, hoping the act of swallowing would induce vomiting. She drank, but wasn't interested in the biscuit.

As late afternoon gave way to evening, he decided he couldn't leave her alone in the house again, just in case she took an abrupt turn for the worse. So he clipped a long horse lead onto her collar and took her out to the barn with him. She came along willingly but slowly, far more subdued than was her usual nature.

Back in the house, he prepared a snack of crackers and humus. Sooner came to sit by his stool, staring at him pleadingly with eyes of liquid gold. A good sign, surely. He offered her a cracker. She took it lightly between her teeth, rolled it around on her tongue a couple of times, and then spat it on the floor, her nose wrinkling. *Odd*, Grayson thought. It wasn't like her to refuse human food. Maybe she just didn't like humus.

When it came time to retire for the night, Grayson didn't feel confident enough to let her sleep in the bedroom. The contents of her stomach could be ejected at any time. He could roll up the area rugs, but what if she got into something else while he slept? He toyed with the idea of taking her crate upstairs, but his back was sore from chores and the crate was heavy. No, best not to overdo it.

He rose from the stool he'd occupied half the day. Sooner lifted her head from the floor where she'd been lying, but she didn't try to get up. Not until he reached for the leash. But even then, her movements were atypically slow. He took her outside one last time. She peed, but didn't poop. Normally he wouldn't have thought too much about it, but today her bowel movements were of utmost importance. In fact, he was obsessed with them. For nearly fifteen minutes, he walked her, but nothing came of it. Literally.

Finally, he took her back into the kitchen and shut her in her crate. She didn't seem to mind, but he still felt guilty about it for some reason. Like putting a toddler in its crib, then leaving the room as a fever raged inside the child. His conscience heavy with concern, he trudged up the stairs, aware of her eyes following him. He'd done all he could.

Something in him had shifted. This wasn't just about keeping her safe and healthy so he could return her to her owner. In fact, the thought of one day doing that loomed before him like a moment he dreaded. Dreaded because this was not just a good deed he'd done to lift his spirits. And not just because he owed the dog for saving his life. No, it was something far deeper. More permanent. If that was even possible.

It was like the prospect of life without her was somehow... incomplete.

A dog.

He shook the feeling off. It was only guilt gnawing at his conscience for having left her alone.

Upstairs, he took a blanket from the linen closet. It smelled faintly of softener sheets. When he'd first arrived at his uncle's house, he'd had every intention of purging the entire dwelling of all its contents, furniture and linens included. But when Sooner unexpectedly showed up, all his plans had come to a halt. Not a slow grinding halt. A screeching, toppling, bone-slamming halt. His focus had turned to the dog and other animals. It wasn't until just now that he became aware of how much more distant New York City and his life there seemed. His aspirations, his possessions there, everything connected with it, even his marriage to Fee, had become less important to him. Less... *real* than this place.

In Manhattan, everything hinged on a goal. Everyone was on a schedule. It was life lived in the future, where the goalpost, every time he got near it, was picked up and moved a little farther away. Here there were no goals, no plans, no deadlines. Just the daily rhythm of chores and the connections to the animals. Most of all this neurotic, overly exuberant, very complicated dog.

Grayson removed a pillow from the bed, taking it and the blanket downstairs. After reassuring himself there was nothing in the kitchen Sooner could get into, he let her out of her crate. She crawled under the table, sank down with a groan, and rolled onto her side. Her eyes drifting shut, she appeared more content and peaceful than distressed. All the same, he was going to keep a close watch on her.

He snapped out the blanket then put it on the floor next to her along with the pillow. A knife of pain stabbed through his bad knee as he knelt. He straightened his leg, waited for the pain to pass, then stretched out on the cool, hard floor. Sooner's eyes blinked open only a second before drifting shut again.

The worry should have kept him awake, but knowing he was close enough to hear her breathing calmed him. Sleep came within minutes.

When he heard the sound of a dog retching at three in the morning, he awoke not with disgust or anger, but relief. Groggy, he sopped up the mess with paper towels, noting the jumble of contents and wondering what had possessed her to eat rancid meat, rotten vegetables, and to chew up and swallow plastic. Then, somewhere in the soggy bits of her vomit, he found part of a familiar food jar wrapper: peanut butter.

Sooner heaved again. This time, her bile was clear. Her stomach had been emptied.

"So," he said, "was it worth it?"

She watched for a moment as he wiped up the new puddle, then gave the tiniest groan, as if to say, 'Not really'.

As he sprayed the area down with disinfectant, then washed his hands, he noticed Sooner moving around more freely, her eyes brightening.

He sank to his knees in front of her. Took her face in his hands. "I hope you learned your lesson."

Shaking her head loose from his hold, she sneezed several times.

He knew she'd do it again, if tempted. It was up to him to make sure she didn't have the chance.

SAY WHEN

—oOOo—

It was five minutes past nine AM when the ringtone on his phone awakened Grayson.

He rolled onto his back to stare up at the ceiling while he cleared the cobwebs from his brain. The ring broke through his fog again. He swiped at the floor, found his phone, and pressed it to his ear.

"Yeah?"

"Grayson, did I wake you up? I thought you'd be done feeding the horses already."

It was Doc Hunter. The horses did need fed, but he'd get to them when he was ready. "Just haven't had my coffee yet." Which was true. After he struggled to his feet, he retrieved the empty coffee pot from the drying rack.

Sooner was lying on the bottom part of his blanket, stretching her legs as she yawned cavernously.

"So which end?" Hunter said.

"Pardon?" Grayson had turned the water spigot on, not sure he'd heard correctly. "Which end what?"

"Which end did… whatever come out of? The dog's, I mean. You didn't call me in the middle of the night, so I figured things must've worked themselves out."

"Ah. They did. She puked it up. Seems getting every last bit out of the peanut butter jar meant devouring the container itself." When the water reached its mark, he slid the pot into the coffee maker and filled the filter with grounds. He pushed the button to start it dripping before escorting the dog out the back door to do her morning business. "One question, Doc: Why? Why do dogs do stupid stuff like eat trash? Even the parts that aren't edible. You'd think it wouldn't feel good going down."

While Sooner sniffed out a suitable spot—and ended up squatting in the same area she always did—Grayson could hear the bleating of lambs on the other end of the phone. Or maybe it was baby goats, kids. He couldn't really tell the difference just by listening.

Hunter chuckled. "You were expecting her to behave like a human being when you took her in?"

"Not exactly. I just want to know why a dog would do something like that? Something that doesn't make sense."

"She's a dog."

"Obviously."

"Look, Grayson, if there's one thing I can say with any certainty, it's that dogs are good at, well... being dogs."

"That *still* doesn't explain it." He went to lean against the fissured bark of the crooked oak tree that dominated the side yard of his uncle's home.

"Sure it does. It explains everything. There may be a lot of ways their behavior doesn't make any sense to us, but there're also ways dogs are better than us. Wiser, if you will."

"How's that?"

The pause that followed stretched out so long Grayson thought the line had gone dead.

"How?" Hunter echoed. "When's the last time you saw a dog holding a grudge? Never. Do they live by deadlines on the calendar? No. When you come home at the end of the day and your dog is waiting for you, do they sulk because you were thirty minutes late? No, they're overjoyed *because* you came back."

Grayson chewed on that for a moment. The morning sun's rays lit puffy wisps overhead, striping the horizon in bands of pink, purple, and fiery orange. To the west, a bank of clouds was building. Darker, denser. The rain would be a welcome reprieve. Temporarily, at least. Later on, the moisture would saturate the air and make it even more humid.

Then, suddenly, Hunter added, "Dogs have a lot to teach us, you know."

Unable to help himself, Grayson scoffed. "If anything, you'd think *she* should learn something from it. I fail to see what the lesson was for me in this."

"Are you sure about that?"

"What? Of course I am." Grayson didn't like it when people spoke cryptically. He liked solid, practical answers.

"Maybe you're looking a little too closely at the situation. Take a step back, take in the big picture. Take a look at yourself, even. It may come to you in time. Perspective is everything."

Sooner sat at Grayson's feet, squinting at him. From this angle, her nose was rather pointy. And she, the dog, looked like nothing but trouble.

With a twinkle of mischief in her eye, she bounded off, the hitch in her stride now only faintly evident. Diving, she scooped a stick from the ground and circled back. When she returned, she sat squarely in front of him to present her prize, an obvious expression of pride on her bunched-up cheeks, as if she'd done nothing at all naughty the night before, the slate of her offenses wiped clean.

"Say," Hunter began, "the scan confirmed it was the dog missing from Brandy Anders' accident. My receptionist gave you all the info, right?"

"Yes, she did."

"Did you contact the owner?"

"I called, but the inbox was full, so I dialed the alternate contact the microchip service had listed for someone named Paul Anders. A family member, I assume." What Grayson left out was he'd taken his time on the matter. Despite the fact he didn't have a job yet, he was happier than he'd been in a long time.

Hunter broke through Grayson's thoughts. "You got a hold of someone then?"

"Unfortunately, no. It just rings and rings, but no one picks up. I even tried at odd hours. Still no answer, and there's no voicemail set up. Texts have bounced. But given what the newspapers said about her having several broken bones and needing surgery, I can't imagine she'd be up for a conversation. Even for good news."

"Keep at it. Hopefully, you'll get through eventually."

"I will."

After the call was ended, Grayson took the stick from Sooner and tossed it as far as he could. She limped happily out to retrieve it. Without a job, what better thing did he have to do today than play with a dog? Actually, he wouldn't have minded if every day from now on was like this.

chapter 16
Brandy

Play, Brandy had learned, was the key to training Sooner. As long as work was disguised as a game, the dog would do anything. With absolute focus and unbridled enthusiasm. Without fear of being wrong. But never the same thing more than a few times. If Brandy asked her to sit in front on a recall for a fourth time, it might be one time too many. And then Sooner would start getting creative with her responses—darting around to heel, dropping halfway to her, sticking on her stay, or performing a play-bow six feet away. The message was quite clear: *Why do you keep asking me to do the same thing over and over? Did I do it wrong the first several times?*

Brandy was thinking of that because on this particular day, she was being asked to do her physical therapy exercises for the fourth time. They weren't difficult—under ordinary circumstances, anyway. But nothing about Brandy's life was ordinary anymore. It might never be again. Every day, every moment, was filled with pain. The simplest tasks were impossible. Things she used to take for granted, like getting out of bed, required help. She tried to tell herself she was lucky to be alive, but sometimes it felt like the alternative might have been better. The only thing that had kept her going was the hope that her dog, Sooner, was out there somewhere and they'd eventually be reunited.

Although she hoped for the best, she feared the worst—that Sooner had been hit by a car and killed or, wounded from the accident, had been attacked by coyotes. Either was possible. Maybe her dreams of Sooner had been nothing more than glimpses of her spirit on the other side as she waited faithfully at the Rainbow Bridge.

It was time she accepted her circumstances, then learned to deal with them as best she could. She wasn't in any state to care for a dog anyway. When she'd nodded off at the wheel and crashed her van into the ravine off the interstate less than an hour from home, she'd broken her left femur, dislocated her left shoulder, cracked three ribs, and fractured her pelvis and two vertebrae. She now had so many screws and pins holding her together that she would never be able to walk through airport security again without setting off the metal detector.

For a while, it had been doubtful whether she'd even be able to walk again. The day she wiggled her toes was a monumental breakthrough. For her doctors and nurses, at least. For her, it still felt like she was miles away from the finish line.

And now here she was, struggling to stand between a set of parallel bars, hanging on for dear life. Her arms shook with the strain. Her upper body slouched forward, her neck unable to support the weight of her own skull. Her legs were like flimsy lengths of cardboard, collapsing beneath her with the slightest shift in weight. Her whole body was tired. Unbelievably, unbearably tired.

"One step, Brandy." Emalee stood at the end of the bars, her hands outstretched, ready to catch her if she fell forward. The problem, as Brandy saw it, was what would happen if she fell backward. Or just straight onto the floor. Which was the most likely scenario.

"You can do it, Brandy," Emalee cheered. All she needed was a short skirt and a pair of pompoms. "Just lean forward and swing your leg—simple as that."

If Brandy would have had the means to, she'd have smacked that obnoxiously optimistic smile right off that smug twenty-four-year-old's face. Walking six feet may have seemed simple to someone who had never broken a dozen bones in her body. It may have seemed simple to someone a good twenty years younger than her, someone blessed with good genes and the physique of a marathon runner. It was *not* simple to her.

"You *can*!"

No, she couldn't. She'd failed more than once already today. Her day-to-day progress had been abysmal. Besides, having lost her best friend due to her own negligence, she didn't have much reason to go on trying. There had been no confirmed sightings of Sooner. The few messages that had come in had turned out to be false leads—dogs that definitely weren't hers. Each disappointment had dashed her hopes further, until it seemed impossible Sooner might have survived at all. Even if by some miracle she had, there was very little chance she could get by in that vast wilderness, let alone survive attacks by coyotes or bears or a bullet from a well-aimed shotgun.

Before Brandy had regained consciousness and several times since then, she'd dreamed of Sooner. But those dreams had only been memories of what once was, wishes for what might have been. Without her best friend, all she could see ahead of her was a life full of struggle. What was the point of even trying?

Brandy's phone dinged from where it sat on the chair next to what she'd deemed her torture apparatus. Her brother maybe. Or a coworker. Definitely not her dad. Not in his condition. He'd never texted before, anyway. He wasn't in the sort of shape to suddenly start doing it now, either. Unless maybe someone had sent it for him. No, it was more likely he would've had someone at the nursing home call for him. Although the last time she'd spoken to him over the phone, he'd barely been able to do more than grunt a reply back to her.

"You want me to check that for you?" Emalee asked.

"Could you?" Not that Brandy was all that interested. Or believed it might be her father. But she welcomed the interruption if it gave her a reprieve.

"Stay where you are," Emalee ordered. "See if you can take some of the weight off your arms and support yourself just a teensy bit more with your legs. I'll be right beside you. Let me know if you're having trouble."

Having trouble? Did this girl think she was being lazy? Brandy faked a smile. "Sure, no problem. I'll just hang out here. But make it quick. I'm cramping up." Which she was.

Emalee laughed as she ducked past the bars before picking up the phone. Brandy's hands were locking up. Her arms and shoulders ached with the strain. If she did collapse, at least it would prove a point—that Emalee was pushing her too far, too fast.

"Hah." Emalee cocked her head as she peered at the phone in her hand. "Not a number that's in your contacts. Want me to read it to you? I don't want to blurt out anything personal." She glanced sheepishly around the room. The other patients and therapists were preoccupied with their own business, but sound carried readily in the high-ceilinged room.

"Go ahead. Unless it's someone from one of the online dating sites asking for a second date. I'm a little tied up at the moment." She hadn't been on those sites, ever, but it was her best attempt at a joke.

"Okay." Emalee read the text to herself. Her eyebrows lifted. "Oh... honey, you'll definitely want to hear this."

An impossibly long pause.

"Read it," Brandy prompted.

Emalee walked a couple of steps down the length of the bars. "Someone named Grayson Darling. He's asking if this is your dog."

Hope warred with doubt. Could it be another false alarm? Some stray that simply resembled Sooner? Brandy didn't want to get her hopes up. She shifted her weight to the left, heaved her right arm forward, caught the bar, and then dragged her left leg along. Twice more, she staggered forward until she was within arm's reach of Emalee.

"Let me see that." Brandy leaned to the side to get a better view of the screen, her discomfort momentarily forgotten. "Make the picture bigger."

Emalee pinched the picture out. A dog, a red dog, came into focus—and then went blurry. Tears stung Brandy's eyes. Hot, prickly tears. She lowered herself clumsily to the floor, her head barely missing one of the bars as she landed ungracefully on her rump. Pain cascaded through her. She was aware of it, yet not focused on it. She brought her hands to her face, catching a waterfall of tears in the pools of her palms.

"Honey, are you okay?" Emalee crouched beside her. She placed a hand on Brandy's quivering shoulder. "I'm so sorry. It wasn't your dog after all, then?"

"No… it…" Brandy swallowed back a sob. Tamped down the deluge of emotions so she could force out an intelligible response. "It was… *is* her. He found her. He found her. She's safe."

chapter 17
Sooner

There it was again. That sound. The feeling.

I sensed it long before it occurred. A static in the air. My nerves on edge.

A storm was rolling in. I could smell the rain already.

In a matter of seconds, a steady breeze rose to a gusty roar. Outside the kitchen windows, the branches were lashing at one another, throwing warped shadows against the kitchen wall inside where the yard floodlight shone in. The movement of air tickled at my whiskers and lifted the fur along my spine. Grayson had left the windows cracked to keep the house cool. He'd regret it tomorrow.

The first rumble was far away. Then there was another, and another… and another. Each one was louder and longer than the one before. Lightning flickered faintly. By the time the rain began, the wind was blowing fiercely. It buffeted the siding of the house, rattled the gutters, and knocked a plastic chair over on the porch with a terrible clatter. Then, suddenly, the floodlight was extinguished. Even the faint orange light on the display of the oven went off. The buzz of the refrigerator was silenced. For brief moments, the world was thrown into bursts of dazzling light followed by utter darkness.

I hunkered down in my crate, knowing I wouldn't sleep that night. At Brandy's, I'd slept next to her bed soundly, knowing she was close by. Whatever the reason, Grayson didn't seem to think I belonged upstairs where he slept.

I didn't like this arrangement—so I let him know.

Pitching my head back, I let out the plaintive howl of my coyote cousins. The song of my kin.

Aroo-aroo-arooooooo!

Walls of rain slapped at the windows, some of it dripping over the inside edge of the windowsill. The wind hammered harder.

Aroo-roo-roo-rooooo!

A flash of white. Blinding. The air exploded. Sizzled. Jolted my heart. Separated every hair on my body one from another.

I plastered myself against the back of the crate, desperate for escape. Outside, just beyond the kitchen window, a bough of the giant sprawling oak tree creaked. An eerie groan was followed by a massive cracking sound as the bones of the great tree splintered and then gave way. Branches crashed against the ground with an unearthly *woompf!*

Run! my instincts told me. *Get away!*

Energy rushed through me, gave me strength. I rammed my paws between the bars of the crate door, pulled and pulled. Thrashed about. Yowled my anxiety, calling for help.

I didn't feel safe here. Wanted out.

Run! my instincts screamed at me. *Find a hiding place! Stay alive!*

Harder and harder, I threw my body against the sides, dug at the door, bit at the wires.

"Sooner?"

Grayson's voice, meek and perplexed, wafted from upstairs. Then his feet padded down the treads. My anguish increased. By the time he got to the dining room, he was pounding across it in his stilted gate.

His fingers flipped the light switch. Nothing.

"Hold on, girl. Hold on." He opened a drawer next to the lifeless fridge. A click and a narrow beam of light followed. "Oh… my."

My heart beat wildly, then skipped. I panted shallowly, my head abuzz, every nerve stripped bare. He was going to set me free. Save me!

I yipped for him to hurry. Whined inconsolably.

He knelt before the crate, undid the latch, and yanked open the door. Grabbed my collar and pulled me into his arms. I twisted in his hold, fought for freedom. But he only held me tighter.

"Shh, shh. It's okay, Sooner. I'm here. It's okay."

Even as I struggled in his arms, he stroked and soothed me. Spoke to me calmly.

Outside, the flickering continued. I shuddered each time the sky boomed.

He sat with me for a very long time. Until the blasts of sound became less frequent and the flashes diminished. Which was a very, *very* long time.

At last, my nerves settled, although my heart was still pounding in my ears. But in the growing tranquility, I was aware of a new sensation: the strong beating of his own heart as he held me to his chest.

I tucked my snout against the crook between his neck and shoulder. Flicked my tongue at his ear.

Thank you.

"I know," he whispered, his fingers scratching lightly behind my ear. "You must've been frightened out there alone for so many days. But everything's all right now. You don't need to worry anymore. You're safe here."

Finally, he let go of me. Exhausted, I lay down, my chin on his thigh as he sat on the floor with his legs outstretched.

"Come on upstairs." He stood, a grimace on his face as he

reached down to rub at his lower leg. One by one, he closed all the windows downstairs. I followed him. "But don't expect me to hold you all night. I could really use some sleep. Between you and this farm, I'm all worn out."

His hand beneath my collar, he guided me up the stairs. Once inside the bedroom, he closed the door.

Without waiting for an invitation, I bounded up onto the bed and sank into its welcoming softness. After making a few circles to find just the right spot, I lay down with a grunt. In the middle.

Grayson rolled his eyes. "Make yourself at home, Sooner." He peeled back the covers and slid underneath, then poked me in the side. "The least you could do is scoot over. You're taking up half the bed, if not more."

I had no idea what he was trying to tell me, but it sounded like he was being affectionate. So I slurped at the side of his face to let him know the feeling was mutual.

Good human. You're starting to understand.

—oOOo—

"Sooner? Hey, Sooner, where are you?"

Hiding, obviously.

"Come here, girl. I have something for you… Soooooner!"

How dumb did he think I was? I'd heard it rattle. I could detect the sound from a mile away—pills hitting the inside of a plastic bottle. I knew what was coming next.

"Sooner? Sooner, Sooner, Sooner!"

I was hiding upstairs in the bathroom because he'd been acting suspiciously. Did he think I was going to come running? That I didn't know any better? That I'd fall for his false overtures again?

His feet tapped across the kitchen floor, the dining room and living room, then plodded up the stairs in that uneven gait of his.

When he hit the landing, he went momentarily quiet. He'd figured out I wasn't going to come running. Then he descended the stairs, unhurried.

From somewhere, the snap of my leash chinked. Floorboards creaked as he made his way back to the bottom of the stairs.

"Hey, Sooner," he called up the stairway. "Want to go for a walk?"

A walk? I peeked around the toilet, dared a look into the hallway. I wanted so badly to dash down the stairs, sit to have my leash clipped on, and take *him* for a walk. He needed the exercise.

But...

I hadn't forgotten the rattling sound. Hadn't forgotten the bitter taste, the chalkiness, the lump in my throat. How the pills made me want to puke every time. Since I'd spit that first pill out, he'd tried hiding them in rolled-up bologna, globs of peanut butter, bowls of yogurt, chunks of cheese, and even small squares of steak sandwiches. Whenever he took an interest in watching me eat, it was a tip-off there was a hidden pill. As much as I loved human food, swallowing those pills was not worth any price.

"Let's go! Time for a walk."

If I remained where I was long enough, there was a chance he'd forget about it or just plain give up. But he could also get busy with some other chore and forget about the walk, too. He might even go without me.

Walks were all I had these days. A chance to stretch my muscles and work my limbs. And the smells! This house smelled of dust and old wood, but outside... outside I never knew what fantastic smells I might discover.

The things I could roll in—

"Soooooner!" He rattled the leash again.

I couldn't help myself. Adrenaline flooded my veins, propelled me out of the upstairs bathroom, down the stairs, spinning at the bottom to change direction. At the end of the dining room, I turned again, slowing, my hind feet kicking up the corner of the big rug to bunch it behind me.

Grayson stood at the front door, smiling, the leash held lightly in one hand. I skidded to a halt, ducking my head slightly so he could more easily find my collar. He took hold of my collar and clipped the leash on.

We were going outside!

Walk, walk, walk! I barked. *Walk, walk, walk, walk, walk—*

"Quiet, Sooner. You're hurting my ears."

Walk, walk—

He clamped both hands on my muzzle. "All right, I get it. But first"—he kept his grip on my nose with one hand and slipped the other inside his shirt pocket—"you have to take your morning antibiotic."

I crumpled to the floor. Flopped over. Went belly up. Locked my teeth shut.

No. Way. Not happening.

He shoved two fingers inside my lips, cranked my jaws open, and plopped the pill inside. Before I could spit it back out, he held both hands on my muzzle.

"Swallow, swallow."

I waited. Looked at him innocently. Wiggled a little to let him know I wanted up. The bitterness was making my eyes water.

"Did you swallow it, huh?"

I whined softly. He could interpret that however he wanted.

He let go of me. I scrambled to my feet. Went to stand by the door, looked up at him, and—

I hacked the pill onto the floor. Darn it.

I'd tried to keep it tucked between my tongue and the roof of my mouth until we got outside and he wasn't looking, but my taste buds had rejected it.

"Aw, Sooner. It's going to taste worse the second time."

He was right about that. It tasted even worse the third and the fourth time. He finally shoved it so far down my esophagus that the only way to eject it would have been to toss up my breakfast along with it, but somehow, amazingly, that didn't happen. It lodged itself halfway down, a dry lump blocking my innards. He patted me between the shoulder blades. I coughed and gagged, but instead of bringing the pill up, it went down.

"Doc Hunter says you have to finish all the pills so your wounds won't get infected and they'll heal more quickly. Every last one. To be honest, I don't like making you take them. But if it makes you all better so you can go back to your owner…" His words trailed away.

Mercifully, he fetched my water dish and let me drink my fill. The medicine sat in my stomach, its bitterness dissolving as I fought waves of nausea.

I'd let him believe he'd won this battle. For now.

He stroked my head, then ran his hand down my back. "Ready for our walk now, girl?"

Ready? Yes, there was another word I knew. It meant pay attention, because we were about to do something important.

He flung the door open. Together, we walked out into the sunshine. To take in a new day. A new beginning.

I forgave him for jamming the pill down my throat. But I wouldn't forget.

—o0Oo—

Grayson had been asleep for hours. Snoring softly at intervals. The window open wide. A welcome breeze lifting the curtains. Outside, crickets chirped a symphony.

Our walks had become increasingly longer. But they came with a price—I had to swallow a pill before we went outside. Nasty things. I didn't understand why Grayson insisted on forcing them down my throat. They never sat well in my stomach. Eventually, however, I learned the less I fought him, the sooner our walks began. Last night, however, the pill had made me especially nauseous. Not even the piece of bacon Grayson fed me from his plate and the leftover gravy drizzled over my kibble could make the nausea go away. It had kept me up half the night. So I gazed around the room, considering my life as it was now.

Every time the curtains fluttered high, I saw stars from where I lay, bright white against the blue-black bowl of the sky, winking down at me. There was so much here on the farm that was different from the life I'd known before. So much quiet. So much predictability. So much... boredom.

But in the mundane was a peace with which I was uncomfortable. It made me restless. Like a part of me was missing—that part that made me feel alive with purpose. The purpose Brandy had given me: precision, obedience, loyalty, speed, accuracy, instinct.

She had always asked so much of me. And I accepted willingly. Even when I was unsure. Because I always knew she would help me understand. She was good at that. And Brandy was proud of me.

Grayson, on the other hand, asked so little. Nothing almost. While I welcomed the lazy days and slow pace as I healed from my ordeals, I also bristled at it. It got under my skin like a bur. Irritated and frustrated me. He often wandered around aimlessly, no hurry in any task and even less focus. He cared for the horses on a loose schedule, but there was a disconnect there. He didn't understand them, nor they him. I couldn't entirely blame him. They were massive animals, powerful and sometimes temperamental. I myself didn't dare go in the stalls alone with them. When he did, he was very tentative. It wasn't that they were mean, not without cause. It was their sheer size.

With me, however, he was different. Clueless still, but determined. Caring, even. As if he really was trying. I'd give him time.

Provided I survived the boredom.

Stretching, I flopped over onto my back and closed my eyes, let the breeze cool my belly. Let sleep carry me to another place, another time…

"*Over!*"

I raced to the next jump, gathered the power in my muscles, sprang upward, over, landed on light feet, pivoted, took three more strides, over the next jump, stretched low, ducked my head, flew through the tunnel—

Buzzzzzzz!

Brandy threw her arms wide. I leaped into them. She hugged me hard and then let me down gently.

"One more second, Sooner. So close! But don't worry—we'll run again soon. I promise you we'll get to do it all again."

Waking with a start, I raised my head to look around.

Brandy was just here. She was! We'd been running agility together. I'd heard her. Felt her arms around me.

I got to my feet. Searched the room. Sniffed under the closet door. Checked under the bed. Looked in the bathroom. Even out the window. I searched for her, listened for her, smelled for her scent. She wasn't here. She wasn't, as far as I knew, anywhere.

It was still night out there. The window open. The breeze now faint. The crickets quiet. The stars were dimming as night ebbed and morning approached.

Grayson, too, was still there. No longer snoring. His face stuffed into his pillow, sleeping on his stomach. He wouldn't be up for hours yet. Even when the sun came up, he would sleep on. Eventually, he'd rise at his leisure, shower, and take his coffee while he watched the morning news.

Just as I was about to lie back down, that sickening feeling washed over me.

After watching him for a while to make certain he was deep in sleep, I crept into the bathroom. I stood over the throw rug that spanned the floor between the toilet and sink, then stretched my neck until—

Blech!

Ah, last night's supper, bacon and all.

I felt relief and… guilt. Grayson would be displeased. Just like when I was a tiny puppy and my owners yelled at me for not holding my pee or poop after they'd ignored my subtle cues. It was an awful dilemma for a dog to suffer. Dogs were supposed to make these messes outside, but the humans were the doorkeepers, letting us out only when it was convenient for them. I could only hold it in for so long before I felt like exploding. As for puking—there was no holding that back. It came when it came, wherever I might be.

After rearranging the rug to hide the mess since I couldn't bury it, I slunk back to my spot beside the bed, circled until I was facing in just the right direction and had crumpled my blanket up sufficiently, then drifted off to sleep again, feeling much better physically than I had a short while ago.

I didn't fully awaken again until I heard Grayson from the bathroom.

"Nooooo! Oh, Sooner. Why didn't you wake me up?" He mumbled to himself some more, then shuffled into the bedroom. "Really? This whole upstairs is hardwood floor, and yet you puked on the rug—why? It's almost like you were aiming for it."

The displeasure in his voice made me cringe. Before I could dart under the bed, he took me by the collar, gently but firmly, and led me to the bathroom rug where he pointed at the crumpled rug and puddle of partially digested kibble.

"I know you can't help it if you're sick, Sooner, but it's my fault. Maybe I shouldn't have given you that bacon and gravy." Crouching beside me, he pointed to another part of the floor. "Next time, though, aim for any place *but* the rug, okay?"

Bracing my legs, I waited for him to shove my snout in the mess, to shout at me, or to haul me downstairs and banish me to my crate again. But the punishment never came. Instead, he hugged me, his hand stroking lightly from my withers to my rump, over and over and over.

Without another word, he cleaned up my mess: sopped up the vomit, carried the soiled paper towels downstairs and deposited them in the big trash can there, and put the rug in the washing machine. When he came back up, he lifted my chin with a finger and said, "If you're done, you can hang out with me for a while. But *please* let me know if you feel another upchuck coming so I can scoot you over to the edge of the bed, okay?"

Then he went back to bed, patted the mattress beside him, and called my name.

I placed a paw on the mattress, but hesitated. I wasn't sure. Was he sure?

"Up, Sooner. Up."

I knew that word. After I jumped up on the bed, I stretched out beside him.

"You know, as much trouble as you are, some days now, you're the one bright spot." His fingers found the tickly place on my belly. My hind leg kicked involuntarily. He chuckled as he scratched all the places I couldn't reach. "It's been a rough year for me, Sooner. Hell, really. I hope I never go through another like it. Have I told you about it? Geesh, where should I start? Did I tell you about my wife—*ex*-wife, Fiona? She was… *is* beautiful. We met when…"

And he proceeded to tell me the story of his life, starting in the middle somewhere.

Dogs didn't understand every word humans said. Truth was, humans had way too many words. They were an emotional mess, all of them. They held onto grudges. Even though we didn't understand everything they said or did, we just liked the sounds of their voices and being with them.

Whatever their problems, dogs would always listen. We never judged. We didn't give unwanted advice.

We were just there. And that alone could make everything better.

chapter 18
Grayson

The benefit of taking care of the animals to the point of exhaustion was Grayson didn't have time to feel sorry for himself. Sometimes hours went by in which he didn't think of his divorce or the fact he didn't have a job. Then there was the matter of his lease. It was due to run out next month. He'd even asked himself if perhaps he could let it expire and find something more modest and less expensive, even if it meant a longer commute. Perhaps a row house in Brooklyn close to a park or a quaint cottage-style on Staten Island with a yard big enough for a dog—

He flipped a bucket over and sat on it. A cloud of barn dust rose from the ground. Where had that notion come from—him with a dog? This thing with Sooner was only supposed to be temporary. Eventually, her owner would take her back. They'd both be overjoyed to be reunited.

Maybe though… maybe there was a stray in a shelter somewhere that needed a home? Or a dog returned to its breeder that hadn't worked out with someone else? Or a senior dog whose elderly owner had passed away suddenly?

Standing back up and stretching his arms above his head, he pushed the thought away. There were a million dogs like that. Cats, even. He couldn't save them all. Besides, he wasn't really a dog person. He enjoyed the metropolitan lifestyle: thrived on the long hours at work and a rising career, the dinner parties, the theatre tickets. Well, more the first two things than the latter. He wasn't much of a socialite, but Fee had forced him to get out on occasion. Not having responsibilities that tied him down allowed a lot of leeway. Unlike his present situation.

Right now, for instance, he'd been searching for a coffee can full of U-nails to repair a section of fencing that had pulled away from the posts. He remembered seeing the can just a few days ago. He was sure he had. So far, he'd wasted half an hour looking. Not what he wanted to do with his time, but if he didn't fix it, the horses might go on a walkabout.

Yet, even as much time as they robbed him of, there had been moments when being with the animals had given him some satisfaction. Sooner made him laugh almost daily. She was an intelligent dog—too clever for her own good, really. She also aggravated him frequently because she was so easily bored. He hadn't yet figured her out, except she generated more energy than the Hoover Dam.

The horses were less work in some ways than the dog, more in others. He could leave them for hours at a time, the entire day even, and not be worried they needed something from him. Yet when they did, it was backbreaking work. He was still afraid of being hurt when around them. Magnificent creatures, but they also didn't know their own strength. Loretta was the horse person, not him.

Every day, he went to bed sore and tired, but he was also developing calluses where his hands had been soft before and rebuilding muscles that hadn't been used for decades.

Still, he hadn't come to Kentucky with the intention of staying—although being here had already changed him in ways. Renewed him. But it was only a stage in his upended life. A life with a plan that no longer seemed as clear as it once had.

After three times of searching through every corner and cubby hole in the barn, he walked outside and started looking around the yard. Sooner trailed after him. If he didn't find that can within the next five minutes, he might as well admit defeat and drive to the hardware store.

There was at least one thing he could sort out. He dialed Rex Franzen, surprised when he picked up the phone on the second ring.

"Martina?"

"Who?" Grayson said. "No, this is Grayson Darling, Skip Dalton's nephew."

"Oh, yeah, yeah. Sorry about that. I was expecting my secretary to call. Come to think of it, she wouldn't have phoned the landline. Right now, I'd appreciate a text, hell, even a telegram from her. Her vacation's gone on a little longer than planned. What can I do for you, Gary? Horses getting along fine? Hard work, ain't it? All that shoveling and tossing around hay bales. Builds muscle and burns calories, though. Definitely an upside to it."

Grayson resisted correcting him about the name. "You said to call you back. I've had a few"—he glanced at Sooner, who was snuffling through the grass beneath one of the smaller oaks in the backyard—"diversions lately, so I'm just now getting around to it. What's the word on Skip's financial holdings? Did you get it sorted out?"

"About that…" The pause was filled with the sound of drawers sliding open and cabinet doors banging shut. "I've had a few diversions of my own. Martina had to take an extended leave of absence, so the clerical work around here is… Let's just say I didn't know how reliant on her office skills I was until recently. My wife Vanessa always refers to her as my work-wife. Used to say my life would be total chaos if Martina ever quit or retired. Also said I'd be more devastated by that than if she divorced me. Hate to admit it, but she might've been right after all. Anyway… I'm on to a few leads. Just don't want to give you partial information and mislead you in any way, if you follow me. Why don't I give you a shout when I have something more solid?"

"When do you think that will be?"

"When?" Another pause. The creak of door hinges, the rustle of papers. "Oh, hard to say, but I anticipate soon. If you don't hear from me, ring me up."

"I'll check in with you first thing next week." Grayson wasn't going to let him avoid the issue forever. He didn't know how long these matters usually took, but from his point of view, it had already gone on long enough.

"Sounds good. Ah, is it eleven already? I have a lunch date in half an hour with Vanessa at Fox Hollow. Long-term care facility close to town here. She's the admissions director there. At least, I think that's her title. If we don't squeeze in an hour when we can, some days we barely see each other, let alone actually have a discussion." There was a succession of soft thumps, like books or dense file folders being dropped onto a desk. "Oh, by the way, if you're still wanting to move the horses—and I expect you are—check with Tucker down at the feed store. Sometimes he knows a person or two looking to buy. Worth a try."

"Sure." Before Grayson knew it, the call was over. Except for reminding Rex he'd promised to help resolve matters, nothing had been accomplished. Once again, he'd tried to move forward with his life and put things back in order, only to have his plans swatted away like a lethargic housefly barely hanging onto life on a chilly autumn day.

After circling the barn, he drifted toward the house. He still hadn't found that darn coffee can. He'd retrieved it when he first noticed the fence bowed out. Where had he put it?

Still holding onto his phone, he dialed another number. One he knew by heart, even though he'd hoped he would never again need to speak to the person.

"Grayson? Are you back in town now?"

"Dr. Philipot, hello. No, I'm still here. In Kentucky."

"Oh, are you staying there then?"

Grayson paused. He didn't know why. The answer should have been simple. "For now, I suppose. I'm still trying to find homes for the horses. The vet here, Dr. McHugh, says I'd be better off selling them privately. I have an ad in the paper and a card up at the local grocery store." He'd had two inquiries the first week, but so far those people hadn't called back to follow up.

"So once the horses are gone…?" Dr. Philipot left the question unfinished.

"I… I don't know."

"Do you want to come back to the city? Have you had any more interview requests?"

"No, none lately. I haven't had time to look much or send out more resumes."

"So you've taken to life on the farm then?"

Grayson had hoped he'd move on from that topic. It was so much more convoluted than he'd expected. "I'm not sure. I came here expecting to just sell the horses in a week or two and be gone. But I guess it's like trying to sell a house in some areas—it depends on how many people are looking and if the fit is right. But there's also…" He stalled there. Because he had a tough time admitting to Dr. Philipot that he'd taken his preposterous advice, however accidentally. "There's a dog. I've taken her in. It's only temporary. Until her owner gets better. She was in an accident. They both were actually—the owner and the dog."

Just as he rounded the back steps, his foot struck metal. The coffee can toppled over, nails spilling onto the ground. He stooped over to gather them up, then set the can atop the railing. Ah, yes. He'd placed it there two days ago when he'd stopped to inspect a plank that had come loose.

"Is the owner paying you?" Dr. Philipot asked

"Oh, no. I wouldn't take any money for it."

"Why did you decide to do it then?"

"Isn't it obvious?"

"You'll have to tell me your reasons, Grayson. I know you pretty well, but I'm not very good at reading minds."

His mother would've called Dr. Philipot a smart aleck, but that would've implied an attempt at humor. "Because it was the right thing to do. I mean, if I had a dog and couldn't take care of it for a while, I'd want to know it was in good hands."

"That's a very selfless act, Grayson. I'm sure she'll appreciate it greatly." A pen scratched audibly on paper. "How are you and the dog getting along?"

Grayson chuckled. "Rough start, I guess you'd say. But we're getting to know each other."

That was a nice way of saying she was a pain in the ass most of the time, and he was a bumbling first-time dog-sitter.

"I don't remember you ever mentioning having had a dog before. Did you have one before you got married?"

"When I was very young. We had a small dog. A Yorkie, maybe. They gave it to me for my sixth birthday. But my parents were always too busy to walk him and I was too young to remember to, so he messed where he wasn't supposed to. When I came home from school one day, he was gone."

"Did he run away?"

"That's what they told me, but I never believed them. They just didn't want him anymore."

"And how did you feel about that—that your parents gave your dog away?"

Grayson knew the answer to this. He remembered it distinctly. "Angry."

"Because they lied to you?"

"No. Because it was *my* dog." He realized as he said it, though, that there was much more to it. Odd, but even though he hadn't thought of it in years, he realized he was *still* angry about it.

When their talk was over, Grayson leaned against the trunk of the big oak. He watched Sooner digging, lost in the moment. Clods of dirt clung to the feathers of her forelegs, and her muzzle was smeared with fine particles of earth. Every time she lifted her head to look around, her cheeks bunched into a smile of pure and complete happiness. After a few pants and a snort to clear her nostrils, she'd go back to her excavations, immersed in her goal of uncovering whatever it was she was searching for. Was there a mole tunnel somewhere underground? A grub or earthworm?

He should've told her to stop it, but she was just being a dog. She was good at that.

He may have even loved her for it.

—o00o—

Hunter McHugh bent lower, squinting as he tugged the stitch free with a pair of tweezers. He dropped it into a small plastic bowl along with the other cut threads before snipping another.

It had been three days—no, four—since Grayson had spoken on the phone to Dr. Philipot and in that time he hadn't seen a single human being, except in cars driving down the road. Chores had kept him busy, as usual, and the animals had kept him company. Still, it was refreshing to talk to another person face to face.

Sooner was lying on her back on the kitchen floor, her initial apprehension long since replaced by a drowsy expression. Grayson stroked her bunched-up cheeks. She wasn't often this calm, but he'd noticed Hunter had this effect on animals, as if they were mesmerized by his touch.

Grayson had arranged to have the vet come out when he'd noticed Spark had a crusty goo around one eye. Hunter had confirmed it was an eye infection, then treated it accordingly. The visit was convenient because it was also time to remove Sooner's stitches. Hard to believe she'd been with him for almost two weeks now.

More than a medical visit, this was also a good opportunity to ask questions, because Grayson, frankly, was at his wit's end.

"How do you do that?" Grayson asked.

"This?" Hunter cut the last thread from the mended wound on the inside of her right back leg, then sat on the floor. "Practice, I suppose. I get a lot of it."

"No, I mean how do you make them so calm when you're doing all sorts of things to them? I've seen you pry open a horse's mouth and practically grab their tonsils. Yet, they barely bat an eye. And Sooner, she's never this still for me. You have no idea what it was like the first few days just getting a pill down her throat."

Laughing, Hunter dabbed some antiseptic on a cotton ball and swabbed Sooner's scar. She didn't even flinch. He tossed it in the bowl, too. "Sometimes they do put up a fight. You just haven't seen those. As for Skip's horses, they're used to me. They trust me."

"But how? *How* do you get them to trust you? Sometimes I feel like the dog is the one running the show, and I'm just here for damage control. Look at what she did to that crate when a storm came through."

It was still sitting in the corner, wires mangled.

"Sounds to me like you're asking more than one question—and there's no easy answer to any of them. It's a process, really."

"Okay, so tell me the first steps. I'd like to get through this without her destroying the house or running off."

Hunter started on another smaller bite wound, meticulously cutting and tugging at the stitches. They had all healed remarkably well. "For starters, the storm and her destroying the crate… those are different situations. I don't know if she had this problem before—you'd have to ask her owner about that—but it can be generalized anxiety or even something like PTSD."

"Dogs have those problems, too?" Grayson wondered if they ever suffered from depression. And exactly what would a depressed animal act like? Could a person tell if their dog were feeling blue?

"Any animal can. Some are born with a propensity toward nervousness, just like some people are. Their brain chemistry is different. They're always on the lookout for danger."

"So how do I fix that?"

"I'm not sure you ever can."

"That's not very encouraging."

"I know, but it's the truth. One thing you can do is figure out what her triggers are. For her, it's thunder and lightning. She may even be sensitive to a change in weather. Like some people get headaches when the pressure drops or a front rolls in. If she's highly aware of those conditions, it may send her into panic mode. She just wants to go somewhere where the storm can't affect her, even though she's not sure where that is. So her brain is telling her to run away. If you can remove or reduce the triggers, that will help, but you can't control every situation. Unfortunately sometimes, the more it happens, the more heightened their reaction can be."

"So it's hopeless? She'll always be like this?"

"Not necessarily. There are a few things you can do to help. One is let her have a quiet, safe place when the storms come. Is there a basement here?"

"Just a crawl space."

"Hmm, okay. So maybe put her in a room without windows. Or just someplace she feels more secure. Close the windows and drapes.

You can also leave the TV or music on, loud enough to help drown out the thunder. Give her a bone filled with peanut butter to keep her mind occupied. And if needed, I can supply sedatives in pill form. Something mild to start."

That seemed a little extreme to Grayson, but he didn't want her to destroy anything else, or worse yet, hurt herself or run away. Her owner would never forgive him. Still, he had this thing about pills. Especially lately. He'd rather solve problems without them. Even if it was the hard way.

"I'll keep all that in mind. Thank you. But what about the fact that she never stops moving? It's rare to see her sleeping. If I even move in bed, she's up and alert. It's been hard keeping her busy. I didn't know dogs had so much energy or I—" He stopped short of saying he wouldn't have signed on for this. There was no way he could've known. At any rate, he needed to know how to better deal with it. "I can't keep up. She's always a step or two ahead of me."

"Well, that one's easier. Not only does she have a lot of energy, but she also processes input at a very rapid rate. Think of it this way: she's like Alison Felix the sprinter and Einstein all wrapped up in one. She's an athlete and a genius. She was used to having an outlet for her energy and activities that kept her mind occupied."

The last stitch removed, Grayson emptied the bowl in the trash for Hunter and then offered him some iced tea. Since technically he was in the South, he felt compelled to have it on hand for visitors. To make it as authentic as possible, he put a ridiculous amount of sugar in it, until the last few crystals would no longer dissolve no matter how much he stirred it. As Hunter took the first few sips, Grayson watched his face.

"Too sweet? Not sweet enough?" Grayson asked. Sooner was still lying on the floor, looking all too relaxed.

"Perfect."

But Grayson wasn't sure if he were being honest or merely polite.

In New York if he'd asked anyone that, they would have told him the truth. Here—he could never tell.

Hopelessly trying to process everything Hunter had just told him, Grayson sat at the kitchen table. There were marks where Sooner had gnawed on one of the table legs in a fit of boredom. She'd also emptied the upstairs bathroom trash can and shredded every last tissue or piece of paper in it, stolen cookies off the counter, rolled in horse manure, treed multiple squirrels, and emptied his coffee cup when he'd left it on an end table. It was worse than having a toddler in the house.

Sitting across from him, Hunter slid a copper penny across the table. "For your thoughts?"

How to phrase it like he wasn't rife with regret and desperately wanted to unload the dog. "I'm not sure where to start. It's all a bit overwhelming. I feel like I've inherited two-year-old quadruplets."

Hunter gave a hearty laugh and Sooner shot up from the floor, rushing to him to see what was the matter. He ruffled her mane. "I can see where you'd have that impression. These dogs were bred to think on their own, Grayson, with limited direction, but also to work in partnership with their humans. I've had several in my lifetime. Each one is different, but they can be frighteningly intelligent and a handful. It doesn't matter so much *what* you do with her, but that you just do *something*, if that makes sense? Does it?"

"Yes, but again—what? Give me a starting point."

Sooner began sniffing around for crumbs, even sticking her nose at the counter edge until Hunter gently reminded her that was not acceptable.

"All right." Hunter took a long pull of his iced tea, thinking. "Start with the basic obedience commands: sit, down, stay, come, heel."

"She already knows those."

"Yes, but do you?" When Grayson gave him an indignant look,

Hunter explained further. "What I mean is that it matters *how* you tell her those things, as well as how you praise or correct her. Tone and timing are important." Patting his leg, he called Sooner to him. She launched herself from across the room, her paws scrabbling on the slick floor as she built momentum. She barely pulled up short in time to keep from crashing into Hunter's knee.

"Sooner, sit!" he commanded.

She sat.

"Good girl. Lie down."

She dropped to the floor.

"Good." Then he nodded across the table at Grayson. "See. She's very obedient. You try now."

The dog was staring at Hunter like he was a god. Grayson called, "Sooner, over here."

"Come," Hunter corrected. "You have to be consistent with your words. 'Come' is a common command."

"Okay, okay," Grayson muttered. "Come?"

Sooner ignored him.

"Say her name first, then the command. And say it confidently. It's an order, not a question."

"Right." Grayson tried again. "Hey, uh, Sooner… come."

Her ears twitched. She gave him a sideways glance, but remained where she was.

"One more time. She's learned she doesn't have to comply. You've done a lot to confuse her so far, I'd imagine. My guess is she considers herself above you in the pecking order. In other words, she doesn't respect your authority."

That rankled Grayson just enough so his words came out more forcefully this time. "Sooner—come!"

Maybe too forcefully.

Tentatively, she rose to her feet, slunk to him with her head down, and stopped just beyond arm's reach.

"It was your tone," Hunter informed him. "She can sense your emotions, so she thinks she's in trouble now."

Aggravated, Grayson put his head in his hands. "I give up."

Standing, Hunter moved to clap him on the shoulder. "Don't. Like I said, look up video tutorials for basic commands. I'd suggest a dog training club, but the nearest one is in Lexington over an hour away, so basically, you're on your own. The good thing about videos is you can go at your own speed. The bad part is you won't have anyone to offer suggestions tailored to you. Not all dogs are the same. Anyway, that should get you started." After gathering up his supplies, he put them in a leather bag. Together, they went to the front door, Sooner trotting along behind them. Hunter turned to Grayson. "As for all that excess energy she has, why don't you help her burn some of it off? You have a hundred acres here. Take her on hikes. Toss a Frisbee or ball. Or better yet, go for a run with her."

"A run? I don't know about that. I'm not sure I could." It would be too painful. Not just physically, but emotionally.

"I'm not saying start with a marathon. She's still recovering from her ordeal, but she could use some gentle physical therapy. Start with a mile walk. Do that for a few days. Then switch to two minutes jogging, two minutes walking, and so on for ten minutes. Gradually make the runs longer. Build up slowly. A few miles a day will give her an outlet. It'll do you good, too."

Was he insinuating Grayson was out of shape and soft in the middle? Okay, maybe he was, but it wasn't exactly polite to point it out.

Grayson opened the door, but made Sooner stay inside. The door swung shut and she pressed her nose to the screen, letting out a pitiful whimper. The two men walked down the steps and out to Hunter's truck.

"Do you always prescribe rigorous exercise for your patient's caretakers?" Grayson asked pointedly.

Hunter gave him a sincere look, the kind that friends did when they were about to say something serious but not entirely welcome. "Only when the person needs it as much as the dog does." He turned in a semicircle to view the farm, like he needed a few moments to arrange his thoughts. "Look, Grayson, I don't know your whole story, but I get the sense you could use a—how should I phrase it?—a reason to get up in the morning. Something to look forward to every day. Animals are a lot of work. A lot of times, it can seem like they're not worth the trouble. But they can give back to us in unexpected ways. Usually when we don't expect it. I know it sounds cliché, but I'm a big believer in making the best of a bad situation and learning from it. You hadn't planned on inheriting this farm. You hadn't planned on meeting Sooner, let alone taking her in. But those things have taken your life in a completely different direction from whatever you had planned before you came here. I think you two"—he pointed at Grayson, and then at the front door where Sooner sat watching loyally—"were meant to cross paths. The dog needs direction; you need a purpose. She needs exercise to build her strength back up…"—he tossed his bag onto the passenger seat, climbed in the truck, and rolled down the window—"and you need to get your butt out the door and stop moping around for whatever it is you don't have anymore."

Wow, and Grayson had thought New Yorkers were blunt.

When Hunter started up the truck, Grayson tapped on the door. "Wait, shouldn't I pay you?"

"This is Adair County, Grayson, not the Big Apple. I'll send you the bill when I get around to it. I trust you'll pay me when you can."

As his truck rolled down the driveway and out onto Troutwine Road, Grayson ambled back to the porch. He sat down on the steps, realizing for the first time what a beautiful day it was. It was the comfortable warmth of a late summer morning, cooled by a gentle breeze. The sparrows were chattering in the junipers by the fence row, and the robins were plucking nightcrawlers from beneath the blades of dew-damp grass. If he took Sooner out for exercise now, they could beat the heat.

Then again, he was already behind on that list Loretta had given him. A list that never seemed to get any smaller, no matter how hard he worked at it.

Behind him, Sooner scratched softly at the window screen. She yipped. Grayson studied her.

"All right. You win. We'll go on a walk. A *short* walk. Just don't expect it to become a habit. I may not always have time."

Sooner wiggled her entire body in a curlicue, as if to say she wasn't going to let him off the hook easily.

—o0Oo—

There was so much of Skip Dalton's property Grayson hadn't yet seen. He wasn't quite sure where to start. So he let Sooner decide. In hindsight, that might've been a mistake.

He should've worked on the training first.

The only athletic shoes Grayson had brought with him was a worn pair of sneakers more fit for lounging on the green at Central Park than any sort of real exercise. The soles had lost their cushioning, the uppers were beyond broken in, and the ends of the shoestrings had frayed. Also, the tabs on the heels were rubbing blisters on his Achilles within the first half mile.

He'd taken so long to prepare for their outing—finding lightweight clothes he could move in, hunting for his misplaced wristwatch, looking for a Thermos to carry water in—that by the time they got started, it was past midmorning and already building steam in the air.

Sooner was somehow aware this was more than a break to relieve herself or a trip to the barn, so she practically bolted out the door, dragging Grayson along. He gripped her leash for dear life, afraid she'd tug free of his hold and be gone forever.

How would he face her owner then? What would he tell her?

It happened so fast.

I didn't know she was so strong.

I thought she'd come back.

He couldn't let it happen. Maybe they should turn back. Maybe… maybe he wasn't suited for taking care of this dog. He wasn't a dog person. Not an animal person of any sort. He didn't even have children of his own. He was only used to taking care of himself. He couldn't get her to do what he wanted. He wouldn't know what to do if she ran away.

Didn't. Couldn't. Wouldn't.

Grayson grimaced. Maybe he shouldn't let a mere dog get the better of him.

They topped a short rise in an empty pasture, then started down a long slope that dipped into a broad flood plain. Sooner was out at the end of the leash, pulling hard.

"Whoa, slow down, girl. Slow down."

But she kept on pulling, head low, ears back, cheeks wide in a joyful smile. It wasn't so much that she had somewhere to go, just that she was going *somewhere*.

"Easy, Sooner. Easy!" Grayson pleaded. To his immense relief, she slowed. Every once in a while, though, she glanced back, as if to make sure he was still there.

When they came to the narrow creek winding through the flood plain, Sooner leaped across with ease. Grayson, however, wasn't quite so agile. He landed in the middle, the water halfway up his shins. Water splashed everywhere, soaking his shoes, his khaki shorts, and his T-shirt up to his navel. Tumbling onto the opposite bank, he fell to his knees.

"Damn it, Sooner! Not so fast!"

Before she hit the end of the leash, she heard him and rushed back. After a few quick kisses to confirm he wasn't hurt, she took one look at the running water and dived in. Like a bunny, she hopped around, flailing water in all directions. Then she stuck her nose in and snorted bubbles.

"What are you—?"

Lifting her head, she tensed her shoulders.

"Oh no. No, no, no. Don't you d—"

She shook her whole body, shoulders rotating side to side, spine twisting, fur flinging droplets in an arc ten feet or more... showering Grayson.

He flung his arm up, too little and too late. As he lowered it, laughter spilled forth. His hands were red from gripping the leash, his feet were tired from all the pounding even though they hadn't gone more than half a mile, his shoes oozed with mud, and his clothes, his hair... his entire person was drenched. He was out of breath, but it was a good kind of breathless—the feeling of having pushed his body past its limits. And he didn't mind being wet because it was already getting unbearably hot out and he would've headed straight to the shower anyway when they got back.

Instead of going on, Grayson sat for a while with his feet in the creek, shoes off, socks laid out to dry under the rays of the rising sun. The grass on the bank was thick and cushiony, like an overstuffed pillow. Little darts of silver flashed in the rippling water. A minute later, he realized they were minnows. His gaze followed the creek downhill, until he saw where it joined a bigger creek, just beyond the fence that marked the property line. Come to think of it, he wasn't entirely sure where the property line was. He'd have to ask Rex Franzen—

Rex. The lawyer was supposed to have called Grayson back to give him more details. He patted all his pockets before remembering he'd left his phone in the house. No matter. It could wait.

A lot could wait. He didn't have to make any decisions about whether to stay or go yet. He still had almost a month on his lease back in the city. Still had time to find the horses homes. Still had time before Sooner would need to go back to her owner.

The dog stretched her feet out, front and back legs splayed so she was lying like a frog. With a cavernous yawn, she placed her muzzle between her forelegs.

Grayson lay back, hands across his chest. Filamentous clouds were laced across the sky, barely moving. The lightest of breezes brushed his face. The sunlight poured down, warm and powerful.

He closed his eyes to shut out the brightness. Let his chest fill with country air, heavy with the scent of grass, sweet clover, moist earth, and, of course, animals and all that went along with them. All in all, it did smell better here than in the city. He'd gone nose-blind to the everyday stench there. If he went back now, he'd notice it. If…

Birds trilled in the distance. The neighbor's cows lowed. Somewhere, a truck rumbled down a bumpy country road…

—o0Oo—

Grayson awoke to snot blowing in his ear.

"Sooner… stop it." He swatted at her without opening his eyes.

Her tongue flicked across his closed eyelids.

"I said stop it. Go away." He didn't want to get up. This nap was the closest thing to heaven he'd known in years. Decades, maybe. It was probably like what Fee had wanted their vacations to be—total relaxation. But he'd always taken his briefcase with him, always been e-mailing or returning phone calls. For the first time, he realized he didn't miss going to work every day at the same office. He still missed Fee, but more and more, it was that he missed having someone he could talk to, someone just to *be* with.

When he heard the slurp of Sooner drinking from the creek, he decided it was finally time to get a move on. Sitting up, he became aware of a burning sensation on his exposed skin. He scanned his bare arms, lifted the edge of his sleeve—

"Ow. Ow, ow, ow."

Alerted, Sooner jumped up from the bank, then pounced on his sunburned legs.

"No, get off!"

She backed away, her ears flattened.

"I'm sorry." He extended his hand. "I know you didn't mean it. That just hurt. Normally it wouldn't, but…"

Inching forward, she sniffed his hand. Then she curled around` and slid under his arm to sit beside him. Her leash was still attached to her collar. He must've let go of it when he'd fallen asleep. She'd had every opportunity to run off, but she hadn't. Or maybe it was just that she hadn't noticed.

He hugged her. "Feeling more comfortable with me, are you? Well, I'm feeling that way with you, too. What do you say we finish our walk, then have some lunch back at the house?"

She licked his chin vigorously.

They continued—Sooner leading the way, Grayson trying to slow her down—until they came to a fence-line with no gate in sight. When he turned around to find an alternate route back to the farmhouse, he realized it was a good way away. Probably close to a mile.

It was early afternoon. He'd slept longer than he first thought. Grayson started down the hill at an easy trot, sure he'd have to tug back on the dog or yell at her to go easy. To his surprise, she fell back to his knee, occasionally glancing up to check on his position. At the bottom of the hill, he stopped to rest a minute before resuming. They walked a little more, Sooner pulling impatiently. He began to jog again, and she eased up. As much as it hurt from how out of shape he was, it also felt exhilarating. His knee ached, but only a little.

How many years had it been since he'd felt the ground fall away swiftly from beneath his feet? Felt his heart drum proudly inside his chest? Had his muscles burn so exquisitely? Or the air rush down his windpipe into his lungs and then out again in a constant thirst for precious oxygen? His joints threatened to collapse, his muscles were turning to jelly. A flush spread over his skin, and every inch of him was soaked with sweat.

It was the best he'd felt in a long time.

Free. Strong. Alive.

But his body kept reminding him that although he remembered what it was like to run fast and be light of foot, it could not, at present, comply with the youthful wishes of his mind.

They did this dance of start-stop-start until, at last, they reached the front porch. Grayson almost sank down to rest, wanted to collapse right there in fabulous exhaustion, but knew he might not get up for some time if he did, so he made himself continue inside. At the kitchen sink, he filled a bowl with cool water for Sooner before getting himself a glass of iced tea.

Outside, Grayson set the water dish next to Sooner. Side by side, they sank down onto the front steps. He tucked the end of her leash under his leg—not that it was enough to stop her if she wanted to take off, but it was there.

The dog slurped, her long tongue flicking water over her front legs, onto the porch steps, and as far as his thigh. When she was done, she lay in a sphinx position with her tongue lolling to the side. Her cheeks were bunched in an expression of utter delirium and her eyelids were half closed. A pair of robins landed in the yard, squabbling, and she didn't even glance at them. He noticed how content she seemed. Gone were the nervously shifting eyes, the restless tension coiled in her muscles, the ears flicking every which way. She was as worn out as a hound that had pursued a fox for many miles.

Eventually, Grayson realized, Sooner's owner would also be well enough to take her back. But he didn't want to think that far ahead. In the meantime, they had a lot of work to do if they were ever going to fully understand one another. Although, truthfully, he had no concept of what that might entail.

For now, she was happy enough to lie next to him, gazing out over the countryside, no cares or worries. He felt the same.

There weren't any tomorrows or yesterdays. No burdens or regrets. They weren't on anybody's schedule or trying to fulfill anyone else's expectations.

They just… were.

chapter 19

Sooner

We went running nearly every day. At first, it seemed hopeless. He was old… well, not old-old for a human, but older than Brandy. Past his prime. He shuffled and stumbled, heaving for air like he was racing up a mountainside carrying twice his weight on his back, not jogging through soft grass at a leisurely pace. I almost gave up on him several times. *He* wanted to give up. The first few times, he'd stop often, hands on knees as he stooped over to catch his breath, sweat dripping from his chin onto the ground. Sometimes I wondered if he wasn't going to keel over dead right there. Then what was I supposed to do? So I'd nudge at the back of his knees until he told me to stop, lick his face in encouragement, tug in the direction we'd been going, and whine in impatience. Eventually, he'd start to walk. But why walk anywhere when running was an option? After his breathing had evened out, he'd start running again, some foolishly persistent determination awakened in him.

It didn't take me long to recover from all my cuts and bites and bruises. I was starting to feel more like my old self again: curious, eager, energetic. I wanted to explore this new place, sniff every chipmunk hole and rabbit trail and pile of horse manure I could find so I knew who else had been there, how long ago, and sometimes what they'd eaten. I rolled in the grass and drank from the stream. When Grayson wasn't paying attention, I even dug at the earth to see what small, slimy creatures I could find. This farm, all spread out, was all so excitingly new to me.

I'd long since given up on finding Brandy. Besides, she hadn't come back to find me, even though I'd been there by the van, left, and come back to wait some more. At times, I wondered if this was how it would be for the rest of my life: one home after another, new places, new people, new rules. Did people tire of their dogs and trade them for new ones? Not care if they lost them? Did a dog ever stay with one person forever?

As each day passed, it became achingly clear. This man, Grayson, he was my person now—for however long that might last. And even though he was terribly inept at communicating with me, he tried. He was getting better. I let him know when he was right and ignored him when he was wrong. That was how Brandy had taught me. The relationship I had with Grayson was mostly one of confusion and frustration, but there were moments, more and more, in which we did seem to click.

Grayson stood up from the oversized desk in the upstairs spare bedroom where he'd been hunched over his phone listening to a small voice speaking from a tiny moving picture. The words had been familiar. Words a good owner said to his dog. Words any decently educated dog ought to know.

He held a dog biscuit in the air above my head. "Okay, let's give this a try, shall we? Sooner, sit?"

The word was right, but the intonation was entirely off. I sat, then lay down. *Try again, buddy.*

"No, I said sit! Sit, Sooner, sit. Sit, okay?"

Was I supposed to do it the first, second, or third time? And if 'sit' was what he wanted, why did he throw in the words 'no' and 'okay'? Those meant entirely different things.

Exasperated, I flopped over onto my side. Where was that new squeaky toy he brought home yesterday? I arched my neck back, scanning under the furniture. Oh, there it was! Right beside that shelf with all the dusty books on it. I inched toward it on my belly, preparing to pounce. Maybe I could get him to play? He was awful at training.

"No, Sooner. What are you doing?"

I leaped to my feet, attacked the toy, tried to kill it, and then dropped it at his feet. *I'm a good hunter, yes?* I sat, waiting for him to catch on and throw it for me.

"Hey, good sit!"

Oh. He noticed. Brilliant of him. I slammed the toy down with my paw so it let out a great and wonderful squeak.

He pointed at the ground right in front of the toy. "Down."

I lay down. *Pick it up. Pick it up, pick it up, pick it up. Throw. It.*

"Wow, you did it! Hey, that was really good. Good girl, Sooner!" He thumped me on the head, then gave me the biscuit.

Of course I did it. I know a lot of things. Now throw the toy!

He groped through his pockets. "Shoot, I'm out. Need to stock up on biscuits today." Then he picked up the toy, holding it above my head. "Sit up."

I snorted. Which did he want? 'Sit' meant one thing, 'up' another. When Brandy said 'up,' she wanted me to jump up on a pause table or the bed or in the van or—

"Come on, Sooner. Sit up." He dangled the toy tauntingly.

I looked around the room. Since he couldn't make up his mind, I took a guess. Maybe if I guessed right, he'd throw the darn toy.

Before he could change the rules of the game, I vaulted onto the bed, spun around, and did a play bow, my rear end waggling.

Throw it. Throw it! I barked.

"No, no, no. Get off, Sooner."

Okay, that was clear enough. I hopped off and sat because that must've been what he wanted.

Toy! Toy!

"Ah, look, will you? Your feet are muddy." He scowled. "Bad dog."

Say what? Bad dog? But how?

I hung my head in shame, not even sure what it was I should be ashamed about. Was he displeased at me for trying? Brandy would never have done that. She would always repeat the command until I understood what she wanted, then told me what a good dog I was. Even when Grayson used words I knew, they didn't always mean the same thing.

Grayson stomped over to the bed, then inspected the quilt. He ran his hand over it, gathering a ball of fluff, which he showed me. "See this? You're shedding, too. How is it possible for one dog to lose so much hair?" After dropping the wad of hair, he paced in a small circle, stroking his chin. When he stopped, he studied me for a while. "Since your stitches are out, I think it's time for a bath. Maybe a good dowsing with warm water will loosen up some of that fur coat of yours."

Three things I didn't like about his speech. One was the look on his face. He was obviously unhappy with me. Two was his tone. Again, I'd done something terribly wrong. And three, I clearly heard the word 'bath'. That was a word in my vocabulary I would rather didn't exist.

His phone made a strange chirping sound in his pocket. He took it out, tapped at it, and scowled more. "What? No, totally unacceptable. Who does he think he is, putting me off like that?"

His mood wasn't improving, and neither was mine.

"No time for a bath today." He pointed at me. "Stay there."

I knew the word 'stay,' but I had a bad feeling there was more to it—as in this wasn't going to result in any pets, praises, or treats. As soon he marched out of the room and started rummaging in the bathroom, I looked for an escape route. I was headed toward the door, ready to dash down the stairs, when I heard him coming back. I dived under the bed. It was a tight squeeze. Cobwebs hung down from the old wire springs of the framework, tickling my face as I pushed through. There were several shoe boxes under here, some crumpled socks, random bits of paper, two dead spiders, and—

Be still my heart. It was a bone!

I'd lost that bone last week. It must've gotten kicked under here after I'd lain beside the bed chewing it while Grayson stared at his computer. As tempted as I was, I'd leave it for later. It was always good to hide bones in many different places for safekeeping. I never knew when there might be a shortage.

Grayson's feet appeared in the doorway. "Sooner, where'd you go?"

Pulling my hind legs farther under, I then lay very still.

Easily fooled, he left and went to the big bedroom. As he called my name over and over, I explored more of my surroundings with my nose. It smelled overpoweringly of dust. I discovered a piece of hard candy, smelling faintly of the human who had lived here before Grayson. Taking it in my mouth, I bit down. It made a loud crunching sound, but Grayson was apparently too far away to hear. Fearful he'd return and find me, I swallowed it quickly, but the two halves caught in my throat partway down. A cough rose from my chest. I hacked the candy onto the floor, sure he'd hear, but by then, his footsteps were cascading down the stairs.

"Sooner? Hey, Sooner! Soooner?"

Over and over he called my name. I knew it was bad not to go to him, but I hadn't forgotten how he'd said the word 'bath'. While I loved swimming, the cool water surrounding me as I floated weightlessly, I didn't like standing in the slick tub and having soap worked into my coat and running into my eyes, then the blasting heat and ear-boring wind of the hair dryer. Not to mention once I got 'clean,' I was forbidden from rolling in the grass or digging in the dirt. Not worth it, even if it meant going on a car ride.

Then again... car rides meant new and wonderful places. Excitement. People, other dogs. Parks, pet stores, dog shows.

They also meant veterinarians.

No, I'd stay here for now. Be safe. Take a long nap maybe. Loyalty did not equate to stupidity. This new human couldn't be entirely trusted. He'd fooled me one too many times with those pills.

It grew quieter downstairs. Minutes slipped by. He must've given up. The darkness beneath the bed comforted me. Sleep called. What better way to pass the time than with a nap?

Through the window, I heard birds singing, the wind rustling leaves, the faraway chug of a tractor. Smells drifted to me on that late summer breeze: hay freshly cut, the perfume of roses, clover crushed beneath hooves, the growing mound just outside the barn of straw mixed with manure... Every muscle in my body relaxed as I drew air in. I stretched my legs out, yawned, closed my eyes...

"Sooner?"

I opened my eyes with a start. It was Brandy calling my name!

She stood at the top of a hill, waving her arms at me, the sun beaming down on her. "What are you doing over there?"

My muscles quivered with excitement. Inside my chest, my heart throbbed against my ribs so hard I was sure it would burst. I, too, was standing atop a hill. Between us was a broad valley, grass fluttering in a lazy breeze. The horses—those I'd come to know as Persephone, Spark, Clifford, and Goliath—munched on stacks of hay and clover, roses braided into their manes.

A lone oak stood in the trough of the valley. Beneath the shade of its canopy stood Grayson, turning in a circle, hands cupped to his mouth, his lips moving but making no sound.

Brandy tilted her head. "Never mind. I can see you're not done. Be a good dog, okay? He needs you more than I do."

I could hardly believe my eyes! She seemed so far away—and yet, I could hear her so clearly. As if she were right next to me.

I took a step forward. Then another and another, the slope of the hill beckoning me downward and onward. I was running now, my legs churning fast, my heart light with joy. The grass was so tall I had to bound high. The effort tired me. My legs grew heavier with each stride, my leaps flatter to the ground. After several heartbeats, I glanced up in search of Brandy. I had to stand on my hind legs to see. She was tiny. Far away. I was no closer than before.

"Ah, no, no, no, Sooner." She shook her head in disapproval, then pointed a finger at me. "Sit!"

I stopped in my tracks. She couldn't possibly mean that. Not when she was right there.

But there was no mistaking the look on her face. Confused and disappointed, I sat.

"Now lie down—and stay."

I did as told. Even though I could no longer see her.

"Sooner? Here, girl. Sooner! I know you didn't leave the house. The doors are locked. Sooner?"

I jumped up so abruptly I hit my head on the underside of the bed. My head rang. A slit of light appeared before me. Eyes now open, I saw the socks, my bone, the scraps of paper, all shadowed by the bed above. Beyond that was the upstairs bedroom. I remembered where I was and why I was hiding. Lowering my chin to the floor, I focused on staying quiet. Grayson padded up the stairs hurriedly, like he had somewhere to go. Just as he hit the top step, I noticed something small and square peeking out from beneath one of the socks. Sniffing, I sorted out the scents swirling around in my nose. I had a vague recollection of what it was: salty, oily, crunchy yet on the stale side. A Frito!

I wiggled toward it, my nose quivering as I inhaled its tantalizing promise, dust filling my nostrils. I snorted softly to clear my nasal passages. It was dangerously close to the end of the bed. Did I dare risk exposing myself?

Grayson's feet shuffled across the doorway, pivoted, paused. "Sooner, you in there? Be a good dog and come on out."

I froze in place. Although he was trying very hard not to sound angry, there was an edge of irritation to his voice.

"Hmph, guess you don't want to go to the feed store. They have things for dogs there. Balls, squeakies, bones… biscuits, even. Good dogs get biscuits."

If he was mad at me *and* taking me to the vet, there was no way I was coming out now—biscuits or no biscuits.

Anyway, I'd been told to stay. I remembered at dog school when Brandy used to put me in a sit or a down, then told me to stay as she walked across the ring and another person rolled a ball past me. I'd failed the test the first few times, but I soon caught on. No matter how tempted I was, when Brandy told me to stay, I stayed. So that was what I was going to do.

Grayson moved on down the hall. He opened and closed a cabinet door in the bathroom, then made his way to the main bedroom. I took the opportunity to scoot closer to the Frito. Reaching a paw forward, I curled a nail over it and slid it toward me. Puffs of dust exploded in the wake of my paw, tickling the inside of my nose. A sneeze built inside my head, the pressure straining to be released. Grayson began to move again, out into the hall. I held my breath, waited for the urge to pass. He passed the doorway, started down the stairs. And then—

Achoo!

Water filled my eyes. I sniffed. Sneezed three more quick times.

"Sooner!"

SAY WHEN

A hand grappled in the darkness, hooked around my collar, and pulled me out into the light. I sneezed again.

"What are you doing under there?" He nudged me over onto my side before attacking my feet with a fluffy towel and rubbing vigorously between my toes. It wasn't until he stopped that I realized how much I'd been enjoying it. Then, he glanced at his watch and tossed the towel aside. Starting toward the door, he slapped at his leg. I followed.

"I need to go to town. You might as well come along. Pretty sure they'll let you in the feed store and as for Rex… well, I don't care. He and I need to have a face-to-face conversation."

Again with the irritated tone. But I sensed it wasn't directed at me, so I relaxed a bit. In the kitchen, he took a big carrot from the refrigerator and tossed it to me, then poured himself a glass of iced tea and chugged it.

"I did not come all this way," he ranted in between swallows, "just so some small-town lawyer could dump this place on me, then ignore me. I'm going to give that rat a piece of my mind." He placed the half full glass in the sink, grabbed his phone and wallet off the counter, and stomped out the back door, holding it open just long enough for me to slip through. I stopped briefly to relieve myself before catching back up to him. We were on some kind of mission. Whatever it was, it was my job to supervise.

Just as he put his hand on the car door handle, Grayson stopped dead, a stunned look on his face as he gazed down at me.

I sat, patiently waiting for him to open the door.

"Your leash." He glanced at his empty hand, then at me. "I forgot to put your leash on, and you didn't run away." Smiling, he patted me on the head. "Good dog, Sooner. Good dog. But since we're going into town, let's go back in and get it. Keys would be good, too. Can't drive a car without the damn keys."

We went in the house to retrieve my leash and his keys from their usual hooks next to the door, then came back out and got in the car. After he turned the key in the ignition, he glanced at me in the rearview mirror. Then he twisted in his seat and stared at me straight on. "You know, it's like every time I turn around now, there you are—next to me, behind me, sometimes on top of me. And you haven't even been around that long. But don't think for a moment I'm getting used to it. I still don't appreciate the dog hair in my coffee, or the scratches on the hardwood floor, or the crack-of-dawn potty outings."

I tilted my head at him, trying to sort out his words, but nothing made sense except for 'potty'. Was he asking if I needed to? Had he not noticed I'd done that the first time we went out the door?

He turned back around. "Now, ready to go get those biscuits?"

I woofed softly.

"At least you're a good dog. Most days."

Ah, good dog. I lived to hear those words. Straining forward, I licked his ear. *Thank you.*

This was one of those moments in which things were definitely right between us.

chapter 20
Grayson

"Be with you in a few—"

"No, sir. Not a few." Shoving the door to Rex Franzen's office open wide, Grayson stormed in.

Sooner was close at his side, her eyes darting as she took in the unfamiliar surroundings. Grayson found the space overwhelming in a cluttered sort of way: the faded wood paneling, the patchwork of certificates and degrees lettered with fancy script adorning the walls in their mismatched frames, the billiard-green carpet with threadbare paths, the towering bookcases with row upon row of binders labeled with names and dates in ballpoint pen and law books with gilded volume numbers on their spines.

The dog tugged toward a low filing cabinet, where a coffee maker sat with an empty carafe. On a saucer beside it was a cup of cold coffee and a half-eaten cheese Danish. She sniffed the air and sat, her quivering nose inches from the tempting pastry.

"No, Sooner. Leave it." Grayson snapped the leash lightly. Head low, she padded to him and sat at his side. He was beginning to understand that her tendency to rush toward new things wasn't willful defiance, it was merely a confident curiosity, like a child seeking to understand the world around her. The videos he'd been watching were helping. He was learning to redirect her attention and follow it with praise, but he had to remind himself regularly. Being a good dog trainer was not intuitive for him. He reached down to pat the top of her head. "Good girl."

"I'm sorry… Mr.…?" Rex Franzen had the desperate look of one meeting up with an old classmate but at a loss for his name.

"Darling. Grayson Darling. Skip Dalton's nephew."

"Oh, right, Gary. I should have recognized your face. It's just that"—he waved a hand at Grayson's attire: a pair of loose-fitting jeans with grass stains, new but smudged running shoes, and a short-sleeved green and blue plaid shirt that Grayson had picked up at the feed store—"you're dressed like one of the locals now. You must've assimilated." He winked in jest, but the joke fell flat. "Threw me for a moment, but go on—what brings you here?"

It took every bit of restraint Grayson had not to throw Rex Franzen out the window behind him. The striated light coming in through the blinds behind the desk blinded Grayson momentarily, sparing him the outburst.

Rex rifled through the piles on his desk in search of an elusive scrap of paper. Appearing not to find it, he lifted his hands in defeat. "Did we have an appointment? Ever since—"

"No, but we should have—a long time ago." Grayson flapped a stack of papers in the air before slapping them down on the lawyer's desk, its shellacked cherry wood surface marred with nicks and scratches. "I've looked through all these. Standard stuff: a will, a deed to the property, bonds, bank statements. Some of the numbers are outdated, maybe a few minor inconsistencies, but I don't see anything that could be causing a holdup. You said there was more that you were looking into, and I've been waiting to hear what that was. You've been putting me off for how long now—four weeks? Five? Do you know how many interviews I could've had in New York City in that time?" Grayson didn't mention that his options thus far had seemingly run dry. If he'd had the incentive to look, he might've found something, though. "I put off sending out more resumes because I was led to believe that my uncle's estate was going to get squared away within the month. And now I've wasted all this time and for what? Waiting for you to *not* call me back? Meanwhile, I'm days away from losing a lease on a rent-controlled apartment and am paying for a car that until I came here, I had no use for.

"Have you even looked into Skip's other investments to determine the state of his finances, whether he owed money or had it coming to him? I've left half a dozen, maybe seven or eight messages on your machine, but I haven't gotten so much as a courtesy call. I finally resorted to e-mail and got some automated message. Do you treat all your clients this way—or is it just me you're avoiding? How do you even stay in business in this town?"

In the fifteen minutes it had taken him to drive to town, Grayson had worked up a hefty dose of ire. In his years of arranging loans in the biggest city in America, he'd worked with all sorts of people: dodgy businessmen, filthy rich elites, philanthropists out to save the world, honest working-class folk just trying to save up to send their kids to college, immigrant entrepreneurs with lofty dreams… Their problems and plans had run the gamut, but none had ever frustrated him to the extent that Rex Franzen had. Grayson had started out being polite with the small-town lawyer, only ratcheting it up to pointedly insistent when his messages had gone unanswered. Eventually, assertiveness had transformed into something bordering on outrage— an emotion he'd only ever flirted with, quickly tamping it down when the prospect of losing all control offended his sense of decency.

But this time was different. He'd wasted days, no *weeks,* waiting for a callback and some kind of resolution.

Elbows on the desk, Rex steepled his fingertips together. "I take it you haven't heard the latest scuttlebutt through the grapevine, maybe while you were down at the feed store?"

"That's my next stop. But no, what are you talking about?"

"Martina, my receptionist, the one who kept this operation running like a well-oiled machine… she skipped town with my accountant, Magnus Jorgensen. He was everyone's accountant in this half of Adair County, actually. The tax preparer, too. Seems those two had been engaging in some hanky-panky for well over a year and decided to run off to Costa Rica so they could shack up indefinitely. No telling if they'll get hitched once both their divorces go through. There's a betting pool going on down at the senior center as to how long they'll last before one of them breaks it off. Magnus is easy enough to get along with, a happy-go-lucky sort of fellow, but Martina is quite the drill sergeant. I had no idea how many details she dealt with on a daily basis as far as records and billing and"—he waved a hand toward the reception area beyond the open door—"well, all that business-related mumbo-jumbo. I just figured she was one of those OCD-types. I have a whole new respect for the job she did. Her job, mind you. Lost all respect for her as a human being, the way she up and—"

"Okay, okay, I get it. Faderville has been rocked by a scandal that would put Hollywood to shame. But enough of the soap opera. You're my deceased uncle's attorney, which by default now makes me your client; therefore, you and I have business that needs attended to. Couldn't you at least check your messages? And how hard would it be to find a replacement for her? At least someone to answer the phone and reply to e-mails, for crying out loud."

"I'd be offended by your lack of sensitivity and civility, sir, if I thought you understood the extent of my problem. You don't replace someone like Martina on a whim."

At this point, Grayson was beyond frustrated. If it hadn't been for

Sooner having snuck around the desk and lain her head on Rex's knee to gaze up at the lawyer with pleading eyes, he might have lunged across and grabbed him by the shirt collar. Instead, he flattened his palms on the desk and leaned forward. "I didn't come here to hear excuses. You owe me some answers. I want this business wrapped up, so I can get on with my life."

"Fair enough, Gary."

"My name's *not* Gary. It's Grayson." His eyes darted to a certificate from Rex's law school with more legible lettering. "*Reginald*," he growled.

"Ah, touché… *Grayson*. Touché."

Rex leaned back in his cracked leather swivel chair, as if to put a little more distance between himself and Grayson. After a pause, he laid a finger on the stack of papers, tapped it a few times. "I did tell you this wasn't everything, right?"

"That's what you said." They stared at each other for several seconds, neither one yielding, before Grayson spoke again. "So what do you have—anything?"

It was more a challenge than a question.

"I might."

"Might's not good enough."

"Well, I don't have all the specifics yet…"

Grayson restrained himself. "Then tell me what you do have."

Sighing, Rex scooted his chair back and rose. Sooner followed him as far as the leash would allow before he went out into the front room. Drawers slid on their metal rails, then banged shut one after another. One minute stretched into two, then three.

The ache in his knee growing with each passing minute, Grayson sat in one of the two visitors' chairs facing the desk. The high back, padded arms, and deep cushion comforted his tired body. He was becoming more efficient with the daily chores and had developed new calluses, but his runs with Sooner were becoming increasingly longer.

It wasn't the runs themselves that were testing his limits; it was the ruggedness of the terrain and the steepness of the hills.

"Found it." Rex dropped a manila folder in Grayson's lap, then reclaimed his chair and kicked his feet up on the desk. It was the first time Grayson really noticed his boots: part cowhide, part crocodile, intricately stitched. Not new, but certainly not inexpensive. They went hand in hand with the turquoise bolero he wore in place of a tie and the sterling-silver belt buckle. "Martina had some kind of complex system for filing papers away, all indexed and cross-referenced on her computer. She could pull up a file lickety-split, but I kept getting sucked down rabbit holes before I finally got some inkling as to how it worked. Anyway, your uncle Skip did make some totally lame-brained investments with the horses, lost an embarrassing amount of money on them. But…" He pulled open a desk drawer, took out a pack of gum, and offered Grayson a stick. "Want one? Black licorice. Or maybe it's clove. The old-fashioned kind. Doesn't last long, but it has bite. Been hooked on the stuff ever since I gave up cigars."

"Thanks, but I'll pass." Grayson skimmed through the papers. "I'm no lawyer, but these look like some sort of business contract."

"They are. Keep reading, though. It gets better."

By the time Grayson got to the last page, he was more confused than when he'd started. "I don't understand what these all mean. The first set looks like from when he bought into his restaurant franchise. Some other related papers. And his original stock purchases. Is that right?"

"So far, so good."

Grayson shrugged. "So what? He got out of that business ages ago when he got involved with the horses."

"Indeed, he did. Your uncle worked like a dog in his younger days, but he hated the hours. He was good at it, though. Damn good. He helped establish Rutherford's as one of the most successful chains not just in Kentucky, but the entire Southeastern United States. He didn't just own the one restaurant in Somerset. He owned eleven of them—from Virginia to Arkansas and on down to coastal Alabama."

A quick scan of the papers led Grayson to find that it wasn't just one business listed in the sales contract, but almost a dozen. The final sales price was staggering—over ten million. Still...

"He used this money to buy the farm, didn't he?" Grayson asked.

"An equine estate, you'd call it. But yep, he did. Bought the finest horses, employed some trainers and grooms, travelled the continent..."

So much for that, Grayson thought.

Rex unwrapped a stick of gum, then popped it in his mouth. "Your uncle did do one smart thing, though."

"What?"

"He held onto his stocks."

Grayson studied that paper one more time. Skip had bought in low. He might even have been one of the first on board. That only meant something if... "So what are they worth now?"

"I don't have the foggiest idea, Grayson. I figured, you being the financial wizard, you ought to know. Got a wild guess?"

"I worked in the loan department of a nationwide bank. I mostly dealt with business loans, but sometimes mortgages and personal loans, like autos, and the financial side of creating business plans. Stocks are far from being my specialty. I really don't pay attention to the market myself, but I do know a few people who could look into it." He lifted the stack of papers up. "Can I—?"

"Sure. Let me make some copies for you. Martina probably has another set somewhere, but I stopped looking when I found these." Rex came around the desk to take the papers and head out again. He wasn't in the front room ten seconds when he came back in. He hitched a thumb over his shoulder. "Right, slipped my mind. There's some sort of doggone error message flashing on the copier. Been that way for four days. Technology is my Achilles. Would you—?"

Rex disappeared back into the front without waiting for a reply. Sooner returned to Grayson's feet, nudging at his hand with her nose. It was a familiar signal to him by now. She wanted him to get a move on. They had places to go, things to do.

He smoothed the hair on top of her head. "Yeah, yeah. I know. I promised you a trip to the feed store. Don't worry—we'll get there. It's just…" There was so much he didn't know right now. A couple of months ago, he'd been determined to keep pushing in one direction. Had wanted his life to go back to being what it had been before, Fee included. More recently, he'd felt trapped by his circumstances, stuck on the outskirts of some backwoods Appalachian town that wasn't even big enough to have a movie theater. But now he felt on the precipice of another monumental life change. Not worse. Not necessarily better. Just… a change. He wasn't sure what it meant.

"Maybe I won't be stuck here after all, Sooner."

She tilted her head side to side, as if contemplating the implications of his statement. Then she stood, shook herself head to nubbin, and headed toward the door as far as her leash would allow, pulling Grayson to his feet.

A few minutes later, he had unjammed the papers from the back of the copier—papers that had likely been there for more than a few days.

"Say, uh…"—Rex looked over Grayson's shoulder as he collated the papers—"I know you said loans were your area of expertise, but do you know general accounting and tax prep? I'm just inquiring because this town is now short a number-cruncher and—"

"No." Grayson handed him a set of copies.

"Pardon?"

"I wasn't planning on sticking around here. Either way." Copies in hand, he headed for the front door.

"No problem-o. Just figured I'd toss that out there. Keep it in mind. Hell, you wouldn't even have to take over his office. You could just work out of your home."

"Thanks, but… it's not my home. Good day." Grayson nodded, more out of politeness than agreement. "And thanks for the paperwork. I'll follow up on it."

—oO0o—

Grayson stepped out into the glare and sticky heat of a late morning sun. The smell of diesel fumes hit him as a semi and two pickups rolled past on the main street, then chugged to a halt at the stoplight a block away. There, on the opposite side, was a narrow office in the lower level of a brown brick building. The arched lettering on the big glass window, which looked like it had once been the display window of a storefront, said 'Jorgensen Accounting Services,' then beneath that in smaller block letters: 'Business and Personal Finances'. Hanging in a lower corner of the window was a printed sign that said: 'Free tax prep'.

A lure. Grayson knew the tactic. Lasso them in by offering to write down the obvious numbers in the right place, then point out that with a little extra attention, plus a nominal fee, more tax deductions could be found. Typical gimmick when there was no competition to speak of.

A young woman walked toward them on the sidewalk. The toddler in the stroller she was pushing waved her hands excitedly. "Goggy!"

"Yes, Claire, that's a doggy." The woman slowed to give the little girl a better look. When her daughter reached out a hand, the mother gently pulled it back. "No, no, sweetheart. You have to ask. That doggy doesn't know you." Then she glanced at Grayson and asked, "Can she? It's okay if you say no. I understand."

He glanced down at Sooner. Even though she was sitting, her hind end was wiggling. She didn't appear the least bit nervous or stressed by the enthusiasm of a small person. "I think she's fine. Go right ahead."

"He says it's okay, sweetie. You can pet the dog. But be gentle."

The little girl extended her hand. Sooner sniffed it, working her way up the girl's arm until she was practically nose to nose with her. Then Sooner licked her cheek. Two quick licks, just enough to tickle. The toddler bunched her shoulder to her ear, giggling contagiously.

"Thank you…?"

"Grayson. Grayson Darling."

"Thank you, Mr. Darling. I'm Becca Mays. Poor Claire here has been cranky all morning. Seems I interrupted her nap to come downtown here to ask Mr. Jorgensen a few questions. My husband and I just opened our own restaurant last summer—The Apple Orchard."

"That place on the hill, just off the interstate?" He remembered seeing it when he first came to town.

"The one and only. The orchard was started up by his grandpa. When his father died and his mom retired in Arizona, she left it to him. The orchard itself is barely enough to live on, but I told Hank, 'What if we opened a restaurant?' He's always loved to cook—makes *the* tastiest barbecue this side of the Ohio River—and I make some mean apple dumplings. Won the baking contest at the Adair County Fair four years running now."

"Impressive. I can barely follow the directions on a box of mac and cheese." It was true. Suddenly, the thought of food made him remember he'd only had two cups of coffee that morning. "Maybe I'll stop by for a meal soon."

"Love to have you. We're open until ten, for those who get the late-night munchies."

Grayson had often eaten dinner at that hour, but he'd also forgotten to eat altogether at times. As long as he was here in Faderville getting Uncle Skip's farm and finances sorted out, he might as well enjoy the pace of life. "Is there much of a dinner rush if I come by around five?"

"Never more than a ten-minute wait unless a tour bus pulls off the highway and unloads. Harris's Outdoor Café probably doesn't like the competition, but I figure folks in this town need some options. Otherwise, they all hightail it to Somerset on weekends and for special occasions. Well…" Glancing across the street at the empty office, she sighed. "Guess I should've just called and saved myself the trip. I'll have to make an appointment over in Somerset myself now, although I don't know when I can manage that. My neighbor is watching the twins right now—they're ten months old—and my son gets off the bus for kindergarten in"—she glanced at her watch—"Oh, crap… sorry. Here I am shooting the breeze and I have less than twenty minutes to get home. Anyway, thanks for the bright spot. At least Claire's in a better mood."

As she wheeled the stroller on and hurried to her car, half a block down, Sooner spun in place, watching. Becca set Claire in her car seat, then packed the stroller away in the back of her minivan and drove away. Sooner let out a plaintive whine.

"You sound like you have a leak, Sooner."

She looked up at Grayson briefly, then back to the road, the van getting smaller and smaller in the distance. Her head dipped. Her ears folded to the side. Finally, she lay down in the shade of a mailbox, head between her paws. She seemed like the little kid whose older sibling has boarded the school bus for the first time, leaving her behind.

It almost broke Grayson's heart. He wondered if she'd played with kids before when she was with her owner. It would help to know those things about her, so he wouldn't have to guess. He knew he should call her owner up, rather than just text, but he hadn't worked up the courage. He wasn't sure why he hadn't yet. Except for where it might lead.

Anyway, he would. Later today. Or tomorrow. He owed Brandy Anders that much.

First things first, though. He was hungry. The dog probably was, too. After all, he had promised her biscuits.

chapter 21
Grayson

Grayson paused before the large plate-glass window of Kerry's Donuts and More. Beside him, Sooner put her paws up on the brick ledge beneath the window to peer inside. Three glass cases formed a U. To the left on the bottom were birthday cakes. Not as ornate as some he'd seen in New York City, but they were artfully decorated. Above them on wire racks were pies, their contents marked with hand-printed labels. The right-hand case held melamine trays full of cookies and muffins. In the center case were more trays loaded with donuts and pastries.

After checking his wallet and finding himself low on cash, he did some adding in his head and weighed whether to buy himself two oversized muffins or half a dozen donuts. He wasn't sure what such things cost here, but his stomach was twisting with hunger.

Inside, a plain-faced woman with her hair pulled into a tight bun beneath a hairnet spritzed the glass case and buffed the fingerprints away with a rag.

A flush of embarrassment fanned upward from his chest to his neck to his face. It took a moment for him to realize the woman was smiling at him. Probably because he was staring. Either he needed to move on and never return, or go in and buy some donuts.

Just as he put his hand on the door latch, he pulled it back. There were two small plaques in the center of the door. The first said 'No shirt, no shoes, no service.' The second said, in all caps, 'NO PETS ALLOWED'.

The dog—he couldn't bring her inside.

After walking Sooner to the closest parking meter, he tied her to it. He wasn't entirely sure about leaving her unattended in public, but at least he could see her through the window from here.

"Sit," he commanded. Sooner's ears perked. She sat. If he wasn't mistaken, she looked rather pleased with herself. A trickle of sweat worked its way down his sternum. The day was heating up rapidly. He'd do his best to hurry. Raising his palm, he commanded firmly like he'd seen in the videos online, "Stay."

He walked away, turned around, waited. She hadn't moved. Didn't look like she was going to.

A bell tinkled behind him. The donut store clerk held the door open. "For heaven's sake, dog's gonna melt if you leave her out there on the sidewalk. Bring her on in."

"But the sign says—"

"Meh, don't mean nothing. That's just there for the sake of the health inspectors and I don't see any around, do you?"

"What if your boss comes by? Won't you get in trouble?"

"Boss?" She laughed. "I *am* the boss."

After untying Sooner and stepping inside, he said, "You must be Kerry, then."

"Ah, no. Kerry was my late husband. I'm Gertrude—after my grandmother. Thought about changing the name of the store when he passed ten years ago, but Gertrude's Donuts didn't have the same ring to it. People call me Gertie, for short, by the way. But I also answer to

'Hey, you!'" She scurried behind the cases, lifted a tray of cream puffs from a counter to the rear, and slid it into the center case. "Anyway, place has a good reputation and name recognition is everything. Don't mess with what ain't broke, right?"

Sooner pressed her nose to the glass, ogling the goods.

"Sooner, get back," Grayson said.

The dog took three steps backward as smoothly as if she'd practiced the move, which Grayson was pretty sure she had. There was probably a lot about this dog he hadn't yet discovered. Unfortunately, she'd left a wet nose print squarely in the center of the glass. He was about to ask for a paper towel to wipe it off when Gertie interrupted his thoughts.

"What can I get you—half a dozen cream puffs? You look mighty hungry."

He was, but the truth of the matter was he only had so much money on him. "As good as that sounds, how about a couple of glazed? Or do you recommend the Bismarcks? I can't decide."

"Tough call. My glazed are the most popular, but the Bismarcks were voted the best in Adair County." Leaning across the case, she curled a finger at him like she was about to reveal a deep dark secret. "Some folks tell me, though, that you haven't really lived until you've had one of my cream puffs, but don't just take my word for it. Ask around."

"Thanks, but I'll go with a glazed and a Bismarck, plus a small decaf."

She turned around to pour some coffee. "You don't like cream puffs?" Her voice had an indignant edge to it.

"I do, actually. It's just that I only have four dollars in cash." A sorry thing to admit, but she was pushing the cream puffs rather aggressively. This lady could hold her own with any New York street vendor.

Setting the cup on top of the case and snapping the cover on, she regarded him for a few moments. Gradually, the sternness in her face softened to something more like pity. "Well, why didn't you just say so?"

Gertie stuffed the two donuts and a cream puff in a white paper sack, then slid it to him. "That'll be a buck seventy-five."

The math wasn't right. He wasn't sure whether to correct her, but it didn't seem right to underpay on his first visit. "I don't think that's—"

"Cream puff's on the house. So's the coffee, by the way."

"But I didn't ask for a cream puff—no offense."

"None taken. Anyway, consider it a sampler. We're famous for them—ask anyone. I know you'll more than like it. Then you'll come back again for more. It's how we build our clientele in small towns like Faderville."

He opened his wallet, taking out four dollar bills and holding them out. "Really, I insist."

"It's okay, honey." She plucked two from his hand and gave him a quarter. "I know what it's like to be out of work. Kerry and I were both laid off from the bottling plant twelve years ago before we opened this place. Just paying it forward."

"But I'm not..." He left the statement unfinished. Because he *was* out of work. Had been for close to a year.

"And don't even dream of leaving a tip. Because if you do, I'll just give you more donuts. That would be a dangerous precedent to set. You'd end up thirty pounds overweight. Like me." Gertie patted her round middle. Although thirty pounds was a conservative estimate. "Here's my tip to you—if keeping the pounds off is a struggle, don't open a bakery."

Just this once, he was going to be humble. And he was going to appreciate the small things that people did for him. Things he used to take for granted.

"Thank you," he said. He meant it.

The next thing he noticed was Sooner sitting up, her front paws crossed, begging.

"Would you look at that?" Gertie marveled. "Some dog you got there."

Another trick he didn't know she knew. Sooner was a regular circus dog.

"What do you call her?" Gertie asked.

"Sooner."

"Wait there, Sooner." Gertie disappeared in the back before coming out with a metal tin. She popped it open and produced a biscuit, then tossed it over the case. Sooner caught it in midair. Laughing, she threw her another. "You bring this here dog back anytime… I'm sorry, what's your name?"

"Grayson. Grayson Darling."

"Anytime, Grayson. She's an absolute peach. That is, unless you're just passing through."

"No, I… I'm staying at my uncle's place until it gets sold."

"Uncle's place, you say? You wouldn't be Skip's nephew, would you?"

"I am."

Her face lit up. She clasped her hands together, brought them to her heart. "Oh, what a wonderful man he was. So generous. Taught my daughter how to ride. Most patient 4-H leader in the county. She was scared to death of falling off, but by the time he got done with her, she looked like a regular cowgirl. I was really sorry to hear about his passing. He used to pop in here every Sunday morning, sometimes once or twice a week extra if he was running errands in town. I don't think he wanted coffee and donuts so much as he just wanted to flap his gums. Boy, he used to tell the most fascinating stories about his life, but then"—she waved a hand dismissively—"you've probably heard them all ten times over."

It would have been strangely awkward to admit he'd barely ever spoken to his uncle, couldn't even remember what he'd said when they had met, so Grayson said nothing at all to Gertie. He had discovered a lot of mementos that told a fragmented tale of his uncle's life: a guidebook for 4-H leaders, photos of a woman he'd been married to for less than ten years, and then the newspaper clipping of her obituary after she'd died in an auto accident, a uniform from a brief stint in the army, and a sizable collection of fossils, geodes, and gemstones. Maybe someday he'd try to find someone who personally knew more about him—then again, he probably wouldn't be around long enough to form that kind of casual relationship with this woman or anyone else. For now, she was just a business owner, and he a patron.

"Thank you for the cream puff." With a nod, he headed for the door.

"Let me know what you think of it," she called after him.

He pushed the door open, stepped out, and made his way down the sidewalk. Sooner trotted alongside him. He could feel her gazing up at him with those pleading puppy-dog eyes.

"Nice try," he told her, "but you're not getting any."

—o0Oo—

Grayson took a few sips of coffee before placing the pastry bag in his car. Although the car was good on gas, it didn't work well for hauling sacks of feed. He could only get two in the trunk. Using the backseat was impractical, since it was a coupe. Plus, there was the problem of how to transport lumber and other supplies needed for a farm. If he was going to stick around for a while, he'd need something more practical. But he was starting to think the easiest thing to do would just be auction off the horses and go back to New York—with the dog.

Then it struck him—he wasn't even sure his lease allowed dogs. He'd seen a couple of cats, but no dogs in the complex. The more he thought about it, the more convinced he was it didn't. He'd check on it. Soon.

A soft whine drew him from his thoughts. Sooner had lain down in the shade of the car, her tongue hanging long from the side of her mouth.

"Let's go in," Grayson said. She followed him, but her enthusiasm was waning by the minute. For mid-September and not yet noon, it was getting unbearably hot.

Inside the feed store, Sooner pepped up a little, obviously revived by the cool air blasting from the overhead vents. She walked calmly alongside the cart, sat when Grayson stopped, and sniffed the air but resisted stealing the basted rawhides sitting temptingly on the lowest shelf. Grayson couldn't decide which biscuits she'd like, so he put three different kinds in the cart.

"Now that's a nice-lookin' dog."

A man about ten years older than Grayson stood at the end of the aisle. He was wearing a dark blue apron that had a pair of scissors and a black Sharpie peeking from the pockets on the front of it.

"Dog have a name?"

"Sooner." Grayson wondered why people always asked about the dog. Maybe it was just a polite way of breaking the ice without getting too personal.

The man made eye contact with the dog. She lowered her head slightly in a submissive gesture, her hind end wiggling as she struggled to restrain her congenial nature. Being more of an introvert, Grayson didn't quite understand the feeling, but he could appreciate it. However alien it might have seemed to him, having a dog was turning out to be an unexpected advantage. It wasn't so much that he didn't want to get to know people; just that he didn't always know how to strike up a conversation. Sooner made that easy just by being herself.

The clerk smiled. "Well, hello, Sooner." Then he looked at Grayson, as if finally remembering his job. "Looking for anything in particular?"

"Dog food," Grayson said.

"What kind?"

"I don't know." Hunter had given him a bag when he took her home. He'd emptied the contents into a plastic bin and tossed the bag before noting what it was. The only reason he knew what to feed the horses was because Loretta had written it down. "What do you have?"

The man—whose nametag said 'Tucker'—gestured for him to follow. "Let me show you."

Grayson wheeled the cart around the corner after him as the man kept talking.

"We got just about everything. Fancy no-grain, limited-ingredient kibble made from duck, wild boar, and even kangaroo for dogs with food sensitivities"—slipping into aisle four, he gestured toward the stacks to his left, then to his right—"and there's the high-protein food the guys down in the hollers feed their hounds. Poor things are skin and bones, but then they do run for hours at a time."

"Oh." Grayson stared at the rows and stacks of food, overwhelmed. "I don't think she has any allergies. But I do want to feed her something healthy."

He turned so he was facing the sacks on the right. Peered at the prices marked beneath. He could buy a week's worth of groceries for himself for what one bag cost. "These seem expensive."

"Because they are." Tucker moved toward them. "Frankly, folks that buy this stuff got more money than brains. Best off just picking something in the middle. If she don't like it, bring it back and I'll give you a refund."

"For an opened bag?"

"Sure. Better that than you driving over to Somerset and shopping at that mega chain store where you save a couple bucks a bag but spend more on everything else."

"Thanks." Grayson wasn't sure if what he said was just a sales pitch. At any rate, Sooner was almost out of food. He studied the bags some more. Had no idea what he was looking for. "What do you recommend?"

Tucker tapped on the end of a bag next to him. "This is what I feed my boys."

Still cost enough to fill his gas tank almost twice, but bartering didn't seem like a possibility. "I'll take that then."

Tucker loaded the sack onto Grayson's cart, then bent down to fawn over Sooner. She curled into a pretzel shape as he scratched at her back.

"When will you be getting some more of that horse feed in the yellow sack again—the one with a picture of the bay and the foal on the front?" Grayson asked, remembering the other reason he'd come here. He'd been in the only aisle with horse feed and hadn't seen it.

"Should be in tomorrow," Tucker said. "I'll give you a sack of the premium feed at the same price to tide you over. Sound okay?"

Grayson hesitated. Loretta's instructions had been specific. He didn't feel comfortable changing things up without her approval, yet he didn't feel like calling her up over such a seemingly trivial matter. He nodded, still a little reluctant, but grateful not to have to pay the extra.

"Say," Grayson began, remembering something Rex Franzen had suggested, "would you happen to know of anyone looking to buy a horse or two? My uncle left me with several, and I'd like them to go to homes where they're going to be well cared for."

"Not at the moment," he answered matter-of-factly.

Disappointment sank Grayson's hopes. Another door closed. With his finances being up in the air, he didn't want to *give* them away, but he was willing to compromise. "I wouldn't ask much."

"Can't say as I do. Now if you had some feeder calves you wanted to sell for FFA, I could hook you up with some folks." Tucker grabbed a sack of horse feed off the display in the main aisle, then added it to Grayson's cart. Before Grayson could start tallying up the damages to his credit card, Tucker walked toward the register. "How many you got?"

"Calves? None." Grayson followed him with the cart.

"Wasn't talking about calves."

"Oh, dogs then? Just this one. And she's not really mine. I'm just watching her for someone while they're in the hospital."

Stepping behind the register, Tucker snorted. "Wasn't talking about dogs, either. I meant horses. How many *horses* you got?"

"Oh. Four. But they aren't mine, either. Well, I guess they are. For now. Otherwise, I wouldn't be selling them, obviously. They belonged to my uncle. He died recently."

"Skip Dalton?" Tucker began ringing the items up.

"Yes, you knew him?"

"Who in this town didn't? He practically paid for my son's college, back when he had a full stable." The brightness faded from his face. "Then he got older. Just like the rest of us, I s'pose. Keep telling myself I should slow down, too, think about retiring. But ol' Skip was a little better off than I am. Nope, I'll be working until the day my ol' ticker stops beating." He thumped the heel of his hand against his chest, then narrowed his eyes at Grayson. "Whatcha got as far as those horses? Just in case anyone asks."

"Only three are available, actually. I'm holding onto one until the lady who's going to take him gets back in town." Which made Grayson start to wonder when that was going to be. She'd told him a general timeframe, but he couldn't hold onto Goliath forever. Or the other horses, for that matter. He gave his phone number to Tucker, just in case, along with a brief description of each horse, and paid.

After putting Sooner in the backseat, he loaded the two bags into his undersized trunk and set the biscuits on the passenger seat. The dog food would last him a while, but not the horse feed. If he had more cargo room, he wouldn't have to make so many trips to town.

Maybe it was time he quit paying on this rental car and buy something more practical.

—o00o—

On the edge of town, Grayson slowed his car as he approached the used automobile lot. Multicolored pennants hung from the lampposts, fluttering in a muggy breeze. Balloons tied to the side mirrors of some of the cars bobbed on their strings. A banner above the street entrance heralded "End of Summer Blowout Sale".

Without making a conscious decision to do so, he pulled into the lot and parked in an empty spot far from the sales building.

Sooner scrambled to her feet in the backseat, her nose practically shoved in Grayson's ear as she panted with excitement.

"Don't get your hopes up," he told her. "Just seeing how far a dollar goes in these parts."

She woofed softly. Windows lowered to let the breeze circulate, he finished his pastries, all three, and savored his coffee. He figured he'd earned the calories, exercising the dog. Sooner whined. He slipped her a few dog biscuits.

Because he expected to be pounced on the moment he opened the door, Grayson stayed in the car, watching. No salesman emerged from the building or walked the lot. If one made a beeline toward him, he was going to start the car up and drive off.

He opened the car door cautiously. A quick survey of the property showed a lot devoid of people. He let Sooner out, then walked with her to the nearest line of cars. None of them seemed practical, not even the bigger ones. Two rows down, he discovered the trucks. He couldn't imagine the gas mileage on any of them was very good, but he needed something with more cargo space. On the end were a few vans. No, not his style. Besides, he didn't intend to start up an airport shuttle or package delivery business.

He moved along to the last row: the SUVs. Designed more like a car in front, but roomier in the back, he could haul a few things in one of these while he was on the farm. He zeroed in on a mid-sized SUV in an attractive metallic red. It was long enough to put a few boards in the back, deep enough to carry as much as a dozen sacks of feed, but not so high off the ground he would've felt like he was driving a bus.

"Seats fold flat on that one."

Grayson spun around to see a man barely in his thirties in navy slacks, a crisp white button-up shirt, and a red tie with stars on it. All he needed was a couple of sparklers and an Uncle Sam hat to look like the Faderville Fourth of July parade grand marshal.

"And lucky for you"—the salesman hit a button on the key fob and pulled open the driver's side door—"this one's fifteen hundred off. But only until tomorrow when the sale ends. Can't believe this beauty hasn't sold yet. One owner, non-smoker. Low miles. Tires are practically brand new." He kicked at one for show, then extended the key to Grayson. "Care to take it for a spin?"

The salesman was doing exactly what he'd hoped to avoid. Grayson backed away a few steps—at the same time, the man stooped forward and put his hand out to Sooner. She lunged forward eagerly, almost jerking Grayson off his feet.

"My, my, but you're a friendly one." The salesman ruffled the fur on top of her head. "Well-mannered, too. What's your name?"

"Sooner," Grayson answered for her.

"Well, hey there, Sooner. Such a pretty dog. And a good dog, too, I bet."

Sooner did a happy dance. She was enjoying this jaunt about town, meeting so many people.

Then the salesman stood up. "You can take the dog along, of course."

Which hadn't even been on Grayson's mind. "Oh. I'm just looking. Really. Don't want to waste your time."

"I understand, I understand. But please, don't ever feel like you're imposing." Pulling a business card from his back pocket, he smiled with a set of teeth so unnaturally pearly white they practically glowed. "Feel free to stop by whenever you want, even if it's to admire the rims on our newest additions to the lot—or to just have a cup of coffee and chat. We're open nine to nine daily. If I'm not here, one of my business partners will be. Gotta spend some time with the family. And sleep."

Grayson glanced at the card before tucking it in his own back pocket. Mac Kendrick was the man's name. Somehow, it suited him. He had the lean muscular look of a high school quarterback now grown but still lifting weights to maintain his physique. Not the sort of guy who would beat someone up in an alleyway, but the kind who would use his muscle to help move a neighbor's furniture or change a tractor tire. When he'd pulled in here, he'd been reluctant to speak with a salesman. Hadn't wanted to at all. But somehow, Mac's manner had put him at ease. Even with the sales pitch.

Or maybe it had everything to do with the dog. She was proving to be a good judge of people.

Grayson stuck out his hand to shake Mac's. "Appreciate the offer, but again... just looking."

"I do that myself sometimes. You have a good one...?" He let the words trail away into a question.

"Grayson. Grayson Darling." And with that, Grayson turned and started back toward his car. Halfway there he paused, turned around. Mac was still there, buffing dirt specks from the hood of the SUV with a handkerchief.

"Say, just thinking, but..." Grayson walked back toward him. "If it's still here a few days from now, would you consider, I don't know, maybe twenty-five hundred less?"

Mac gritted his teeth, drew in his breath through his nose. After a pause, he said, "I don't know if I can go that low." Then he rubbed his chin. "I'd have to ask the manager… He might say no."

Grayson nodded. "Okay, just figured I'd ask."

But the two men understood they'd struck a deal. They would meet in the middle. That was, if no one else was gullible enough to pay sticker price before then.

—o0Oo—

Half a mile from home, Grayson saw a ragged line of runners slogging up over a distant hill, coming in his direction. He could tell by their youthful build they must be the members of the high school cross country team. The same group he'd seen his first day in Faderville.

A pool of sweat dampening the back of his shirt, Grayson cranked the fan up on his AC. He glanced at the clock on his dashboard to see it was mid afternoon. Had he really spent so much time in town, talking to strangers? Then again, they weren't entirely strangers anymore. He knew their names, and they knew his.

But it had all started with the dog. They'd asked *her* name and spoken to her first. Which made Grayson wonder—if he hadn't had the dog, would they have been so friendly toward just him?

He shook the notion off. It wasn't like he, Grayson, was *un*friendly. He talked to people all the time back in New York. Every day. At work. When he ordered food. If he needed the building custodian to fix something in his apartment…

Basically, when he had to. Which suddenly made him feel… like something here was different. Or maybe *he* was different.

These connections he was forming with people, however small—with Loretta, Rex, and all the other people he'd met today—were like pieces of a jigsaw puzzle, all laid out on a table, waiting to be assembled. He wasn't exactly sure just yet where he fit in, or if he even did. Then again, maybe he was only grabbing at straws. Trying to justify his poor luck at being stuck here. And yet, the cloud that had hovered over him when he first arrived in Faderville had long since gone. Not like a storm blown abruptly away on strong winds. But gradually. Like a fog dissipated by the barest of breezes and a rising sun.

As he drove toward the oncoming runners, lithe and effortless as he'd once been, he took in the view around him—the rolling hills a hundred shades of green, the contentedly grazing cows, the weathered barns with their patched roofs, and the well cared for but modest homes. He saw it so differently now. Saw the tranquility. The simplicity. The beauty of it all.

Why had he not seen it before?

There was no denying that his life had changed drastically. He no longer had his work to bury himself in. Didn't pay attention to the clock or even what day of the week it was. Hadn't thought of sending out his resume in… two weeks? Three? A month? He almost asked himself what he'd been doing all that time, but he recalled clearly: mending the fence, painting outbuildings and shutters, sorting through his uncle's belongings, pulling weeds, mowing, grooming the horses, and training Sooner.

A warmth circled inside his ear. It took a moment for him to realize Sooner's muzzle was resting on his shoulder, her breath brushing across his neck, tickling his ear. He smiled fondly. All those people today—they'd reached out to him because of a dog. *This* dog.

Still, it was like there was something missing. Some piece that would make it all—the farm, the dog, the people of the town—come together in some meaningful way.

As the runners came close, he slowed down. Sooner scurried over to press her face against the opposite window to get a better view, her body quivering in excitement. She whimpered.

"Later, okay, girl? We'll run when it cools off a bit." Not that it would much. But he wasn't about to take her out this time of day.

Six runners glided past in a tight pack as the road leveled out.

Then came the seventh, eighth, ninth, tenth… Mostly boys, but some girls, too. A small gap. Three more. Four girls not far behind, chatting in between breaths as they ran. A few more, each running alone. Some struggling slightly, but working hard. Their faces set with determination, focus, the agony of exhaustion.

Grayson remembered all those things. Envied them their young bones and strong muscles, their fluid joints. Remembered the pounding of his heart. The rhythm of his breathing. The steady cadence of his stride. The intense effort of running hard. The joy of having run fast.

He missed it all. The burning muscles. The drain of energy. Even the sweating.

"Tonight," he said as much to himself as to the dog. "We'll run tonight. The whole way."

And as they ran, maybe he'd find that thing that was missing. Or not. Because he wasn't even remotely sure what 'it' was, let alone where 'it' might be.

—o00o—

The restaurant was busy when Grayson arrived, but not overcrowded. He'd driven home to drop off his purchases and the dog, then returned to town for an early supper. A relic from olden days, the restaurant resembled a general store, both inside and out. A long covered porch bedecked with rocking chairs stood at the front entrance. Just inside, behind the counter on which the cash register sat, were rows of shelves selling nostalgic items, handmade goods, and old-fashioned candy.

Becca spotted him before the hostess could take his name. After greeting him like an old friend and then fetching her husband, Hank, from the kitchen to meet Grayson, she showed him to a table and suggested the daily special: breaded pork chops with apple-cranberry-pecan stuffing and green beans with bacon and pearl onions. It was cheaper than the fried chicken platter, so he took her up on it. He didn't regret his impulsivity. The portion size was so ample he was satisfyingly full two-thirds into it. Still, he ate, unwilling to let one delectable bite go unappreciated. It was as good as—no better—than anything he'd ever had in New York City.

As he was cornering the last juicy lump of his apple dumpling, Becca came around. Small talk turned to business, and they spent the next hour hashing out a viable business plan to grow her and her husband's client base. Grayson was just as enthusiastic about the restaurant's potential as Becca was. He may have even offered his accounting and tax services. He quoted her a modest fee far below what he was used to getting paid, but it gave him enormous satisfaction to know he was helping little Claire's parents on the path to a brighter future.

A year ago, he'd primarily known his clients as figures on pieces of paper: bank statements and credit ratings and income tax returns. But today, for the first time, he'd seen what those numbers meant and envisioned what they could lead to. He wasn't just dealing with numbers. He was affecting lives.

The shift in his perspective was seismic. The rewards were limitless.

Grayson took the dog on a run that night—a whole mile, nonstop—and went to bed exhausted and content. Two days later, because he didn't want to seem overly eager, he returned to town for cream puffs and coffee and more bags of horse feed. His last stop was at the car dealer's. After some requisite haggling and a modest down payment, he bought himself that SUV. There was even room for Sooner to stretch out on the second-row bench seat for a short nap on the way home.

Now he just had to figure out how to swing the monthly payments with his depleted savings, not to mention how he was going to return the rental car. Both were bigger problems than he wanted to think about. So he didn't. Instead, he pondered how freeing it was to be impulsive—and how utterly frightening.

When that became too much to bear, he thought about all the new people he'd met recently and how he was getting to know them. People who might possibly become friends. If he stuck around long enough.

In the meantime, he needed to start running with the dog more regularly. He had to come up with a training plan that would ramp up gradually, so he wouldn't overdo it. There were no championships or personal records to aim for. The goal—in the beginning, anyway—was simply to get fit. And to tire the dog out. But Grayson was pretty sure he might never reach that last goal.

chapter 22

Sooner

Our runs, at first, had been short. Painfully slow. With a lot of huffing and stopping and Grayson bending over to rub at his knee. He tired so easily. When we reached the trees, he'd rest, offer me water, wait a while. Then we'd go back. Slower and more haltingly than before. I nearly died of frustration.

And yet, it was the most wonderful thing I had ever done—and I had done a lot of fabulously exciting and fun things during my life before Grayson. But the things I'd done with Brandy always came with some sort of... expectation. A certain way of doing things, rules I was never wholly privy to. Whether it was rally, obedience, or agility, the order of obstacles and exercises changed. The places we did them changed. The noises and sights were an ever-present distraction I was never allowed to explore and was expected not to react to. Being a good dog meant being an obedient dog, even when I was worried about whether I would get my part right. Loyalty and willingness were part of my DNA. But the pressure and stress of competing were a constant.

I'd loved Brandy more than life, and I'd lived to please her. But it wasn't until my life with Grayson began that I remembered what it was like to be a puppy again and how wonderful it could be to just... *be*.

That was why I loved running with Grayson so much. The joy was in the doing. Even if I had to slow down and be patient for him. I suspected he'd either suffered some terrible injury in the past or been born with a weakness in that one knee. And so I tempered my enthusiasm and ran slower out of sympathy for him. In the days after Brandy was lost to me, I had nearly died. But in surviving, I had grown more resilient. Somehow, at some time, life had knocked Grayson down hard, perhaps more than once. Taught him the fight could not be won. It was up to me, in this one small way, to show him otherwise.

So I learned to wait for him, to encourage him, to reward his efforts with wags and licks and occasional yips of joy. Sometimes the training of a human was not for the dog's benefit, but for our person. We were selfless that way. The pack was only as strong as its weakest member.

And that was what Grayson and I were now—a pack. A pair. A duo. A team. Partners. It didn't matter so much who was in charge. Just that we were together. Because being alone was not something I ever wanted to be again. I sensed it hadn't suited Grayson well, either.

Day by day, our runs became longer, less broken up. We would rise at first light or head off as the sun was sinking to avoid the heat of the day. I knew the shoes he put on and the clothes he wore when he was preparing to run. Sometimes, I'd hurry things along by bringing him my leash and then, smiling at me, he'd clip it on and we'd head out the door.

Grayson's first steps were always stiff and plodding, just like the heavy striking of Goliath's massive hooves on packed dirt. By the time we reached the crest above the gulley where the little creek ran, he would loosen up. While the songbirds announced the break of day, we trotted through dew-laden grass and drew crisp air into hungry lungs. Moisture soaked my legs and belly, but it kept me cool. I went gently through the shallow creek, slowing to a walk so Grayson wouldn't stumble on the slippery stones. I always thought he was overly cautious, but then, he only had two feet to stand on, not four.

To my surprise one day, we went beyond the shady grove to circle around the far pasture before turning back. The next day, we joined the creek farther up and ran beside it for a while. Then the day after that, we went through a rusty gate Grayson had replaced the latch on a few days earlier and over a hill bigger than any we had in our own fields. At the top of that hill, we paused for the first time on our run and gazed out at a sky full of gathering clouds. As a blustery breeze tickled my whiskers, I lifted my nose and sniffed. Dark clouds were gathering on the horizon. There was rain coming, but for now, we were dry.

Sinking to the earth, Grayson stretched his legs out. I sat at his side, surveying our kingdom like lions atop the mountain. Gray morning light glistened off the water in the twisting creek far, far below. We watched in silence. He didn't give me commands; I didn't demand his attention. We were simply in each other's presence. Two parts of a whole. As if it had always been that way.

"None of this is what I planned." Leaning back, Grayson gazed up at the sky, his fingers laced together on his chest. "I thought Fee and I would be married forever. That we'd hit some magical age and retire somewhere warm but not too wet, like California or Arizona. I just wanted to be comfortable. To not have to worry about money. So I let that fear drive me while I took Fee for granted. I suppose she was right when she asked me when I was going to start really living. I wasn't even sure what that meant. I suppose I figured if I wasn't hurting anybody, if I was just being a good law-abiding, tax-paying citizen, then that was all I had to do. Now I can see that maybe that wasn't enough. Guess I had to get away from that life to see it clearly."

He closed his eyes. When he didn't move for a while, I lay beside him and rested my chin between my paws. Wind rustled the grass on the hills.

Then Grayson spoke again, lowly. "I wasn't making the world a worse place—but I wasn't making it any better, either." He turned his gaze on me, his breathing deep and even. "No, this is not what I planned at all. It's so much less and yet... so much more. Thanks for making me feel important every day, Sooner." He smiled. "And for saving my life. You taught me to appreciate what is, instead of toiling away on what ought to be. Love you, girl. Just like you are."

I licked his whole face. I loved him, too. Faults and all.

Plus, he gave me peanut butter.

Down below, the horses grazed lazily. Around them, the grass undulated in a sea of green. Across the road in the woods, wind shook the leaves on their branches. A cloud of blackbirds burst upward from the treetops, a scribble of dark crescents against a darkening sky. They moved as one above the pasture, swooping and turning, until they settled atop the roof of the barn, their raucous caws piercing the air.

I could have sat there all day... except I wanted to run again. Standing, I nudged Grayson in the shoulder. He, evidently, was not so inspired. Within minutes, he was asleep.

Not one to defy him—not anymore, anyway—I slept, too. One eye open, of course. Someone had to watch for trouble.

—o00o—

Plop... Plop. Plop, plop...

I smelled it before I even opened my eyes. Raindrops pattered upon the ground, their rhythm rising to a steady percussion. I lifted my nose, inhaled, squinted against the assault. There was a chill in the air that had not been there this morning.

I nudged Grayson. Did it again more insistently. Grumbling, he rolled onto his back and gazed at me with one eye open.

Plop, plop, plop-plop-plop.

I listened closely, but heard nothing beyond the drip of rain, didn't feel the sky shake. No, it wasn't that kind of rain. Not a summer storm that rolled in fiercely, bellowing thunder and throwing bolts of terrifying light. It was the kind of rain that might go on for days. The kind that signified a change in the seasons. The return of autumn, the prelude to winter. I didn't like the cold—except for snow, which was magical—but winter did mean more time inside together. Which was a good thing.

Standing to stretch, Grayson tugged the zipper of his jacket up higher. "Race you back to the house, Sooner?"

I waited for him. To pick up the end of my leash. To lead me down the hill. To go back home before we were both soaked and frozen.

Instead, he unclipped my leash. Folding it up, he tucked it inside the waistband of his sweatpants. "Go on. You know the way."

This was some sort of trick. A test.

He waved an arm toward the house. Still, I waited. I felt the need to make sure he got home safely and remembered the way, even though it wasn't all that far. He was a human, after all. As far as I knew, they couldn't follow a scent trail to save their lives.

Sighing, he shook his head and started down the hill. A cautious shuffle at first, but he eventually picked up steam as I followed. Then the ground flattened out and he was pushing the pace, his arms pumping, his knees driving uncharacteristically high. While neither graceful nor fast, he was as near to sprinting as I'd ever seen. He even looked happy, although every now and then, he'd land in a shallow hole, his knee twisting, and a grimace would flash across his face. But still, he pushed on.

It was a glorious feeling to run hard beside him as a cool rain fell. Down the hill. Up another. Across the creek. Past the horses.

When we turned onto the final stretch of our path not far from the farthest corner of the horse stables, I spied a furry creature ambling from beneath the board fence. It was mostly black with a little white and a big bushy tail that waved like a banner above its back. Ugliest cat I'd ever seen, but I knew it didn't belong here and I intended to run it off with a warning it wouldn't forget.

So I took off at a dead sprint, head low, legs churning as I left Grayson behind. Laughing, he urged me on. "That's it, girl. Go! Meet you on the porch."

He must've seen the cat and wanted me to do my job.

Encouraged, I picked up even more speed. But I stayed quiet, not wanting to startle the intruder. Cats could be almost as quick as dogs and were often more agile. Last thing I wanted was for that cat to hear me coming and scramble up a tree to safety. If I could, I'd nip it in the tail so it never returned.

I was bearing down on the animal when I heard Grayson screech. "Sooner, no! Leave it! Noooooo!"

Too late. It saw me. And turned, flicking its back end in my direction, tail straight up.

That was when I discovered it was no cat. Because not only were cats not that needle-nosed and ugly, they didn't smell *that* bad.

I had only a fraction of a second to turn my face away as the vapors it released hit my eyeballs and were sucked into my nostrils. I skidded, tumbled, and rolled sideways. Didn't come to a stop until my ribs slammed against the planks of the barn. Air whooshed from my lungs.

Momentarily stunned, I blinked away the vapors that stung my eyes. When I tried to draw air back in, the smell was so repulsive I nearly choked. Saliva filled my mouth. I coughed, then retched. Great globs of foamy drool dripped from my tongue.

SAY WHEN

The... whatever it was, shook its tail one last time, then began to scurry away. Twin strips of white ran from the top of its head down the length of its back to the tip of its fringed tail, a harbinger of its noxious aroma.

As it scampered down the lane, the urge to pursue it well off the property flared in me, but quickly dimmed. I wanted nothing to do with its kind. Ever again.

But I couldn't allow it to leave without letting it think I'd rip it to shreds if it ever returned. So, I scrambled to my feet and barked the most ferocious string of barks I had ever barked.

Go away! Go far, far away! And don't you dare ever come back! Or I will kill you! Dead! Dead, dead, dead, dead!

Human feet plodded to a halt. "Sooner, you did not—"

I whipped around to see Grayson standing by the end of the barn, a sour expression on his face. His hands flew up to cover his mouth and nose. "Oh, no way," he grumbled. "You *did*. I can't believe you just got skunked."

Proud I had chased away the unwanted vermin, I began to trot in his direction, eager for his praise.

"No!" Spinning, he ran back a few steps the way he'd come. Then, his face turned away, he flailed his hands at me. "Stay right where you are. Don't come any closer. Just... stay."

I paused in my tracks, confused. He didn't want me near him. Had I not done right in chasing that *thing* away before it could throw its stink on Grayson? I hadn't known it when I charged at it, but I'd sacrificed my own wellbeing for him. Taken the hit. I thought I was protecting the farm.

Rain dripped softly from filamentous clouds, coloring the world a watery gray. Whimpering, I folded to the ground. Slunk on my belly toward him. He was unhappy with me. I wanted to make it up to him.

Eyes wide, voice stern, he pointed at me. "Stay!"

Ashamed, I halted. The stench was horrible. I couldn't even stand myself. I hadn't meant to do anything bad. Hadn't known...

I watched him hurry into the house, the inside front of his jacket pulled up to cover his mouth. Rain drizzled down, its misery seeping deep into my heart. I'd disappointed him. It was almost more than I could bear.

The horses eyed me from behind their fence, Goliath staring down that long, dark nose at me, haughty and judgmental. Then he stomped a giant hoof, swished his tail, turned, and trotted away, the presentation of his broad rump a statement in itself. The rest of the horses followed suit. All except Persephone, the quiet, pensive chestnut who always kept her distance. She seemed to understand my hurt and sense I'd gotten myself in some sort of unenviable predicament.

We studied each other for a while through the dreary veil of rain. I wanted to go to her, touch noses, make a truce, one that said I will not harm you, or you me. A friendship, of sorts. But I knew if I went so much as halfway, she would turn tail and run from me, just as Grayson had done.

Then Clifford nickered at her. Just like that, she turned and joined the others.

Out of the corner of my eye, I saw Grayson striding across the yard. He wore a bandana covering his mouth and tied at the back of his head and a pair of goggles that he used when cutting wood. On his hands were rubber gloves that reached up to his elbows. In one, he carried a trash bag filled with something and in the other... a bottle of dish soap.

I knew what this meant—a bath. And there was nothing I hated more than a bath. Except the blow dryer. I was always sure that contraption was going to strip the fur from my flesh.

The urge to run gripped me. But I knew if I tried to escape, Grayson would be mad at me. Madder than he already was.

Avoiding me at first, he went into the stables. When he came back out a minute later, it was without the bag. As he marched at me, I could sense the anger in his steps.

I didn't budge. Not one inch. Just waited as he came, clipped my leash on, and led me to the hose that stretched to the horses' water trough. He tied the end of the leash to the fence. There I stood, awaiting my punishment.

My fur was already damp from the rain, but when the water from the hose hit my skin, I shuddered from the cold blast. The whole time I suffered through the humiliation, Grayson was muttering under his breath. Nothing about his touch was kind or even business-like. It was gruff and hurried.

"Damn it, Sooner. Damn it, damn it, damn it." He coughed. Water ran from his eyes. He tried blinking it away, but they only watered more. "Don't you know what a skunk is, for Pete's sake? That big white stripe is a warning flag, okay? It means 'stay the *hell* away'. Got it?"

The rain grew heavier, steadier. Grayson worked the suds into my fur. He was careful around my eyes, but the soap still ran into them, an even sharper sting on top of the persisting duller one. Between the suds running into my eyes, the rain, and an itch that seemed to stretch from the tip of my nose to the nub of my tail, I couldn't hold off any longer.

I shook.

Mounds and dabs of soap bubbles splattered everywhere—including on Grayson. Cursing, he rubbed his face against his upper arm, then went back to working the suds in, more vigorously than before. When he seemed satisfied to have covered every inch of me in bubbles, he rinsed me off. At some point I thought my torture was nearly finished, but then he soaped me up and rinsed me twice more.

I had never been so wet, cold, and miserable in my entire life.

Grayson looked pretty wretched, too. As if at that particular moment, he regretted ever taking me in.

Then, without another word, he untied my leash and led me to the same stable where he'd first found me. Once inside there, he shut the door and took towel after towel from the trash bag he'd carried outside. He rubbed me dry—or as near to dry as he could manage. In the corner of the stall, he'd spread a low mound of straw and put a blanket on top of it.

"You're staying here until I can get the supplies to properly de-skunk you." There was disappointment in his voice. "And until you air out some more. Sorry about your luck, but there's no way you're coming in the house smelling like you are."

Then he went. The weight of my loneliness settled on me.

A short while later, he put the horses in their stalls, brought me some food and water, and left again quickly, no words of comfort or kindness, just a scowl.

I turned in circles until I found just the right spot, then lay down on my blanket. In the stall across from me, Persephone nickered to let me know she was nearby. I whimpered in reply. She rattled the metal handle of her water bucket. In the next stall, Goliath tapped lightly at the dirt floor with a hoof. In time, the horses grew quiet and night fell. This time as I drifted off to sleep, I dreamed not of Brandy, but of Grayson, running beside me.

If I'd thought a bath was the worse punishment I could ever receive, I was wrong. What was worse was not being with Grayson, even though I understood why he wouldn't want me in the house like I was. Still, no dog should ever be without their person—

Yes, that was what he was. *My* person. He may not have been perfect, but he was all mine.

I wanted to run with him every day. Sleep beside him every night. Ride around in the car with him on errands. Take naps on the hilltop next to him. Eat the bits of sandwich he didn't want. Chase the squirrels away when he was out working in the yard. I loved it when he talked to me and even when he said nothing at all.

SAY WHEN

He'd taught me that *just being* was a good and wonderful thing. That when I sat there quietly and took the world in, I noticed things I never would have if I were busily headed somewhere.

And maybe, just maybe, I'd taught him a few things, too.

chapter 23

Sooner

Four sleeps and two more baths. That was how much time went by before Grayson allowed me back in the house. Even then, he confined me to the kitchen. I stayed behind the gate, despite the fact I could have gone over it easily now if I'd wanted to. I didn't want to be relegated to the crate, or worse—banished to the stall again. While I respected the horses, they were their own pack, not mine.

During the week following what Grayson came to refer to as 'The Great Skunking,' it did nothing but rain. Every day. Every night. For hours on end. Even when rain didn't fall from the clouds, it dripped from the tree leaves, which were now changing colors and starting to fall to the ground. It filled the ditches and made the creek run over its banks. The ground was soggy. The air, Grayson's bedding, and even my fur were damp. The sky was so gray it was hard to tell when daytime ended and night began. The sun had gone into hiding, taking its light and warmth with it.

We didn't go outside to run. Grayson liked being wet even less than I did. So we stayed inside. Doing nothing. Which, for a day, was fine. But a day stretched into two, then three, then four… until I lost count.

Whenever it was time for Grayson to do his chores outside, he'd suit up in a rain jacket and pants and go to the front door—without me.

After several times of this, I grew agitated and rushed to the gate. I'd been sequestered in the kitchen ever since The Great Skunking. He only joined me when it was time for meals or he needed a drink. Otherwise, I was all by myself. The solitude was almost unbearable. I hadn't realized until then all the interesting things humans did. Simply watching them and trying to make sense of it was highly entertaining.

Take me, I barked. *Take me with you!*

"Sooner, stop," he commanded tersely as he zipped up his jacket. "No bark."

I barked some more. *I'm bored. Bored, bored, bored!*

I didn't like being ignored. Didn't like being left out of the excitement. Grayson needed me to look after him. He needed my company. What if another wild animal came onto the property? What if a stranger showed up? What if he fell and got hurt? Or just needed to talk?

"I said no! Now stop." He flipped his hood up, then pulled the drawstring tight. "You'd get muddy if you went out to the barn. Besides, every time you get wet, you stink again. Doc Hunter said that could go on for months. So I'm trying to keep you as dry as possible, so maybe, eventually, you can sleep in the bedroom again."

Bedroom! I barked. *Yes, bedroom. Tonight?*

Scowling, he slammed the door behind him. How rude.

Hey! You forgot me! Take me with you! Come. Back. Here. Now.

I barked and barked and barked and barked. He had to have heard me. Because he eventually *did* come back. Although he didn't look happy.

He unzipped his jacket. Pulled off his boots. Stepped out of his pants. Never breaking his glare at me.

"I heard you the entire time I was out in the barn," he said. "I got the message, loud and clear."

I wagged my hind end. Flashed my most charismatic grin. Sneezed adoringly and dipped my chest in a bow.

Play? I woofed softly.

He stood there, fists clenched, nostrils flaring.

This was going to take some convincing. All this rain was putting Grayson in a foul mood.

I spun around, searching for a ball, a squeaky, even a leash we could play tug with. Anything to lift his spirits. But he'd collected all the toys earlier in the day and stuffed them in a basket, which he put in the living room, saying, "You're wearing them all out, Sooner. And I'm tired of tripping over them every time I come in here."

I had nothing to offer him. No toys. No sticks. Not even a rock he could toss for me. Nothing, except—

A dish towel hung temptingly from a drawer pull. After grabbing it, I ran back to the gate. Even though he always discouraged it, I put my feet up on top of the gate so he could see I had something for him.

His brow furrowed. I wasn't sure what that meant. When he didn't move from where he stood, I went in search of something else. This time, I took a plastic bottle from the recycling bin. When I clamped my teeth on it, it made a wonderful crinkling sound. I returned to the gate, raised myself up, and crunched the bottle. Loudly. Several times.

The furrow disappeared from his brow. He regarded me curiously.

How could he not like the bottle? All this time, he was throwing away perfectly good toys I could've chewed on or we could've played fetch with. Clearly, he wasn't getting my point.

Running out of options, I lowered myself, searched again. Then I saw it—brightly colored and perfectly round.

I ran to the far end of the kitchen, balanced on my hind legs, and, without setting my feet on the counter, took an orange from the fruit basket.

Before I got to the gate, Grayson burst out laughing.

"Hold on." He went into the living room where he rummaged around in the toy basket. Then he brought my tennis ball. The one with the fraying fuzz and the bald spot and the grass stains.

And for a gloriously long time, we played ball in the kitchen. He rolled it under the table legs and chairs. Bounced it off the cabinets. Landed it in the recycling bin. We played the 'Wait' game where I couldn't take it until he said 'Okay!' and the 'Find it' game where he placed it under one of three upside-down plastic bowls, shuffled them around, and told me to find the ball. They were easy games, but I always teased him, pretending not to want to wait or taking my time to show where the ball was. I had to let him think he was winning sometimes, for his own benefit. Otherwise, he might get discouraged and not want to play anymore.

When the games grew wearisome for us both, I showed him my tricks. He caught on more easily this time, but he sometimes gave each move a different name than I was accustomed to. Once he repeated them a few times, I responded to his unfamiliar words. 'Say your prayers' became 'You should be ashamed,' and 'Circle left' or 'Circle right' became 'Spin'. Grayson didn't care which way I turned, just that I did. It wasn't that Grayson couldn't learn, it was just that he was different from Brandy.

We understood each other now—well enough, anyway—and that made *everything* better.

—oOOo—

One day, after he'd afforded me more freedom to move about the house again, the clouds cleared and the sun rose strong and bold.

There was still a chill in the air, but it was the crisp cold of autumn and not yet the biting cold of winter.

When I heard the jingle from the snap of my leash, my excitement was nearly uncontrollable. I jumped up and down in place in front of Grayson. I'd learned, quite abruptly one day, not to jump *on* him when he jerked his knee reflexively upward to block me.

"Whoa there, you crazy kangaroo." He laughed. "I know you know what the leash means, but I can't get it on you if you won't be still. Now, sit!"

I sat as he snapped my leash on. When we got outside, I expected to follow our usual path and started that way, but he tugged me toward the car and put me in the back. I didn't quite understand. Grayson had his running clothes and shoes on. He never wore both at the same time unless that was what we were going to do. Maybe we were going to the feed store to see Tucker, or to get donuts from Gertie, or stopping at Becca's restaurant so I could lick the jelly from Claire's chin and so Grayson could eat some apple pie and sneak me a few French fries. None of those things were equal to running, but they were exciting, too.

At any rate, the rain had stopped and we were going *somewhere*. Being stuck inside with Grayson hadn't turned out as awful as it could've been, but I needed to be outside to stretch my legs.

Grayson drove on roads I had never seen. There were houses and hills and barns and wooded places unfamiliar to me. That in itself was intriguing. I stayed alert, barking at a field of cows as we passed to make Grayson aware of the huge beasts. It was my job to keep them at bay and ensure Grayson was safe. It was always good for a dog to sound as fearsome and big as possible—that way if we met any dangerous creatures or strangers who might do our people harm, they would be warned of our intent to protect at all costs. My duty as a dog was to guard my person. One of many duties, but perhaps the most important. I would always keep him safe and be his source of comfort.

The car slowed, turned. We were pulling into a… a park?
Yes! A park, a park, a park!

Woods surrounded wide grassy areas and trails led into and through them. Brandy had taken me to parks many times. Sometimes we would practice our obedience exercises with 'distractions'. Squirrels were an unfair diversion. They were annoying and should always be dealt with immediately. At other times, we just took long walks through the woods. She would put me on a longer leash, and always kept me on it to be considerate of other dogs and because, well, squirrels. I couldn't be held accountable for my disobedience if one of those pesky rodents zigzagged across my path, dashed up a tree, and then clung there upside down, taunting me with its obnoxious chatter.

After Grayson let me out of the car, I scanned the area. Birds flitted from tree to ground and back again, but no squirrels dared show themselves. Perhaps some other dog had come before me and justifiably dispatched of the nuisances.

Grayson took an impossibly long time tying his shoes. I watched intently, not because I was interested in what he was doing, but because I couldn't help but wonder why humans bothered with them at all. Were their feet not made for running, just like mine? I'd seen young children running barefoot in the park, but after a certain age, the practice seemed to be discouraged.

Finally, Grayson started jogging toward one of the paths. I paid close attention to his pace, adjusting my position as he labored up a short hill and then sped up slightly on the downward side of it. The trees closed in around us, the woods dense on either side. The path, however, was wide and while fairly smooth, the occasional root or rock had to be avoided. Grayson stepped carefully at first, but in time, his stride evened out as he learned to navigate obstacles with ease.

A fallen tree blocked the path ahead. Grayson slowed only slightly, gathering himself at the last moment as he told me, "Over!" In unison, we jumped over the log, both landing deftly on the other side before continuing.

Lower and lower the path went, the sound of rushing water growing gradually louder. The scent of greenery and damp earth mingled with the decay of fallen leaves and rotting wood. Here and there, I smelled traces of rabbits and birds, raccoons, and yes, squirrels. I heard some of the creatures rustling through the underbrush or scrabbling amongst the limbs high above, but I kept my eyes on the path and the swing of Grayson's feet next to mine.

I glanced up at Grayson's face as we ran, seeing a happiness that hadn't been there when I first met him. When had he changed? I couldn't be sure, but it had been a gradual thing.

We ran in perfect sync, our paces matched, his stride becoming faster and smoother. We were a matched pair. Partners. A team. It made me happy because it made *him* happy.

For a time, we went along a shallow river. Sunlight glinted on its surface. The path eventually opened to meet the river at a broad pebbly shore. Water swirled in eddies around scattered rocks, lapping at the ragged banks.

Grayson bent over to catch his breath. Thirsty, I pulled toward the water.

A lone runner dashed along the path, gliding lightly, arms churning in an unbroken rhythm. His dark shoulder-length mane flowed behind him. He never turned his head to look at Grayson and me down by the water. Just stared ahead at the path before him, secure in his zone. Moments later, he was a fading blur of motion.

"Go on." Grayson unclipped my leash. "Get a drink. Cool your feet off."

Wading out into the cool water, I took a deep drink. When I'd had my fill, I turned back to Grayson. He had a stick in his hand.

Throw it! Throw it! I begged.

"Fetch, Sooner!" He tossed it into the water, not far from me.

The stick arced low and landed in a shallow area with a *plop*, then bobbed at the surface. Bounding to it, I clamped my mouth on it before the current could carry it away. Over and over, he threw the stick. Again and again, I brought it back. I was no dummy. This was his way of tiring me out in hopes of being better able to keep up with me on the uphill return of our run.

It wasn't until an entire crew of runners appeared on the path in the direction we'd been heading that he stopped throwing the stick. He patted his leg. "Sooner, come."

I trotted obediently to him, then let him clip my leash back on.

The runners, five of them, slowed as their leader veered off the path and swung toward us.

"Hey, cool dog," the leader said. Like the rest of them, he was lean and long-legged, not quite a man, no longer a boy. His skin was a golden brown, his hair black and sleek. He studied Grayson. "Does he run with you?"

Grayson nodded. "She. Yes, she does."

"Ah, sorry. Couldn't tell with all the fur. That's cool."

"Today's our first three-miler." Grayson patted my head. "Dog's doing great, but I needed a break."

"Yeah, man. We hear you," another one said. He and the boy-man beside him laughed. "Coach sent us out for ten. Ought to be a taper week, but seems like we're training right through this race."

"Taper?" Grayson perked. "Is it post-season already? Big meet coming up?"

"Naw, not this week," their leader said. His eyes were so brown they were almost black. He walked closer, crouched, and extended his hand. I sniffed his fingers, which smelled of sweat and dirt. He smiled at me. I could tell he was a good person. "Just league. Should be a breeze, but Somerset has a couple of beasts."

"When's state?" Grayson asked.

"Beginning of next month," the leader said.

"You're assuming we'll get there?" one of them said from the rear of the group.

The boy beside him elbowed his ribs. "We're doing it for Tervo, remember?"

"Right. For Tervo."

A cloud fell over them all. Their leader dropped his gaze to the ground somberly. I licked his fingers, trying to provide comfort, but he seemed not to notice.

Finally, Grayson broke the silence. "So, you've got a shot at state, do you? What kind of times are your top five running?"

The leader shrugged, stood. "We have seven under eighteen."

"You're full of it, Cruz," the boy in the rear said, stepping forward. "Say it like it is." He wiped the sweat from his forehead, then nodded a hello at Grayson. "Cruz here runs high fifteens without anyone on his tail. Me and Dusty are in the low sixteens. Got three other guys can do seventeens, easy. Keen's gonna crack eighteen any time now. Then there's Mateo." He nodded toward the path ahead on which the lone runner had gone minutes before. "He has superpowers."

Several of them nodded.

"Won't matter if we can't put it all together on the same day," another said.

Grayson had an excited air about him. "State's coming up, huh? Maybe I'll come and watch."

"You got a kid at the high school?" Cruz asked.

"No, I don't."

"Then why come? Nobody comes to watch some skinny dudes traipse through the woods. I mean, we've got the best record of any sports team in the school, yet we get no recognition. Zero. Folks think we run just 'cause we're afraid of getting flattened in football."

"We are," a shorter boy off to the side joked. They all laughed.

"At least those big galoots can't catch us," another added.

Cruz nodded. "Yeah, they just corner us in the locker room, then beat the snot out of us when no one's watching."

"It was that way in my day, too," Grayson said. "I used to be… I *am* a runner. I went to state when I was your age."

"Oh yeah? Cool." Cruz lifted his chin. "How'd you do?"

Grayson opened his mouth, but nothing came out for a breath or two. He glanced down at his shoes, splattered with mud, then off into the tangle of trees. "I won."

"State? You *won* the state meet?"

"It was a long time ago." Grayson shrugged. "Another life, practically."

The boys drew in closer, regarding Grayson with admiration. They asked his name, barraging him with other questions as they took turns petting me.

"Did you get scholarship offers? A full ride?"

"Where'd you go to college?"

"How many miles a week did you run in high school?"

"Seventy, eighty miles? A hundred? More?"

He gave short answers, as if he were uncomfortable with the attention. But he answered them all, until—

"Did you run all four years at Bowerman? Was your team good?"

His face drooped. He looked back up the path the way we'd come. For the longest time, I thought he was done, that he was going to say goodbye and leave. I didn't want to go right away. As much as I wanted to run more, I was also enjoying the attention. Living on the farm now, I didn't get to meet many people except when we went into town on errands.

"I had an accident," Grayson said flatly, "just before the start of my senior year. Got hurt pretty bad. Haven't run since, until a few weeks ago. Another one of my teammates…" Reeling me in closer, he stepped back from the group. "I should probably go. Nice meeting you guys. Just… be careful out on the roads. Some drivers don't pay attention."

"Sure, man. Thanks," Cruz said. He turned to his teammates. "So how far ahead do you think Mateo was this time? That guy's a freak of nature."

"You just wish you were him," someone in the back said. Then in unison, they all turned and took off running.

As Grayson and I started back the uphill path, one of the boys called over his shoulder, "Hey, if you come to the state meet, look us up!"

Grayson lifted a hand in a wave. Picking up our pace, we pressed up the hill along the winding path through the woods. The sound of the boys' footsteps on packed dirt carried briefly before fading away as they continued along the river. We went faster, Grayson leaning into the incline and lifting his knees as he dodged roots and rocks. Excited, I pulled ahead. It became a race. The faster I went, the faster he went, until only the tautness of the leash held me back. Not once did he correct me.

Ahead lay the fallen log. Grayson, I could tell, was tiring. He slowed to step over it, rather than jump it. I vaulted atop the log, then jumped down as he swung his legs over. He landed with one foot, then brought the other forward. But instead of resuming his pace, his foot hit a shallow hole. His knee buckled. He stumbled, twisted sideways, and landed on his hip.

Before I could check to see if he was okay, Grayson staggered to his feet and lurched onward. His gait was uneven. He grimaced in pain. Yet, he said nothing, just kept going. Slower than before, but for some reason unwilling to stop.

When we reached the car, Grayson bent and clutched his knees, his breath coming in labored gasps. He dropped to the ground, covered his face with shaking hands, and wept.

"Why him? Why... *him*? Justin had everything to live for. Why was *I* given a second chance?"

I didn't like it when my person was hurting inside. It made me hurt, too.

Slowly, carefully, I crawled to him, rooted under his arm to slide my muzzle close to his face. Licking the tears from his face, I whimpered, *I love you. More than the sun and the moon and the stars.*

Grayson's arm encircled me. "I love you, too, you crazy dog. Guess I don't have 'nothing' after all. Because I have you. For now, anyway. That should count for something, right?"

We sat together like that for a good long while—him stroking the fur along my spine, me licking the snot and tears from his salty face.

"It's time I made a phone call," he said. "Someone's been waiting to see you."

Then we got in the car and drove home. Grayson didn't say a word the whole way. He just kept glancing in the mirror at me like I was something special. Like he couldn't live without me.

chapter 24
Brandy

"Hello," said the man's voice. "Is this Brandy Anders?"

Brandy swallowed hard. She hadn't been expecting *him* to call first. In actuality, she'd been trying for days to summon the courage to call Grayson for almost two weeks, putting it off over and over again. Yet every time she'd written the text asking when would be a good time, she'd deleted it, overcome by emotions that were yet raw. She desperately wanted to see Sooner again, but being able to take her back was a long, *long* way off. That reality was almost too upsetting to consider.

On some days, the thought of getting well enough to be able to let her dog in and out or take her on walks alongside her wheelchair kept Brandy going. She insisted on doing as many small tasks for herself as she could, like pouring her own glass of water or putting on her own shirt—but healing bones had a way of making the simplest things nearly impossible. Her progress had been painfully slow. The doctors had warned her it would be that way in the beginning, that there would be setbacks. She still didn't have the upper body strength to get in and out of her wheelchair unassisted.

Then, three days ago, her orthopedic surgeon had informed her she would need full time care for months yet. That meant either staying in a rehabilitation facility like she was now or moving in with her brother in Dallas—far from her ailing father. She'd prefer to spare her brother the inconvenience and stay here—the staff had been good to her—but the costs were prohibitive. She didn't want to be in debt for the rest of her life. Yet, the humbling fact was she needed help. Neither option allowed for a dog—and that made Brandy sick at heart. She'd been putting the decision off, just like she'd been putting off talking to Grayson or seeing Sooner again.

"Hi, Grayson," she finally managed in a thin, weary voice. She forced herself to speak louder, to sound more cheerful than she actually felt. "How are you?"

"Shouldn't I be asking *you* that?"

He'd posed the question in the kindest of ways. Still, she didn't like talking about how hard her life was right now. It only made her more depressed.

"I'm well enough," she said, not knowing what else to say, "considering."

"Oh, right. Sorry." Grayson was quick to put her at ease. "I realize when you asked the question first that the polite thing would just have been to say 'fine', but then… Honestly? I can't imagine how hard it's been for you. Not just being in the hospital and all the complications from the accident, but being without your dog. She really is something special."

This was why she'd avoided calling. Because sooner or later, it would come around to this—him taking care of Sooner for her and how much longer he'd need to do that. She wanted to both cry and rage at the same time. But she couldn't. Not now. Not to him. She needed to get through this conversation without letting him know she was falling apart inside.

"How is she?" She refrained from asking Grayson to hold the phone to Sooner's ear so she could talk to her because that would only shout 'Crazy Dog-Lady'.

"Right now? Tired. A good tired, though. We just finished a brisk run. She *loves* going running!"

His voice had pitched with enthusiasm, which made Brandy feel a little less guilty about this stranger looking after her dog. Still, she needed to know more about him. It was important Sooner be in the right hands. If he wasn't a good fit, maybe one of her friends from the dog club could take her in.

"So you're a runner, huh? Planning any marathons?" In high school when the PE teacher made them run a mile, she'd considered it the worst kind of torture. She was built for short bursts of speed. Couldn't imagine running a whole twenty-six plus miles at a stretch. Slogging around the track for four laps only made her knees ache and gave her blisters. Not to mention the sweat. She admired people who had the focus to go for miles, though.

"Right now, I consider myself a jogger. But I used to be a serious runner. Back in college."

"Why'd you stop? Work? Family?"

"No, I… I was… injured. Hit by a car, actually."

"Wow, really? You're lucky you weren't killed. Did the driver get cited?"

Dead silence on the other end. She almost thought the connection had been lost, except she could hear a TV faintly in the background.

"Grayson? Did I say something wrong?"

"No, you—" He broke off, inhaled, let it out slowly. "My best friend was with me. He died."

It was her turn to be silent. Her gut twisted in pain for him. Scars weren't always on the outside. A rush of guilt welled up in her.

"I'm sorry," she offered. "I shouldn't have…"

"Don't be. You had no way of knowing." After a short pause, Grayson continued, "Anyway, enough of dark secrets and apologies. Would you like to talk about something, I don't know, a little more uplifting, maybe?"

"Please. I could use more of that."

"Great." His relief was audible. "Let me tell you about Sooner then. Both the good and the not-so-good."

Honesty. She was liking him more and more. "Do I want to know?"

"You'll laugh, I promise."

He told her not only about how Sooner had given him reason to keep up with his running and get back in shape, but also how she'd gotten into the trash and he'd stayed up all night with her, how she'd tried to defend the farm from the skunk and lost, how he'd watched YouTube videos on obedience and trick training, and how quickly she picked things up.

Brandy found herself laughing along with him, just as he'd promised. But when he'd exhausted his stories twenty minutes later, she fell silent.

"You miss her, don't you?" he said.

A knot formed in her throat. "Like crazy."

They used to do so much together—she and Sooner. But all those wins and titles didn't mean one iota as much as the bond she had with that dog.

"So let me ask you a question: Why the name 'Sooner'?" Grayson said. "Are you originally from Oklahoma?"

"No, I'm not. I didn't name her, actually. She had two other homes before I ended up with her. Seems she was something of a wild child."

"I can imagine. So where'd the name come from?"

"When you're getting ready to leave the house, have you ever beaten her to the front door?"

"No, she always gets there sooner than... Oh, I get it. It does fit her."

"It's also because she was the last left in her litter. The breeder, Violet Tulley, kept saying, 'Sooner or later, someone's gonna come along who's just right for you.' Guess that was me. Better late than never, though."

"Lucky for you it worked out that way."

Luck. Lately, Brandy felt like she'd had the worst luck of her life. But now, she realized how fortunate it was that Grayson Darling had found Sooner. Still, there was something she needed to know. "Can I ask *you* a question now?"

"Shoot."

"Don't take it wrong, but... why did you wait so long to get in touch with me?"

"Wait? As soon as I got your number, I tried calling. But it kicked over to voicemail and said your inbox was full. Same with the texts. Eventually, they wouldn't go through at all."

"Oh." It hadn't occurred to Brandy that when she'd finally gotten a new phone and checked voicemail, that her friends and family had left multiple messages, all trying to figure out how she was doing. "I'm sorry, I... Never mind. It was a dumb question now that I think about it. My phone was destroyed in the accident. It took a while before I could get a replacement and even then, I wasn't in the frame of mind to clear out my messages. Getting by was a day-to-day thing. And then, the news about my dad..."

"Paul Anders?"

"Yes, how'd you know his name?"

"He was listed as the alternate contact for her microchip. I called that, too, over a dozen times, but no one ever answered. Did something happen to him?"

Overcome with emotion, Brandy wiped tears from her cheeks. She swallowed hard several times, trying to keep herself from dissolving into sobs. Now wasn't the time to pour out her emotions. Not to someone she barely knew. But already, she'd learned so much about Grayson. He'd done exactly what he should have in trying to reach her. He hadn't stopped until he'd gotten through. She would've understood if someone had given up by then, but he hadn't.

She grabbed a tissue to wipe her eyes and nose. "He had a stroke a couple of weeks after my accident," she finally managed. "I haven't seen him since."

Even though Grayson didn't speak for a few moments, she sensed his compassion. It was a silence that didn't need to be filled with words.

"I was just thinking…" Grayson finally said. "Actually, I've been thinking about this for a long time. Why don't I—we, why don't *we*—come and visit? Whenever it's convenient for you, that is."

"We?" Panic crashed through her chest. She knew what he meant, but she was stalling.

"Yes. Sooner and I. That way if it feels strange talking to someone you barely know—meaning me—you could just send me to the cafeteria to fetch some coffee and spill your heart out to the dog. I've discovered she's an excellent listener—and she always keeps her opinion to herself. Wait, I shouldn't say that. She lets me know when I'm wrong. She's just very subtle about it. A raised eyebrow, a snort… If she could roll her eyes at me like a teenager, she would."

Her panic subsided. Honesty, integrity, a love for dogs, *and* a sense of humor. This guy was ticking all the boxes. Too bad she wasn't in the market at the moment. Anyway, he was just being a kind soul. She shouldn't read too much into it.

As much as she desperately wanted to see Sooner, though, there was a downside to it: When the visit was over, she'd have to say goodbye. For a long time. Maybe forever.

"So… this weekend?" he asked. When she didn't answer right away, he added, "Or I could wait until—"

"You… you could come, I suppose. But… this *is* a hospital. Sooner's not a certified therapy dog—she wouldn't be allowed."

"I don't understand how that matters." He sounded genuinely baffled. "She's your dog."

"It matters a lot. In short, she doesn't have the credentials to visit a hospital. Therapy animals have to go through training and pass tests to prove they can handle things like wheelchairs and people on crutches. If that wasn't required, then any animal could be brought in: a wild animal, a diseased rodent, a terrified cat, an unruly dog—"

"Okay, okay, I get it. Although I have to think there's a way around it… Anyway, name the day and, if nothing else, I'll share pictures of Sooner with you. I wouldn't mind getting away from the farm. It's been too wet around here to do much outside anyway. Monday okay?"

She didn't have any excuses left. Besides, it would be nice to be able to thank him in person. "Okay. Monday."

"Great! See you then."

After they hung up, Brandy held the phone to her chest for a long while. It would be a few days before he came. She had that much time to sort out her life and figure out what to do with Sooner. It wasn't fair to the dog to keep bouncing her from home to home.

But giving her dog up—if it came to that—would be the hardest decision of her life.

chapter 25
Sooner

Humans didn't realize how intuitive dogs were. We sensed things, subtle cues: a slight movement, a change in tone, a way of carrying oneself.

I grew suspicious that something was afoot when Grayson became increasingly preoccupied over the next several days. He'd look at me fondly, sigh, and then frown. So I stayed by his side, there if he needed me. I waited for him to talk about whatever it was that had him so concerned, but he didn't say much. In between sleeping and eating, we went on our runs and took care of the horses. He checked his phone more often than was normal for him, as if the answer to his problem was somewhere inside that little black device that he carried with him everywhere.

And then one day, he gathered up my leash and took the car keys off the hook by the back door.

"Would you like to go for a ride, Sooner?"

Ride? Yes, yes, a thousand times yes, I barked.

He opened the door, and I raced out ahead of him. Long gone

were the days when he didn't trust me off leash. I'd proven my dependability. In turn, he'd given me more and more freedom, even allowing me to wander about and explore around the farm as he did chores. Most of the time, though, I followed him wherever he went, just because I enjoyed his company.

As I waited at the car and he came my way, he smiled sadly. Sad because even though his mouth was curved upward, his eyes didn't crinkle. When he reached the car, instead of pulling the door open right away so I could jump in, he crouched before me, my leash bunched in his hand.

"We're going to see Brandy, your owner," he told me.

I cocked my head, unsure if I'd heard right. Had he really said Brandy's name? I hadn't heard it spoken aloud in a very long time, although I'd far from forgotten it.

"Brandy's in a physical rehab facility near Lexington, getting the care she needs. She's sorry she couldn't take care of you lately, but she had to have some surgeries and it's going to be a long time still before she's well enough to take you back. She didn't want you to come just yet. Not because she doesn't love you still, but she thought it would be too hard. I mean, she didn't say it in so many words, but I could tell… Anyway, I got the administrator's okay and we're going to surprise her. I think she needs you more than she knows. It will give her a reason to get better."

He drew me into his arms then, burying his face in the fur of my neck. For a long time, he held me like that, his breath shaky. Then abruptly, he stood and opened the door for me.

I hesitated. Something about this didn't quite feel right. Like today was both good and bad at the same time.

"Go on," he urged. "Get in. We're already running late."

I did, only because he told me to.

Normally we turned left out of the driveway to go to town, but today we turned right. At first, I watched out the window, but as the minutes wore on, the motion of the car as it rolled up over the hills and down into the valleys lulled me to sleep.

By the time I woke up, there was a tall and sprawling building before us, surrounded by other buildings, some attached by covered walkways, others standing separate. The car was sitting in the midst of a parking lot with lots and lots of other cars.

A mournful wail cleaved the air, rose in a shrieking pitch, then fell low before rising again. It continued like that, growing gradually louder and closer. Fear rippled through me as a white truck with flashing lights pulled into the parking lot before speeding toward the sidewalk by the glass doors.

I growled at it.

"It's okay, Sooner." Grayson twisted in his seat to reassure me. "Just an ambulance. They won't hurt us. But we can wait a few minutes before going inside, if you want. I don't mind. I need to sit here for a while myself anyway." Turning back, he lifted a finger toward a three-story building that stood apart from the bigger one. "Besides, we're not going into the hospital. We're headed over there: the post-operative physical rehabilitation facility. To see Brandy." His eyes met mine in the rearview mirror. "You want to see Brandy, don't you?"

Stop it, I barked. *Stop teasing me!*

"You do, do you? All right then. Let's go see Brandy."

I couldn't understand why he kept mentioning her over and over. Did her name mean something else to him?

As he fumbled with his seatbelt, readjusted his wallet in his pocket, then zipped and unzipped his jacket, I noticed something: the siren had stopped. I turned toward the ambulance. It was still there, but two people had hopped out and were removing a bed on wheels, of sorts. On it was a person, tucked beneath a blanket.

Something about it made me think of the mechanical bird that had lifted Brandy from the ravine.

This was where they'd brought Brandy? The realization smashed into me like a landslide.

She's here! She isn't lost after all!

I clawed at the door, eager to get out so Grayson could take me to her.

"Hey, hey," he chided. "Not so fast. Remember your manners."

Hurry! Hurry up, up, up! Hurry, hurry—

"Whoa!" Reaching back, he grabbed my collar and snapped the leash on. "Don't you dare bolt out into traffic. I know you're excited, but I'd appreciate it if you minded your manners like the trained dog you are—or else they'll boot you out of there. I told them you were well-behaved. Practically a PhD, as far as dogs go. Don't make a liar out of me. They usually don't let any animals except certified therapy dogs in. They made an exception for you, Sooner."

He got out and opened the back door partway, making sure to grab the leash before I could barge past him. I stood, but hesitated. Why was he being so *slow* about this? It was like he didn't want to take me inside to see her—

Oh. I understood. While I was overjoyed to believe Brandy might be inside that building, he was saddened by it. Why?

"It's time." He tugged on my leash, throwing me off balance. I leapt to the ground ungracefully. After shutting the door, he started toward the building, jerking me forward, his steps forced. "Brandy will be so happy to see you, Sooner."

By the time we reached the entrance, I was the one leading him. The glass doors whooshed magically apart as we approached, opening up into a lobby that seemed more like an oversized living room than a waiting area.

Inside, I scanned for Brandy. An older couple occupied a pair of recliners before the TV, the man's hand resting on his wife's, her eyes closed as she napped and a pink blanket with fringe spread across her lap. A younger woman wearing fuzzy slippers and a bathrobe over dark gray sweats sat on a couch next to a gas fireplace, playing cards fanned in her hands as she chatted with a woman in blue scrubs.

I lifted my nose, sniffed hard, let the smells linger in those places inside my muzzle that remembered scents. The smells of many humans were here, but I couldn't be sure…

"You must be Mr. Darling," a woman said from behind the counter next to us. "Welcome. I'm Cherise."

Grayson nodded, then tipped his head at me. "This is Sooner."

"I figured as much." She half stood to peer over the edge at me. "What a pretty dog. But he's shaking. Is he scared?"

"She. Sooner is a she," Grayson corrected. He ran a hand over the top of my skull. I was trembling: excited, worried, confused, happy—so many things all at once. His touch soothed my nerves, even as I sensed his own worries. "And she's not scared. Just anxious. It's been months since they've seen each other. Could you imagine being away from a loved one for that long, wondering if they were even still alive?"

Smiling, she sat back down. "No, I couldn't. It's good you brought her, though. Miss Anders has talked so much about her dog, I would've known it anywhere. You'd be surprised how many of our patients never have—"

"I don't mean to interrupt, but can you call her down here?"

"Oh, dear, no. She can't…"

The words hung suspended, like bubbles floating in the air, fragile enough to be burst with a child's fingertip or even a puff of breath.

"Can't what? Isn't she here still? She should be expecting us. Well, me at least. I didn't exactly let on that I was bringing the dog."

"I mean she can't come down here. Not without a lot of trouble, anyway. I take it you haven't been to see her yet?"

"We've talked on the phone, but yes, this is my first time here. The dog's, too."

"Why don't I show you to her room then? Betsy," she said to the woman in the pale blue scrubs playing cards, "can you watch the desk for a few minutes while I show this handsome gentleman and his lovely dog to Miss Anders' room? The orderly is on break."

"Sure." Betsy laid her cards on the coffee table. "Gin… I think."

As Betsy made her way behind the counter, Cherise motioned for Grayson to follow her. We walked down a quiet hallway to an elevator. "We're only going to the third floor, but everything here is designed for the disabled. Many of our patients are bedridden. Miss Anders is one of the luckier ones. She can at least sit up."

She punched some buttons on the wall. Moments later, a set of doors opened. We stepped into the elevator.

"Is she…? "Grayson stumbled for the right words as the doors closed and the car lurched upward. "Can she use her legs at all?"

"Not yet, but she's very determined." We exited the elevator, then found ourselves in a new, busier hallway.

"So she's a…?"

"Paraplegic? Technically, yes. But that doesn't mean it's permanent. She has some feeling in her legs, so the doctors are hopeful. As for Miss Anders, well, she's been a little frustrated. People often think recovery should be quicker in the beginning, but these things can take a long time. Years, even. Just understand she's still processing what happened and the changes that have occurred in her life because of it." Suddenly, Cherise waved her hands in front of her, then clasped them over her heart. "Listen to me—talking like I'm her doctor and you're her next of kin. I tend to step outside my bounds, but stick around here long enough and you soon learn some are more special than others. Besides, I'm making it all sound more dreadful than it is. She's been a wonderful patient, really. She's always nice to me. Always. And her therapists constantly tell me how cooperative she is and how incredibly hard she works. Qualities like that make more of a difference than a person's medical condition." She turned toward the end of the hallway. "Follow me."

We passed door after door, some closed, some open. Through the open doors, I glimpsed the occupants, some with sad or pained faces, others brightening at the sight of me. A few of the people had tubes attached to their bodies, like I'd had when I was at Doc Hunter's, so I knew they weren't well. Others appeared a little abler. One was sitting in a chair by the window, an open book resting in her lap as she turned a page. Another man sat at a small table, sifting through pieces of a jigsaw puzzle.

Grayson gripped the end of the leash tightly, even though I was walking with slack in the lead. For some reason, I sensed, he needed me right next to him. Needed to know I was his and he was mine. That we were partners now, working together.

Then Cherise stopped. She indicated the door before her, slightly ajar. "This one." Inside, a TV played. She lowered her voice. "Do you want me to go first, announce you're here?"

Swallowing, Grayson rubbed at my ear closest to him. "I think we've got this."

"I'll be at my desk if you need anything." A faint smile on her full lips, Cherise stepped to his side and headed back toward the elevator. She tweaked his sleeve as she passed him. "Good luck."

"Thank you."

For close to a minute after she left us, Grayson gazed at the floor. Then, finally, he reached out and knocked three times, so softly it was a wonder any response came from the other side.

"Yes?" Bedding rustled. The volume on the TV lowered. "Come in."

That voice. Could it be...?

As he pushed the door open, I glanced one last time at Grayson. The worry and nervousness that had plagued him all day melted from his features. Something different, something more hopeful, had replaced it.

"Grayson... hello. I've been waiting—"

Sitting in a hospital bed, her legs covered with a blanket, Brandy froze in midsentence as her eyes fell from Grayson's face down to me. For a few moments, she remained like that—mouth open, hands holding the edge of her blanket. Then, her lip began to tremble and everything crumbled. Her hands shot up to cover her face, and she broke into uncontrollable sobs.

Grayson unclipped my leash. I rushed to her, stopping just short of launching myself up onto her bed like I'd done hundreds of times before.

I'd waited so long to see her. Thought I never would again. To know that at long last I'd found her—my heart swelled with so much love I could barely contain my enthusiasm.

But as much as I wanted to jump into her arms and cover her face with a thousand kisses, I stopped myself. Instead of flinging myself joyfully at her, I placed a paw on the edge of her bed, almost—but not quite—touching her leg.

Something about her was very, *very* different.

chapter 26
Grayson

No matter how many times he'd imagined it ahead of time, Grayson wasn't quite prepared for the scene that had begun to unfold before him, yet seemed to have frozen partway. He'd been nervous all week—about meeting Brandy, about whether to bring Sooner, and then once he'd decided to do so, about how ecstatic they'd be to see each other.

Yet, that last point wasn't at all playing out the way he'd expected it to.

There had been a moment in which Brandy and Sooner had seen each other. A moment of disbelief. And then... he wasn't sure how to describe it, other than it wasn't the glorious reunion he'd expected. At least, not yet.

As soon as they'd laid eyes on each other, he'd unclipped the leash. Sooner, rather than jumping onto the bed and throwing herself at a sobbing Brandy, had paused next to it, one paw gingerly resting beside Brandy's leg. It was as if the dog sensed something about her had changed profoundly.

As he waited for something to move forward, to find the proper words, it was the dog who took the initiative. The same dog who'd challenged him daily, who'd dragged him on runs until he was aching and breathless, who'd quivered in mortal fear of a thunderstorm—that same dog walked quietly around to the other side of the bed where there was more room and jumped up. Not with her usual raucous energy, but deftly, like a cat positioning herself on a narrow fence rail. With a weighty sigh, Sooner lay down, rested her chin between her paws, and watched. Waited for a signal from Brandy. Whether to get off or to come closer.

Brandy must have felt the mattress shift, because she couldn't possibly have heard the dog above her sobs. Slowly, she lowered her hands. Tears streaked her lightly freckled face. Her eyes were red, her cheeks puffy. The tiniest drizzle of snot leaked from one nostril over her upper lip. Grayson found it adorable that she loved this dog as much as any mother would a child. He liked that about her already.

And then... her fingers grazed Sooner's head, rested briefly at the top of the dog's neck, found that sweet spot just behind an ear, and scratched ever so gently. The dog leaned into her touch.

"Sooner..." Brandy croaked through her tears, "I've missed you sooo much. So, very, *very* much."

The dog licked her fingers, letting out the tiniest whimper, as if to say, *Me, too.*

Then Brandy drew her hand back and patted a space farther up on the mattress, closer to her. Sooner crawled forward to burrow in that narrow space. She lay incredibly still as Brandy stroked her fur, her sobs giving way to sniffles and then to murmurs of praise.

As Grayson took in her outpouring of love for the dog, he studied her features: barely tamed red-gold curls surrounding a heart-shaped face, the fine fanning of crow's feet at the corners of earthy brown eyes, and skin as translucent as alabaster. Even in her hospital gown and a peach-colored robe, she looked strong and vibrant, a woman young at heart, but old enough to know her direction in life.

"You didn't go far from the van until they took me away, did you?" Smiling through tears of joy, Brandy pressed Sooner's cheeks between her hands. "Were you trying to find me, then? I know you were. You're such a good dog. The best dog in the whole wide world. Ever. Since the beginning of dogs. Better than Lassie and Rin Tin Tin and—"

As he stood there in the doorway, watching their love reignite, he couldn't help but think that he was, bit by bit, losing the dog that had come to mean more to him than he'd ever believed a dog could. It both filled his heart with love and emptied it at the same time.

In bringing Sooner back to Brandy, for the first time in his life he was doing something for someone else, without regard to how it might affect him. He knew he had to let the dog go, and yet… it was the last thing he wanted right now. Still, there was no other solution. It was the *right* thing to do.

In the last couple of weeks, he'd come to realize that even if he never landed his dream job, even if he never returned to New York City, everything would be all right.

"Grayson?" Brandy said in the slightest of Southern accents. "Why are you just standing there?"

He blinked until her words registered fully. "I… I should've let you know I'd be bringing her. But I was afraid you'd say no, not to. I did clear it with the hospital administrator, by the way. She said they'd make an exception in your case, based on Sooner's accomplishments and all."

She motioned for him to come closer. He did, but apparently not close enough.

"Over here. I don't bite. Promise." She laughed, just a little.

He couldn't help but smile, even as much as his insides ached. Something about her was contagious, though. An energy. A light.

But there was something else. Something inside *him*. He couldn't quite describe it. It was just a feeling. Like the subtle buzz of electricity when a hand was touched to the outside of a machine and the vibrations from its inner workings were sensed. There was also an odd kind of… fullness. Like his heart had expanded inside his chest. It was strangely exhilarating and thoroughly uncomfortable all at the same time. He had to avert his eyes.

Somehow, his feet carried him across the space between them. Around the foot of the bed. To the other side where Sooner had tucked herself against Brandy's broken body.

"Are you…" He swallowed. Studied the rigid brace that encased her middle and the one on her left leg. "Are you in much pain?"

Her smile slipped away. "Sometimes. Kinda comes and goes. Every day, they make me get up out of this bed and move around—as much as I can, anyway. They tell me it'll make me stronger. That I'll heal faster that way… although I'm not so sure about that." She glanced at the IV drip beside her. The labeling indicated it was a painkiller. A powerful one. "I can understand why people get addicted to this stuff. They keep saying I can control how much I get and I'm allowed to have more, but… I don't know. I'm not sure it's worth it. If I could stand it, I wouldn't have any at all."

"But if you're hurting, why wouldn't you want some more relief?"

Brandy fixed her gaze on the sunlight coming in through the window. She breathed in and out several times, her face tightening as if a wave of physical discomfort was surging through her before she continued. "Because it reminds me that I'm alive. That I survived. And that, for now, even though I'm not what I was, I *will* get better." Her fist clenched around the hem of her blanket, then went slack. She exhaled audibly. "Just because it hurts like hell today doesn't mean it will tomorrow."

Her words hit Grayson hard. There had been a day when he thought he had nothing left to live for. A day during which he thought all his endeavors had been in vain. A few moments when he was sure his pain would go on forever. Maybe even drag him deeper into some interminable purgatory. But it hadn't been so. Serendipity—a dog in desperate need—had saved him. Someday, he'd tell Brandy that story. Maybe. But not today.

Suddenly, Brandy shook her head, then tried to pull her body up a little higher against the pillows stacked behind her, but all she did was rumple the sheets beneath her. "Sorry, didn't mean to bare my soul to you. We hardly know each other. Guess I'm just overly emotional these days." She smoothed the fur on top of Sooner's head over and over.

"Don't be."

She blinked at Grayson. "Huh?"

"Sorry—don't be sorry. You've been through a lot. Talking helps us make sense of things."

She forced a laugh, but it sounded fake. "Yeah, says who? Sometimes even *I* don't know what I'm talking about."

"Says my therapist."

She didn't say anything to that. Which was a relief to Grayson. As comfortable as he felt with Brandy already, it seemed too sudden to learn everything about each other on the very first day. There was no rush. There would be time—later.

"So, I have to ask," he began, desperate to change the subject, "who does your hair?"

She laughed. For real. A bubbly, from-the-heart sort of laugh. Then her cheeks flushed. She tugged at a golden-red curl. "I do my own. But… I did have help today. A little. Ronelle, the nurse's aide, helps me wash my hair and get most of the tangles out. After that, there's a lot of scrunching involved. I can't go to sleep until it completely air dries or I end up with the worst case of bed-head you've ever seen."

"Sounds like a lot of work, but I'd say you have it down to a science." Grayson admired her wild crown of ringlets. The sort of unruly bright red locks that other kids would have made fun of—and every grown woman must have envied. "You have beautiful hair."

It wasn't like him to be so bold, but then, he wasn't the person he used to be. Before he came to Faderville. Before Sooner saved him.

She looked down at her lap. "Thank you."

Sooner nuzzled beneath Brandy's hand, urging more pets. The dog hadn't so much as glanced at Grayson since they entered the room. But then, he hadn't paid much attention to the dog, either.

"As long as you're here"—Brandy nodded toward the oversized chair in the corner—"have a seat."

"Actually, I probably shouldn't stay long. I don't want to tire you out. All that physical thera—"

"Oh, please." She rolled her eyes. "Your visit is the most exciting thing to happen to me today. Heck, this whole month. And I'm not just saying that because you brought Sooner along. I'd like to get to know the person who's looking after my dog."

When he hesitated, she pointed at the chair. "Sit."

He complied. It was comfortable, but felt strangely too far away. He scooted it forward. Then he put his elbows on his knees and opened his mouth to speak before thinking better of it.

"What?" Brandy prompted.

"Nothing." He fought a smirk.

"You were going to say something. I know the look."

"Well, it's just that… I was waiting to hear you tell me to 'stay'."

They both burst out laughing at the same time. Sooner's head popped up. She glanced from Brandy to Grayson and back again. Her little nub wagging, she slathered Brandy's left hand and wrist in kisses.

When Brandy's laughter had finally subsided, she wiped the tears from her eyes. "I thought about it. I really did. But I wasn't sure how you'd take my sense of humor."

"I'm glad to know you still have one." Because he wasn't sure he would have, under the same circumstances. He'd lost his job, yes. But she'd almost lost her life. Come to think of it, he almost had, too. More than once.

For more than an hour, they talked—joking, asking questions, sharing stories—Sooner snuggled by Brandy's side. She told him about her father's poor prognosis following his stroke. He told her about the farm and the horses. She spoke about her physical therapy and how hard it was to do even the simplest things that she had once taken for granted. He told her how he'd been downsized from his job and come to Faderville to settle his uncle's estate, but hadn't quite left yet.

Brandy never asked why he had a therapist in the first place, or if he was still seeing one, and he didn't volunteer any details. Grayson didn't ask if she were at all depressed by her situation—because if it were him, he most certainly would have been. There seemed to be a line, without it ever being said, over which neither of them dared to cross just yet.

Grayson stayed longer than he'd planned, simply because Brandy seemed so heartened by Sooner's presence. It couldn't be because of him. He was merely the dog's ride.

But when Brandy stifled a yawn, he could tell she was growing tired. The pauses were getting longer. Her eyelids heavier. He decided, reluctantly, that it was time to take his exit.

"We ought to go now." He stretched his legs and then stood, his thumb on the clip of the leash, ready to attach it to the dog's collar. "Sooner, come here."

Instead of heeding his command, the dog flattened herself to the mattress, as if she could weave herself into its fabric and become part of it.

Brandy gave the dog a nudge. "Off, Sooner. Off."

Ears pinned to her head, Sooner tossed her a wounded look, then slunk off the bed. Grayson snapped the leash on before Sooner could jump back up.

"You'll come back soon, I hope." Tears pooled in Brandy's eyes, but she bravely kept them at bay. "If you can, that is."

"Of course we'll be back. Not like I have anything else going on lately—except for the farm. But I can always make time." *For you*, he nearly added. But that seemed inappropriately forward for someone he'd just met.

"Tomorrow?" she blurted out. Then, "Oh, I'm not thinking. Sorry. It's a haul from Faderville to here. You obviously can't do that every day."

"The day after, maybe?" It would give them both something to look forward to, he figured.

Her face brightened. "Sure."

"What time?"

"You tell me. Not like I'm going anywhere."

"Noon? That'll give me a chance to finish morning chores."

"Noon would be perfect. I can't wait." Brandy kissed the fingertips of her right hand, then stretched them toward the edge of the bed, where Sooner was resting her muzzle. She touched the dog upon the nose. "Love you, princess. More than the sun and the moon and the stars."

Sooner sniffed her fingertips to take in her scent, then licked them gently.

"The one thing that kept me going, even as I was hanging upside down in that van, only half-conscious, feeling like I wanted to die, was you, Sooner. Sometimes I dreamed of you, and I knew you were still out there. Even when they kept telling me that you hadn't been found. I knew… I just… knew."

She raised her eyes to meet Grayson's, her voice an airy whisper. "Thank you. For finding her. For taking care of her."

He simply smiled. He would do it a thousand times over now, even though he hadn't been sure about doing it in the first place. Because it was worth it. Not just to her. But to him.

Then he tugged on the leash and left, his steps hurried but heavy.

All the way down the hall and even as they exited the main doors, the dog kept glancing back.

Back in the SUV, he sat for a long time, the key clenched in his palm, the car idle. Sooner sat with her nose pressed to the window, whimpering.

He knew, ultimately, what he would have to do. And in doing so, he would be tearing his heart in two.

chapter 27
Brandy

The look in Grayson's eyes when he called Sooner to him to leave and she'd resisted had shot a pang through Brandy's heart. He'd rescued the dog, cared for her, spent every hour of his day with her at his side. It was understandable he would have come to rely on Sooner's company—maybe even love her.

Sooner wasn't the dog for just anyone. She was… needy, in a way. Needed to be exercised and entertained. Needed a job to do. Needed an owner who viewed all of that as a positive, not a problem. Brandy had been her third owner for good reason. Not because she was a bad dog, but because she was exceptional. Capable of extraordinary things. Certainly smarter than her first two owners.

Yet Grayson had kept her busy on his uncle's horse farm just by letting her follow him about as he did chores and taking her on runs. Simple activities that had kept her mind occupied and spent her excess energy.

There was so much more Brandy wanted to ask Grayson, yet

most of the questions that came to mind seemed too personal, so she kept them to herself. For some reason, though, she felt like she already *did* know him—that they'd met before. It sat there on the edge of her memory, just beyond reach.

Brandy flipped through channels mindlessly, barely registering what was on TV. In the hour since Grayson and Sooner had left, she'd done a lot of soul-searching. When she'd been on the way home from the last trial with Sooner, she'd been reveling in all that they'd accomplished in so short a time: the ribbons, the titles, the high scores, the accolades from judges and fellow competitors. It had filled her not only with pride, but also a certain amount of smugness. She'd taken the unruly, overly exuberant dog and shaped her into a high-drive performance dog, a possible contender for national championships and international teams. If she'd thought all that had been the measure of the dog's worth, she now saw how misguided that was.

The titles and ribbons had meant something to *her*, but nothing to the dog. Not any more than the dog might value stacks of dollar bills or a diamond-encrusted collar. What had mattered to Sooner were the hours spent by Brandy's side, the words of praise, the pats on the head, the quiet times spent at home lounging on the couch next to her. All those were the very things Grayson had given her. By the way he talked about Sooner, Brandy could tell the dog had come to mean a great deal to him. She sensed there was some deep and abiding connection between them that he hadn't fully revealed to her.

She lifted her phone from the bedside table, opened the contacts. Her brother, PJ, had been expecting her to call back. She'd told him she needed a few days. It had been four.

A volunteer wheeled a cart full of food trays into Brandy's room.

"I forget. Did you want the turkey with mashed potatoes today—or the meatloaf?" The older woman lifted a tray from the top shelf and winked. "I'd strongly suggest the turkey."

She set a tray on Brandy's adjustable table, peeled back the lid, and placed utensils and a napkin beside it. Brandy thanked her and poked at her food with her fork, taking a few quick bites of the turkey so the woman would move on and leave her to her thoughts.

Once alone, though, Brandy almost wanted to call her back. Anything to put off calling PJ. She'd always gotten along well with him and his wife, Tyana, a nurse who was taking time off to raise their infant daughter. It was Tyana, in fact, who'd suggested Brandy come live with them. The problem was they lived in a swanky high-rise in Dallas. Even if the landlord would make an exception for a dog, she couldn't expect Tyana to take Sooner out several times a day, on top of caring for her daughter and helping Brandy. No, it was too much to ask. The most practical thing, the *best* thing, to do would be to accept PJ's offer and allow Sooner to remain with Grayson. But after six months or a year or however long it would take to get back on her feet, if she even could, would it be fair then to ask for the dog back? It seemed like a selfish thing to propose.

Still, that dog had been her pride and joy, her best friend, her sounding board. Her heart-dog. How could she live without her?

"Excuse me," Brandy called out to a nurse passing in the hallway.

The nurse popped her head in. "Do you need something, honey? More to eat? Another blanket? Can I pour you a glass of water?"

"No, I don't need anything. Just the blinds and door closed. I'd like to take a nap."

"Of course." After closing the blinds, the nurse flicked off the overhead lights and pulled the door shut.

With no witnesses, Brandy let go. Dissolved into a maelstrom of emotions.

When every tear was wrung out of her, she gazed at the suspended ceiling, noticing a small divot in one of the acoustic tiles, like someone had jabbed a pair of scissors into it and loosened a chunk.

It might not have been fair to ask so much of Grayson, but it also wasn't fair to think she could so easily give her dog up. She *needed* that dog. Needed her in order to have a reason to get better. Needed her to cope with how different her life was going to be from now on.

And then, she couldn't think about it for one second longer. There would be plenty of time for her to make up her mind. Time to give her brother an answer. Time to get to know Grayson better, to gauge whether he even wanted to keep Sooner indefinitely.

She set the phone in the drawer. Put the decision off for another time.

Time. Lately, she had far more of that than she wanted.

chapter 28

Sooner

Time couldn't go fast enough on the days in between our visits. Yet on the days we did see Brandy, it slipped away in a blink. Every night when we went to bed, I hoped and dreamed that on the next day we'd get in the car and make the long drive to the place Brandy now lived. I couldn't quite figure out the arrangement, but it seemed like only the one small room in the building Grayson called the hospital—or sometimes the rehab center—belonged to her. I wondered if Brandy and I would ever go back to the little brick house in the neighborhood where we once lived? Would she ever take me for walks again? Or run agility with me? Or train with me for obedience, perfecting our turns and signals and stays?

Mostly, I wondered why she couldn't just come and stay with Grayson and me. There was plenty of room in the house on the farm. He always seemed so lonely. Like he needed someone besides me to be with. If only humans would act as they truly felt...

The more visits we made to Brandy, the longer each one lasted. Which made my heart happy. It made Grayson happy, too. But also very nervous. Because again, being a human, he wasn't acting the way he truly felt—which was that he liked Brandy. A lot. Only he didn't seem to want to show it.

It was harder to tell how much Brandy liked him, though. She'd always been friendly to everyone she met from the outset, whereas Grayson found it harder to let his guard down. Still, there was something different about the way she looked at him. When he spoke, she'd gaze at him, waiting until he returned his attention to her. Then their eyes would catch and linger, until one of them broke the contact. More than a glance, less than a stare. Like some kind of test, the point of which had no purpose. As if there was an invisible line, a duration of time neither was quite ready to cross. Both waiting for the other to do or say *something*. But it would always end with an awkward pause, followed by an even more awkward attempt at changing the subject.

What were they so afraid of?

Grayson was a hot mess that morning. That was how I knew we were going to see Brandy today. He'd lain in bed an excruciatingly long time, alternately glancing at the clock on the nightstand and then staring up at the ceiling, fingers laced together on his chest. When the intensity of my own stare didn't get him up and moving, I crawled across the bed to snort in his ear. He flopped over. I licked his neck.

Pushing me away, he grumbled, "Stop it."

I tried to wait. I really did. But it was morning, and my bladder was full.

So I hopped off the bed, stood at the door, and woofed softly. *Go see Brandy?*

"Hold your horses. I have to pee, too."

Pee? Well, yes, that. But more than anything I wanted to go see Brandy today. I knew Grayson did, too. I just didn't understand why we couldn't see her every day, why we couldn't stay longer, why she just didn't come back here with us and—

"I just..." Grayson pulled the sheet up to cover his head. A second later, he flipped it down. "I don't know. What if I'm entirely wrong? Like… what if she thinks I'm some weirdo, a creep? Oh God, this sounds so grade school. I'm a fifty-year old divorcee, for crying out loud. Aaaagggh!"

With that outburst, he leaped out of bed, pounded down the stairs in nothing but his boxers, and let me outside. A few minutes later when he let me in, the coffee pot had been started, and he had his running clothes on. After letting the horses out, we went on a short, fast run around the farm.

Frost sparkled on the grass. Wherever we went, we left a trail of footsteps. The wind was cold enough to bite at my face as we broke out into the open beyond the horse barn. Even in the frigid air, running felt good. It made my heart beat bolder and my muscles stronger and my lungs bigger. Grayson no longer huffed or gimped. As we raced up the highest hill, he drove his knees and pumped his arms hard. At the top, he pivoted, and we raced back down.

Too soon, our run was over. I waited by the bathroom door while Grayson showered and dressed. As he made his way down the stairs, I dashed to the front door.

"Not yet," he said and went to the kitchen, where he drank his coffee and ate his toast while I had my breakfast.

The moment he got up to put his dishes in the sink, I rushed to the front door again.

"Too early, Sooner." He sat on the couch, then turned the TV on. "Visiting hours don't start until ten."

Let's go, I barked. *Let's go! Let's go! Let's go! Let's—*

"Stop. It."

Let's—

A throw pillow sailed through the air, then hit the floor close by me with a *woompf!* Taking the hint, I lay down with an exaggerated sigh. Every time Grayson moved—to aim the remote or readjust the couch cushions or stretch his legs—I sat up. But then he'd scowl at me or shake his head and I'd sink to the floor, weighed down with disappointment.

I'd finally drifted back off to sleep when I heard his footsteps fading toward the kitchen. The TV had been turned off, the relative quiet amplifying his every move. He set his coffee cup in the sink. The car keys jangled. The clip of my leash rattled.

I was at his feet in a blink, jumping up and down, spinning in circles.

We're going! We're going!

"Yes, Sooner. It's time. We're going to see Brandy."

It was my dream come true: Brandy, Grayson, and me—all together. I only wished it could be that way every day.

—o00o—

Brandy was waiting in her wheelchair when we got to her hospital room. She was all dressed up in nice clothes, with little smears of pink on her lips and dabs of sparkly gray on her eyelids. She also smelled like flowers. Which was an odd coincidence because Grayson had stopped to buy her some.

"I... I wasn't sure which kind you liked, so I got the arrangement that had pretty much everything." Clutched between his two hands was an explosion of color: whirls of pink in different shades, buttons of sunny yellow, lacy white flowers, and spots of red and blue and purple. "Now that I think about it, maybe I went a bit overboard."

All four feet on the floor, I greeted Brandy with wags and whines of excitement. She ruffled the fur on top of my head, then tweaked one of my cheeks. I licked her palm, but what I really wanted to do was jump in her arms. Somehow, without ever being told, I knew it wasn't appropriate anymore. It was hard not to do, but I was sooooo happy just to be with her.

"They're perfect." Brandy held out her hands to receive the huge bouquet. "You know why? Because I don't have a favorite. I love all flowers. You made the right choice." Bringing them to her nose, she inhaled deeply. Smiling, she laid them in her lap. "Ready for our walk?"

Walk? Did Brandy say we were going for a walk? But... how could she walk with her legs like they were?

"Are you sure you want to?" Grayson's brow folded in concern. "It's a bit chilly out. I could just push you up and down the hallway. Maybe we could hang out in the activity room and—"

"Grayson," she interjected, "what do you think I do when you're not here? I've been up and down the hallway a million times. I want to go outside. Feel the sun on my face. The wind in my hair." She flounced her red curls. "Now, if you'll just hand me my coat..."

He retrieved her coat from a hook by the bathroom door, then helped her put it on. Which wasn't easy, because her movements were constricted by the braces she still wore on her leg and back. Once she had both arms in the sleeves, Grayson attempted to close the buttons in front, but the two sides of her coat couldn't quite reach.

"Don't worry about that. I'll be fine. It's not *that* cold yet." She tugged the blanket that was in her lap up higher over her middle. The flowers almost tumbled to the floor, but she caught them. "I think we need to leave the flowers here, though."

"Oh." He looked at her blankly as she offered them back. "Of course. But... right. I forgot to bring a vase. Maybe they have one over at the gift shop in the hospital... Should I—?"

"Don't bother. Just stick them in the water pitcher. It's the flowers I treasure, not what they're sitting in."

He wedged the stems of the bouquet in a tall plastic container half full of water. The moment he drew his hands away, it started to tip. He grabbed it just before it fell sideways. Then he wedged the base of the container between a lamp and stack of books with the wall behind it.

"Perfect," Brandy said. "The room looks so much more cheerful now."

Satisfied Brandy seemed pleased with his gift, Grayson maneuvered to stand behind the wheelchair. Placing his hands on the handles, he gave it a nudge. It didn't move. He pushed a little harder, and Brandy snickered.

"Sorry." She put her hand over her mouth to contain her laughter. "Just wanted to see how hard you'd try before it occurred to you the brake was on."

"Very funny." Reaching down to the side of the chair, he lifted a lever. "At your command, Mistress Anders."

She turned her hand palm up. "First, the leash. I'd like to walk the dog."

Walk, yes! I woofed softly, mindful this was a quiet place and loud repetitive barking would be frowned upon.

"You know that word, don't you?" Brandy smiled at me. I spun in a tight circle, then did my happy dance.

"Which way?" Grayson handed her the leash.

Brandy pointed to the right. "I suggest we ride the elevator to the ground floor. I can take the bumpiness of the stairs, but it's murder on the wheelchair."

They laughed. Such a lovely sound. They were happy together. Which made me happy.

If only it could always be like this, but I was getting the sense that life was ever-changing. Even when things were going totally right, something, anything could happen to send it spiraling out of control. I wanted to hang onto this day forever.

He wheeled her into the elevator. I rushed in, wary of the doors that shut on their own. Soon, I had that familiar sinking feeling that told me we were going down. When the motion stopped and the doors slid open, I rushed back out. Brandy tugged back on my leash, and I fell back in line beside her.

She and Grayson chattered nonstop as we went out into a little courtyard. The small trees and bushes that surrounded it were nearly bare of leaves. He wheeled her around the perimeter once before stopping at a bench. The air felt cool on my nose as I settled down between where Grayson sat and Brandy's wheelchair. There was a lightness and a rhythm to their words. But there was also comfort in the brief spans of silence.

"A computer programmer?" Grayson cocked his head. "I never would've pinned you for that."

"Why—because I'm a woman?"

"No, not at all. Because of your sense of humor. I think of tech geeks as talking incessantly about gigabytes and code and all sorts of things that don't make any sense to me. Being on a different plane of intellect, I guess. I knew some through my work, and I never felt like I spoke the same language as them."

Her left eyebrow arched. "I feel that way about your kind."

"My kind?"

"A numbers man, as we used to call the people in accounting. But we're not all that different, are we? Our work is just one part of who we are. If we start reducing people to what they do or where they come from or what kind of clothes they wear, then we're failing to see the parts of that person—parts we may connect with."

They stared at each other for a while. Like they were sharing thoughts.

Grayson opened his mouth as if to speak, then shut it. Elbows resting on his knees, he laced his fingers together and waited a few breaths before saying, "I was like that before I came to Faderville."

"Like what?"

He shrugged. "I thought I had nothing in common with the people who lived here. That we were from different worlds. They didn't belong in mine, and I didn't fit in theirs."

"And now?"

SAY WHEN

A pretty young woman with thick dark hair opened the courtyard door from inside, then held it open for an older man with a walker. They both nodded a hello before beginning a slow walk around the outside of the little garden. The old man had on a red hat with lettering. His spine was bent, and he moved as if his knees could barely hold him up.

With every step, the woman encouraged him. "Look at you, Dad. Last week, you could barely walk across the room. Those new knees of yours are practically bionic."

When the father and daughter reached the far corner of the courtyard, Grayson continued. "Now? I think the people in Faderville have helped me discover parts of me I didn't even know were there. Or maybe... maybe it's just a new me."

Brandy reached across the space between them, then put her hand on his knee. Taking her fingers in his, he squeezed lightly.

She held his gaze. "I like people who are always trying to figure themselves out. Growth is good. Even when it comes at the cost of humility."

They didn't talk for a while. Just sat there staring at the bare branches and dried up stems and gazing up at the sky.

"So," Brandy finally said, "tell me about your family."

"That's easy. I don't have one. Nobody close, anyway. Both my parents have been gone for a while now. They were older when they had me. I was an only child. And you?"

"One brother in Texas. He has a wife and one-year-old daughter. He and his wife suggested I come live with them. Until I'm well enough to take care of myself, that is."

Turning to stare off in the distance, he hesitated. "When will that be? For how long?"

"If you're asking when they're going to release me, they haven't said... yet. As for how long I might be in Texas, who knows?"

"Oh." He kept his face turned away from hers, but I could see his jaw twitch. "Are you going to? Go live with them, I mean."

"I haven't decided yet. Plenty of time to figure it out. Although I did sell my house just outside Lexington last week. My friend from the dog club, Jaelynn, had a son looking for a starter home, so it worked out for him. It was an older two-story with both bedrooms upstairs. Neither the front nor the back door was set up to accommodate a wheelchair ramp, and the bathrooms… Let's just say I'd have had to park my chariot in the hallway and crawl to the john. Forget using the shower."

"Selling your house must've been a hard decision."

"Yes and no. The neighborhood was nice enough, but the house itself wasn't anything fancy. I figured it was time to accept my reality, which is that I have too many limitations to be able to keep up with a house and yard right now. Probably didn't get as much as I could have, but now I have that money to help with my medical costs and long-term care. My insurance is decent, but it will far from cover—" She covered her mouth with a hand briefly. "Oh gosh, I'm so sorry. I don't mean to saddle you with my problems. They aren't yours to solve. Anyway, I'll miss my house, but it seemed like the right decision for now, things being what they are."

"Brandy, it's okay, really. I don't mind you telling me. After all, we are friends, right?"

"Yeah, I suppose you could call us that. We're more than acquaintances, anyway."

"So, what about your parents? Do they live far away, too?"

"My dad doesn't. But… he had that massive stroke and…"

"Your mom—is she still around?"

Lowering her eyes, Brandy bit her lip. "No, she died when I was young. Fifteen, to be exact. She overdosed on prescription meds."

Grayson paused. "Accidental?"

"I don't think so. I mean, no one ever said for sure, but she hadn't been right for a long time. She'd been in a funk for months.

Years, maybe. Like any kid, I was kind of wrapped up in my own world. All I knew was she was somehow different from other moms. It wasn't until later that I found out she took pills for anxiety and depression. When I found her that day—"

"*You* found her?" Grayson was facing Brandy now, his full attention directed at her.

Swiping at a tear, Brandy nodded. "I'd come home early from school. It was an exam day, but she must've forgotten. A friend dropped me off at home. I found her in bed… I thought she was asleep at first. I almost shut the door and left because I had softball practice. But something just wasn't right. She was lying on top of her blanket. The TV was on, really loud. Then I saw the open pill bottle… the empty bottle of rum…"

Grayson slid as close to her as he could, reaching to enclose her in his arms. Feeling her sadness, too, I laid my chin on her knee as she cried softly. A little while later, Grayson offered her a tissue. She wiped her eyes and blew her nose.

"If she was hurting inside," Brandy said, "why didn't she tell someone? Didn't she understand what being without a mother would do to *me*?"

"Probably not. People who are depressed… The mind does crazy things to them. Sometimes, it even convinces them the whole world—even those they love—would be better off if they weren't in it, pulling everyone around them down." Grayson's gaze slid to the ground. "Brandy, I… I never told you the full story about the day I found Sooner."

She waited for him to go on, but it took a long time for him to get the words out. So long that the old man and his daughter got up, walked halfway around the courtyard, and left.

"A year ago," he finally went on, "after my divorce, I lost my job. No matter how hard I tried to put my life back in order, nothing ever seemed to go my way. At my ex-wife's insistence, I'd been seeing a therapist. I used to resent my appointments with him, but at the time, I thought it would save my marriage. It didn't do that, but I suppose it gave me someone to talk to. Then when I came here, even that feeble thread broke. I didn't know anyone, didn't have a purpose or a future, didn't have any friends to turn to because I'd spent the last twenty years of my life investing in my career... I had nothing but time on my hands. It was only caring for the horses that kept me getting out of bed every day, but even that wasn't enough. A string of blue days turned into a suffocating cloud. It's hard to describe what depression feels like, but most people figure it's an emotion you can shirk yourself of voluntarily. That all you have to do is slap yourself out of it by adopting a positive attitude. But it's not like that at all. It's a physical feeling. A heaviness. Like being hopelessly lost or drowning. You want it to stop—to go away forever. But it only drags you lower and lower.

"So one morning, I opened a bottle of sleeping pills and... I heard the horses raising a ruckus. There was a dog barking in the barn. And I thought... I thought, 'I can't leave the horses to get hurt by a stray dog or starve in the barn. I have to save them. Give them a chance.' So I spit out the pills and went out to the barn—where I found Sooner.

"In a matter of minutes, everything changed. When I found her in that stall—all skin and bones, her fur matted, gashes in her skin—and she looked at me, I forgot all about my troubles. I *had* to save that dog from dying. Had to find out who she belonged to."

Brandy studied her hands in her lap. "Had you ever thought of, you know... doing that before?"

"Ending my life?" Grayson said frankly. "No. But at the moment, everything just seemed so dismal, so hopeless. Like I was sinking in quicksand and there was a boulder on top of me, pushing me beneath the surface. If someone had thrown me a rope just then, I wouldn't have reached out for it. I just wanted to stop the feeling. Wanted a way out."

She raised her eyes, waited for him to look at her. "Sooner saved you?"

He nodded.

"And now—how do you feel about your life now?"

A burst of wind swirled around us, tossing a strand of hair across Brandy's face. Grayson reached out, tucked it behind her ear, and lingeringly brushed his fingers across her cheek. "Like everything's going to be all right. Maybe even great someday."

He drew his hand away.

"Do you believe in fate, Grayson?"

"Can't say I do."

"I can't see how you couldn't. I mean… your marriage broke up, you lost your job, got displaced to a locale totally foreign to you. And yet, it all seems to be working out for you. Like it was meant to be."

"Brandy… if you accept that, then you have to accept that your accident was fate, too. That you were supposed to get hurt and suffer and lose the use of your legs. No, Brandy. I have to think that sometimes crap just happens. Even to good people like you. I can't believe that something so horrible was ever meant to happen to you."

Her mouth tilted in a half smile. "But is it truly horrible if something better comes of it?"

"Like what?"

She shrugged. "I don't know yet. But someday, I will."

"Maybe…"—he looked up at the sky, as if searching for something there, then at Brandy—"maybe it's not so much that fate happens to us, like we're on some kind of raft in a stormy sea. Maybe who we are, deep down inside, determines where we end up. Like our character is our rudder."

They stared at each other for an uncomfortably long time.

What I'd heard was a lot of 'Blah, blah, blah, blah… blah, blah.' Like I said, humans used way too many words. They'd be better served to act on those words, and, if they felt something, which I was sure they did, they needed to. Those two liked each other. A lot. But instead of showing it, they just kept talking and talking and talking. It almost put me to sleep.

Dogs had it right. If we didn't trust you, we'd growl. If we were still sizing a person up, we'd study them from a safe distance. If we liked them, we'd wag our hind ends and lick them all over. Once our mind was made up, we weren't shy about showing how we felt. What was the point of holding it in? Life was too short not to let someone know they were loved.

Yawning, I stretched in a play bow. It had to be left to the dog to point out the obvious, apparently. First, I licked Brandy's fingers. Just as she raised her hand to pet me, I moved to Grayson and rooted at his hand.

"Grayson," Brandy said, "I think she's trying to tell us something."

"You're right." He stood. "Need to go potty, girl?"

Potty? What? No.

Before I could give them more clues as to what they *should* be doing, Grayson led me toward a patch of mulch. This wasn't grass. I'd always been taught to do my business on grass, even if it was covered by snow. Exasperated, I ignored him.

"Go potty. Hurry up."

Finally, I squeezed out a few drops, then pulled him back toward Brandy.

"Looks like she's ready to go," she said.

Go? I looked from Brandy to Grayson, then spun in a circle. *Go home! All go home!*

Brandy laughed. "Let's go then."

No matter how hard I pulled toward the lobby once we went inside, they weren't getting the message. We went not outside to the car, but back to the elevator and up to Brandy's room, where they spread a blanket atop the little table there and shared a lunch from a

SAY WHEN

picnic basket. Grayson slipped me the crust from his sandwich, just like he always did, while Brandy pretended not to notice.

After a while, I forgot the fact we were still at this odd place that had become Brandy's home for now. It wasn't quite what I wanted, but home was wherever my people were.

And there *was* food involved.

I wanted this *every* day—to be with Grayson and Brandy together. I didn't want to stay with just one or the other. I loved them both in ways that were different and equal. I didn't even care if Brandy and I never did the things we used to do again. I could run with Grayson instead. That was more than good enough.

Their love was enough.

chapter 29

Grayson

Grayson didn't recognize the truck parked in front of the stables. For a moment, he considered phoning the sheriff, thinking someone was trying to steal the horses while he was off the property. Then he wondered if the guy he'd started buying straw and hay from had a new vehicle for delivery. He was about due to show up, but the bed of the truck was empty. Maybe he'd already carried the bales in.

All his questions dissolved when Loretta walked out of the stables leading Goliath. The reins were draped loose between them, the horse ambling along behind her, his nose inches from the back of her head.

Loretta waved, and Grayson waved back. Instead of parking in front of the garage next to the house like he normally did, he turned the wheel and stopped the SUV near the horse barn. When he got out, a man Grayson didn't know emerged from the stables. By then, Loretta was walking Goliath around the outside of the riding arena, talking to the gentle giant like she would a child, occasionally patting him on the nose and then pushing it away when his lips nibbled at her hair.

The stranger nodded. "Howdy! You must be Mr. Darling."

"Grayson's fine." He stuck his hand out, noticing a second too late that the man's right hand was a prosthetic.

"I'm Clayton, Loretta's husband." He returned the handshake as if it were no big deal. "Back from Florida a week early. Loretta wanted to swing by on the way home to see how you were getting on. She said looks like you picked it all up like a natural." He leaned in close, his voice lowered like he didn't want his wife to overhear, even though she was a good fifty yards away by now. "Don't take it wrong, but she was a little worried about you tending to the horses, being a city slicker and all. But you gotta know Loretta. She doesn't think anyone but her can do things right."

"Um… thanks, I think."

Sooner trotted up to sit slightly behind Grayson, peering past his knee, as if she found a measure of safety there. When he'd first let her out of the car, she'd been concerned with Goliath, watching the big horse from a safe distance.

Clayton clapped Grayson on the shoulder in a friendly manner. "Don't worry. You did fine." He leaned sideways to get a better look at the dog. Sooner shrank back. "That the dog that was lost before we left? The one from the accident?"

"Yes, this is her. Sooner's her name."

"Well, I'll be. She looks a lot healthier than when I last saw her." He cupped his good hand to his mouth. "Hey, Loretta! Come here. Look what showed up."

Looking over her shoulder, she guided the horse in a U-turn. As she neared them, her eyes settled on the dog. A crease formed between her eyebrows, then disappeared as a smile transformed her face. "Is that who I think it is, Clayton? The one you almost caught?"

"Sure is," Clayton said. "She looks a sight better, don't she?"

"I'll say. She was a sack of bones when you had her cornered in the garage. Hello, Grayson."

"Hi, Loretta. How's your daughter?"

"Good, good. Still has some discomfort, but she recovered faster than expected. Turns out once she could do things for herself, Clayton and I were just getting in the way. So we came home. I wanted to see Goliath. You took good care of all of 'em. Too good, maybe. A might generous with the feed, weren't you?"

"Guilty. But they always look so hungry."

She rolled her eyes.

"Hey, I kept them alive."

"That you did. Truth be told, except for them being a little stouter around the girth, you did fine."

"I told you," Clayton said in an aside. Loretta gave him a look that instantly cowed him. He kicked a stone loose in the dirt. "Excuse me while I hunt down a pair of wire snippers I left here months ago."

After Clayton went back into the barn, Loretta dropped Goliath's reins and bent to scratch behind Sooner's ear. The dog remained glued to Grayson's side, although she seemed a little less leery of Loretta than she had her husband.

"Just look how full and shiny her fur is," Loretta cooed. "And she's got some meat on her ribs now. Sure didn't look like that when we saw her before."

"Not too fat?"

"Not at all. She looks fit."

"She should. We've been running together."

"You don't say." Standing, she dusted bits of straw from her jeans. "Did you locate her owner?"

"Just came from there, actually," Grayson said. "The hospital, that is."

"She's still in there? Wow, must've been pretty bad."

Grayson told her what he knew of Brandy's injuries, but when it came to the prognosis, he was admittedly fuzzy on that.

"So she doesn't know how long it will be before she can go

home?" Loretta asked.

"They don't exactly know yet. I figured taking her dog to visit would help speed her progress along."

"Her dog, huh? So she's taking her back at some point? You're just keeping the dog until then?"

"Well, yes, I suppose so." Although that was another matter he hadn't sorted out. Along with a host of others. The entire way home, he'd been mulling a list of things he needed to decide on. The problem was there were too many, and he didn't know where to start. Lately, his feelings toward Brandy herself were complicating matters even further.

"But I thought you were planning on going back to New York? Heck, the reason I made Clayton stop here before we went home was so I could check to see if the horses were even still here. The whole time I was gone, I kept wondering if you'd really meant what you said—about giving Goliath to me—but I thought it would be pushy to ask until I got back and could actually take him. I figured we'd show up and the place would be empty. Or someone else altogether would be living here. I was surprised to see things looked pretty much the same. I texted you when we were on the way here today, but you didn't answer."

Clayton exited the barn again, carrying a pair of wire snippers. He put the tool in the truck, then joined them.

"Oh, sorry." Grayson pulled his phone out before tapping at the settings. "I turned the sound off when I was at the hospital, and I forgot to turn it back on. Yes, I see it now. I'm glad you stuck around, though. And yes, I meant what I said about Goliath. He's all yours if you still want him."

Her smile beamed wider. "Oh, I do. I sure do. But we have to patch up the lean-to and fix a few holes in the fence first. What about the rest of them, though? I thought you were going to sell them."

"I was, but… I just never got around to it, I guess. Rex Franzen said I could sell them quickly at auction, but then I wouldn't have any say in who bought them. When I put a sign up at the grocery, I got a few calls. Most just asked a couple of questions but never followed up. Anyway, I should probably do more about that. Are there any 4-H groups I can let know about them? I'd rather sell them to a kid at a bargain price than someone who didn't care about their welfare." He'd wanted top dollar at first. Had thought he needed it. But over time, he'd concluded that money didn't matter all that much.

Loretta gave Clayton a pleading look. He shrugged his shoulders and said, "Go on. You know you've been thinking about it."

"As luck would have it," Loretta began, "I volunteered to advise a riding club next year. Figured as long as I had time on my hands, I'd do something useful with it. Some of the kids live in town and board horses at various places. It would be a lot easier if there was one place they could all meet and learn to ride. A place kind of like this. With a few spare horses." Hands in her back pockets, she cast her glance around the farm. Goliath had wandered off about ten feet to nibble on some grass next to the fence.

It took a few moments for Grayson to catch on to her drift. "Oh, *here*, you mean? I, uh, don't know. I'm still not sure how long I'll be here."

It was only lately he'd stopped being fixated on getting back to New York. Every attempt to find desirable employment there had fallen through. Meanwhile, circumstances kept steering him in this direction. He wasn't sure if fate was trying to clobber him over the head with 'signs' or if he'd merely given up. It had been a couple of months, almost three, since he'd left New York. A lot of positions could've opened up in that time.

But then, there were the horses to consider. And the dog. And Brandy.

Brandy... Her smile had been undeniably warm. That she could set her discomfort aside and engage so fully with him made him marvel at her. Simply being in her presence had made him feel hopeful, for reasons he couldn't pinpoint. The farm outside Faderville was a drivable distance from the hospital. If he took the dog for regular visits—

Loretta batted at the air to get his attention. "Forget I even mentioned it. You have your own life to live. But... if you *do* decide to stay here in Faderville, Clayton and I were just daydreaming about how this would be the perfect boarding stable and that we'd be happy to help out." Gathering up Goliath's reins, she began to lead him toward the gate to the pasture. The other horses had been watching with vague interest, but as she lifted the latch, Spark's head came up. Moments later, she and the others were trotting to greet Loretta. "Just something for you to chew on. Don't feel pressured or anything. Sometimes I get crazy ideas."

After she walked Goliath into the pasture, she removed his halter. Spark and Clifford ambled up to her, snorting and nickering happily. Persephone hung back, as if expressing her displeasure at Loretta's extended absence. The halter slung over her shoulder, she started for the barn.

Clayton muttered to Grayson, "I could tell you stories about her. Crazy ain't the half of it."

"I heard that, Clayton Porter Hoberty," she said without turning around.

Goliath kept his eyes on Loretta, following her as far as he could on the other side of the fence up to the point where it stopped and she went into the stables.

Clayton and Grayson stood in the fading sunlight, a clumsy silence stretching between them. The situation required small talk, a skill which Grayson had never entirely mastered.

They glanced at each other, smiled, looked around them. Sooner nudged Grayson in the back of the knee, as if to suggest they move away, preferably inside the house, where this stranger posed no threat.

She must've remembered the incident when Clayton tried to capture her. Still, Grayson wasn't about to let her off the hook by putting her away. If Loretta was going to be around a lot, Clayton was, too. The dog might as well get used to him. And Grayson might as well get to know him.

"So"—Grayson peered into the dark tunnel Loretta had disappeared into, as if she might suddenly reappear and spare them both—"how was Florida?"

"Florida? Florida's just fine, I s'pose. Some folks like it. I can see why. You could practically get drunk on the sunshine. But to me, it's all flat as a pancake. They don't have real dirt either. Just sand. Year-round bugs. Frogs, lizards. Gators and crocs. Sharks and jellyfish. Whatever you do, don't go near the water. Don't go outside if you can help it, either. You know what people say—nice place to visit, but I wouldn't want to live there."

He spat at the ground. "Loretta… all she did was talk about home. Not to our daughter or the grandkids, mind you. They've all been citified—oldest granddaughter has a panic attack if she's more than ten miles from a shopping mall. But we're country folk to the core. Loretta missed the horses. Heck, she'll even get up at the crack of dawn just to feed 'em. She's kind of like the little girl who never grew up when she's around them. Guess they make her feel young. Nothing she loves more than teaching a kid how to care for and ride them.

"Now me, on the other hand, I don't get the fascination. I'd rather spend my cash on a new truck or a bigger TV or fifty-yard-line tickets at a bowl game. But you know what? Them critters make her happy, manure and all. And"—smiling broadly, he scratched at his paunch—"they keep her out of my hair a good part of the day. A man needs time to nap and watch sports, don't you agree?"

Grayson nodded politely.

Sooner crept from behind Grayson's knee. Neither man said a

word as she extended her neck to sniff cautiously at Clayton's shoes. When she sat at Clayton's feet and tilted her head up at him, he raised his eyebrows at her. "Don't you worry, sweetheart. I'm not gonna steal you. Right here's where you belong. Right here. Lil' slice o' doggie heaven."

Grayson studied Sooner. She was still a little guarded, but confident enough that Clayton wasn't going to try to nab her this time around. But yes, she appeared content with her surroundings. Happy with her life here. With him. Even though just a short while ago, she'd been reluctant to leave Brandy's side.

A few long minutes later, Loretta appeared. "We'll be back first thing in the morning if that's all right with you? But we can't take him right away. We still need to fix some fencing. And the shed has a few leaks in the roof. Not sure how long all that'll take, though. Depends on the weather… and the help." She tipped her head toward the truck. Clayton took the cue, moving to follow her to it. "Besides, the horses could use some exercise. I'll come out once or twice a day to do that. They can get lazy if'n someone don't make 'em move."

"Oh, right. Sure then. Come out anytime. You don't even have to call or tell me ahead of time. Just don't let yourself inside the house without knocking. I've been known to amble around in my boxers."

They both laughed.

"Thanks for the warning." Loretta got in the driver's seat while Clayton climbed in the other side. She rolled the window down. "Just let me know before you up and leave, will you, so I can say goodbye—assuming you leave, that is."

Before he could answer, she drove away. Grayson lifted a hand in a wave, even though he wasn't sure if either saw or returned the gesture. He couldn't have answered her, anyway. Because he didn't know what he was going to do—even though he knew what he *should* do.

A couple of years ago, his life had seemed so straightforward:

put his head down, work hard, and someday he'd get his reward. That focus had come with a price, however. He'd sacrificed his marriage. Frittered away opportunities for friendships and memories. Then when his job went away… he had nothing ahead of him and no one to turn to.

Not having a prestigious job or money hadn't been the worst thing, though. Being alone had.

Then along came Sooner. Challenging him. Testing his patience. Helping him make new friends. Sharing the re-found joy of running with him. Listening to his problems and all his regrets as they sat together on top of the hill overlooking everything.

Heaven—Faderville and this farm had become that for him as well. It wasn't a place he would ever have imagined himself being. Yet, it had been exactly what he'd needed.

He could see himself staying here indefinitely. But… not all by himself.

—o0Oo—

Every time Grayson glanced in the rearview mirror, he expected to see Sooner there—if not staring back at him, then curled up in a ball on the backseat, snoozing contentedly. It was a little like the first few months after Fee left him. He'd roll over in the morning, expecting to find her stretched out beside him on the bed, blissfully slumbering. But there hadn't even been the indent of her head on the pillow.

He readjusted the mirror of his rental car. Yes, Rex was still there, tucked in behind him on I-75 in Grayson's new-to-him SUV. Having given the rental car a thorough cleaning, he'd put Sooner in the SUV to be Rex's passenger during the drive to Lexington. He liked the looks of his new vehicle. Not quite the workhorse a pickup was, but still more functional than the tiny two-door he was driving right now. The rental company had told him that, for a reasonable fee, he could drop it off in Lexington, rather than drive it all the way back to New York City. It was worth the cost to save himself days of driving. He could've taken it back, then cleared out his apartment and returned in a box truck, but then there would've been the problem of how to get the truck back. In the end, it seemed more important to stay where he was for now, so he could take Sooner to visit Brandy often.

Meanwhile, he planned to hire a moving company and put his things in storage. When he had time, he'd go sort through them, but the truth was he hadn't missed his possessions much. They were a reminder of the life he no longer lived. They may as well have belonged to someone else. Which gave him a thought... Maybe he could donate his stuff to a halfway house or shelter—someone who might need the items more than he did.

Because he wasn't going back to Manhattan. Not anytime soon, anyway.

—o0Oo—

After dropping the rental off and squaring up the final bill, Grayson took over driving duties in the SUV. In the few seconds it took him to buckle up and turn the key in the ignition, the scent of spearmint nearly overpowered him. If he didn't know better, he'd swear someone had dumped an entire bottle of mouthwash in the backseat.

"What's the scoop?" Rex waved a stick of spearmint gum at him.

Grayson declined his offer before cracking both front windows. Cool, fresh air poured in. The trees lining the parking lot were a patchwork of bronze, crimson, and russet. It carried him back to his college days: frosty mornings, a trail beside the woods, his breath an icy cloud, three-quarter-inch spikes sinking into muddy earth, the clop of feet from somewhere behind, pursuing him, spurring him to run faster...

He hadn't realized until recently how much he missed that part of his life. It had given him both drive and purpose, as well as connected him to others. He gazed at the reflection of his own eyes in the rearview mirror. Where had that person gone?

Readjusting the mirror, he caught a glimpse of Sooner, already lying down in the backseat like a seasoned traveler. He then moved his seat forward, tilted the steering wheel at a comfortable angle, and fixed all the mirrors again. Rex was half a foot taller than him. Everything was messed up. Even the floor mats were out of place.

Rex tilted his cowboy hat back, stretching his long arms wide. So wide his left hand now rested on the back of Grayson's seat. Grayson shifted to the left as he glanced sideways at Rex's intruding limb, but Rex didn't catch the hint. Instead, Rex slapped the back of the seat. "Fess up, now. You said you'd give me the scoop on the stocks on the way to the hospital. I'm guessing you're worth a fortune—am I right?"

Grayson backed out of the parking space. The rental facility was on the far side of town from the hospital. It would take a good thirty minutes in traffic to get there. "Not exactly."

"Okeydokey, not billions, then. A cool few mil?"

"Not even that."

"Say what? I thought—"

"Yes, I thought that, too—or hoped, anyway. I tracked down Skip's business lawyer in Louisville, who directed me to his broker in New York. Turns out the stocks had been split at some point, so they aren't currently worth a lot. He'd also sold some to finance his equine investments, just like you said."

"But his franchises? That's one of the most popular grub chains this side of the Mississippi. How could he not be rolling in dough from those? I don't get it."

"He kept reinvesting in new stores until he had himself spread pretty thin. Some restaurants turned a healthy profit, but most didn't. He was unflinchingly loyal to his employees and customers, so he did his best to avoid closing the struggling locations. In the end, he had to.

It was a blow to the communities his establishments served, not just because of those he employed, but also because of the local charities he funded: boys' and girls' clubs in disadvantaged neighborhoods, domestic abuse shelters, addiction counseling services, refugee resettlement charities… He even supplied uniforms for a youth track club in Nashville. Running those businesses wasn't just about turning a profit; it was about lifting up those who needed a hand the most. All told, I'll get a few hundred thousand out of the stocks. Enough to keep up the farm for a while. If I don't sell it, that is."

"So are you going to? I know a good real estate agent who—"

"No offense, Rex, but you couldn't even fill me in on the full extent of Skip's finances. I had to hunt it down myself."

Rex puffed his chest up. "Look here, corporate law and stocks are not on my list of specialties. Not much call for that in a humble lil' town like Faderville. I serve the basic needs of common folk, not hoity-toity bigwigs like you were used to cavorting with. Besides, Skip barely mentioned that end of things when he came in to set up a will. He made it sound like it was all cut and dry. He handed off the papers, Martina filed them, and that was that. Same as any other honest guy getting his life squared away before the man upstairs called." Rex was talking louder and faster, as if the volume and overabundance of his words could convince Grayson to back down. "I didn't see him in my office again after that—just around town or down at the fairgrounds whenever there was a sale or a riding event. Hell, Gary, if I'd thought for a second—"

"For the last time, it's *Grayson*!" Grayson hit the brakes at the precise moment he shouted his own name. The stoplight ahead had turned red. Not that it had come as a surprise, but his attention had been so focused on trying to keep up with Rex's barrage that his mind hadn't been on his driving.

Rex slapped both hands flat against the dash, as if to stop himself from flying through the windshield. "All right, all right! I *may* have been a little out of the loop on Rex's dealings. I… apologize. And that ain't an easy thing for a proud man like me to do, mind you. So I'm sorry I let you down on that account. It's just that Martina is the only assistant I ever had. I didn't realize until she up and left that she was the cog that turned the wheel, so to speak. In fact, I'll be the first to admit she *may* have left, in part, because I didn't pay her well enough for all I expected of her. The hard truth is she's not coming back, and I have to move on."

Grayson never liked it when people blamed others for their own failures, but he did feel a little sorry for Rex. A little.

The light turned green. Grayson turned left and headed toward the highway. "I haven't decided yet. About the farm, that is."

Several miles later, Rex said, "It's a shame you can't keep the farm *and* use that money to help kids in need or something. A crying shame."

It was several miles down the highway before an idea came to Grayson. There was a way to keep up the farm *and* continue his uncle's humanitarian legacy, actually. But it would take more than just him to do it. Someone like Loretta, maybe.

chapter 30
Grayson

Even though they'd come from a different direction than normal, the moment Grayson turned the last corner before the hospital, Sooner popped up from her makeshift bed in the back of the SUV. By the time they found a parking spot in the hospital lot, she was turning circles and whining with anticipation.

Grayson got out, clipped her leash on, and locked the car. Rex offered him another stick of gum.

"How many packs a day do you go through?" Ignoring the offer, Grayson started toward the main entrance of the physical rehab facility.

"I don't keep count." Rex stuck the pack back in his suit pocket. "It's a habit I picked up when I gave up cigars—twenty-two years and ten months ago. All because Martina said she couldn't work in a place that smelled like an ashtray. She also helped assemble my wardrobe, scheduled my car maintenance and home repairs… I'm lost without that woman. Lost, I tell you. Feel like I'm on a blow-up pool raft in the middle of a hurricane in the Atlantic."

This was exactly what Grayson had dreaded when he'd asked Rex to help him return the car—too much information interspersed with hyperbole. Rex Franzen was one of those people who couldn't stop talking, no matter what. Grayson could only hope that being in Brandy's presence would provide some relief. He'd told her they would stop at the hospital on their way back. It would have been a wasted trip to come all this way and not do so—even if he had to tow Rex along.

"Maybe I ought to try to find her," Rex said as they crossed the parking lot. "I know a private investigator over in Bowling Green who could do the job. I'll double her salary if she... Wait, no. I can't quite afford that. I'll give her a twenty-percent raise. If she balks, I'll offer twenty-five. Then maybe she'll reconsider her situation and—"

Grayson's phone rang, sparing him. "Excuse me."

Rex gave him a thumbs-up as Grayson stepped away. The area code was from New York City, but he didn't have the number in his contacts.

Taking Sooner to a patch of grass, he gave her the command to go potty.

"Hello?"

"Hello, this is Terrence Hawkins again from Attovan Investments. Am I speaking to Grayson Darling?"

It took a second for Grayson to find his voice. "Uh... yes. Yes, it is."

"Look, I know this is unexpected, but we decided to touch bases with you about something. An opportunity."

"Did your candidate fall through?"

"Oh no. She joined us right away."

A small wave of relief washed through him. Not getting the job he'd wanted hadn't been such a bad thing after all. He was growing accustomed to his life in Kentucky. Had even found himself making plans—

"Actually, I have a better proposition for you," Hawkins continued. "I don't know if you're still in the market for employment, but we have another position available to head up a small department that deals in loans for start-ups. Basically, it's to help people who don't have a lot of capital, but do have a solid business plan and want to expand—"

Grayson listened as he detailed the duties of the position. It sounded like what he was doing with Becca and her husband, only a lot more volume and potentially bigger companies. When he got to the part about salary and benefits, Grayson was left speechless.

"Are you interested?" Hawkins asked.

Grayson leaned against a tree to hold himself up. Sooner was at the end of the leash heading back toward the main doors, staring over her shoulder at him.

"When do you need to know by?"

"By next week, at the latest. You were the best candidate for the position, but we need to fill it as soon as possible. You'll let me know?"

"Yes, of course."

For a full minute after he hung up, Grayson pretended to remain on the phone, waiting for a decision to come to him, some undeniable sign that would steer him in the right direction. But the longer he stood there, the more uncertain he felt. Sooner, tugging impatiently, wasn't helping matters.

"Did you go yet?" In all honesty, he'd been so taken unawares by the call he hadn't been paying attention to the dog.

Sooner woofed softly and leaped in the direction of the door, bucking at the end of her leash.

"All right, all right. Brandy's expecting us. Not like she's going to up and leave without telling me."

When Grayson rejoined Rex, the lawyer raised an eyebrow at him. "That's not the face of a man who just won the lottery. Bad news, partner?"

"No, not bad. I was just offered a lucrative position at one of the premier loan companies back in the city."

Rex clapped him on the back hard. "Congratulations, my man! Congratulations. Our little town could've used your talents, but can't say anyone would blame you for taking a bite out of the Big Apple."

Grayson didn't try to explain he hadn't automatically accepted the offer—or even knew if he would. He really wanted to talk to Brandy about it before he decided. Find out if she was going to move in with her brother. Only that discussion wasn't going to happen today. Not with Rex in the picture. It definitely wasn't something he felt comfortable discussing over the phone, either. No, it would have to wait until his next visit here in a few days—and he *would* decide by then.

He'd been waiting on an offer like this for a long time. An entire year. The pay was enough to afford a better apartment, closer to work and the park…

The more Grayson thought about it, the more he realized there really wasn't all that much to think about.

—o00o—

As expected, Rex dominated the conversation. Brandy was a good sport about it, though, and every so often, Grayson would catch her rolling her eyes or making funny faces if Rex turned his sights on the TV or out the window.

There was one positive about Rex: he hit it off with the dog. Apparently, they'd bonded on the trip to Lexington. Sooner always was a tolerant listener.

"My, that is impressive." Rex rubbed Sooner's ear, and she leaned into his touch. "Twenty-three titles, you say?"

"Yes," Brandy said, "if I counted right."

"Whewee! Dog's got more degrees than I do." He winked at Brandy. "Can she manage a law office? I've got an opening."

"Hmmm." Brandy tapped at her chin with a finger. "She can't type, file papers, or use the computer, but if you pay her in kibble, she'll happily play ball with your clients."

"Deal." Rex stuck out his hand. "As long as you give her some assistance with the computer aspect. It's time I joined the twenty-first century and put all my client files on hard drive. Or up in the clouds, whatever it is they're using these days."

Suddenly, Sooner hopped off the bed and stood by the door, a look of urgency on her cherubic face.

Grayson knew the signal. "Excuse me. I need to run her outside. Either of you need anything while I'm in the lobby? Rex—a pack of gum, maybe?"

"Nice of you to ask, but"—Rex patted the inside pocket of his suit coat—"I never go anywhere without backup."

A quick trip down the elevator and Sooner emptied her bladder on the first patch of grass they came to, but then she started to do the circle dance, which meant she was working on a bowel movement. They had to walk clear to the end of the sidewalk and halfway back before Sooner did her business. After he bagged her waste, he got to the front door to find no trash cans outside. Remembering one by the side door halfway around to the back, he went there. By the time he got back inside, Grayson figured a good ten minutes had elapsed. He'd apologize to Brandy when he had the chance. First, he needed to quench his thirst.

In the lobby, he paused at the counter that served as a snack shop for visitors and residents. The clerk was adding bags of chips to a display, and hadn't yet noticed him. He decided he'd pick up a drink on their way out.

When he returned to Brandy's room, Grayson expected to find Rex talking a blue streak. Instead, he found himself looking at Rex's back. He was speaking lowly to Brandy. Something made Grayson pause in the doorway, and Sooner automatically sat. It had been part of her training with Brandy, and Grayson found it convenient whenever they walked in town and had to stop at a crossing. On this occasion, her quiet obedience gave him a few moments to observe the interaction between Rex and Brandy. He almost cleared his throat to announce himself when he noticed Brandy had her arm extended. Rex was holding her hand close to his heart. Tears glistened in her eyes, and there was the faintest hint of a smile on her face.

Before they could notice him, Grayson stepped back into the corridor, pulling Sooner with him. He couldn't quite digest what he'd just witnessed. The two of them were acting as if they'd known each other for much longer than half an hour.

No, he had to be reading too much into it. Rex, being the amicable person he was, was just offering Brandy comfort. Besides, even if Rex had tried to flatter Brandy, she wasn't the sort to be so easily wooed. Grayson ought to know. Plus, Rex was married. He wouldn't be making overtures to Brandy—would he?

They were laughing now. Raucously. Like old, dear friends. What could possibly be so—?

"Mr. Darling! Are you lurking in the shadows?"

Grayson looked up to see Cherise bustling toward them, clipboard clutched to her side. She was a short stout woman of mixed heritage who could've passed for any of a dozen ethnicities, but with a congeniality that made everyone who met her instantly feel welcomed.

"I see you brought my favorite redhead today." Cherise crossed in front of Brandy's doorway, then bent to pet Sooner. The dog curled around so Cherise could scratch her hind quarters. "That's the spot. Isn't it, girl? Right there."

Grayson could barely hear her next words over the thumping in his chest.

"Looks like Miss Brandy already has a visitor." Straightening up, she leaned sideways to peer into the room and waved at Rex and Brandy. Then she scooted closer and whispered, "Fine-looking gentleman, but I don't think you have anything to worry about." She winked. "Miss Brandy practically glows whenever she talks about you."

"What... what do you mean?"

Sighing, she rolled her eyes. "Typical man. You haven't been paying attention." She tapped the tip of her finger to his chest, her words hushed. "She makes out like it's all about the dog's visits, but it's more than that. A girl can tell these things."

A flush of embarrassment washed through Grayson. He felt the sudden urge to explain the situation, to set Cherise's mind on less personal matters. "Rex came with me, actually. To drop a car off across town. I just came back from taking Sooner out."

At the mention of her name, Sooner did a little dance, pulling toward the door.

"Hmph, in that case, maybe you should hurry back in there before they get any friendlier. Bye now." Cherise moved along to the next doorway, then popped inside. "Hello there, Mrs. Palmer! Dr. Capelli will be along soon to talk to you about—"

Sooner lunged through the doorway, taking Grayson along with her. Rex and Brandy turned to look, Brandy's mouth open as if they'd been caught in the middle of an intimate conversation. She shut it abruptly, smiling in a polite way.

"That took a while," she said. "Everything come out okay?"

"The usual." Grayson unwound the leash from his hand, allowing Sooner to hop onto the bed. "I think it's time we got Rex back home. I'm sure he's got a stack of work to catch up on."

"Nothing that can't be attended to later," Rex said.

Grayson glared at him. "We don't want to wear Brandy out before her physical therapy."

"It's Saturday, Grayson," Brandy chimed in. "My physical therapist, Emalee, is off for the day. Which means I am, too."

They were making this difficult. Grayson took a five-dollar bill from his wallet. "I forgot to get myself a drink for the drive home. Rex, would you mind getting me a can of that peach sweet tea? Get yourself something, too, if you want. It's on me." He shoved the money into Rex's hand. "I'll meet you in the lobby in a few. Just want to say goodbye to my friend here."

Rex stared at his palm. If Grayson could've shoved him out the door and down the hallway, he would've.

"Will do," Rex finally said. He plucked up his hat from the table by the window, put it on, and tipped the brim to Brandy. "Delighted to have met you, Miss Brandy. I sincerely hope it's not too long before I see you again. Call me if you need anything." With a wink, he pressed a business card into her hand and sauntered out the door.

Not until after the elevator dinged and the doors opened and closed did Grayson speak. "Whatever you do, don't hire him as a lawyer."

"Rex? Why? He's so charming."

Charming? Grayson cringed. Overbearing was more like it. "Just trust me on this. Friendly and competent don't necessarily equate."

"If you say so." Brandy squeezed each of Sooner's front paws in turn. Her voice took on a wistful tone. "She's happy with you. I can tell."

The sentiment took Grayson so off guard that all the things he'd been planning on saying were flushed right out of his brain. "But she misses *you*. Every day."

"I know," Brandy whispered. Tears welled up in her eyes. She banished them with her fingertips, leaving little smudges of mascara underneath. *When had she started wearing makeup?* Grayson wondered. Without looking him in the eye, Brandy continued, "I've come to believe that people—and dogs—come and go in your lifetime for a reason. They each teach us something, as long as we're open to it.

My mama taught me that life is precious and even when we think we don't matter to someone, we do. I even believe there's some good in everybody—even an overblown lawyer who talks incessantly because he's afraid of silence. Are you sure Rex isn't a used-car salesman?"

"Positive. The car salesman in Faderville is much more subtle."

"Point taken about Rex. Although I still think he's a nice guy." She narrowed her eyes. "Was there something you wanted to say privately? You chased Rex off like a little brother intruding on a date."

"Well, mostly I just wanted to set up our next visit. I was afraid if Rex was here, he might invite himself along." He knew he ought to tell her about the offer now, and about how his whole outlook on life had changed and that she'd been a large part of that. But it was so complicated. And personal. "Anyway, I—"

"Good afternoon, Miss Anders!" A short dark-haired man strode into the room, flashing a brilliantly white smile. "How are you today?"

"Great, Dr. Capelli." Brandy pushed herself up higher on her pillows.

He flipped through her charts, his ragged black eyebrows lifting toward his hairline. "Ah, yes. I see. Uh-huh. Very good progress. Very good. I'm hearing wonderful things about you from PT, Miss Anders. They say you'll be in tiptop shape for the downhill slalom by the next Winter Olympics, yes?"

Brandy giggled. "I don't know about that."

The doctor turned to Grayson. "And who is this fine gentleman—husband, fiancé, boyfriend…?"

"Dog-sitter," Grayson answered. He could've said he was just a friend, but he didn't want Brandy to think that was all he ever wanted to be. Because the truth was he'd begun to think of her differently.

"Practically family then." The doctor shook his hand, then returned his attention to Brandy. "So, you've been here a while. Made considerable progress. But obviously, there's still a good way to go, yes?"

Brandy nodded.

Dr. Capelli flipped the edges of his lab coat open before slipping his hands in his pockets. "Perhaps we should talk about what lies ahead for you."

The mood had shifted abruptly from congenial to somber. Grayson felt like an intruder. He wanted to ask if Brandy wanted him to stay, but even that seemed presumptuous.

Shuffling backward a couple of steps, Grayson cleared his throat. "Uh, Brandy, I probably ought to rescue the snack shop attendant from Rex. I'll message you soon."

"Okay." She wiggled her fingers in a wave, then patted her chest to invite Sooner closer. When the dog was tucked against her, she gave her a longer-than-usual smooch on top of the head. "Be good, princess. Love you more than the sun and the moon and the stars. Forever and ever."

Sooner slathered her face in kisses, until Brandy abruptly thrust her away.

"Go," she ordered, the slightest quiver in her jaw. "Just… go."

Confused, Sooner cocked her head. When Brandy turned her face away, Sooner slunk from the bed and to Grayson's feet. He snapped her leash on, taking a second to ruffle her fur.

Grayson nodded at the doctor, then at Brandy. "See you next week, Brandy."

She forced a weak smile, but said nothing. Something in her had shifted, but maybe she was just nervous about what Dr. Capelli might say. If Grayson had felt it was his place to do so, he would've stayed with her. He wanted to. With all the difficulties she'd endured, she could use some support. But both Dr. Capelli and Brandy had gone silent, as if awaiting his exit.

He took the cue and left. He'd talk to her about it next time. By then, he'd have it all sorted out anyway.

chapter 31
Brandy

Good and bad. That was how Brandy had received the news from Dr. Capelli. She'd had a full day to let it all sink in, but she still wasn't sure how her life would unfold in the coming year. She *would* get better—he'd assured her that much. But by how much and how quickly remained to be seen.

The nerves along her spine had been severely damaged. Only time would tell if she would regain functionality of her lower limbs and to what degree. At worst, she would be wheelchair-bound forever and perpetually plagued by pain. At best, she would undergo a recovery that could last for years, but in which she might eventually be able to walk again. *Might*. But Dr. Capelli told her if that happened, she could expect to have a limp. She would only get to that point, he stressed, if she worked hard at it, without falter.

Her bones, for the most part, would mend. Eventually. The real problem, however, was that her spirit—who she was as a person—wasn't the same. Her future was a vast unknown. A void into which to toss her hopes and dreams. To everyone else, she likely appeared indomitable and determined. But inside, she was struggling. She'd always been a fighter, but she'd never been as exhausted as she was by *this* fight. It was like waking up every day knowing she had to climb the same enormous mountain over and over again. Instead of growing stronger and having it get easier, she felt more worn down each day.

Until Grayson began to visit with Sooner. That was enough to lift her up and make anything seem possible. Seeing her dog again filled her with a love so big she *wanted* to get better. Although she'd felt like giving up numerous times, she hadn't. She had persevered.

Something else had developed during those visits. Something entirely unexpected. She'd grown fond of Grayson. Felt a connection to him that was more than mere gratitude and deeper than friendship. Seeing him, talking to him, just *being* with him—it brought on a whole host of emotions that both energized her and threw her off balance. It was easy to be open with him. She loved to hear him laugh. Loved seeing the adoration he had for Sooner. The way he smiled every time he came into the room and saw her. The sigh of regret he made every time he left…

It also complicated things. When Grayson told her about the day Sooner showed up at the farm, she'd been presented with a different struggle. She'd looked forward to a time when she could take Sooner back permanently. Yet knowing what Sooner meant to Grayson—how she'd saved his life and he'd saved hers—it seemed selfish to ask for the dog back after he'd done so much to care for her. Brandy could never give Sooner the life that Grayson now did. He ran with her almost every day. Sooner accompanied him on chores around the farm and rode with him on errands into town. They were good for each other.

If Brandy took her back, she'd need to find an apartment she could afford that would accept dogs. That meant she wouldn't have a yard for Sooner to run in. She could hire someone to walk the dog, but after having discovered running long miles with Grayson, would short walks by a hired dog walker be enough? Not likely.

Brandy would also be depending on others for transportation, so jumping in the car at whim to go to the park or pet store or training club was out of the question. How could she give Sooner the exercise and stimulation she needed if she couldn't go anywhere or do anything with her? The dog would be bored to death.

In the past, Brandy had always been critical of people who re-homed their dogs. It was like giving up for adoption the child someone had raised from infancy. How could anyone be so heartless? Why on earth, she used to wonder, did dogs end up in shelters, or rescue, or getting returned to their breeders? Sooner had been taken back to her breeder twice as a puppy when her previous owners had deemed her to be too much trouble. They'd given up on the dog. But that wasn't what she was contemplating now. She wanted to do what was best for Sooner.

It had taken her until now to understand the dream she'd had while trapped in her wrecked van. More than a dream, though, it had been a vision. A glimpse into the future. A future in which Sooner and Grayson were forever together.

If only she could be a part of that.

Her phone, lying on the small table beside her hospital bed, vibrated with an incoming call. When she glanced at the caller ID, a wave of relief flushed through her chest.

"Peej?" It was her nickname for her brother, Paul Junior. Everyone else called him PJ.

"You mean you haven't blocked my number yet?" he jested.

"New-ish phone. I couldn't figure out how."

"Right. While I've got you cornered, I have some time off coming up. Any chance they might spring you soon?"

"Funny you should mention it." Brandy surveyed her room. She had every inch of it memorized. Had the routine down pat, too, including which nurse or physical therapist was on what shift. Still, it had always been temporary. A place to sleep while she got better. Better enough to have some degree of independence anyway. "When can you come by?"

A few minutes later, she ended the call. There were details to iron out still, but everything would work out in the end. At least, she hoped so.

Brandy understood now, though, why some people *couldn't* keep their pets. The death of a loved one, financial hardship, a terminal illness, divorce, an accident... Life could change in a blink. She would become *that* person. The one who gave up her dog.

Only... her dog already had a home—and she couldn't have imagined a better situation for Sooner than to live with Grayson on the farm, or in New York City, or wherever he landed. For that, she was extremely grateful.

But it still hurt like hell.

As she lay there staring up at the ceiling, her phone dinged with a text. It took a good two minutes before she finally looked at it.

It was Rex.

That thing I told you about? he wrote. *It's on. Let me know if tomorrow is too soon. Will call later with details.*

She called her brother back. "Peej? Slight change of plans."

chapter 32

Sooner

Grayson wanted to pretend our visits were all about taking *me* to see Brandy, but I was just his excuse to spend time with her. For the life of me, I simply couldn't understand why he didn't make his feelings plainer. Dogs were never so obtuse.

Ever since Grayson took that phone call outside the hospital, he'd been acting particularly distracted. Strange, even. For all the words humans have conjured up to express themselves, they often still lacked the ability to use them to any good effect. Usually while we rode in the car, he'd talk to me. Sometimes he'd use words I knew, but a lot of times, he'd just babble. Like he was thinking out loud, analyzing his problems. I didn't mind, I liked the sound of his voice. In fact, his voice was so soothing to me I often fell asleep during his monologues. As I did on the way home from Gertie's the day after visiting Brandy.

Until, teetering on the edge of consciousness, a phrase I knew caught my attention.

"…go for a run. Would you like that, Sooner? I could use a long run. Got a lot of things to think about. Decisions to make. We'll even go to the park."

I sat up. Stared at him in the mirror. Saw his eyes crinkle in a smile.

"That's a 'yes,' I take it?"

Run, yes! I barked.

"All right, then. We'll do that."

I gave him a big lick on the ear in agreement. Running made me happy. Grayson made me happy. Brandy made me happy.

Now if only Grayson could make Brandy happy...

—o0Oo—

I breathed in cool, fresh air as we ran along the trail of the park. Underfoot, leaves crunched and twigs snapped. Squirrels scrabbled up and down the trunks of trees, acorns clenched between their long rodent teeth. Here and there, a few birds chirped in complaint of the cold.

Above it all, Grayson's words as we ran drifted through a muted landscape, unhindered, unanswered.

"...realize it now. Why have I been so, so... afraid to just *live*? To feel? To slow down and look around me and appreciate what is, instead of pining to make things better, to be more successful, to feel financially safer? As if nothing else mattered. God, it hurt like hell to hear it from Fee, but she was absolutely right about me. I'd shut down my feelings because, well, sometimes they hurt. It was easier not to delve into them than to admit to my own faults. You know what I've figured out since then? That first life whispers to you where you're going wrong, but if you continue not to listen, eventually it hauls out a baseball bat and slugs you a good one. That farm wasn't just some burden for me to unload; it was an opportunity to reassess things. The fact that you"—smiling, he glanced down at me—"showed up precisely when you did, well, that was nothing short of a miracle, wasn't it? You saved me, and then you led me to Brandy. Like it was meant to be all along."

He stopped dead in his tracks. So fast, I'd slingshotted forward and hit the end of the leash before realizing he wasn't moving with me. He stared into the distance, his mouth agape. I cocked my head, peering where I thought he was looking. Searched for a hint of movement. Listened for a sound. But there was nothing there. Nothing out of the ordinary, anyway. Just a few squirrels, a blackbird cawing, the faraway tinkle of the river flowing over rocks.

Grayson sank to his haunches, then cupped his head in his hands. I sniffed his head, rooted beneath his arm, breathed into his ear. When he didn't respond, I tugged forward, encouraging him to run with me some more.

Finally, he raised his eyes. "I have to tell her how I feel when I go back. I *have* to tell her."

Then he pulled me close, kissing the top of my head. "Thank you for bringing her into my life, Sooner."

—o0Oo—

On our way back up the trail in the park, the sound of light, rapid footsteps approached us from behind. Grayson paused to look. There, at the bottom of the winding path, a lone runner began to climb the hill. He seemed far away, but by the time Grayson and I resumed our run and neared the top, he had caught and passed us effortlessly.

Just beyond the top of the hill, the runner bent and clutched his knees, his breathing deep, but not labored. Grayson and I stopped close to him. It was only then I recognized him as the one who'd been ahead of the pack we'd met here in the park before.

"You're on the Faderville High School cross country team, right?" Grayson said. "Mateo, is it?"

He shrugged, lifted his eyes. "Maybe. You a coach?"

"Oh no, no. Just an old runner. I spoke to your teammates last time I was here. They said you're headed to state."

"The team, yeah."

"They seemed to indicate you're pretty fast. That right?"

"I like to run alone." He had a different way of saying his words. They rolled off his tongue rapidly. But he also spoke softly, as if he wasn't comfortable with his speech. "Easier out front."

"I agree. Are you a racer or a pacer?"

Mateo squinted at him.

"I mean do you sprint to the front and just hold them off—or go by pace and hit your splits evenly, letting the pack fade back to you?"

He shrugged again. "What's it matter how you do it? You just got to get to the tape first."

Grayson nodded. "True." Then he tilted his head. "But why not go for the course record? Bold doesn't get it if you don't race smart."

"Eh. If it happens, it happens." This time, Mateo lifted one shoulder in a nonchalant half-shrug. "Tervo send you here to put a bug in my ear?" He cracked a smile, but quickly hid it.

"If you're going to win, nail the record. Make sure they remember you. At the end of it all, you don't want to have any regrets."

"I just want a scholarship, man"—he wiped the sweat from his face on the shoulder of his shirt—"to make my father proud."

"As long as you run your heart out, I'm sure he will be when he sees you come in first."

Mateo scoffed. "He won't get to *see* me do anything."

"Why?" Grayson sounded genuinely confused.

"My parents—they're not together."

"Ah. Does he live in another state?"

"Yeah, Chiapas."

"Where's that?" Grayson said. "Mexico?"

"Yeah. Almost Guatemala." Mateo stared at the ground. Said nothing for a while. Then he met Grayson's eyes. "You should coach.

Tervo says he's getting old. Might retire next year. We told him no, but… he *is* old. He used to run with us—the slow ones, anyway. Then he biked. Now? He just sits and waits."

"I don't think I'm coaching material. Anyway, sounds like he knows what he's doing. I will come and cheer you on, though. Go for the record?"

Mateo shrugged. "Maybe."

Before Grayson could say anything else, Mateo turned and jogged the last of the trail.

We walked the rest of the way, allowing time for our breathing to return to normal. An engine rumbled to life. An old truck, its bumper missing, exited the parking lot, Mateo in the driver's seat.

Standing at his SUV, Grayson watched him go. "I have the feeling that kid has got more guts than brains when it comes to racing." He opened the door for me. After I jumped in, I laid down. Grayson hung in the doorway. "Sometimes, though, that's not a bad thing."

—o0o—

A few days later on the way to the hospital, Grayson rolled the window partway down so I could stick my nose out and inhale all the smells from outside. He'd changed since we started visiting Brandy. Become happier, more carefree. I'd like to think part of that was my doing, too. Every day, I tried to let him know this was not the way to live. Play was important. Noticing and paying attention to the things around us was important. Being with loved ones was important.

And that day, as we walked from the car to the place where Brandy now stayed, it was like he'd been carrying a great weight since I'd known him, but now it was gone. His steps were lighter and quicker. He spoke in rapid bursts, excitement pouring out with his words.

"Sometimes when life throws you a curveball, Sooner, you've just got to buckle down and take a swing; otherwise, you'll never hit a home run and you'll end up striking out." He sighed, then laughed. "Listen to me, will you? Talking in baseball metaphors. I don't even watch baseball. Too boring. All that waiting for *something* to happen..." The main doors parted, and we walked into a bustling lobby. By now, all the staff knew Grayson and me. He waved at each of them in turn as they exchanged hellos. Once on the elevator, his fingers scratched lightly at my head. "Let's put it this way then: You can't win the race if you don't even go to the starting line. Hell, you can't even finish the race."

The elevator stopped at the second floor—which wasn't Brandy's floor. I could tell because the smells were different. No one got on. Eventually, the doors closed again.

"I'm going to tell her about Attovan." He nodded several times. "If you think about it, it was a blessing in disguise really. Forced my hand. I've been floundering in indecision when, in fact, I've known all along what I should be doing. I just didn't want to listen to my gut because, well, this wasn't part of the plan." His grip tightening on my leash, Grayson peered down at me. "So I'm going to tell her what I decided and why. I mean, either she'll stare at me like I'm the biggest nut job on the planet or—"

The elevator dinged. The doors slid open. Grayson took a step forward, but stopped when he saw Cherise waiting to get on.

"Oh, hello," she said, a V forming between her eyebrows. Her clipboard clutched to her chest, she took a step back. "What are you doing here today?"

We exited. "The usual. Why?"

The excitement that had buoyed him up since he'd awoken that morning began to drain out of him.

Cherise's eyes darted around as she searched for words.

"What is it? Is Brandy okay?" My leash fell from his hands. He gripped Cherise by the shoulders. "Tell me!"

Her chin sucked back, she gawked at him. "She's fine, as far as I know. Better than fine. They released her this morning. She left with her brother—PJ, I think his name was." Her hand flew up to cover her mouth. "Oh dear, I forgot. I'm not supposed to share that sort of information with non-family members."

Grabbing the upper part of her sleeve, he guided her into an alcove and spoke softly. "Where were they headed?"

She shook her head. "I... can't... tell you."

"Back to his home in Texas? Come on, Cherise, give me a clue. I need to find her. It's important."

"No, I mean I can't tell you—because I really *don't* know. Even if I did, I'm not supposed to say. You understand, surely? That's personal information. I can't share any of it. But in this case, they didn't say and I didn't ask."

Grayson leaned his back against the wall. His head sank to his chest. "Why didn't she tell me?" After a few breaths, he said, "Or maybe... maybe she didn't want me to know."

Cherise touched his elbow. "Follow me."

We trailed after Cherise to the third-floor nurse's desk. She spoke to the man sitting there, and he handed her something.

"She left this for you." Turning around, Cherise laid an envelope in Grayson's hands.

For a few moments, he merely blinked at her. For a few moments more, he stared at the envelope. Finally, he opened it and read. It didn't take him long. He put the letter back in the envelope, then closed his eyes briefly.

"I won't ask you what it says," Cherise said, "because it's private. But if you want me to pass along a message for you, I could probably find a way."

Grayson faked a smile. "That's all right. I have her phone number. I just... In the letter, she said Sooner was meant for me all along. That the dog belongs with me." His gaze fell on me, and I sensed a deep sadness in him. Like all the joy that had been there only minutes ago had somehow been swept away, banished into oblivion. "I just… I just thought maybe it could be the three of us… Maybe. I mean, that was up to her. Given time and all. But I figured… Anyway, I finally knew that was how I felt… what I wanted… hoped for…"

One of Cherise's eyebrows arched. "So she's giving the dog to you?"

He nodded.

"That's all she said? Don't tell me if you don't want to. I'm just asking as a friend, of sorts."

"Pretty much. She said she'd get in touch with me when she was all settled in her new place—wherever that is."

"Oh." Cherise smiled weakly. "I'm sure she'll call soon. Or maybe you can call her?"

"Maybe." Grayson scanned the corridors as if desperately hoping Brandy would appear in a doorway. But she wasn't there. His face sank. "She took all her things? She's not coming back?"

"Everything. Not that she had much. A few changes of clothes. Some books. Not much else you need here. You want to see her room?"

"No, no, that's fine." Turning, he started back to the elevator. Stared at the buttons as if he'd forgotten what they were for. "I, uh, I guess we'll go now. Thank you—for everything you've done."

Before he could go, Cherise shuffled to him and pulled him into a hug. "I thought this was going to all work out. Like some kind of fairytale ending. Maybe it still will, huh?"

Grayson didn't say anything. Just hugged her back lightly, then tore himself away and jabbed at the buttons. The door sprang open and he slogged inside the elevator, dragging me after him.

I couldn't understand why we hadn't seen Brandy or where she could've gone.

Whatever had happened, Grayson needed my comfort. As my

job, I took it seriously. I would do everything in my power to make him feel better.

Deep down, though, I knew there were some problems even a dog's love couldn't fix.

chapter 33
Grayson

The drive from Lexington back to Faderville had never taken so long. Grayson was sure time was churning in slow motion. It didn't help that traffic was unusually heavy. At some point, he was trapped behind a semi passing another semi. 'Passing' wasn't the right term, though, because the two trucks went down the highway side by side for miles and miles.

Until traffic stopped entirely.

Grayson inched his SUV onto the left shoulder to get a better view. As far as the eye could see, cars were backed up bumper to bumper. Every once in a while, he was able to crawl forward a few feet, but each time he swung out to see if the jam was breaking up, there was no sign of it getting better anytime soon.

"As if this day wasn't crappy enough," he grumbled. Even though he knew he shouldn't, he flipped his phone over to see if Brandy had answered the texts he'd sent before leaving the hospital. Nothing.

Sooner was asleep in the backseat, completely oblivious to their situation. As soon as they'd gotten back in the car at the hospital, she'd clung to him more than normal, trying to lick his ears and snuffling at his shoulder. He hadn't felt like receiving her sympathy, so he'd scolded her for standing on the center console and told her to 'get in the back,' a command she knew well by now.

When he'd awoken that morning, the world had seemed bright, his path ahead clearly laid out. He was going to tell Brandy about the offer he'd received, explain why he wasn't taking it. And then he was going to tell her how he felt about her. Just put it all out there. See how she reacted. It was ridiculous how much he felt like a junior high boy trying to summon the courage to ask his crush to a dance, but he couldn't go on without knowing how she felt about him. The thought of her rejecting him had nearly made him physically ill. But conversely, the prospect she might feel the same—it had been worth the risk. At least, he'd thought so.

Maybe, somehow, she'd already sensed his feelings for her. And by leaving, she *was* giving him her answer.

If Grayson had thought he couldn't feel any lower than he had the morning he'd stared into that full bottle of sleeping pills, he'd been wrong. The hurt he felt now was so devastating it was as if a black hole had opened up right beneath his feet, and he hadn't yet stopped falling.

What had made her so determined to put distance between them? Had he said or done something to put her off? He couldn't think of anything. By all accounts, their last visit had gone well enough. He hadn't mean to leave her with Rex for that short stint, but Sooner had needed to—

A horn blasted behind him. The semi ahead had rolled forward, and it was picking up steam. He'd been so mired in his thoughts he hadn't noticed. Lifting his foot from the brake, he moved forward.

By the time traffic resumed a normal pace, a question had worked its way forward in his mind until he couldn't ignore it any longer: Had Rex said something to her?

The more he thought about it, the more likely it seemed. Rex had told Brandy he was going to take that job.

Suddenly, instead of drowning in despair, Grayson was angry. Angrier than he'd ever been at another human being. So angry, he wasn't sure what he was capable of.

Grayson wove in and out of traffic, one foot on the brake, the other on the accelerator. The speedometer ticked over seventy-five, eighty, eighty-five… Sooner was sitting up, whimpering, as if pleading for him to slow down. Only when he swerved into the right lane and she went toppling over did he let up on the gas.

"You okay, girl?"

Sooner's head popped over his shoulder. Her tongue flicked nervously at his ear a few times, then she retreated and plastered herself to the back of the seat, her legs braced and a look bordering on terror on her face. Grayson reduced his speed, making sure he wasn't tailgating the slowpoke in front of him. He really needed to get a sturdy airline crate to let her ride around in. She might not like having her freedom restricted, but if it kept her safer, it was worth it. He also needed to put a lid on his temper so he wouldn't accidentally cause a wreck or rearrange Rex's face.

As hard as he tried, though, he couldn't cool down. How dare Rex tell the person he loved something that wasn't true? He needed to give him a piece of his—

The person he loved…

He did. He *loved* her.

Only… he wasn't sure she loved him.

Rex had ruined his chance of ever finding out—and he was going to make the bastard sorry he'd ever meddled in his personal life.

—o0Oo—

Grayson stomped on the brakes, then swerved into a parking space on the block on which Rex's office was located. He barely took the time to pull the key from the ignition before jumping out and yanking the back door open for Sooner. He didn't even bother to clip her leash on or make sure to lock the car. Leash laws be damned. The dog wasn't about to run off. And if someone in Faderville wanted to commit grand theft auto for the first time in ten years, let them. He had a score to settle—and it just might be him who got arrested for assault and battery as a result.

Every time his feet impacted the concrete, the thought reverberated in his bones: *I. Will. Kill. Him.*

The anger fueled superpowers in him. He could've punched through a cement block wall and not felt a thing. It also blinded him to anything but his purpose—Rex Franzen was going to regret what he'd done.

As Grayson turned the corner, he was so focused on reaching Rex's office he almost plowed into a stroller. Little Claire Mays, her face framed by a hood fringed in faux fur, stared up at him, her mouth open in an O of fright. Her lower lip trembled. Tears welled in her round eyes. Soon, short puffs of air morphed into blubbery sobs, broken only by the ear-piercing wails of an inconsolable toddler.

The shock of it jarred Grayson back into the bigger world. The one beyond his inner core of smoldering revenge. The sharp edges of his determination softened the tiniest bit.

Becca Mays rushed around the stroller to lift her daughter out. She cradled Claire's head against her shoulder, stroking her hair.

"Shh, shh. It's okay, Claire. Everything's okay." Her motherly voice was soothing, but the glare she aimed at Grayson could've lasered through steel. "She was sound asleep. I think you startled her, that's all."

Although her words were carefully chosen, the implication was Grayson should watch where he was going.

"I'm sorry," was all he could get out.

Becca bounced the little girl on her hip a few times before setting her back down in the stroller, upon which she produced a lollipop from the small cross-slung bag at her hip. Claire gasped in delight, her displeasure at being woken instantly erased.

"See? All better now," Becca said to her daughter. Then to Grayson, "See you around. Be careful."

Grayson might have nodded, but he wasn't sure.

Then they were gone, as if they'd never been there at all. Discombobulated by the encounter, he stood transfixed by a crack in the sidewalk. Became aware of a cool gust of wind barreling down the tunnel of the main street of Faderville. Heard the chug of a semi accelerating from a four-way stop. The *clink-clink-clink* of a rope against a flagpole. The click of footsteps from behind—

A hand alighted on Grayson's shoulder.

He gasped. Snapped his head to the right.

"You okay, pal?" Gertie stepped back to study him. Her baker's apron peeked from beneath the hem of her worn brown coat. "I'd say you look like you just lost your best friend, but she's right next to you."

It wasn't until then Grayson remembered Sooner was still with him. The dog gazed up at him, concerned.

"You stopping by the donut shop while you're in town? I made some raspberry cream-cheese Danishes fresh this morning." She rubbed her ample tummy in a slow circle. When Grayson hesitated, she added, "First one's on the house. You just give me your honest opinion."

"Sure," he finally managed without even being wholly aware of what he'd just agreed to.

Gertie rattled on some more about the cold snap coming and how there were rumors of Starbucks building a store at the interstate exit and all the harm that would do to the community if they did. Grayson blinked at her, his focus meandering. He nodded as if he were listening, even though what he was really doing was trying to re-gather all the forceful words he'd meant to lob at Rex Franzen.

By the time she finally moved on, Grayson had regrouped. He'd come here for a reason and socializing with the locals definitely wasn't it. He glanced down, made sure Sooner was still there, then slapped his thigh for her to follow him.

As he reached for the doorknob to Rex's office, the smooth metal slipped in his hand. The door flew open before he could even push it. A figure clad in plaid flannel and wearing knee-high mud boots blocked his way.

"Hello, Mr. Darling." Tucker from the feed store flapped a thread of tickets at him. "Can I interest you in my church's raffle? Only twenty or so tickets left. Proceeds go to help local families in need. We're giving away a pair of roundtrip plane tickets to anywhere in the continental US. Consolation prize is a fancy barbecue grill. Being a homebody, I'd prefer the latter myself, but some folks want to get away from it all from time to time. The drawing is next week at our annual Night at the Casino fundraising event."

"Uh, I don't—"

"Ten bucks for the lot of 'em."

Grayson had the distinct feeling Tucker wasn't going to budge from his gatepost until Grayson paid the toll. After digging a twenty out of his wallet, he stuffed it into Tucker's calloused hand. "Keep the change."

"I'll do better than that. I'll put your name on our Honor Roll of Donors in the church program." He unrolled the last of the tickets, split them down the middle, and handed Grayson a pen.

Grayson stared at the pen in his hand. "What's this for?"

"To write your name on them—and phone number, so we know who to call when we pull the winning tickets. Got a gut feeling it's gonna be your lucky day, Mr. Darling."

For a moment, Grayson thought about correcting him. Far from being lucky, this had been about the worst day he could remember in months. Years, even. Maybe even worse than the day Fee asked him for a divorce.

But he'd come here for a reason. The sooner he dispensed with Tucker, the sooner he could unload his grievances on the very cause of his troubles.

Grayson scribbled his name in barely legible slashes of ink on the backs of twenty tickets, along with all ten digits of his out-of-area phone number. He handed the string of tickets back to Tucker. "Rex in there?"

"Yup. You have an appointment?"

"No and I don't need one for what I'm about to tell him."

Sidestepping Tucker, Grayson plunged into the dimly lit front room of Rex's law office. Sooner slipped in behind him. It was notably tidier than the last time he'd been there. As he stomped across the front room, he could hear Rex on the phone at his desk.

"… anytime you want. We could even meet over dinner. The wife works until—"

Rex looked up from the folder in front of him. "Pardon me, Mr. Zimmerman. A client just walked in. Looks urgent. I'll call back as soon as I can. Meanwhile, you tell those grandkids of yours how impressed I am with their accomplishments… You, too. Have a great day."

Pushing his roller chair back, Rex stood and pointed at the leather chair across from his desk. "Grayson, have a seat. Something the matter? Can I get you a drink? No alcohol on the premises, but I learned how to make a decent cup of coffee this week. I also have bottled water for the dog and soda for you, if you prefer—red pop, root beer—"

"I didn't come here to chitchat." Grayson circled the large executive desk to stand within arm's reach of the lawyer. It took all his restraint to not grab him by the bolero and shove him up against the wall.

"Something about your uncle's farm, then? If you've got a problem, I'm all ears. You know I want to get that all straightened out as soon as—"

"Why did you tell her?"

For a few heartbeats, it looked like someone had just plopped Rex down in an alternate universe. "Tell who what?"

"Brandy. Why did you tell her I was going to take that job?" Grayson didn't even wait for an answer. He had a lot bottled up inside him, and he didn't want to hear some lame apology. "Today I showed up at the hospital to talk to her about… about things I'd been thinking about. About her. About us. Things I'd decided. And here you go and jump in the middle of it all without for a second even considering if it was your place to share personal information. If I'd known you were going to blab it to her, I never would have mentioned it. But I trusted you to keep your nose out of business that was never yours to begin with. You shouldn't assume you know everything, because you don't. That was rude and presumptuous of you and…"

Words eluded Grayson. All the steam he'd built up on the drive here seemed to have dissipated. Instead of volleying back excuses, Rex had let him vent without interruption. He hadn't even so much as taken a step back in case Grayson threw a punch.

Settling himself back into his chair, Rex drummed his fingers on the armrests. "You done or just taking a breath?"

Grayson realized then Rex knew it as well as he did—Grayson didn't have it in him to physically assault someone. He couldn't even do a good job of lambasting him. Still, he needed to speak his mind. "It wasn't your place."

Rex pointed at him. "Normally, I'd agree with you, but Grayson… it pained me to see you floundering around like you have been."

"What?"

"In the time you were gone letting the dog take a dump, I got the whole scoop on Miss Anders' prognosis—something you haven't managed in the hundred or so times you've been with her."

"Hundred? I haven't—"

Rex held out his palm. "Let me finish, will you? You're sweet on that gal. Can't even be in the same room with her without going all soft and gooey on the inside, am I right?"

Without being told again, Grayson claimed the seat across from Rex. He had flashbacks of being in Dr. Philipot's office. "That's personal."

"Maybe it is, but you know what, Grayson? I *care* about my clients. The gentleman I was on the phone with when you barged in—his thirty-two-year-old daughter is in hospice. Terminal breast cancer. And that ain't the worst of it. She has three kids under the age of nine. Divorced her louse of a husband a couple of years back because he liked to do a little dating on the side. To boot, he's been in and out of jail for the past four years, so Zimmerman is trying to make sure he gets custody of the little ones and not one of the father's lowlife kin."

"What's your point?" Grayson prodded.

"My point is I asked Miss Anders how soon they were going to release her and what her plans were. Nothing personal about that, either. Just taking interest in a fellow human being. You're all concerned about going slowly and being cautious, but good heavens, son, take a risk every once in a blue moon, will you? If you like a gal, don't be so damn shy about it—or she'll assume you're not interested and move on. I've seen sloths at the zoo move quicker than you do."

That irked Grayson. Not the insult about sloths, but that Rex was meddling in his personal affairs and playing matchmaker. "That's nice of you, but again, you're assuming—"

"How long did you think she was going to wait around for you to get up the nerve to even ask her on a date?"

"It's not that simple."

"Why? Because she's wheelchair bound?"

"That's not what I meant."

"Then what *did* you mean?"

Grayson didn't have a ready answer. It was far too complicated to get into right now. His relationship with Rex was of the business variety, not a personal one. Come to think of it, he didn't even want this man as his attorney if this was his idea of attending to legal matters.

They stared at each other a good long minute—Rex waiting for a response while Grayson tried to sort out a dozen scrambled thoughts and roiling emotions into something logical and orderly. Nothing came to mind. Nothing that sounded right, anyway.

The velvety softness of a dog's muzzle slipped beneath Grayson's right hand, which until then, had been resting on his knee. Sooner gazed up at him with eyes that were more gold than green. Amber, almost.

She made a sound between a whimper and a growl. *Say what's in your heart,* she seemed to be trying to say.

Why was it so much easier to talk to her than the people in his life? He drew in a breath, scrounged for the courage to hurl the words forth. The dog licked his fingers as if coaxing him.

"I think I... I think I love her, but..."

Rex propped an elbow on his desk, rested his chin on his fist. Stared at Grayson like he was the biggest fool this side of the Appalachian Mountains. "I see now why you're divorced."

Grayson clenched the arms of the chair. "That was cruel."

"But true... and necessary." Rex opened a drawer, then grabbed a set of car keys. "I've handled a lot of breakups in my day, Grayson. Most times, people are so fixated on what's wrong that they can't push through and see what's right, let alone say it out loud." He walked toward the door. "Grab the dog and come with me."

"To where?"

"I'm taking you to where my wife works. Place called Fox Hollow."

The only thing Grayson knew about Fox Hollow was that it was a home for old people just outside of town. A picturesque sort of prison.

Grayson hung back, offended Rex would order him to follow without letting on why he should. Even though he'd spent a lifetime setting aside his feelings in favor of a roadmap for success, something deep down inside told him Rex was going to pit him face to face with the very thing he was afraid of finding out.

He might've stayed in that chair, defiant and willfully ignorant, until Rex was long gone—and good riddance to him—except Sooner was following Rex out into the street.

chapter 34

Sooner

I sat in the middle of the front seat between Rex and Grayson in the big truck. The view up here was great, but I didn't like not having a window seat. This unexpected ride out into the country would've been a dream come true if Grayson had just traded spots with me and rolled the window down. Then I could've ignored the tension between them, stuck my nose out into the fresh air, and played a game of 'guess that smell'.

"All I can say"—Grayson gripped his knees like he needed something to hang onto—"is this had better be good."

Rex said nothing for a while, which was unusual for him. We flew over a series of hills, around several corners, down into a wooded valley, then back out onto a wider road that extended straight ahead for miles, flanked by fenced pastures. Just as I spotted a herd of cows and scooted over to crowd Grayson to get a better view, Rex finally broke the silence.

"I'm going to say something you might take as impolite, but I'm an honest man, so I'm going to put it out there."

Grayson drew a hand over his eyes. "Here goes. Out with it then."

Rex glanced sideways at him. "When you came here—to this little one-horse town—did you kinda see us all as—how do I put it?—unsophisticated? Like this place was lacking in amenities? Like we had less education and skills than the folk you were used to brushing elbows with?"

Grayson swallowed. "It's not what I was used to."

"That isn't what I asked. Be honest now."

He blew out a breath, nodded. "I suppose so. It's a… a very different way of life."

"There are a lot of different ways of living. We folk here like things wide open, not so busy. We like to get to know our neighbors. We help them out. Sure, sometimes we gossip about them. We can be guilty of a little *schadenfreude*, too. But if your coworker's cousin falls on hard times because their spouse is drug addicted, you pitch in and donate a baby swing for their little one. You offer a ride to the doctor to your ageing neighbor, frankly because you know they shouldn't be behind the wheel and there's no good way of saying it. You help the farmer down the road round up his wandering goats when a storm takes the fence down."

"People in New York help each other, too. We help absolute strangers. Like during 9-11."

"So do we. So do we." Rex slowed to a stop, checked left and right, then turned onto another road. "Our way of life is every bit as good and valuable as what you were used to. We just focus on fewer things at a time, so we can give those things and people the attention they deserve. More of a minimalist approach to life, I guess you'd say."

"And your point is…?"

"My point is I know it was probably hard for you to get used to. You wanted to unload that farm and those horses so you could get back to all that glitz and glamour and leave us simple folk behind. But then, things changed for you. You found a dog. You met a gal… And then you didn't know which was better: going back to that old life you knew—or starting a new one."

Something hard seemed to break inside Grayson. Fractured down the middle. He turned his face to the window and slid lower in his seat, only the belt buckle stopping him.

Rex gave him some time before continuing. "One thing I learned in my business is how to read people. I may talk a lot, but I also pay attention—something you might be well advised to do yourself. It matters just as much how people says things as it does what they don't say at all. Me—I'm a straight shooter. I say it like it is and then some. You, on the other hand—you weigh every word. You keep most of them inside, afraid of what might happen if you let them out. Afraid, even, of the feelings behind those words. So when you came barging into my office today, guns a-blazing, I knew she meant the world to you. Hell, I knew it when we stopped to visit her. At the sight of her, you grinned so big I thought your head was going to split in two."

Grayson sat up straighter. "Oh, come on. How did you know? I didn't even know for sure—not until I got that job offer from Attovan, anyway. How could you possibly tell?"

"Son—can I call you that? It's not short for Grayson, in case you're wondering. Around here, it's what we call anyone younger than us."

"You probably only have ten years on me, Rex. But sure, call me 'son,' if you want. It beats 'Gary'. Anyway, how did you know?"

"How? All I had to do was pay attention, just like I said." Rex pulled into the parking lot of a long brick building and parked. It was one of many brick buildings on a sprawling property surrounded by swaths of manicured lawn and perfectly spaced spruce trees. It sort of looked like the neighborhood I used to live in with Brandy, only with virtually no traffic. Rex winked at me. "Right, girl?"

I barked. Because I wanted out, so I could figure out why we were here.

As soon as Rex opened the door and the scent hit me, I knew. *She* was here.

—o0Oo—

"Brandy, hi." Grayson stood in the doorway, his feet fixed to the welcome mat on the front steps. He looked past her, like he was searching for something—or someone else. "Why... why are you here?"

Rex gave him a gentle shove from behind, and we all piled inside. It was like a little house, only with wide doorways, no steps, and very little furniture. The living room, kitchen, and dining area all ran together. I bounced to Brandy, gave her fingers a few licks, and wandered off to explore, sniffing. Mostly, it smelled of cleaning fluids.

Behind Brandy's wheelchair stood a man I didn't know. He had hair the same shade as hers, although only a fringe of it from one ear to the other around back. The top of his head was bald and shiny, and he had wire-rimmed glasses.

The man extended his hand to Grayson, regarding him with a hint of suspicion. "You must be Brandy's friend, Grayson. Hello, I'm Paul Anders, Junior, Brandy's older brother. PJ for short."

"Hello." Grayson shook his hand. When he tried to pull it back, PJ held onto it for a moment, like he was sizing him up. Grayson turned to Brandy. "Can we talk alone for a few minutes?"

Before Brandy could answer, Rex hooked an arm around PJ's. "Say, driving in here, I saw some of these places have a back patio. Mind showing me?" He guided him toward a set of double doors, but then lingered as PJ continued in that direction. Rex pointed at Brandy. "The whole story, mind you. Don't leave anything out."

She nodded.

When the two men had gone outside, Grayson crouched in front of Brandy to be on her level, like he did with me sometimes. "Okay, tell me. Why are you here? Rex wouldn't tell me anything on the way. Isn't this a retirement home? And why didn't you answer my texts or calls? I showed up in Lexington for a visit, and you'd cleared out of there without a word. Cherise wouldn't give me any details. Just said you left with your brother, so since you'd been talking about moving in with him, I just figured, well… that you'd gone to Texas. Then I read your letter about needing to make choices and how you thought Sooner was better off with me. Honestly, even though I knew I'd miss her like heck, I was looking forward to the day she could go home with you."

She rolled her wheelchair back, turned it, and moved to sit in front of the big picture window in the front of the living room area. Grayson followed her and sat in the middle of the couch across from her, but beyond arm's reach. Like he was keeping his distance for the moment.

"I didn't know what to do, Grayson. I'd already decided to leave Sooner with you. I figured it was best for her—and you."

"But she's *your* dog. You've done so much with her. Sooner loves you."

There was confusion in his voice, and it worried me. I trotted over to him, then laid my muzzle in his lap.

Brandy shook her head. "I can't do those things anymore. I don't know if I'll ever be able to again. You two… you *need* each other."

He sat back. Studied her hard and long. "You're afraid of what I might do if she's not around?"

"Maybe… I don't know."

"Brandy, I'm not in that place anymore. I don't think I ever will be again."

"You don't know that."

"So that's why you left and didn't answer me? You don't want to be around if…" He stood up, paced a circle around the room, hands in his pockets. "You, of all people, should understand this is why people don't talk about depression."

She expelled a sharp breath. "Oh, Grayson. I think we've gotten off on the wrong track. I'm just saying it can happen to anybody at any time. And before you condemn me for running away because I couldn't face that part of you—I didn't. This is where I live now. Because I wanted to stay nearby."

"I don't understand."

She sighed in the same way Grayson did when I didn't get what he was trying to tell me. "When you left the room last week, Rex asked about my prognosis. I told him what I knew at that point, but mentioned you'd never really asked about it. He asked if I thought you were afraid of me being discharged and moving away. Until that moment, that hadn't really occurred to me, but when he asked that, well, a lot of things made more sense then. That snowballed into him hinting he could tell you liked me, as in *liked*-liked me, in a girlfriend sort of way, so I told him I felt the same way. That as much as I wanted to accept my brother's offer, I'd been wanting more time to see where things went between you and me, but I was having a hard time gauging how you felt. I knew if I moved to Dallas, it could get too comfortable there for me in my brother's house. So I told Rex I'd rather stay nearby in Kentucky somewhere if I could, but I hadn't looked into it yet. That's when he told me his wife worked here at Fox Hollow, and said he'd check on openings for me.

"As luck would have it, after you left, Dr. Capelli told me I could go home in a few days. No one was more surprised than me. The next day, Rex let me know there was an unexpected opening here. It was like everything was just working out the way it was supposed to. Things moved so fast I didn't have time to get in touch with you. There were a lot of details to take care of. A lot. It was exciting and scary and overwhelming." Drawing in a deep breath, she went on. "Just before Peej and I left this morning, I had a meeting with Dr.

Capelli and had my phone on silent. Then I put it in my suitcase and simply focused on the fact that my life was finally moving forward. We also went to see my dad. I'm not sure he even knew who we were. But we stayed for two hours and I told him all about the past few months—even about you and Sooner. So, you see, I wasn't intentionally ignoring you. But those were all things I had to do on my own—for myself, by myself. You have no idea what it's like to feel so dependent on others."

He resumed his seat on the couch. "You're right. I don't. But... why *here*? I mean, I understand there was an opening, but isn't this a retirement community?"

"It also has units devoted to people recovering from traumatic medical events like strokes, amputations, or accidents. People like me. I have my own space here, but there's also help if I need it. Which I will. For a while, anyway."

"What about your job?"

"I made arrangements with my employer to work from home, as long as I can make it to meetings once a month. They have a van here that goes to Lexington weekly. It works out perfectly."

"Still, why here when you could be in Lexington somewhere?"

She sighed. "Because of you, Grayson. You. Because of us. Or what could be 'us,' actually."

As if struck by shyness, he dropped his head. "Oh." A long minute later, he raised his eyes. "So Rex didn't tell you about Attovan?"

"I don't know what Attovan is."

"You don't?" Something in his demeanor shifted—lightened, almost. Like an anger he'd been clinging to had suddenly been snatched away. He glanced toward the sliding glass doors, beyond which Rex and PJ could be seen immersed in conversation, then back at her. "Attovan is a big loan company. They called the other day, offered me a lucrative job back in New York. A really good one.

Right before we came up to see you that day."

A blank expression on her face, Brandy shook her head. "Believe me, he didn't say anything about a job offer."

Grayson flattened himself against the back of the couch. "I owe Rex an apology—a big one."

"I think I missed something."

"Never mind." He waved a hand in the air like he wanted to redirect her. "It's not important. I'll explain later. Brandy, would you—?"

The glass door slid open, and Rex popped his head in. "You two kids done yet?"

Grayson glared at him. "Get lost, Rex."

"Hint taken. Carry on." He slid the door shut.

Grayson scooted to the end of the couch, reached out, and took Brandy's hands in his. "Brandy, would you like to go on a date?"

Weaseling my way between them, I poked my head up so their arms were encircling me.

Brandy laughed. "Do we have to take the dog?"

He grimaced. "I think we should—the first time, anyway. She is what brought us together, after all."

"All right. Yes, I will. On one condition, though."

"That being?"

"That you'll tell me what's on your mind. Every little thing."

He smiled. A big smile. "Okay, I'll start right now. You know what I'm thinking?"

"Not a clue. Tell me."

"I'm thinking we're pretty good together—and that I'm lucky I found you. The luckiest guy in the world, maybe. All because of a dog."

epilogue
Grayson

A horde had gathered on the horizon: a riot of blues and reds and oranges and greens. Their shoulders were bent forward, legs braced, fists clenched. Behind them, banners snapped in the crisp breeze, emblems of the lands from which they hailed. Far beyond that, a city of tents waited as gathering points to receive them after their impending ordeal. Before them stood a man in all black, his pistol pointed skyward.

Grayson hadn't forgotten the feeling, not a moment of it. Not the miles run in solitude, whether in oppressive heat or bone-biting cold, nor the sensation of flying over the earth, his feet barely touching the ground as he crossed the finish line, arms raised in victory.

Today, though… today, it was someone else's dream either come to fruition or crushed into dust. All in a matter of minutes—but built upon months or even years of grueling work. This was the state high school cross country meet, an event which had drawn hundreds of the most qualified competitors and thousands more fans to a fairground surrounded by open fields and patches of woodland in a rolling terrain.

He saw them—the boys from the Faderville cross country team he and Sooner had met on the wooded trail in the park. They wore red and black with a splash of gold, a combination barely distinguishable from half a dozen other teams toeing the line. Since that day, he'd looked up their results and made himself familiar with their names and accomplishments. They'd been humble about their prospects. Theirs was a tribe to be reckoned with. It felt good to root for them, to wish for their success, even though he had no hand in it. He hadn't realized until he'd arrived today how much he'd missed all of this or how much he wished he could relive it all again. Instead, he'd be part of the backdrop—the roaring crowd whose whistles and shouts and clapping hands gave fuel to their adrenaline. It was a different perspective, but a worthy one.

A puff of smoke rose from the pistol's barrel. A fraction of a second later, the shot rang through the air. Knees lifted, drove down. Arms swung. Spiked shoes thrust at firm ground, producing a stampede of bare sinewy legs.

The mass burst forward across the plain as one. Bells clanged. Horns blared. Flags waved and dipped. Voices rose in frantic cheer.

"Go for it, Lucas!"

"Get out front!"

"Pace yourselves!"

"Push each other!"

And then, the wave broke—a lone wolf charging to the front, a pack in pursuit, the brunt of the runners, and finally... a few already straggling behind from a too-early sprint. Faces became distinguishable, blurred, and then moved past.

The onlookers themselves broke apart, raced to other pre-selected vantage points. Others stood idly to await the return of the runners on the looping course. Grayson chose not to wait. He ran from place to place, sometimes only able to see a handful of runners before moving on. His own heart was racing, his muscles drenched in a delirious burn of fatigue.

Minutes later, he raced up the metal stairs and found Brandy and Sooner in the enclosed VIP room next to the announcer's box on an upper level of the grandstands. He'd rented the spot in advance, figuring it provided the best accommodations for Brandy's wheelchair. During the summer, the venue hosted horse shows and tractor pulls amid concessions trailers ribboned in multicolored lights. In late fall, however, it transformed into a gathering place for cross country fanatics. The race course was their battlefield, the victors to be decided by the simplest of human competitions—a foot race over open ground.

"You didn't tell me how crazy this was," Brandy remarked. Sooner was lying on her side next to the wheelchair, clad in the swanky yellow vest with patches that marked her as a service dog in training. "I've never seen so many barely clothed teenagers in one place. Isn't it a tad cold to go around half naked? And look over there. What is that on their faces—war paint?"

"It's a tradition. Not any different from the fans of a pro-football team, if you think about it." Not wanting to block her view, Grayson stood behind her wheelchair. He leaned over her shoulder, pointing into the distance. "There's the leader. See him?"

Brandy shaded her eyes with a cupped hand. "Yeah, I think so. But where's the next guy?"

Grayson studied his watch, counted silently as the seconds ticked by: ten, fifteen, twenty... Finally, he pointed to the wood's edge. "Wait for it, wait for it."

It took a few more seconds before the next runner cleared the woods. Soon after him came a pack in pursuit.

He cupped his hands to his mouth. "That's it, Mateo! You got it! Go, go, go!"

As he watched Mateo glide across the open expanse, his brown-skinned legs churning effortlessly, his spiked shoes chopping at the ground hungrily, excitement surged through Grayson's chest. He could see the second-place runner gaining on Mateo, slowly but steadily. Half a mile to go in the race, Mateo's lead shortened to a dozen seconds.

"Don't look back, Mateo," Grayson muttered. "Don't you dare look back now. *Run*, damn it. Run like they're bearing down on you. Just... *run*."

His heart banged inside his rib cage, threatening to explode. He remembered his own defining moment, just like this one. How he'd heard the amplified breaths of his pursuers, sensed the rumble of their footfalls through the soles of his shoes, seen the faces in the crowd cheering both for and against him. Mateo had a much larger lead on his competitors than Grayson had in his final high school race, but he knew no victory was ever assured until it was won. The greatest of runners had stumbled in the final stretch, their muscles seizing up from a flood of physiological waste products. They had coasted, fooled by confidence, and been overtaken in the last strides. He'd warned Mateo not to succumb to such arrogance. He hoped the boy would not. But he didn't know him well enough to trust he'd follow his advice.

It was impossible to tell from this distance and perspective, so high up in the VIP boxes, whether Mateo was maintaining his lead or losing it more, but Grayson went silent. At this point, nothing he said or did would sway the result. It was all up to Mateo.

Sooner sat up, perked her ears. She scooted close to the railing, her sights focused on the lone runner out front.

The large clock situated less than a dozen feet from the finish line ticked over one giant number at a time. The stadium announcer's voice boomed above the buffeting roar of the crowd: "14:40, 14:41, 14:42... Returning champion Jordan Walsh in second. Mateo Sandoval, a junior from Faderville and first-time participant here at state, still holding the lead. Still holding. Still hooolding—"

Time rushed onward, a tsunami of emotions crashing within Grayson's soul, awakening him. Years ago, he'd buried part of himself securely away, letting his courage lie dormant. True success required risk... and risk sometimes meant failure. He'd been afraid of letting himself get attached to Sooner, afraid of reaching out to Brandy, afraid of stepping off his self-prescribed path and starting over, but no more. Safety meant foregoing life's possibilities. It meant not bearing witness to moments like this or loving so deeply his heart ached.

For a flicker of a second, he thought he saw Mateo glance up at the VIP box where he and Brandy were. He'd told him they'd be there, watching, rooting for him. And then—Mateo raised a fist and pumped it.

No, don't celebrate yet, Grayson thought. *Not until it's over.*

But it *was* over. Mateo had picked up speed, his arms churning in a furious cadence, his effortless stride lengthening. The defender faltered, his shoulders bunching up near his neck, his fists tightening against his torso. The gap behind Mateo widened.

Mateo never glanced back as he ran the final yards. He crossed the finish line, spent and exhilarated. In the chute, he slowed to a halt, turned to watch, and clapped for his competitors. The officials tried to shoo him through to the end, but he just pointed to the oncoming runners as he slowly stepped backward.

"A new course and state meet record!" proclaimed the announcer.

When Walsh stumbled across the line, barely beating the number three man by a second, he collapsed to his knees. Mateo, who by now had made his way outside the chute, ducked beneath the pennants and lifted Walsh up. He helped him through to the end, handed him off to a pair of athletic trainers, and grabbed a cup of water to offer him. Walsh took it, then tipped the cup up. He captured a mouthful of water, but most of the contents spilled down his neck and onto his sweat-soaked singlet. Mateo waited until Walsh had his breath back and had gained some steadiness on his feet. Then he took Walsh in his arms, hugged him, and pounded him on the back in a display of camaraderie and respect. The two then walked out of the finish area together, speaking to one another, smiling—until Mateo was accosted by a small army of reporters, and Walsh slipped quietly away.

"Do you think they'll become friends now?" Brandy asked as Grayson helped turn her wheelchair and they headed to the elevator.

"Possibly." He knew for a fact Mateo and Walsh had never met before today. "Friendly rivals, anyway. If all goes well, they'll meet again in the spring at the state track meet. After that, who's to say? If they both run in college, they could end up in different parts of the country. But it's easier to keep in touch these days than it was in mine. Yeah, I think they'll be friends. They'll definitely never forget today."

Grayson reflected on all the friends he'd made while running in his younger days. They'd been a source of support and shared passion. Those bonds had encouraged him to reach for loftier goals, to go beyond his comfort zone. When Justin died, he'd let that all go, thinking the fewer friends he had, the less likely he was to be hurt again. After that, he'd cast all his attention on Fee—for a while, anyway. The brutal truth was that when people didn't nurture and invest in relationships, they decayed and disintegrated, until they no longer existed.

A dog had taught him that. A dog had made him more caring, more loving, more engaged in the here and now simply by testing his patience and understanding.

Sooner glanced up at him, her golden-green eyes glinting in the slanted rays of late autumn sunlight. She was unfazed by the noise of the crowd and the press of bodies surrounding them. Brandy had tied her leash loosely to the arm of her wheelchair. Whenever she needed the dog to stop or come along, she only had to utter a single softly spoken command.

Grayson couldn't imagine a more perfect day than this—the three of them out and about. Together. His heart was full. And to think, not so long ago, he'd felt he had nothing to look forward to. Now he had more than he'd ever wanted. It would only get better from here on. He didn't know that for a fact. He just decided to believe it.

They stopped before the elevator, a steady stream of parents, teenagers, and coaches flowing past them toward the stairway. The doors slid open. Grayson, Brandy, and the dog got on. Sooner was adept at walking beside the wheelchair now without getting her toes run over.

He'd look up his old teammates when he got home today. Between the internet and the alumni association, that shouldn't be all that hard. He'd find a local road race and sign up for it, too. That would give him some motivation. Maybe he'd make a few new friends that way.

In the brief silence between floors, Brandy spoke. "You seem to really love this sport in the same way I loved competing with my dogs. Do you miss it?"

"Only recently. And I do. A great deal." The doors crept open, and he carefully pushed her out. They wound their way down a ramp and through a crowd milling about on acres of a paved parking lot filled with cars and busses. In the distance, another race was gearing up to start. "I've been thinking…"

"About what?"

"If you don't mind me leaving you and Sooner over by the concessions for a bit, I'm going to find Coach Tervo. I'd like to volunteer to help out with the team next year. He has a lot of kids. Looks like he could use some assistance."

"Oh, sure. But… are we doing something after this, like, I don't know, stopping for dinner somewhere? I mean, I wouldn't mind a Coke right now, but for the price of a pretzel and a slice of pizza here, we could have a nice sit-down dinner somewhere."

"Of course! I wouldn't let you go hungry." Then it occurred to him how selfish he'd been in inviting her here. He wanted to correct his mistake, but wasn't sure how to begin. He felt like a teenager all over again. "You aren't disappointed we came here, are you? I'm sorry. I didn't mean to insinuate *this* was our date. Because it's not. It's just that when I mentioned coming, you sounded curious, then I suppose I got pretty excited telling you all about it and… I guess I may have misread your interest."

"Not at all. I know this was a big part of your life at one time. To be honest, though, I'm more amused by seeing how animated you are during the race than the race itself. It's wonderful you have so much love for the sport."

Just as Grayson veered Brandy's chair toward the end of the concessions line, a woman at the front of the line motioned them forward and insisted they order before her. No one behind them so much as grumbled about it. Grayson thanked her, then bought a Coke for Brandy.

After finding her a spot safely out of the way of foot traffic, Grayson sat on a bench beside her. "Brandy… if you could go anywhere in the country, where would you go?"

"Not the world?"

"That, too. But there's a lot to see right here in America. So play along. Where would you go?"

"Anywhere in the US, huh?"

"Yes, anywhere."

Brandy pursed her lips together, regarding him with intense curiosity. "Is there a particular reason you're asking me this?"

He shrugged. "I may have won some plane tickets in a raffle."

"Ah, I see. No one else will go with you?"

"There's no one else I'd *want* to go with."

Brandy stroked Sooner's neck. "You're just saying that because the dog and I are a pair."

"Maybe." He winked at her. "But I also think we'd make a heck of a little family, the three of us. Don't you?"

"Maybe," she echoed. After a thoughtful pause, she raised a finger. "You know the one place I've always wanted to go, but never had the chance to? Central Park in New York. All that green space and all those people amid all those buildings. I've often wondered what it would be like there—doesn't matter the season. I just feel like I'm missing something never having been there."

"I'll take you to Central Park, then. And any place else you want to see—the Metropolitan, Radio City Music Hall, the Empire State Building..."

"I can already imagine it. When?"

"There's no better time than Christmas. It's... the only word I can think of is 'magical'."

With a flirtatious grin, she said, "I hear it's even more magical when you're with someone you love."

"Funny you should mention that, because"—Grayson bent and kissed her on the lips, softly and fleetingly—"I love you, Brandy."

Not to be ignored, Sooner put her paws on Brandy's lap and wedged her nose between them.

Laughing, Grayson ruffled the fur on top of her head. "Yeah, yeah, we love you, too, Sooner. More than anything."

Brandy squeezed Sooner's paw. "More than the sun—"

"And the moon and the stars," Grayson finished.

author's note

Life can be ugly and hard and hurtful. It can also be kind and beautiful and wondrous. Stories should explore the truths of life, not deny them. I throw hard punches at my characters, but I try to make them come through it wiser so they can grow from it. They learn that things can and will get better.

Emotional pain is as real as physical pain. We should never feel compelled to deal with it alone. Whether you are suffering or suspect you know someone who is—reach out. One act of kindness, one plea for help, can make *all* the difference.

As you muddle through life, just remember this—your dog will *always* be there for you. Their love is unconditional.

about the author

N. Gemini Sasson is a serial remodeler, intrepid gardener, dog lover, and Boston Marathon qualifier. She lives in rural Ohio with her husband and an ever-changing number of animals.

Long after writing about Robert the Bruce and Queen Isabella, Sasson learned she is a descendant of both historical figures.

If you enjoyed this book, please spread the word by sharing it on social media or leaving a review at your favorite online retailer or book lovers' site.

For more details about N. Gemini Sasson and her books, go to:
www.ngeminisasson.com

Or become a 'fan' at:
www.facebook.com/NGeminiSasson

Sign up to learn about new releases via e-mail at:
http://eepurl.com/vSA6z

Made in the USA
Monee, IL
12 January 2020